LUCIFER

Michael Cordy

CORGI BOOKS

LUCIFER
A CORGI BOOK : 0 552 14882 2

Originally published in Great Britain by Bantam Press,
a division of Transworld Publishers

PRINTING HISTORY
Bantam Press edition published 2001
Corgi edition published 2002

1 3 5 7 9 10 8 6 4 2

Set in 11/12½pt Garamond by
Falcon Oast Graphic Art Ltd.

Corgi Books are published by Transworld Publishers,
61–63 Uxbridge Road, London W5 5SA,
a division of The Random House Group Ltd,
in Australia by Random House Australia (Pty) Ltd,
20 Alfred Street, Milsons Point, Sydney, NSW 2061, Australia,
in New Zealand by Random House New Zealand Ltd,
18 Poland Road, Glenfield, Auckland 10, New Zealand
and in South Africa by Random House (Pty) Ltd,
Endulini, 5a Jubilee Road, Parktown 2193, South Africa.

Printed and bound in Germany by
Elsnerdruck, Berlin.

Michael Cordy worked for ten years in marketing before giving it all up to write *The Miracle Strain* and *Crime Zero*. He lives in London with his wife, Jenny.

Acclaim for:

CRIME ZERO

'*Crime Zero* should cement his reputation . . . it's a storming, action-packed thriller, full of big topical ideas and backed up by meticulous research' *Mirror*

'Michael Cordy's techno-thriller is gripping and horribly believable' *Morning Star*

'Energetic and ambitious' *The Times*

'Cordy's energetic and ambitious novel depicts a world in which violent crime has become a global epidemic, with the USA being the fulcrum . . . Credible and imaginative'
The Good Book Guide

'Another splendid thriller . . . What a good writer of thrillers Cordy is. The characters leap straight out of the pages and the plot is always fascinating, fast-moving and believable'
Publishing News

'Fast-paced, politically and scientifically intriguing, *Crime Zero* is a chilling, gripping read . . .' *Shine*

'Cordy's story rides on the back of one man's desperate flight for self-determination. And it rolls at a terrific pace'
Buzz Magazine

'A highly effective thriller' *Crime Time*

THE MIRACLE STRAIN

'*Jurassic Park* meets the quest for the Holy Grail meets *Raiders of the Lost Ark*' *Mail on Sunday*

'A contrived but clever book, playing on millennial fears and expectations . . . [Cordy] spins a taught, gripping tale' *The Times*

'A fascinating and very exciting novel . . . with a massive climax, all of which makes this a truly thrilling adventure story.' *Publishing News*

'Cordy's next-to-incredible story is so tellingly told that it conjures a real excitement . . . Cordy's nicely contrived plot keeps in play moral dilemmas that are both timely and timeless. A hard-thought thriller' *Mail on Sunday*

'Cordy's technologically dazzling first novel is outrageous' *Livewire*

'Based firmly on scientific knowledge already available in top laboratories around the world where the study of genetics has reached the point at which we can recreate man from a simple scrap of DNA, Cordy has given us a new healer with the powers of a second Christ . . . Something that makes *Raiders of the Lost Ark* look like pure hokum. And the denouement must be one of the most surprisingly explosive in contemporary fiction' *The Birmingham Post*

'Great entertainment' *Focus Magazine*

'A good page-turner and an unusual thriller' *Chic*

Also by Michael Cordy

THE MIRACLE STRAIN
CRIME ZERO

and published by Corgi Books

For Jenny

LUCIFER: Lu-ci-fer: from **Latin** – bearer of light (*lux*, light; *ferro*, to bear)

PROLOGUE

The bright circular lamp above the eight-year-old child dims as the anaesthetic kicks in. The little girl reaches for the hand beside hers on the operating-table. It squeezes and she returns the pressure, gripping as tight as she can, fearing that the encroaching darkness will separate them for ever. Like many children she has an instinctive fear of the dark, understanding at some primal level that light divides the universe into two: day and night; visible and invisible; good and evil; living and dead.

But this darkness is merciful. It brings oblivion before the surgical saw cuts into her skull. She can't hear the high-pitched whirr of metal grinding through bone, can't see the fine red mist of bone and tissue refracted in the operating-theatre lights, or smell the blood and disinfectant. She is aware of nothing except her self – her mind – floating in a dark so intense it has a smell, colour and taste of its own. This velvet limbo feels womb-like, safe.

The neurosurgeon lays down the saw and uses a laser scalpel to cut into the softer tissue.

Supremely skilled, his hands are steady but he is aware that this operation is unique: it has never been attempted before. No textbook can tell him where to cut.

After thirteen hours and twenty-seven minutes he allows himself an exhausted sigh as a nurse mops the sweat from his brow. The worst is over. Or so he thinks.

Just seconds later the life-sign monitors by the operating-table erupt in a frenzy of insistent beeping.

At that moment a pinprick of white light punctures the child's velvet darkness. She is no longer floating. Instead she is rushing through a black vortex towards the light. It is just a dot at first but she is moving so fast towards it that the light is revealed as a cone, like the beam of a torch. Then she is inside it, part of the light. She is travelling at such speed now that light seems to stand still around her. It is no longer a solid beam but particles floating past into blackness, brilliant snowdrops of light. She becomes aware of a familiar presence beside her, pulling her, leading her through the silver blizzard towards the peak of the cone, the source. The connection is strong, comforting. She feels no fear now that they are together again.

Then the pain hits her, not physical pain but emotional, psychic pain. Instantly an enormous force yanks her back into the vortex, away from the cone of light, ripping her from the presence beside her. She tries to scream, clinging desperately to the beloved presence that is being torn from her, sinew by sinew, cell by cell, as the receding light reconstitutes itself into a distant and diminishing whole.

Suddenly she is looking down at herself on the table, watching the surgeon and nurses trying frantically to revive her. The operating-theatre is flooded with strong white light. Everything appears so clear, so bright. She stares at herself on the table, transfixed by the slick, gaping wound on the left side of her head and the bundle concealed under the green sheet beside her, and watches the nurse unclasp the small hand that had gripped hers so fiercely. She realizes that for the first time in her life she is alone.

PART 1

SOUL SEARCHING

1

The VenTec Foundation. Alaska.
Twenty-nine years later

Being unable to blink was the worst sensation. That, and the chill fear in her guts from knowing she was going to die.

When she awoke to find herself immobile on the laboratory couch, head shaved and eyes pegged open, Mother Giovanna Bellini knew what fate awaited her. Not only had she witnessed a hundred similar experiments but she had also contributed to them, administering the last rites to the subjects. Unlike her, however, they had been terminally ill. The imminence of their deaths and the act of dying had made them indispensable to the project.

Surely the scientists couldn't be responsible for this. Over the last nine months she had worked with them, helped them in what she thought was God's work. The Red Pope himself had appointed her to perform the last rites, explaining that she was contributing to a great and sacred mission. 'Don't question the scientists, Mother Giovanna, for they, like you, wear the scarlet crucifix of the Church of the Soul Truth on their chests.'

But it had been impossible to remain silent. She had been faithful to the Holy Father since he was a senior cardinal in the Vatican, choosing to follow him when he left to found his own ministry. Now, having been entrusted with this most sacred responsibility, how could she betray that trust by saying nothing?

Stinging liquid was dropped into each eye but she couldn't recoil.

Dear God! Help me!

She willed the words from her lips but no sound came. Even her screams were silent. Her body had been switched off by the paralysing drug, which the blonde woman in the white bodysuit and reflective eye-protectors had injected into her veins.

At the outset, it was understood that Mother Giovanna would leave the laboratory immediately after administering the last rites to each experimental subject, but recently she had lingered outside the tinted glazed doors, curious to observe how they pinpointed the crucial moment of death. After witnessing the final stages of the last three experiments she had felt compelled to contact Sister Constance, her oldest, most trusted friend, and seek her advice. Sister Constance had promised to respect her confidence and encouraged her to go direct to the Holy Father and tell him that the scientists weren't waiting for the patients to die, but killing them.

How did they know she had betrayed them? And how did they dare do this to her, knowing she had the Red Pope's protection?

Even as her upper body was raised and the hollow transparent sphere lowered over her head, she strained to see a flash of red in her peripheral vision – the tell-tale scarlet robes that would signal the arrival of Monsignor Diageo or perhaps the Red Pope himself. But as the glass sphere was sealed round her neck she saw no such sign of salvation.

It was made up of different textured layers and the refracted light shining through them had a cold beauty, like moonlight on a dark desolate lake, and brought her no comfort. The blonde scientist raised the front section of the sphere as if it were an astronaut's visor. Contact lenses, large enough to cover the exposed eyeballs, were inserted in Mother Giovanna's eyes, scratching her corneas. Then a foil tab was stuck with gel to her right temple, making her shaven scalp itch.

Worse than the discomfort, though, was the knowledge that she had unwittingly stood by while others had suffered the same fate. She had been told they were all volunteers who felt nothing before the end, but now she knew that wasn't true. This frightened her more than anything else; she had sinned and needed absolution before she died.

As fear bled into despair she wanted to weep but no tears came.

Where are you, Holy Father? she screamed silently. *Why won't you save me?*

'The countdown's starting soon,' the blonde woman announced calmly.

Mother Giovanna's heart, one of the few

muscles to defy the paralysing drug, pounded in her chest. She panicked, not because she was going to die but because she had not been absolved of her sins.

Forgive me, Lord, and have mercy on my soul. The transparent visor was replaced over her face. Then an odourless gas entered the sphere, bathing the departing world in a green aura. She heard the countdown start and knew that death awaited.

2

Tate Modern. Bankside, London.
Thirty-eight minutes earlier

The mellow sunlight of a mild October afternoon had transformed the Thames to molten gold. The black limousine driving past the Millennium Bridge was a standard Mercedes, except for the heavily tinted windows and custom-built seals that allowed no ultraviolet light into the vehicle. Sitting in the rear seat, Bradley Soames glanced to his left at St Paul's Cathedral, its magnificent dome inspired by St Peter's in Rome. Looking right, directly across the river, a more modern cathedral loomed into view – a cathedral to technology. This angular brick edifice, with a high square chimney in place of a bell-tower, had once been a power station. It now housed the largest modern art museum in the world.

Soames caught his reflection in the heavily tinted glass. He disliked his appearance: the blue eyes and wavy hair, which was the colour and consistency of gold wire, didn't trouble him, but his skin, a pale freckled mosaic of scar tissue, made him turn away. 'Walt, I know most of the press will be in the presentation by now but I still want to use the side entrance,' he said.

'As you wish, Dr Soames,' replied his assistant, from the front passenger seat. Walter Tripp, an elegant, balding black man with round rimless glasses, was dressed in formal dark suit, white shirt and blood-red silk tie. 'The gallery director's arranged the viewing room above the hall as you asked, but there's no UV screening over any of the entrances.'

'No problem, I'll cover up.' Checking his watch, Soames noted that Amber would be starting her presentation in the turbine hall. His own appearance at the launch wasn't scheduled for over an hour but he wanted to observe her and confirm his suspicions.

As the car turned right over Southwark Bridge, he rolled down the cuffs of his lined black jacket until they formed gloves into which he pushed his hands. He grimaced as the fabric caught on the still raw scar on his left hand, where the most recent melanoma had been cut out. He sealed the gloves with Velcro strips to ensure that no skin was exposed then raised the hood and secured it over his head. He put on an oversized pair of tinted spectacles to protect the top half of his face, and attached to the hood a flap that hung over his chest so that it concealed the lower half like a yashmak. When the car pulled up his skin was protected from the autumn sunlight.

Soames stepped out of the car and looked up at the windowless cliff of unbroken red brick that formed the south side of the building before he followed Tripp to the side door. To his left, by the main entrance, he could see banners hanging from flagpoles, announcing the title of the exhibition: 'The Shape of Light'. The sponsorship of this exhibition and a multimillion-pound donation to the gallery had allowed Optrix to take over the turbine hall for today's European press launch of the Lucifer soft-screen.

Two gallery officials recognized Soames from his protective clothing and ushered him through the cavernous main lobby, past the throng of visitors milling around the glass-walled restaurant and the gift shop, and through the crowds waiting to go up to the upper galleries. They got into a lift, and went to a room on the fifth of eight levels. The temporary room had been partitioned off from one of the large galleries and overlooked the vast turbine hall below. It was laid out as he had requested, with a view of the proceedings below, an optical computer with access to the Optical Internet, and a small refrigerator of Coca-Cola.

After the officials had left, Tripp retrieved a pen-sized ultraviolet detector from his jacket and, once he was satisfied that the room was safe, nodded to Soames, who removed his outer wear and focused his attention on the hall below.

It was a breathtaking sight. It was almost a hundred and fifty feet high and two hundred feet long. In place of pillars, iron girders formed a skeletal grid against grey walls and a vault of iron beams supported the soaring flat roof. Black horizontal blinds covered the spine of skylights running down the centre of the roof, and other natural light sources had been similarly screened.

A white banner emblazoned with the Optrix Opto-electronics logo and the corporate tagline 'Let There Be Light' stretched across one end of the hall. Beneath it a raised presentation dais faced a two-hundred-strong audience of journalists, customers and opinion-formers, in regimented rows interrupted only by five luminous sculptures towering thirty feet above them. Commissioned by Optrix from the celebrated artist Jenny Knowles, they glowed in the low light as if pulsing with life. In varying abstract shapes, including a double helix, a stunning interpretation of the Milky Way, and an iridescent twenty-foot-high sculpture of a water molecule, each piece appeared solid although it was no more substantial than light. Soames, however, knew the greater truth behind it: he understood that light was as much a collection of subatomic *particles*, photons, as it was an abstract *wave*.

This duality was embodied in the sixth exhibit, a massive installation that dominated the other half of the hall. It featured two flat parallel partitions seemingly suspended in space, each at least ten feet high and twenty feet wide. The first was white, punctured by two vertical slits. The second was black glass like a television screen. Facing the white partition was a laser cannon, its beam directed at the slits and passing through them to hit the black screen beyond. But instead of creating two vertical lines of light, it produced a zebra pattern of regularly spaced stripes similar to a barcode.

Every few minutes, seemingly at random, the

striped pattern on the black screen would fade and the beam from the laser gun would break up into pulses, like pellets of light. Each single pulse appeared to pass simultaneously through both slits, and as it hit the black detector screen it left its glowing mark on the glass. But instead of forming clusters of light in line with each of the slits these marks gradually re-created the stripes across the width of the screen, as if each perfectly choreographed pulse of light knew its exact place in the pattern.

The exhibit amused Soames. He never tired of exploring and witnessing the anomalies of the quantum world, where particles smaller than an atom defied the physical laws laid down by Newton for the so-called real world.

A hushed murmur ran through the audience below as the ambient lighting dimmed and the sculptures vanished. Only the sixth exhibit was still visible, its single pulses of light continuing to form their magical pattern on the black screen. Seconds later, ethereal music echoed through the cavernous space and one by one each sculpture reappeared.

'Welcome to the light age,' he heard Dr Amber Grant say, from her position on the raised dais at the end of the hall, as the ambient light gradually returned. 'Today, we at Optrix wish to celebrate with you the mystery of light and demonstrate our mastery of it.' She indicated the laser cannon exhibit. 'First the mystery. Imagine the following set-up: two parallel walls, one in front of the other. You make a vertical slit in the first wall and shine a continuous beam of light at it. What do you see?'

She smiled. 'Simple. A single white vertical line on the second wall caused by the light shining through the slit in the first. Now put *two* slits in the first wall and shine a light at it. What happens now?' Amber pointed at the exhibit. 'You don't see two vertical lines on the second wall as you might expect, but a stripy pattern of light and shade. This effect is the result of light waves spreading out from each of the two slits and interfering with each other like ripples on a pond. This famous double-slit experiment, originally conducted over two hundred years ago, proves beyond a shadow of doubt that light travels as a wave.'

Amber allowed a silence to hang in the air. 'Then in 1906 Einstein discovered that light wasn't just a wave but also a collection of subatomic *quantum* particles – what we now call photons. Einstein's original description has become the generic term for the strange subatomic world in which everything from an atom downwards can exist as both an abstract *wave* and a substantial *particle*. But even this duality is not the *real* mystery of the quantum world.'

She pointed at the exhibit, which had resumed sending out pulses of light. 'The sculpture behind you re-creates a modern version of the double-slit experiment. In this experiment a series of *single* light photons are emitted from a source. But instead of passing through one or other of the holes to form a pool of light on the second wall, each photon somehow travels through both slits simultaneously and interferes with itself. As it passes through the slits it gradually forms the zebra-striped wave interference pattern on the detector screen on the second wall, as if it consciously knows its individual place and is choreographed to behave like a wave.

'However, when the experiment is set up with two particle detectors on the other side of each slit we find that each photon behaves as a single particle. Like a pebble, it follows a definite path through *one* slit and strikes only one particle detector.

'These *actual* experiments indicate that photons are conscious. They behave differently depending on how they're observed. And what's even more strange, they appear to be telepathic and clairvoyant too. They know whether to behave like a particle or a wave before they go through the slits. Each photon seems to know how the experiment has been set up and can predict which state it's expected to be.'

She paused. 'So much for the mystery. What about the mastery? We at Optrix pride ourselves on knowing better than most how quantum physics works and have been able to exploit its duality to harness the power of light, which, as we all know, is the ideal medium for computing and communication. Its information-carrying band-width is colossal: a single burst of laser light can transmit the entire contents of every library in the world in a second. It can be split into as many different wavelengths as there are colours in the rainbow, making it ideal for parallel processing.

And, of course, it's fast – there's nothing faster.

'It's been eight years since Optrix launched the first optical computer and transformed the world. If you cast your mind back to the opening years of this millennium, silicon was becoming obsolete as the physical limits of processing power were reached. Even Intel had to concede that Moore's famous law, which claimed processing speeds doubled every eighteen months, was impossible to sustain.

'So when the first optical computer – the Lucifer One – was launched, all the rules were broken. There was no longer a need for a silicon-based processor chip and RAM and a hard disk, because the Lucifer used subatomic light photons to do all these things – to process, memorize and store data. A quartz motherboard of optical circuits allied to a sphere containing processor cells of captured light photons created a computer with the processing speed of the fastest thing in the universe. Light. Optrix turned Moore's law into an anachronism overnight.'

Amber paused and walked across the stage. From his vantage-point Soames found it hard to see her in any detail, but he heard her amplified voice and could tell from the hush that she held the attention of the audience. It had been her charisma as well as her mind that had drawn him to her. That she was physically striking had been largely irrelevant. Her talents, however, would pale into insignificance if his suspicions about her were proven tonight.

Soames looked at Walter Tripp, who was

powering up the optical computer and entering the code for the foundation's Data Security Provider, accessing live video of the experiment four and a half thousand miles away. On the delayed photon screen, which gave a three-dimensional texture to the images, Soames could see the glass sphere being placed over the subject's head. He shifted his attention back to Amber Grant. Confirmation would soon be at hand.

'As chief executive officer of Optrix Industries,' he heard her say, 'I want to remind you of how far we've come in eight years, how far we've entered the light age. I often think that although our logo is "Let There Be Light" it should be "Pushing Back the Darkness" because that's what we're consistently trying to do. In case you've forgotten the leap we've made, the Lucifer can perform a calculation ten to the power thirty-eight times faster than an old electronic Pentium IV computer. In other words, in less than a second, the Lucifer can do a calculation it would take an old IBM ThinkPad the age of the universe to complete.

'The Lucifer design is already a classic. The translucent cube, which contains a glass sphere of photon light particles interacting with memory and processor cells and rests on a motherboard of optical fibre, is a familiar sight in homes and offices around the world. Over ninety per cent of the world's computers, home and commercial, are now optical, produced either by Optrix or our licensees. And the Internet is entirely optical – wireless signals and optical fibres now unite the world at the speed of light. Indeed, many people refer to the Internet as the Optinet.'

Here Amber's tone changed, from triumphant to humble. 'Despite being the public face of Optrix, and credited as the co-inventor of the optical computer, I'm painfully aware that most of the real breakthroughs, the real insights into some of the quantum anomalies of the Lucifer, came from my mentor and the chairman of Optrix Opto-electronics. Bradley Soames is the true genius behind the Lucifer and you'll be delighted to know he's agreed to make a rare public appearance and talk to you later this afternoon.'

Ignoring the buzz of excitement that rose from the audience, Soames glanced at the computer beside Tripp, saw the electrode being attached to the subject's temple. It was close now and, assuming that his suspicions were well founded, Amber would be exposed to the press and the public when it happened. This would make it easier to persuade her to do what was necessary.

'Now to the future,' Amber said, as a low, rhythmic beat filled the hall and the ambient lighting dimmed again, leaving the giant light sculptures pulsing to the music. 'Since the launch of the Lucifer, Optrix have developed new and better ways to exploit the technology. And today's launch is no exception. The Lucifer soft-screen offers a radical new way to present data. Let me show you.'

The tempo of the background music increased and Soames watched her move towards a table at the back of the stage and tap a touch-sensitive control pad beside a translucent glowing cube. A blue rectangular screen bearing the Lucifer logo appeared behind her. It started at no more than a foot high but grew until it was over ten feet high and twelve feet wide. Like the sculptures, it looked solid and opaque but it, too, was formed of light particles.

The screen image changed and the Lucifer logo was replaced by a real-time moving image of Amber. It was as if a vast eight-foot twin stood behind her own five-and-a-half-foot frame, ghosting her every move. The definition was stunning. Her olive skin and thick black hair looked luminous on the screen, and her green eyes were incandescent. She smiled, showing even white teeth, and as her huge alter-ego walked across the stage her Chanel suit shimmered.

'This soft-screen technology literally pushes back the darkness and, within reason, can be whatever size you want it to be,' she said. 'As visible in direct light as conventional LCD and LED displays, it is backward compatible so can be used with all Lucifer models. The display area can be enlarged like now for presentations, or minimized for laptops or personal use.' The screen image shrank down to postage-stamp size then grew again to its full magnificence. 'And, of course, it's portable,' said Amber, her huge luminous image smiling at the audience. She laughed. 'You could say it's the lightest screen in the world.'

The audience laughed with her and clapped; some even stood to applaud, and Soames was swept up in their enthusiasm. Then he heard

Tripp clear his throat and say, 'Almost time, sir.'

Keeping an eye on Amber, he glanced back at the small computer screen beside Tripp. The subject's visor had been sealed and the green caesium and flavion gas was filling the sphere. The scientist in the white bodysuit and eye-protectors held a control pad in one hand. The screen shifted to close-up, focusing on the subject's face within the glass sphere.

Then it happened.

The electrode sparked on the subject's temple. Instantly an even brighter spark – seemingly from the subject's eyes – lit up the gas-filled sphere like a brilliant bulb, before hitting a dark glass oblong embedded in the visor and leaving a stripy wave interference pattern similar to the exhibit in the hall below. It disappeared, lingering momentarily in the sphere's outer layer of optical fibre, glowing like a halo, before it vanished into the ether.

The experiment wasn't interesting in itself: Soames had witnessed a hundred identical experiments over the last nine months and didn't care unduly about today's result. The subject, Mother Giovanna Bellini, was dead, and he doubted the trial had succeeded. What interested him more was its possible connection with what was happening now below him in the turbine hall where the giant on-screen image of Amber Grant was clutching her head and reeling.

At the exact instant the spark had appeared in Mother Giovanna's head-sphere, marking her point of death, Amber Grant had stumbled forward in pain, reaching for her left temple. She was now on her knees and members of the audience were rushing forward to help.

Not taking his eyes off Amber, Soames reached for his cellphone and dialled a number in Cambridge. Someone picked up on the third ring. Soames wasted no time. 'Put me through to the director, please.'

'Dr Knight's in a meeting—'

'Tell her Bradley Soames wants to talk to her. Now.'

In seconds she was on the phone. 'Virginia,' he said, 'it's urgent. The scientist at your clinic I earmarked funds for—'

'Miles Fleming?'

'Yes, he's got to examine Amber Grant – *immediately*.'

'But that might not be—'

'There's no time to argue. Amber needs urgent help. I'll double the funding we discussed for Fleming's NeuroTranslator. She'll be arriving in the next two hours.'

Three minutes later, assisted by Tripp and members of the Optrix staff, Soames was in the hall, standing over Amber who was curled up in the foetal position. Speaking into the microphone, he addressed the crowd: 'Would everyone please move from the hall into the lobby. I'll continue the presentation personally when you return.'

When he was satisfied that the Optrix staff and gallery officials were shepherding the audience away from the stage, he bent down to Amber's rigid form. Lifting her head, he forced two analgesic tablets down her throat and gave her a sip of water.

'Amber, it's me. I've arranged for you to see someone who's going to figure out these migraines. Don't pretend it's no big deal any more.'

He waited for her to say something, but she didn't.

He couldn't remain silent. He had to ask. He had to know. 'The pain in the same place as before?'

'Yes,' she whispered, her pale face contorted in agony.

'Where?' he demanded. 'Point.'

Her hand was shaking as she raised it to indicate the area of pain. But she wasn't touching her head – she was pointing to a position in thin air at least three inches from her left temple.

3

Barley Hall Research Clinic.
Cambridge, England

It was moments like this that restored Miles Fleming's belief in the possible, which had been sorely tested over the last eleven months. He turned to the young man sitting beside him. 'The arm okay, Paul?'

Adjusting the blue latticework Thinking Cap on his head, Paul stared at the anatomically correct figure on the upper half of the split computer screen in front of him. 'Fine, Doc. No pain at all.'

'No trace twinges?'

Paul grinned. 'Nothing.'

'Okay, let's see you move it again. Try raising it above your head.'

Watching the on-screen figure lift its right arm, Fleming checked the horizontal lines spiking furiously on the lower half of the screen. 'Excellent, Paul. Your brainwaves are looking strong. You've got the Alphas under good control now. Lower the arm. Great.' He turned to his research patient, who was frowning with concentration as he willed his thoughts to control the arm on screen. The twenty-six-year-old wore a Nike sweatshirt and faded jeans. His right sleeve hung empty from his shoulder.

Four years ago Paul had lost his arm in a factory accident and until he had come to Barley Hall he had been tormented by severe pain in his absent limb. In Fleming's experience many amputees suffered phantom pain. It emanated from the brain, which had a virtual 3D map of the body in its neural net and often continued to send signals to a limb long after it had been amputated. In Paul's case the NeuroTranslator had helped identify the brainwaves sending pain signals to his missing limb, enabling Fleming to suppress them. He had responded so well to the treatment that a month ago Fleming had decided to extend it beyond stopping the pain signals to boosting the control signals.

'Okay, so you're pretty good on screen.' Fleming turned to the latex mannequin in the corner. 'How about handling Brian?'

Paul grinned. 'No problem.'

'Pretty confident, huh? Let's see you do the egg test then.'

'The what?'

Fleming stood up and went over to the body surrogate. 'Brian' was sexless, but otherwise every prosthetic muscle and joint beneath its latex skin replicated those of the average human body. Fleming retrieved a box from the pocket of his crumpled white coat, opened it and removed an egg packed in cotton wool. He moved to the small table beside the mannequin, placed the egg on one end of the polished wooden surface and the box on the other. Both were within reach of Brian's right hand.

He walked to the other side of the high-ceilinged Victorian room, and stopped at the glass window separating the Think Tank from the observation room. He bent to the workstation, and made some adjustments to the keypad by the translucent cube. 'Right, you're connected to Brian. Ignore the rest of its body. Just focus on the right arm. Lift the egg and put it back in the box.'

'From here?' said Paul, who was ten feet from the egg.

'Just think about moving your missing arm. Like you did with the figure on screen.'

Paul grimaced in concentration.

'Don't try so hard. Imagine that Brian's arm is your arm.'

At that moment the mannequin's right arm bent at the elbow and the hand shot forward, almost hitting the egg.

'Careful. Take your time.'

Slowly the hand opened, moved closer to the egg and gripped it. Paul flashed Fleming a grin.

'Not bad, not bad at all,' said Fleming. 'That's the easy part, though. Now you've got to lift it and put it into the box. Pay attention to the feedback sensors in the fingertips.'

The mannequin's hand raised and moved towards the box. Then it closed suddenly and crushed the shell, dripping yolk and white on to the polished wood.

Fleming laughed and patted Paul on the shoulder.

'Harder than it is on screen, isn't it? Good first effort, though.'

There was a knock at the door and Staff Nurse Frankie Pinner poked her head into the room. An attractive thirty-year-old with dark hair and a wide smile, she was the senior nurse among Fleming's team of doctors, scientists and nurses who helped run his research section in the east wing of Barley Hall. 'Dr Fleming, it's four o'clock. You wanted to check the ward.'

Fleming glanced at his watch. 'Thanks, Frankie. Could you stay and help Paul finish his exercises?' He turned back to Paul. 'Keep practising,' he said. 'Once you've mastered Brian you'll be ready for your own arm.'

He left the Think Tank, turned right into the east-wing corridor and pushed open the first pair of swing doors on the left.

The Barley Hall research ward was an imposing oak-panelled hall with tall lancet windows overlooking the ornamental lake and landscaped lawns to the rear of the clinic. It had been converted from what had been a gymnasium in the Victorian manor's days as a boys' boarding-school. The ward was composed of six roomy private cubicles surrounding an open central area with chairs and a television. It accommodated patients who had to sleep over during clinical trials. Most stayed a few nights before returning either to their homes or to one of the larger specialist hospitals, such as the spinal injuries unit at Stoke Mandeville in Buckinghamshire.

Through the half-open screen doors of the first occupied cubicle he could see a girl lying asleep in bed. A nurse was standing over her. 'How is she?' he whispered. A year ago, two months after her sixteenth birthday, her boyfriend had taken her for a ride on his motorbike. He had walked away from the crash with bruises, but her spine had snapped at the base, paralysing her from the waist down. Yesterday, Fleming's team had inserted electrical implants in her lower spine and legs. With the NeuroTranslator, he hoped that her brain would be able to bypass the damaged spinal cord and control her legs directly.

The nurse looked up. 'She's doing fine, Dr Fleming. Should be ready in a few days' time for her first stint in the Think Tank.'

The adjacent cubicle was Paul's, and the doors to the next two were closed. Fleming opened each a crack to look at his charges. Both occupants were also asleep. He checked their monitors and left them undisturbed before moving on to the fifth cubicle. As he approached this one his usual detached professionalism wavered.

Fleming was only thirty-six but he had become hardened to suffering because he'd seen so much. He knew better than most how a charmed life could be destroyed in an instant. In his career he had come to understand one thing: suffering was arbitrary, and there was no point putting your faith in gods to protect you from it.

For all his fatalism, however, he still found it hard to accept the harsh reality of what had befallen the occupant of cubicle five eleven months ago. It reinforced his conviction that permanence couldn't be guaranteed. His family and friends, particularly ex-girlfriends, often accused him of wanting change for change's sake, but that wasn't true.

He had once been in love when he was at Cambridge, and had been prepared to devote his life to her. But she'd married a lecturer twenty years her senior. Fleming's heart had been broken, but he'd survived. Since then he had enjoyed a number of relationships, although none had yet rekindled in him the spark of true passion. More than one girlfriend had left him because he couldn't commit to marriage. Every time it became serious he shied away. Change was adventure. Change – even bad change – offered possibility, and striving for the possible, regardless of the odds, was his token antidote to suffering.

Most of the patients on this ward, along with the many others he had seen over the last few years, had been told by a doctor that their condition was hopeless, that any form of recovery or positive change was impossible. And he hated that. Particularly when it came to the occupant of cubicle five.

'Miles!'

Virginia Knight was standing in the doorway of the ward. The American director of Barley Hall was in her fifties but looked younger. Tall and slender, she was elegant in her classic navy suit, her fair hair cut short and feathered in a style that softened the angular lines of her long, intelligent face. She took off her glasses and smiled at him. 'Can I see you for a moment in my office? It's kind of urgent.'

Fleming glanced at cubicle five. It could wait. The patient wasn't going anywhere.

4

The director's office

Located in the central section of the Victorian mansion, the office was a grand room with ornate cornices, foot-high skirting boards and a splendid bay window overlooking the front driveway and manicured lawns.

Miles Fleming crossed his arms and sat back on the large chesterfield that the insomniac director often used at night. 'Virginia, you're not being serious! Since when was a migraine urgent?'

Virginia Knight rose from her desk and moved to her Italian coffee machine. She made two espressos and handed one to Fleming. 'It's important, Miles,' she said. 'Trust me.'

Fleming shook his head. 'But I need the Think Tank and the NeuroTranslator tonight. Paul's in there now, and Rob needs to be prepped for his communication trial tomorrow. The research schedule's overloaded as it is. After the success with Jake we're getting huge interest in the Neuro-Translator. We've already got a mile-long queue of research patients and I can't let anyone jump to the front and push the programme back –

particularly someone with a *headache*, for Christ's sake.'

Virginia Knight sighed. 'Miles, you're forgetting that both Jake and Rob jumped to the front of the line.'

'That was different. You can't compare their cases with this.'

'It was different for *you* – that's why I never challenged my predecessor's decision to turn a blind eye to your priority-shuffling – but according to the Barley Hall Trustees' strict research protocol, the rules were bent. All I'm saying is that, as director of Barley Hall, I've got to do what's best for the clinic and you've got to make time for this patient. Tonight.'

Miles Fleming sipped his coffee. He had nothing against Virginia Knight, but she wasn't the reason why he had come to Barley Hall eight years ago after a Cambridge medical degree and Ph.D. in neurology from Harvard. Unlike Knight, who was a doctor turned administrator, her predecessor had been a pure researcher, a true scientist. The great, and now sadly late, Professor Henry Trier had been one of Fleming's professors at Cambridge. And when Trier had taken over the Neurological Trust – a research council set up by private business, Cambridge University and the spinal injuries unit at Stoke Mandeville – Fleming had leapt at the chance to join him.

Eight months ago Trier had had a fatal heart-attack and Knight, who already held numerous executive and non-executive directorships, was appointed his successor. Fleming understood why she had been chosen: she excelled at management, publicity and fundraising, but he worried sometimes that she put commercial concerns above patients and research.

'Setting aside the issue of line-jumping,' she said, reaching for a magazine on her desk, 'let me explain the benefits of seeing Dr Amber Grant tonight.' She passed the magazine to him. 'First of all, you do realize who she is?'

'Sure, I've heard of her.' And that's what concerned him. Amber Grant was rich and celebrated, and in Knight's view that made her especially worthy of treatment. The magazine was *Time* and the front cover featured the airbrushed picture of Bradley Soames that appeared in every publication, and next to him the strikingly beautiful face of his business partner, Amber Grant. Beneath their picture was the line 'Turning the Spotlight on the Light Wizards'.

Fleming flicked through the magazine. On page six he found an interview with Amber Grant, timed no doubt to coincide with the much-hyped launch of the Lucifer soft-screen. Fleming's own NeuroTranslator was based on the Lucifer optical computer and dependent on the technology that Grant and Soames had developed. Despite his annoyance, Fleming was intrigued, and more so when he turned to a profile of the enigmatic and reclusive Bradley Soames – the man many regarded as the genius behind Optrix.

'Go ahead,' said Knight. 'Read it.'

Fleming skimmed the article. Much of it regurgitated the now famous legend of the man, but he was still fascinated by some sections – particularly the one on Soames's early years:

Bradley Soames suffers from *xeroderma pigmentosum*, commonly called XP; a syndrome caused by a mutant gene that means even the shortest exposure to the weakest sunlight causes skin cancers. Born into the wealthy Soames oil dynasty – during a full solar eclipse, so the story goes – many psychologists have wondered how Soames might have developed if he hadn't been so cursed.

He would certainly have been less eccentric but it is doubtful that he would have become so phenomenally successful. It goes beyond irony that this brilliant young man who has lived all his life at the mercy of light should be the one to cage its power and harness its speed.

From his early childhood, confined indoors to protect him from ultraviolet rays, Soames was obsessed with light photons, the subatomic quantum particles of electromagnetic radiation that made up the very thing that imprisoned him. Focusing his intellect on light, he was convinced by the age of thirteen that photons could be harnessed to process, store and transmit data.

At sixteen Soames outgrew even the most gifted private tutors his parents hired to teach him at home, so he attended Cal Tech in Pasadena, one of the leading technical colleges in the world, graduating with top honours two days prior to his eighteenth birthday – younger then than most students applying for the course. But he hadn't enrolled to pass exams: he was looking for a partner. He was seeking someone of sufficiently high intellect to understand his concepts and someone with the requisite drive, social skills and character to do what he couldn't do – go out into the light and help realize his dream. That person was to be a Ph.D. student researching particle physics: Amber Grant.

Many people, including Amber Grant, had thought of developing an optical computer, but their designs had relied solely on optical fibres, which, even had they worked, would have involved a dragon's nest of wires. Soames's approach was different: he proposed using sound to create the strong electrical field necessary to keep electron-hole pairs apart long enough to trap light and the data stored within it before sending it on its way again.

Soames's vision and Amber Grant's dedication, plus a host of relatively minor modifications, each in itself worthy of a Ph.D., led to the invention eight years ago of the world's first practical optical computer. It made Optrix Industries, based in San Francisco, one of the fastest growing companies the world has ever seen.

In addition to his role at Optrix, Bradley Soames increasingly spends time at his private technology innovation facility in Alaska: the VenTec Foundation . . .

'The point is,' said Knight, when Fleming looked up, 'Soames wants to make a multimillion-dollar donation to *your* research.' She smiled. 'You know I'm always talking about the Christopher Reeve effect? Well, you can't deny that stem-cell regeneration of the damaged spinal cord is seen as the Holy Grail of neurological research, which makes it so much easier to get funding for Bobby Chan's genetic-engineering team in the west wing.'

Fleming allowed himself a wry smile. 'Whereas my work in the east wing is still seen as a mechanical Band-Aid and not a real solution – even though, realistically, Bobby's team won't get any practical results for decades.'

Knight laughed. 'Well, that perception's changing fast. Your breakthrough with Jake is making waves. And we've gotta capitalize on it. Bradley Soames is interested in the NeuroTranslator and he's willing to commit serious money to developing it.'

Fleming knew this already: six months ago Soames had approached him indirectly, wanting him to transfer to VenTec. 'And in return for serious funding I have to examine his precious colleague with the NeuroTranslator? Apart from collapsing with a migraine, what's really wrong with her?'

Knight tapped a manila folder on her desk. 'That's another reason you should see her. She's a researcher's dream. Her medical history's fascinating and, as a neurologist, you could learn a lot from her. Don't fight this one, Miles, you're on to a winner. She's only putting back your schedule by a day or so – a minor inconvenience in light of all the benefits she's going to bring.'

Despite Fleming's reservations he was interested. 'Benefits?'

'She's unique,' said Knight. 'I'll release her full medical records to you online, but these topline notes give an idea of what I'm talking about.'

Reluctantly Fleming picked up the folder. Virginia Knight was an accomplished manipulator and he was wary of her. Glancing again at the beautiful woman on the cover of *Time*, he said, 'I still don't see why she should take priority over my other patients. She's not an amputee, is she?'

Virginia Knight leant back in her chair and a broad smile crossed her face. 'Not exactly,' she said, as Fleming opened the folder at the first X-ray and gasped. 'Not *exactly*.'

5

Barley Hall. 5 p.m.

By the time Amber Grant's ambulance arrived at Barley Hall from London it was dark. The crippling migraine had subsided but, as always, she still felt weak. The headaches came without warning and she was resigned to that. However, this last attack had angered her. She had collapsed during an important presentation and the sense of failure lingered. Her work was one of the most important things in her life and she had let herself and everyone else down – in front of the goddamn media. She would miss the key dinner tonight too, *and* the round of publicity and business meetings planned for tomorrow morning before her return flight to San Francisco. Despite the pain she had wanted to return to the turbine hall and continue, but Bradley Soames had insisted she come here. Regardless of what the specialists might say, Amber was determined to catch her flight home tomorrow to see her sick mother, Gillian.

As they drove through the impressive gates of Barley Hall, she peered out across verdant lawns. Even in the gathering dusk and with the onset of

46

winter everything looked more lush than it did in California, and she couldn't help contrasting the Victorian mansion with the featureless American hospitals and clinics she had attended as a child.

Until nine months ago those clinics had been a bad memory. But recently, at the mercy of the increasingly crippling migraines, she had been reacquainted with clinics, doctors and tests. In the last six months she had undergone every test possible, including PET, CAT and MRI scans, but they had revealed nothing to explain her condition. When Soames had escorted her personally from the turbine hall to the ambulance, she had been sceptical about seeing yet another 'specialist'. He, though, had insisted that she see Dr Miles Fleming.

'Amber, you've always nagged me about the damage done to my skin as a child before I got diagnosed with XP. Every two months you stop me firing my dermatologist and insist I take her advice to have another goddamn melanoma or two cut out of me before they kill me. And you know what? You're probably the only person in the whole world I listen to. So now I want you to listen to me. Get your headaches checked out properly. This guy Miles Fleming is smart. His NeuroTranslator is the best application of the optical computer there is – and that includes the new generation of gene sequencers.' Soames regarded most people as fools and the rest as mediocre, so for him to rate the thirty-six-year-old Englishman so positively was high praise indeed.

The orderlies offered her a wheelchair, but she

walked into the elegant reception hall. She hated being regarded as an invalid. Although she spent most of her life working in laboratories she prided herself on keeping fit with early-morning swims in the Optrix pool. Inside, she was greeted by a nurse holding a clipboard.

'Good evening, Dr Grant. I'm Staff Nurse Frankie Pinner. Are you okay to walk? Need anything for the pain?'

'I'm good for now, thanks.'

'In that case, would you mind sitting down in the lounge area while I get Dr Fleming? If you need anything, just let Reception know.'

In a corner of the large hall was a row of back-to-back divans. Amber sat down and retrieved her mobile communicator from her jacket pocket. The device, no larger than a cellphone, opened into two halves: one contained a touch-sensitive control pad, the other a set of numerical keys. She pressed a button on the control pad and a display screen rose from the centre hinge. Just as she was about to check her e-mail and phone messages she heard a sharp intake of breath behind her and a hushed: 'Wow.'

Turning, she saw a small boy leaning over the divan behind hers, peering over her shoulder. He had spiky fair hair, an open, expressive face, and huge grey eyes that gazed at the state-of-the-art soft-screen of her communicator. A woman, too old to be his mother, sat beside him reading a magazine.

'Is that yours?' he asked, resting a small hand on her shoulder and wriggling up the back of his seat for a better look.

She smiled at him. 'Yup.'

'I haven't seen one like that before.'

'It's new.'

'Where did you get it?'

'I made it.' She corrected herself. 'Rather, my company made it.'

The boy looked at her hard and then asked, seriously, 'Are you a genius?'

Another laugh. 'No.'

'My uncle's a genius,' he said matter-of-factly.

'Oh, I'm impressed. What's your name?'

'Jake.'

'Hi, Jake, I'm Amber.'

He flashed her a wide smile. 'What can it do?' he asked.

'Lots of things. Make calls, send e-mails, do computing stuff, check the weather forecast, sports results . . .'

'Can it play games?'

'You betcha.'

'Can it give football scores?'

'Sure,' she said, racking her brains. Sport was a black hole as far as she was concerned. Back home she followed the Forty Niners American football team but only because Optrix sponsored them. 'Who are you a fan of?'

'Man U, of course,' he said, as if only a fool would support any other team. 'I love football.'

'I bet you're pretty good at it too.'

'I'm not so good any more, but I'm getting better again.'

There was something about the way he said it that gave her pause.

49

'Dr Grant.' Looking up, Amber saw that the nurse with the clipboard had returned. 'If you'll follow me I'll take you straight through to the Think Tank. If you need the bathroom or a glass of water, please let me know. We can fill in the admission forms later.'

'Gotta go, Jake,' she said, and stood up to follow the nurse.

When she was on her feet she turned and looked down at the boy. Then she saw why he wasn't so good at soccer any more. She felt a pang – she understood what it was like to be a kid who looked different, but she kept the pity from her face and bent to shake his hand. 'Pleasure meeting you, Jake. Good luck with Man U.'

'Bye-bye, Amber,' he said, with a grin.

The nurse led Amber to the east wing, down a long corridor to the Think Tank, then ushered her into a small chamber next door that contained a desk, a Lucifer optical computer, two chairs and a bank of monitors. A glass window looked into the Think Tank and she assumed that this was an observation room. The nurse poured her some water and left.

Sitting on a soft chair away from the desk, Amber glanced around the room. On one wall there was a corkboard. Pinned to it were what appeared to be thank-you postcards and photographs of patients and staff. One caught her eye: it showed two tanned men in full climbing gear, standing on a white mountain peak against a sky of the most brilliant blue. Similar enough to be brothers, they held their hands aloft in triumph.

Then she caught sight of her reflection in the observation window. She looked pale and drawn. Unconsciously she brushed back her hair, exposing the left side of her face and the thin silver scar running from her temple into her hairline. Now it was apparent that she had no left ear, highlighted by the striking jade and gold earring on her right lobe. She had persistently refused plastic surgery: to eradicate any trace of her childhood operation would somehow be an act of betrayal, she believed.

'Dr Grant? Miles Fleming.'

As he entered the room, she caught herself smoothing her skirt and patting her hair. She recognized him immediately as one of the men in the photograph. He wasn't what she had been expecting. Apart from his unbuttoned white coat he didn't look like a scientist, certainly not the ones she knew, and she was unprepared for his sheer physicality. He was tall, at least six foot, and he moved in that unconsciously graceful way that only the truly co-ordinated can. His dark hair was as unruly as his crumpled clothing and his skin had a ruddy outdoor glow. When he extended his hand towards her and smiled, small crows' feet gathered around his grey eyes. His large hand was warm and gripped hers firmly.

'Sorry to keep you waiting, but we're having to juggle a few things.'

'No problem. Thanks for seeing me at such short notice.'

'Your migraine? How's the pain now?'

'Under control.'

51

'Good. Why don't I outline what we do here and then we'll discuss your problem?'

'Sure.'

'Basically the work here at Barley Hall is divided into two areas. The west wing deals in pure scientific research, focusing on stem-cell regenerative work – rebuilding spinal cords, that kind of thing. Here in the east wing, where my team is based, our research is more practical. We specialize in harnessing the signals in the brain to help amputees and paraplegics regain control of their paralysed limbs and operate their prosthetics.' Fleming smiled at her. 'We also help to manage pain.'

Amber liked his smile but she wasn't ready to trust him yet. 'Oh, yeah? What about pain in a part of the body that doesn't exist?'

'As it happens, that's one of our specialities.'

6

Having read her medical files, Miles Fleming knew of at least two other cases similar to Amber Grant's, one in the United States and one in France, but neither patient had undergone surgery. In all his studies he had never encountered anyone who had endured the operation and survived. And, given her achievements with Bradley Soames at Optrix, Amber Grant had not only survived but come out of the ordeal with her brilliant mind intact.

He turned to the Lucifer optical computer on the desk. It was a translucent cube, housing a pulsing sphere of light on a coil of optical fibre. Behind it was a KREE8 delayed photon plasma screen designed to display what appeared to be three-dimensional images. Angling the screen towards him, Fleming reached for the wireless control pad and retrieved Amber Grant's medical files from Barley Hall's Data Security Provider. The information appeared immediately it was summoned – arriving at the speed of light.

He looked at the X-rays on the screen, then back

at her. There were no obvious signs of the operation, but Amber's hair and eyes drew his attention. Her hair, parted so that it concealed the left side of her face, was as thick as an animal's pelt, blue-black with a lustrous sheen. Her large eyes were shaped like a cat's and the colour was exquisite: irises of the deepest green flecked with gold. She had a fine nose and olive skin. A striking single jade and gold earring dangled from her right ear on the side unmasked by hair. Her full lips were the colour of pale coral. She was one of the most exotic women Fleming had ever met.

'May I see where you had the surgery?'

'Sure.' Amber brushed back the left side of her hair.

Fleming got up and moved towards her. As he bent down to her he noticed her perfume: subtle yet heady, like a rare tropical flower. He studied the neat silver scar that ran from her upper hairline and bisected her temple before running into the hair above the nape of her neck. She had no ear but the scarring was so slight that it looked more like an omission than a disfigurement.

He returned to his seat and looked again at the image on his computer screen. 'Let's talk about your migraines,' he said. 'According to your records they started eight or nine months ago and you'd never had headaches like them before that. Not even as a child.'

'That's correct.'

'You have them about ten times a month.'

'On average.'

'How long does an attack last?'

54

'Depends. If I don't take an analgesic immediately it kicks in, the pain can last as long as an hour. But it's the aftermath that cripples me. I'm so drained I can't function properly for hours.'

'What are you taking?'

'Tylenol Blue. They don't stop the pain but they dull it.'

He nodded. 'Can you describe the pain?'

She shrugged. 'It's like a red-hot needle plunging into my brain, injecting small explosive charges. Lights and stars flash before my eyes and I get nauseous. Sometimes, like today, I collapse.'

Fleming grimaced. 'Sounds fun.' He paused and looked back at the image on his screen. 'The pain's always in the same place?'

'Yeah.'

'Where? Can you point at the *exact* location?'

'There's still a dull throb here,' she said, raising her left hand to indicate the area. 'This is the exact spot.'

Fleming nodded and again checked the image on the screen. She was pointing into space a few inches from her left temple.

'Pretty weird, huh?' she said, looking self-conscious. She picked up the water-glass.

He shrugged his shoulders. 'Unusual, yes, but not inexplicable.'

The picture on the screen from Amber Grant's medical file showed an X-ray of two children facing in the opposite direction to each other. Their skulls were fused together, left temple to left temple, a contoured ridge of bone connecting them. But what made these Siamese twins even rarer was that they were fused not only at the skull but also at the brain. A significant section of their temporal lobe tissue overlapped, and yet, according to the records, both girls had had distinct personalities, exhibiting individual character traits.

Amber Grant placed the glass on the desk, and Fleming noticed how slow and deliberate her movements were. When she sat still she inclined her head slightly to the left, as if listening over her shoulder.

Her file had provided the details of her life: Amber and her twin Ariel had been born thirty-seven years ago to a poor Brazilian girl who couldn't afford to support normal twins, let alone Siamese. They had been dumped in a rundown hospital in São Paulo but, thanks to the intervention of a Jesuit priest, were adopted by a childless Catholic couple in the States.

For the first eight years of their lives they lived happily with their adoptive parents in California. They used to be called the dancing twins because they moved and walked together as if they were waltzing. Ariel was always the strong one, the leader, while Amber was quieter. Then complications arose with Amber's kidneys. The twins shared their blood supply and for a time Ariel's kidneys functioned for both of them. Then it became evident that her heart was subsidizing Amber's and would soon give out under the extra demands placed upon it. If they weren't separated, and Amber's condition treated, not only would she die but she would kill her sister.

There was an additional complication: although they were two separate personalities they shared a key section of brain tissue. There was a remote chance that both girls would survive with their minds intact, but the odds weren't good. However, their parents had little choice but to approve the operation. Within two months of the surgery Amber's heart and kidneys had stabilized and she was given a clean bill of health. But Ariel died on the operating table.

Fleming didn't need Amber's medical notes to tell him she would always harbour guilt for the loss of her sister – who was amputated because Amber was killing her. Presumably this was why she had never had corrective surgery to construct a left ear and further diminish the scarring. According to her medical notes one psychologist had asked her about this. Amber Grant had replied, 'Why should I want plastic surgery? She was the best part of me.'

Fleming looked at Amber and saw her studying him, her eyes challenging. 'So,' she said, 'any immediate thoughts?'

He turned the computer screen round so that Amber could see the familiar X-ray image of her skull fused with her sister's. Pointing to an area of Ariel's temporal lobe, he said, 'The location of your pain is here, exactly where your sister's brain used to meet the section you once shared. At one level it's quite straightforward, and I'm sure other specialists you've seen have told you about it. You have classic phantom pain. It isn't unusual. There's a young man, Paul, in the ward down the corridor who's been suffering pain in his severed arm for the last four years. We've managed to stop it now, using the NeuroTranslator, but it was very real to him. When a part of the body is lost during a traumatic accident the victim may continue to experience acute pain in the missing body part. Often the pain reflects the way the limb was damaged, as if the last distress signal sent to the brain is the one it remembers.'

Amber nodded. 'But I didn't lose a limb.'

'No, that's what makes your case so unusual. You lost a person.' He paused, as he tried to put into words what he was thinking. 'What makes you unique, Amber, is that you possess part of the living brain of a dead person.'

She frowned, transfixed by the image of her twin on the screen. 'I realize that. But what does it mean?' Then she paled. 'Are you saying I'm feeling Ariel's pain? Could she still somehow . . .'

She looked so horrified that Fleming reached across and touched her shoulder. 'No. I can assure you that this is *your* pain. As with Paul's arm, your brain is simply making a link to missing tissue that for some reason it thinks is still there. Ariel is no longer in pain. She's gone.' He tried to make light of it. 'Come on, Amber, you're a scientist . . .'

'I'm a particle physicist, Miles,' she countered, 'and what the quantum world's taught me is that you can't be sure of anything.' Her eyes narrowed, and he knew that she was tired of being patronized by so-called 'experts'. 'All my life I've tried to make sense of what happened to my sister. I've studied philosophy, physics and even theology, and so far

58

all I've learnt is that we don't know much.' She gave a tight smile and leant back in her chair. 'The point I'm making, Miles, is that I'm not in the business of allowing anybody to *assure* me of anything.'

Fleming raised both hands in surrender. He didn't understand how life worked either. But one thing he knew was that when it was over it was over. There was no point wasting any mental energy worrying about the afterlife because there wasn't one. Thank God. 'Amber, I'm not foolish enough to debate the vagaries of quantum physics with you but I do know about the human brain. It can do many strange things and make you believe anything's real, whether it's a pain in a missing part of your body, or the existence of a divine being. Having spent my entire career studying it, I'm convinced that everything we experience in this world can be explained by the electrical and chemical activity in that walnut-shaped organ in our skull. Love, religious belief, our sense of self, all come from our *physical* brain. Our consciousness, our mind, isn't some abstract thing, it's born of the totality of the physical brain, and once the physical is gone the mind's gone too. You're still here, Amber, but Ariel's gone into oblivion. You might be in pain because your brain can still deliver signals to your physical being, but your twin's no longer suffering. She can't because she no longer exists. That's not quantum theory. It's physical *fact*.'

Amber smiled and her tone softened, more teasing than confrontational. 'Since you're talking about the oblivion of death I've got to tell you I'm a Catholic.'

Fleming laughed. 'There aren't many of you left. I thought most Catholics had defected to the Church of the Soul Truth.'

Her smile broadened. 'I'm not real devout, but you know how it is? When your godfather's a Jesuit priest who saved your life and you're adopted by a couple of Catholics, it instils certain loyalties in you.'

'I suppose so,' Fleming said. 'Anyway, you now know that I'm an atheist with outdated Newtonian certainties, and I know you're a Catholic with quantum tendencies. What we don't yet know is exactly why you're having these migraines or how we can stop them. Your brain has to give us the answer to these questions.' He stood and moved to the door, gesturing for her to follow him into the Think Tank. 'Now might be a good time to introduce you to the NeuroTranslator.'

7

'This is the examination room,' Fleming said, 'but everyone here calls it the Think Tank.'

With its lofty ceiling and picture rails, the room seemed antithetical to the extensive state-of-the-art equipment, the battery of oxygen cylinders, medical monitors and other apparatus. On a table on the far side of the room, another translucent cube sat on a thick black base; it contained a pulsing sphere of light the size of a soccer ball. A blue electrode skullcap and a wireless keypad lay next to it; a large plasma screen hung on the wall above it.

'This is where you'll sleep tonight.'

'No bed? So this is a no-frills place, right?'

'Your bed will be wheeled in from one of the ward cubicles. Many of our patients are immobile so it's easier to move them. The intensive-care equipment around the bed bay is for emergencies. Some of our research patients are critically ill, so we don't like to take chances. Anyway, you'll have Brian watching over you.'

'Brian?'

Fleming shrugged. 'It's a stupid name that stuck. In the early days a technical assistant wrote a memo referring to the NeuroTranslator as a brain machine. Anyway, there was a typo and now all the nurses and doctors call it Brian. Stupid, but it stops us getting too pompous.' He walked over and patted the mannequin. 'This is called Brian too. We use it to train amputees and paraplegics how to think commands.' He paused. 'How much do you know about the NeuroTranslator? It's based on the Lucifer, so you probably know quite a lot about the underlying technology.'

She walked over and touched the translucent cube, studying the pulsing glowing sphere inside. 'I assume the optical processor provides the power and speed to translate neural signals.'

'Absolutely. In the base there's also a neural signal amplifier and an optical-analogue converter to enable a subject's brainwaves to communicate directly with the computer.' He picked up the blue skullcap. 'We call this a Thinking Cap. Each node of the interlocking net design carries an electrode to monitor the brain's electrical activity through the skull. All communication from headpiece to computer is wireless. The NeuroTranslator's basic-ally an advanced biofeedback unit, similar to the early Biomuse systems developed by Lusted and Knapp in the early nineties to help paraplegics and amputees.'

Amber nodded. She had read about the Biomuse devices. They were primarily designed to detect and amplify the electrical impulses from residual muscle tissue, and the impulses generated by eye movement. 'But the NeuroTranslator's far more advanced, I guess. For a start, it doesn't use EMG or EOG signals.'

'You're right. It uses EEG signals. About six years ago I was convinced that we could gain far greater control of computers if we exploited the considerably more complex electrical signals present in the human brain. The simple ambition was to harness thought itself.'

Amber smiled at 'simple'. At its most basic level, human brain activity – thought – was made up of electricity racing from the various neural junctions in the brain. As far back as 1929 the German psychiatrist Hans Berger coined the term electro-encephalogram, or EEG, to describe recordings of voltage fluctuations of the brain that could be detected using electrodes attached to the scalp.

Over the decades many continuous EEG signals had been identified: alpha waves could be brought on by actions as simple as closing the eyes; beta waves were associated with an alert state of mind; theta waves arose from emotional stress; delta waves occurred during deep sleep; and mu waves were associated with the motor cortex – they diminished with movement or the intention to move.

Fleming patted the sphere. 'Thanks to your Lucifer optical computer, we were able to identify and analyse all the standard brainwaves and find some new ones to build a detailed map of the brain in action. By amplifying and deciphering these wavelengths, especially the way they worked together to form patterns, we learnt to interpret the electrical impulses.'

Amber was beginning to understand why Bradley Soames had been impressed with Fleming's invention. 'I assume it can learn.'

'Absolutely. In the same way as tuning into radio waves, the NeuroTranslator's neural net seeks out complex patterns of brain activity and correlates them with manifest commands and intentions. Brian comes as close as any entity in history to understanding and expressing a human's thoughts, and mapping their mind.'

'Is Brian conscious?'

Fleming laughed. 'No. Brian uses fuzzy logic and is brilliant at probing our brain and investigating how we think, but it has no will and can't think for itself in the self-aware way we associate with consciousness. If you imagine independent thought as a ball game, then Brian is a brilliant spectator, analyst, commentator and scorekeeper, but it can't play the game itself. The NeuroTranslator primarily analyses and interprets brainwaves, allowing us to boost those that are helpful – for example, the walk-signals needed for an implant in a paralysed or prosthetic limb – and suppress those that aren't, such as pain-signals to an amputated leg.'

Fleming placed the Thinking Cap on his head and pressed a button on the keypad by the cube. The plasma screen fizzed into life and a dazzling spectrum of colours pulsed from the sphere in the cube as different frequencies of light photons performed countless parallel calculations. 'Watch the lines on the screen,' he said. 'They indicate my brainwaves. Now watch the body surrogate.'

There was a sudden spiking of the horizontal

lines on the screen and the mannequin stepped forward with its left leg. Amber jumped. 'You did that just by thinking?'

'By controlling the way I think, yes. It takes practice, but once you get the hang of it it's relatively easy. Brian's a training device. Once our patients have mastered Brian they're given even more sophisticated prosthetic limbs, and in the case of paraplegics even more sophisticated implants. It's still early days but the results have been phenomenal.'

Despite her earlier scepticism about coming here, Amber Grant was encouraged. 'So by analysing my brain waves you hope to identify the signals causing my headaches and suppress them?'

'Hopefully we'll not only suppress the signals but also understand them.'

'And you can do all this tonight? I've got to fly home tomorrow.'

Fleming frowned. 'In one night we'll only be able to start calibrating the machine to your base wavelength signature. It'll take at least a couple more sessions to finalize the preliminary analysis and ascertain what your brain's "normal" resting state is. Only then will we be able to analyse it during a phantom migraine and look at treatment options. Your case is unusual and you should allow up to a month to diagnose and treat it fully. Even then we'll probably need more time.'

'Do it properly or don't do it at all, huh?'

'Exactly. There's a window to start treatment over the next few days, but after that I can't guarantee when I'll be able to fit you in.'

She thought for a second then made a decision. 'Okay, I got to sort out a few things back home, but assume I come back in a few days. What happens now?'

'Frankie, my chief nurse, will set up the first session tonight here in the Think Tank.'

'Will the NeuroTranslator be able to explain why the phantom migraines have only started in the last few months?' Amber asked.

'To be honest, Amber, I don't know. It's usual for phantom pain to occur shortly after a trauma if it's going to occur at all, but your brain is unique. Let's wait and see what Brian can tell us.'

'So when can we start?'

Fleming checked his watch. 'Well, as my old professor at Cambridge used to say, the best time to start anything important is now.'

8

Cape Town, South Africa

Sister Constance had rarely experienced physical fear during her fifty-five years. She felt it now, though, standing on a thirty-foot fishing sloop at dead of night, as the crew threw into the sea a bloody mix of meat and entrails. In the moonlight she could see the ocean come alive with fins cutting through the dark water. She had thought shark fishing was illegal but didn't have the courage to ask the crew if this was true. Pulling her scarlet robes tight around her shoulders she shivered, although the air was warm, tasting salt on her lips from the waves crashing against the anchored boat.

The moon sat full and plump over the distant silhouette of Table Mountain, and she wondered when the Monsignor would come. Each time she had asked the unshaven captain he'd said, 'Soon.'

She could understand why Monsignor Diageo had insisted they meet away from the Red Ark. But why here? She clutched the enamelled red crucifix that hung around her neck, glanced up at the clear night and crossed herself. 'The Monsignor must have his reasons,' she heard herself say aloud, her voice uneven.

Sister Constance had lived a sheltered existence within the Church, a life free of questioning and doubt. Her most traumatic decision had been to follow her headstrong friend, Mother Giovanna Bellini, from the Catholic Church to the new Church of the Soul Truth. But even that had been relatively painless: she had swapped one set of reassuring rules for another. She used to joke that the only real difference was the colour of the robes.

But when Mother Giovanna had called her two days ago and told her about the experiments, Sister Constance had suspected that the Church of the Soul Truth was very different indeed. And yesterday when she had tried unsuccessfully to contact her friend, she had felt concerned. After wrestling with her conscience she had broken her promise to keep Mother Giovanna's secret and had approached Monsignor Diageo on the top deck of the Red Ark to ask if the Red Pope had known of Giovanna's discovery. Clearly shocked, the Monsignor had thanked her for coming forward but refused to discuss this 'threat to everything the Holy Father holds sacred' on the Red Ark.

He had given her clear instructions to board the *Marie Louise* in the harbour then wait for him. The taciturn crew had helped her on board, then ignored her while they took the boat down the coast and went about their business.

Two of the crew passed her, dragging what looked like a cow's rear leg. Grunting, they hefted it overboard, and within seconds the sea was boiling with activity as the frenzied sharks fed off the bounty. Another crew member, holding a boat-hook, prodded the bobbing meat, laughing as the sharks tore it apart. The scene disgusted and frightened her, and she sighed audibly when she heard the *putt-putt-putt* of another vessel approaching. Sister Constance hurried to the stern where her relief turned to joy when the bloodied boat-hook pulled the other vessel alongside and she recognized the man's distinctive face.

'Monsignor Diageo, thank the Lord,' she said. 'Why did we have to meet here?'

'These are sensitive matters, Sister Constance. Have you spoken to anyone else about what Mother Giovanna told you?'

'No, of course not.'

He looked at her closely. 'Are you sure?'

'Yes.'

He gave a satisfied nod. She leant towards him, waiting to be transferred to his boat. 'Does the Holy Father know what the scientists are doing?' she asked. 'Did Mother Giovanna tell him they're killing the patients?'

Diageo looked tired. 'He knows,' he said wearily. He turned his head away but Sister Constance caught a look in his eye that brought her anxiety flooding back. 'He's always known,' he said. Then he whispered, 'I'm sorry.'

Stunned, struggling to absorb the significance of his words, she watched him gaze at the crew, who were still throwing bait to the thrashing sharks.

'As we agreed, there must be no evidence,' he

said, as if she wasn't there. 'Nothing that can be traced back to the Church.'

'I don't understand,' Sister Constance said, as he turned away and she heard the *putt-putt* of the boat's engine start up again.

Then the crew, their bloodstained hands redder than her robes, closed in, forcing her to the end of the sloop. Before she could protest, the man with the hook prodded her hard in the chest, pushing her backwards into the sea.

As the cold water made her gasp and the first frenzied shark bit into her left foot, she still didn't understand why this was happening. Even as the razor-sharp teeth of a Great White ripped into her pelvis, tearing her apart, she screamed out Monsignor Diageo's name, convinced there had been a dreadful mistake.

9

Barley Hall

After leaving Amber Grant with the staff nurse and settling her in to the Think Tank for the night, Fleming turned his attention to two of his other patients. He prided himself on treating all his charges with the same level of compassion and professional care, but Rob and Jake were special.

As he walked to the workshop, he was relieved he hadn't fought too hard with the director against seeing Amber. His curiosity was piqued, and he was convinced he could help her. Also, by putting Rob's trial back till tomorrow, he could give him a surprise that would lift his spirits.

The Barley Hall workshop was the one element of Fleming's research facility that wasn't housed in the east wing. For reasons no one could remember it was located at the far end of the west wing where Bobby Chan's team worked. Here, in an extended shed, science merged with art, where electronics, metal, latex and space-age materials were combined to create prosthetics that behaved and looked like human limbs.

When Fleming entered a technician was peeling

a disconcertingly lifelike arm from a skeleton of metal and wires. Foot and hand moulds lined a wall in ascending order of size. Drums of differing skin pigments were stacked beneath a workbench, and in the far corner of the shed Bill, the chief technician, was honing a shapely left leg. To Fleming's right a series of finished limbs was stacked against the wall. All were wrapped in plastic and bore identification tags, like dry-cleaning awaiting collection. Most were single arms or legs of various shapes and sizes. But slightly apart from the rest was a tiny pair of legs. Each leg was so lifelike that, somehow, Fleming could hardly bear to look at them.

Bill raised his face mask, switched off the lathe and pointed at them. 'I've put the final latex coat on. The feet are moulded from my own boy's.'

Fleming picked them up. As always he was surprised by their weight, although they were no heavier than natural limbs. The detail, particularly of the feet and toes, touched him. 'They look fantastic, Bill, thanks a lot.'

Bill raised his right thumb in a salute. 'Good luck.'

Such was the nature of the clinic that few people commented when Fleming walked back to the east wing carrying the little pair of prosthetic legs. When he reached the other end of the building, he stopped outside the double doors of the physio-therapy suite and peered through circular windows into the large hall with its exercise equipment, walking frames and therapy pool. Only two people were inside.

His nephew, Jake, was sitting on the polished wooden floor with his back to the door, playing with some plastic bricks while Pam Fleming, the child's grandmother, watched over him. Jake had lived with his paternal grandparents since the accident and Fleming had asked his mother to bring him here at six o'clock. She was small and birdlike with short fair hair streaked with grey, but she hovered protectively over her grandson. Both she and Fleming's father had been pillars of support since the tragedy.

Fleming watched as Jake stacked brick after brick until he had created a tower almost as tall as himself. Then he built another and then a third. He admired them for a second or two then knocked them down gleefully.

Holding the legs behind his back, Fleming pushed open the doors and walked into the hall. Jake swivelled round to face him, and the result of the car accident eleven months ago was plain to see: both the child's legs ended above the knee, the right marginally longer than the left. Despite his habitual exposure to similar and worse mutilations, Fleming was still shocked at the sight of his nephew's injuries.

His sole consolation was that at least he had been able to help. He wasn't ideal uncle material – he had a workaholic lifestyle, interrupted only by mountaineering expeditions, and he was a poor role model when it came to stable relationships: every visit Jake made to his townhouse on the river seemed to coincide with the arrival of a new girlfriend. There was one thing, however, that he had been uniquely qualified to do for his brother's son: he had been able to help Jake walk again.

'Hi, Mum,' Fleming said, hugged her and kissed her cheek.

'Everything all right, Milo?' She looked nervous but excited. She had such faith in her son that it frightened him. At Jake's mother's funeral he had overheard her tell a friend: 'Rob and Miles were always close, even when they were little boys. It's so fortunate that Miles can help now.' It seemed to Fleming that his parents had only been able to come to terms with what had happened by investing their fragile hope in him. And he was terrified he might not fulfil it.

He squeezed her hand. 'Everything's fine, Mum. You'll see.' He bent to his nephew. 'Hi, Jake.'

The little boy gave him a sly smile. 'Hello, Uncle Milo.'

Fleming held out the prosthetic legs and Jake's eyes lit up. 'Wow.'

'They're the ones you've been training with, Jake, but we've put the final covering on them so now they look like real legs – *your* legs.'

Jake took them as if he'd been given the best Christmas present in the world. '*Thanks*, Uncle Milo.' Then he fitted the leg flaps over his stumps, connected the implants with practised skill and stood up as if they were part of him. The prosthetic muscles in the artificial legs were instructed by the boy's own thoughts, amplified and translated by computer. Six months ago, five months after the crash, Fleming had downloaded Jake's personal thought-signature from the

NeuroTranslator. He had inserted electrodes beneath Jake's scalp, and with implants and an optical computer no bigger than a wristwatch Jake could walk unaided and lead a near normal life. He had been the first, but already others were benefiting from the technology.

'Right, Jake,' said Fleming. 'Wait here and I'll get your dad. I want him to see this.'

10

The Think Tank. Later that evening

'You made CNN. Saw it when I woke up just now.
You got me worried, Amber. How you feelin'?'

'Not too bad, Papa Pete. What do you mean you
just woke up? Where you calling from?'

'San Francisco.'

'I thought you were in the Vatican.'

'I am, but I'm in a crisis meeting with some colleagues over here.' Her godfather's New York
accent sounded harsh suddenly. 'When the Jesuits,
the storm troopers of Catholicism, start defecting
to the Red Pope you know you gotta problem.'

'I appreciate you calling me, Papa Pete,' she said,
not wanting to get drawn into a discourse on the
Red Pope. 'It's been a long time.' And she knew
why. Ever since her adoptive mother had taken ill
two years ago, and Amber had paid for her to stay
in the best hospice in the bay area, Father Peter
Riga, the man who had saved her life, had
felt betrayed: not only did Catholics not run the
hospice but 'the enemy', the Red Pope's Church
of the Soul Truth, did. Amber had explained to him
that she was determined to give her mother

whatever she wanted, and if that meant staying in a hospice run by a rival church so be it.

'Saw your mother yesterday,' Riga said.

'In the hospice?'

'Sure. She seemed okay.'

'That was kind of you, Papa Pete. She felt bad about you not approving . . .'

'Don't worry. Gave her my blessing. Nice place, too. Just felt ashamed that the Mother Church couldn't look after its own.'

'Things change.'

'They sure do,' he said. 'Anyways, I'm over for a couple days so if you're back on time we can meet up.'

'I'd like that,' she said. 'I'll call you tomorrow.'

'Okay, my child, take care of yourself.'

Amber switched off her communicator and placed it on the table beside her bed in the Think Tank. Earlier when she had switched on the device, it had been loaded with concerned messages from well-wishers. The news was out. One of her early-morning swimming buddies, as well as her best friend, Karen, had called. Even Soames had left a brief message to say the presentation had gone well and to call him if there were any developments.

The one call she had made tonight was to the hospice, confirming that she would be returning as planned. Her mother was in the final stages of terminal cancer and Amber hated leaving her. The thought of returning to Barley Hall, as Fleming had recommended, increased her anxiety. Sitting up in bed, she tried to ignore the video camera staring at her from its mount overhead. She wore the blue latticework Thinking Cap and her scalp tingled where the conductive gel held the electrodes in place.

The NeuroTranslator at the base of her bed emitted a soft hum as it read the electrical impulses generated by her brain; the lower half of the split-level plasma screen showed a grid with individually coloured pulsing horizontal lines, each representing a wavelength in her brain. Some lines peaked violently while others remained virtually flat. At regular intervals the screen scrolled down to reveal other wavelengths, all recording the pattern of her thoughts. The upper half of the screen displayed the stimuli designed to engage her mental processes. Currently she was studying a spatial puzzle. Three lines were overlaid on a nest of concentric squares, which appeared to recede into the distance, and she had to determine which line was the shortest. Despite a suspicion that it was an optical illusion, and the two obviously shorter lines were identical in length, she selected the one on the right.

She had been tackling the on-screen puzzles and exercises for over an hour. They were intelligent and well designed, stimulating most of her brain's cognitive processes ranging from verbal reasoning, logic and numerical dexterity to intuitive guesswork. Earlier, she had been given an injection to stimulate her unconscious neural activity during sleep and so give the NeuroTranslator a clearer read when she started what Staff Nurse Pinner called the 'easy mental exercises'. 'That's when you just close your eyes, drop off and let Brian do all the work.'

Her jet-lag was under control and the puzzles were interesting, but she was finding it hard to concentrate. Her mind kept wandering to her mother and sister. Particularly her sister.

Talking about her twin with Miles Fleming and seeing the medical pictures of when they had been conjoined had stirred up all her old feelings of guilt, regret and loss. Reaching for the bedside table, she retrieved the worn photograph she always carried with her. It showed Ariel and herself embracing in front of a full-length mirror. Because of the angle from which the picture was taken, both their smiling faces were visible and nothing appeared to connect them except their love for each other.

She had spent her entire solo life struggling to resolve her guilt and anger about her dead twin. First she had turned to Catholicism, but however kind and patient her godfather had been in explaining the Mother Church's view of the world she found its judgemental dogma unhelpful. Then she had turned to philosophy and physics to try to understand why things were as they were. Eventually she had focused on the mysterious world of quantum physics, studying the almost telepathic relationships that linked the trillion particles of elemental stardust that made up everything in the universe. So far it had yielded no clear answers but it offered infinite possibilities. And distraction. She might not have found meaning in the vagaries of the quantum world but she had found solace in searching for it.

The sheer intellectual rigour and hard work

required to explore the contradictions and dualities of particle physics diverted her from the guilt and loss that clouded her peace of mind whenever she lay idle for long. But tonight, however hard she tried to contain her unresolved feelings for Ariel, they kept rising to the surface.

When Frankie popped her head round the door the puzzle on the screen changed to a crossword. 'I'm off home now,' she said. 'We've got a big clinical trial tomorrow, but there'll be a nurse in the observation room all night. Everything all right?'

Amber smiled. 'My mind keeps wandering and I'm tired. Does that matter?'

The nurse shook her head. 'Not at all. The stimuli are only used to get a broad read of mental activity and to keep you amused. Brian's fuzzy logic is flexible. If you need to drop off to sleep, don't worry about it. To be honest, for the baseline scan we get the most useful diagnostic data from the sleeping brain anyway. Good night and sleep well, Dr Grant.'

'Night. Thanks.'

She turned back to the screen and completed the crossword. Her eyelids began to droop and she didn't register the puzzles changing on the screen. Drifting in that hyper-lucid state between wakefulness and sleep, her mind returned to her sister.

On and off over the last thirty years she had been disconcerted to feel that her life wasn't entirely her own. Whenever she tried to forge any deep relationship she was frequently accused of being mentally 'miles away' or with 'someone else'. It seemed that, asleep or awake, Ariel was always buried somewhere in her thoughts, as if Amber couldn't let her go, couldn't get on with living her life because it wasn't entirely hers to live. Only when she threw herself into her work and her research had she found peace, a distraction from the other person in her head.

The eight-year-old little girl she had loved more than she loved herself.

The eight-year-old girl who was once part of her.

The eight-year-old girl who had died for her.

11

The ward. Barley Hall

When Fleming entered cubicle five in the research ward, the first place his eyes went to was the ECG monitor. 'How is he, Emma?' he asked the nurse sitting by the apparatus. 'His heart steady?'

The nurse smiled. 'He's stable and should be fine for tomorrow.'

'Thanks. You take a break. I'll look after him for now.'

Turning to the bed, Fleming saw that the nurse had dressed his brother in his favourite faded black Ralph Lauren polo shirt and jeans, and his hair had been cut short in the military style he had favoured when he was in the army. Sitting upright on the motorized bed in his cubicle, Rob still looked good, although the shirt and jeans hung loose on his once powerful body.

Fleming walked round the bed to be directly in line with Rob's good eye. 'Hi, Rob – your cognitive exercises have been great and your heart's behaving itself so we should be on for the trial tomorrow. I've got a great surprise for you now, though. Would you like to see it?' He looked down at the computer screen directly below Rob's face. Sixteen words were displayed on a four-by-four grid. They had formed Rob's vocabulary since he had suffered the stroke to his brainstem, which had paralysed all of his body except his left eye. Using electro-oculographic signals, Rob's eye movements directed a cursor on the screen. When he had chosen a word, he blinked and a computer-generated voice said the word.

'No,' the computer voice said.

Fleming laughed. 'In that case I won't show it to you, you ungrateful bastard.'

He could tell that his older brother was trying to smile – and that the smile was as strained as his own banter. Rob had always been his hero, an action man who was always fitter, stronger and faster than he was. But now when he looked at Rob he felt a crushing sadness and remembered Billy French.

Billy had been a friend when they were in their late teens. They had all shared a passion for climbing, and every summer they bummed around Europe trying their luck on the big Alpine peaks. Rob was already an exceptional climber, while Billy and Miles were merely enthusiastic amateurs. Nevertheless, with Rob as leader, they tackled most levels of climb up to ED, *extrêmement difficile*, and had even scaled a few ABOs, *abominable* ascents. It was on the notorious Nordwand of the Eiger that it happened.

It was the end of the summer. Fleming was nineteen and due to start his medical degree at Cambridge. Rob was talking about joining the

Royal Marines. Billy was still deciding what to do with the future, which stretched out before them, shimmering with endless possibilities.

It had been one of the wettest Augusts on record and the mountain face was plastered with rime and loaded with unstable snow. But they had come to climb the Eiger and nothing could deter them. On the lower reaches, near the top of a buttress known as the First Pillar, Billy made a misstep. His ice axes and crampons sheared out of the rotten ice and he was airborne. The belays should have held him but the ice screws shot out of their moorings.

Rob and Miles dug in deep and stopped themselves being pulled off the face, but Billy fell until the rope went taut, then swung in a pendulous arc and hit an overhang, which broke his neck. In seconds he went from being a fit young man pondering his future to a paraplegic with none.

On the endless, harrowing descent down the mountain, Rob and Miles nursed Billy's trussed body and tried to keep him conscious, hoping to meet someone who could go for help. But no one appeared until they were almost at the base. On the last drop, as they lowered Billy, Rob turned to Miles. 'If this ever happens to me, Milo,' he whispered, his tanned face as pale as the snow, 'just cut the rope and let me go. You're never more alive than when you're close to death. But you're never more dead than when you're stuck in a life you don't want. So let me go. That's what I'd want. A little pain, don't mind that, a little fear and then nothing.' Two days later, Billy died in hospital.

The Fleming brothers had continued climbing together even after Rob married Susan seven years ago. They had travelled round the world in their search for new mountains to conquer, and often felt as though Billy was with them, especially when the going got tough. Fleming had never forgotten his brother's words, and had always thought that if he did come to harm, it would be on a mountain or in combat. It never occurred to him that Rob would have a stroke while driving a Ford Mondeo up the M1 to Leeds.

As he wheeled his brother's bed out of the ward and into the corridor, he told himself again that tomorrow he would help him. He recalled the countless times Rob had pulled him from a crevasse or helped him reach a difficult peak. Now he would support his brother on his toughest climb.

He had already helped Jake to walk again. Tomorrow he would help Rob to talk.

He hoped this was what Rob wanted. Their parents, especially their mother, wanted it. Their mother was an Anglican, who had become even more devout since the accident and believed with an almost blind fervour that in time, with God's love and Miles's skill, her eldest son would be restored to full health.

Fleming knew, though, from witnessing laborious communication sessions with psychologists, that Rob wanted to die. His stroke had caused the car crash that had left him paraplegic, his wife dead and his young son's legs crushed. He had tried twice to broach Rob's depression with their parents, but each time they had been unwilling to talk about it. 'It's just a phase,' they said. 'He'll feel different when he starts to get better.'

And when Fleming had tried to explain that there was no guarantee Rob would get better, his mother had smiled bravely and said that God and she weren't giving up on him just yet. 'God will guide him.'

Like when Rob had had the accident, Miles had thought but not said.

It never occurred to his mother that Rob might *blame* God for what had happened.

For a guilty second Fleming envied Amber. At least she had the solace of knowing that her sister was beyond suffering. His brother's plight had only strengthened Fleming's conviction that there was no God and no afterlife. It had never been clearer to him that the only choice for any man was to make the best of *this* life with its suffering before oblivion took over for ever – and for ever was a long time. Fleming had one simple aim for his brother: to help him in the here and now. He needed to show him how Jake had been helped, and in turn convince him that one day he, too, could be whole and happy again.

'Almost there, Rob,' he said, wheeling the bed down the corridor towards the physiotherapy room.

As they approached the swing doors, the surprise leapt out. Jake was hopping up and down as nimble and agile as if the accident had never happened. 'Dad! Dad! Look at my legs!' He ran to the bed and bounded up to kiss his father's cheek.

Pam Fleming had followed her grandson through the swing doors. 'He was too excited,' she said, with a beatific smile. 'He couldn't wait to show them off.'

Fleming turned to his brother and saw that even his good eye had failed him. Tears were leaking from it and he couldn't use it to choose his words on the screen. 'Save your words for tomorrow, Rob,' he said. 'You'll be able to say whatever you want then.'

12

The Think Tank

As Amber Grant closed her eyes, the video camera and Brian were watching over her. The Neuro-Translator never slept. As it scanned Amber's brainwaves it correlated them with the exercises she had done, comparing her thought patterns to its battery of data, seeking out new patterns that would indicate significant aberrations. All the time it was learning about her brain, mapping the electrical architecture of her mind. Using the Lucifer optical processor that powered its own brain, it performed all these analyses at the speed of light.

While Amber Grant was awake the Neuro-Translator discovered nothing unusual. Nor did it detect anything as she lost consciousness and descended rapidly through the first two stages of sleep. As Amber lingered in the third stage and her body twitched erratically, Brian still registered little outside its normal range. Even as Amber entered the fourth stage of sleep, and perspiration beaded her forehead, the humming mind-reader remained untroubled.

It was only when she entered the state

characterized by rapid eye movement, REM, that Brian registered something unusual in the still uncharted unconscious governed by dreams.

She was sweating. Her forehead was covered with perspiration and her nightdress was saturated. Her lips moved and she mumbled, her words gradually becoming more coherent until she was calling her own name in a child's plaintive voice: 'Amber, Amber, where are you, Amber?'

As she fell into the dream state random movements of her eyeballs were visible beneath the lids. Her body shook as if in distress. Then it became still and her eyes opened.

Memories flashed before her like the jumbled shards of a broken mirror: Father Peter Riga in his Jesuit robes sweeping up Ariel and her in his arms; her father's proud smile when she graduated with top honours from Stanford; Bradley Soames on campus at Cal Tech wearing his tinted mask and protective clothing; her mother stroking her hair and kissing her cheek as she fell asleep; her sister squeezing her hand and whispering goodbye before the surgeon put them both to sleep.

She felt the blade cut into her head. Through white-hot pain she heard herself screaming, her voice mingling with Ariel's, both trying to hold on to the other as they were torn apart. Even now as her mind left her body Amber felt she was attached in some way to Ariel, still being ripped from her. But the pain was emotional not physical, fear, loss, grief and rage combining together. She tried again to scream but she had no voice.

She tried to struggle but she had no body. She was an amorphous entity, enveloped in darkness, rushing towards an unknowable void.

Ahead, a bright cone of light appeared, flickering in the dark, drawing her into its magnetic field. She was travelling so fast that she was soon inside it, a part of it. It appeared to stand still, its beam disintegrating into particles as she merged with it, becoming indivisible from it. Her being was no more than a collection of shimmering packets of light. The light evoked a memory and she waited for Ariel to join her again and lead her to the source.

Then, just as she thought Ariel might be there, the emotional pain spiked to new heights as the last raw connection pulled at her. She wished then that she could cut herself free and float peacefully away.

But there was no escaping the elastic grip that pulled her out of the light, back into the darkness, back to herself . . .

Her staring eyes closed and then opened again as Amber woke with a start. All the time the NeuroTranslator continued to monitor her. And now the night nurse was soothing her, mopping her brow.

She was so focused on her patient that she paid no heed to the pulsing wavelengths dancing across the top half of the NeuroTranslator screen as Brian's neural net assimilated the abnormal aspect of Amber's brain. She rearranged the disturbed bedclothes, relieved that her charge was calm now, and didn't register the twenty-six-second change in tone emitted by the humming device.

When Amber Grant went back to sleep, and the nurse retreated gratefully for a cup of coffee, the NeuroTranslator had returned to its even hum.

13

The Red Ark. Cape Town.
33° 55´ S, 18° 22´ E

Six thousand miles away, Xavier Accosta, the Red Pope, sat alone in his office on the upper deck of the Red Ark. The leatherbound book cradled in his hands looked even older than its hundred years, its spine cracked from being opened too many times at the same page. He let it fall open at the same passage it always did. Breathing deeply, he rearranged his scarlet robes and flexed his damaged left leg, allowing the pain to dissipate. Then he began to read, his dark eyes moving slowly across the page as he savoured each word of the familiar text:

Extract from the *Archives d'Anthropologie Criminelle*, Montpellier, France, 1905

Notes on the experiment between Dr Baurieux and the criminal Languille in which the doctor tries to communicate with the condemned man's severed head immediately after execution by guillotine.

Immediately after the decapitation, the condemned man's eyelids and lips contracted for five or six seconds . . . I waited a few seconds and the contractions ceased, the face relaxed, the eyelids closed half-way over the eyeballs so that only the whites of the eyes were visible, exactly like dying or newly deceased people.

At that moment I shouted 'Languille' in a loud voice, and I saw that his eyes opened slowly and without twitching, the movements were distinct and clear, the look was not dull and empty, the eyes which were fully alive were indisputably looking at me. After a few seconds, the eyelids closed again, slowly and steadily.

I addressed him again. Once more, the eyelids were raised slowly, without contractions, and two undoubtedly alive eyes looked at me attentively with an expression even more piercing than the first time. Then the eyes shut once again. I made a third attempt. No reaction. The whole episode lasted between twenty-five and thirty seconds.

Dr Baurieux, Montpellier, France, 1905

Whenever Accosta read these words he felt both disturbed and excited, imagining what Languille's eyes had seen as his soul departed.

He looked up at four high-resolution holographic plasma screens on the oak-panelled wall in front of him. Two were blank. One showed the looped video of his last service, with the sound turned down, and another the BBC's live coverage of the eighty-thousand tonne Red Ark departing Cape Town harbour to continue its pilgrimage around the world, its blood-red hull and white superstructure gleaming in the African sun. Panning round the pier the cameras captured the crowds straining for a glimpse of the physical embodiment of their Church, the Church of the Soul Truth, the floating city that housed the Red Pope's virtual cathedral, and all the administrative and technical staff that made the world's first e-Church possible.

But as the Red Ark set sail, Cardinal Xavier Accosta ignored the television screens and the spectacular views of Cape Town through the panoramic picture window to his left. He was impatient for the doctor's report on the Soul Project. Time was slipping away, and if the scientists couldn't achieve their goal, all he had achieved since breaking away from Rome ten years ago would be meaningless. And yet, although he wanted to hear from the doctor, he was anxious about Mother Giovanna Bellini. He looked down at the old book and tried not to think about her, but the more he endeavoured to put her out of his mind, the more she dwelt there.

A sudden knock interrupted his thoughts.

Accosta stiffened. 'Enter.'

Monsignor Paulo Diageo opened the door, his powerful body filling the frame. Diageo was similarly attired in scarlet, although his robes were trimmed with a single stripe of gold braid to Accosta's two. Unlike Accosta, who had fine, photogenic features, Diageo's face was heavy and brutish: a low forehead punctuated by dark eyebrows, heavy-lidded recessed eyes and a broad, protruding jaw. His fleshy, almost feminine lips were at odds with the rest of his face and gave his otherwise impassive features a cruel, petulant quality.

Accosta braced himself. 'Mother Giovanna? Any news?'

The Monsignor shrugged. 'It's been resolved, Holy Father.'

Like Monsignor Diageo, Mother Giovanna Bellini had been a loyal follower from the early days. When Accosta had first been promoted to the Vatican twenty years ago she was a lowly nun. She had served him so devotedly that when he was excommunicated a decade later and founded his own Church, she followed him. As a reward he made her one of his first female priests.

Nine months ago, after years of research on the Soul Project, it had been decided to test the technology on dying subjects. Terminal patients with no surviving family were selected from Church-run hospices around the world and pronounced dead before they were taken to the foundation to die. Since a priest was needed to deliver the last rites, and her devotion to Accosta was absolute, Mother Giovanna Bellini had been assigned to the patients on the understanding that she would ask no questions.

But of course she'd asked questions. And when she'd called Accosta, telling him that the doctor and other members of the Truth Council were murdering the subjects, he had already known that the terminally ill patients were being eased into death; it was the only way that the experiments could be conducted. He hadn't wanted to involve Diageo but her questions had complicated matters and the stakes were too high. Diageo had understood his problem, with barely a word needing to be said, and Accosta hoped that once Mother Giovanna recognized the full importance of the sacred mission she, too, would understand.

'So everything's in order?'

'I think so.'

'Nothing I should be concerned about?'

The smallest shake of the head. 'No, Your Holiness.'

Accosta tried to keep the relief from his voice. 'Very well.'

'Frank Carvelli's waiting on line.'

'Put him through.'

One of the holographic plasma screens facing him fizzed into life, and Accosta could see Frank Carvelli picking lint from his black cashmere jacket. He was the second member of the three-man Truth Council that had spearheaded the Soul Project. A delicate-featured man with smooth olive skin and suspiciously blue-black hair pulled back into a ponytail, he had a penchant for dressing in black. Although Accosta thought him vain and shallow, he was a brilliant communicator indispensable to the Church and the Soul Project.

Carvelli was the head of KREE8 Industries, which excelled in everything from communication and presentation software to movie production and public relations. KREE8 had been responsible for creating the holographic plasma screens on which Carvelli's image now appeared. It was also responsible for over 60 per cent of the computer-generated special effects used in Hollywood movies, and specialized in creating virtual movie stars and resurrecting dead ones.

But it was on the Optical Internet, or the Optinet, that KREE8 was supreme, bringing real-time virtual reality to the world. It had been KREE8, and Carvelli in particular, who had helped harness the power of Optrix's optical computer revolution to create Accosta's unique electronic Church. KREE8 WebCrawler headsets allowed millions of people to attend Accosta's services live, as if they were there in person.

Also, Carvelli understood the media. His contacts and muscle had helped make Accosta the phenomenon he now was. Accosta realized this, although he suspected that Carvelli was more interested in supporting him because of the power and exposure he gained from his association with the largest Church in the world than because of any deep-seated faith.

'Your Holiness,' Carvelli said, 'the new equipment is virtually complete. All we need now is a day of your time to upload your image and muscle movements, capture your voice profile and take a full body cast. Just tell me where and when and I'll arrange it.'

'You should speak to Monsignor Diageo about my schedule, but isn't this a little premature given that we haven't even successfully completed the first stage of the project?'

Carvelli nodded. 'A new development has made the Doctor confident of a breakthrough. He told me to get everything prepared so we could move fast when it comes.'

Accosta controlled his irritation. The Soul Project was sacred: it was *his* project and yet the head of the Truth Council, the man who insisted on being referred to by the anonymous sobriquet of the Doctor, was increasingly determining the agenda. 'What is this new development?'

'As you know, the Doctor's a cautious man. He won't tell me until he's more sure but he's confident. And when the Doctor's confident, something usually comes of it. I'm sure he'll tell you more in the next update. I'll liaise with Monsignor Diageo about your availability for the upload.'

'Thank you, Frank.'

After Carvelli had gone off-line, Diageo knocked at the door again. 'Your Holiness, you asked me to alert you fifteen minutes before broadcast.'

Accosta rose from his chair. Straightening his aching body, he stretched to his full height of over six feet and thrust back his broad shoulders. His sixty-eight-year-old frame was still lean and imposing in the scarlet robes. As he felt the adrenaline flow through him, he steeled himself to address his faithful from around the world: the millions of followers who were already logging on to attend his virtual service.

14

Barley Hall. The next morning

'I'm telling you, Miles, I died again last night,' said Amber, looking pale and drawn.

Fleming frowned. 'The nurse said you had a nightmare.'

'It was no nightmare. I don't dream. Ariel used to dream but I never did. That was one of the things that separated us. What happened last night was so real. It was a repeat of the near-death experience I had on the operating table when I almost died. When Ariel did die.'

'But you're not dead, Amber. I'm a doctor. I notice these things.'

He sat behind his desk in his office and tried not to look at his watch. Rob's trial was due in less than two hours and Amber's cab was waiting outside to take her to the airport. This morning he had woken early and, after a jog along the river and a light breakfast, he had left home at about seven. His mother and Jake were staying with him and had arranged to come to the clinic later so that if the trial went well Rob could talk to them. It was an unusually sunny October day and he had left the top down on his ageing Jaguar sports car to speed along the flat fenland roads to Barley Hall. The weather was a good omen for Rob's trial and he had arrived hopeful, expecting to be able to spend the first few hours of the day preparing for it. But Amber had prevented that.

'Come on, Amber, I know you're upset by your dream, but listen to what you're saying.'

'It wasn't a dream,' she said stubbornly, rubbing her ear-lobe.

'Okay, tell me about this dream, this experience.'

'I already told you. I leave my body and rush through darkness to a bright light. I'm moving so fast I catch up with it. Then I'm part of it. And suddenly, as if I'm attached by elastic, I'm yanked back to my body and to life. The only way I can describe it is like a psychic bungee jump.'

'And Ariel featured in this?'

'Well, that's the weird thing. I never saw her but there was a kind of connection – although it's not easy to explain. Like magnets of the same polarity, the more we tried to come together the stronger the force that was keeping us apart became. It was like atoms that attract each other when they're a little distance apart but repel each other when squeezed into one another. We were two people stuck in a revolving door – however hard we pushed to meet up it just wasn't going to happen.'

Fleming smiled sympathetically: by consciously linking the headaches to her dead twin, Amber had unleashed a torrent of repressed memories and emotions from her unconscious, he thought.

'It sounds a lot like a dream, Amber, or a delayed memory. Look, Ariel still intrudes on your thoughts from time to time. Am I right?'

'Yeah.'

'And yesterday when we discussed your headaches you were particularly focused on her. So it's understandable that your subconscious—'

'It was more than that,' she insisted vehemently. 'Some part of her was searching for me, trying to reach me, consciously trying to warn me about something . . .' She trailed off, frowning, as if realizing how strange her words sounded. 'It didn't *feel* like a dream.'

'Dreams rarely do, Amber. Last night Frankie gave you a stimulant to help the NeuroTranslator get a better read off your neural signals, and that often has the effect of relaxing the subconscious – triggering dreams, even repressed ones. It's a good thing – it gives Brian more material to analyse so it can better understand what's going on in there. Amber, dreams are powerful and often seem more real than reality. As we discussed, I suggest you come back here in three or four days so we can complete the analysis. Can you spend up to a month away from your other responsibilities?'

Amber hesitated briefly, then nodded. 'Yes. I want to resolve this. I've *got* to resolve this.'

'And we *will* resolve it,' he said. 'We'll wait for you to come back from California then let the NeuroTranslator finish its initial analysis. We can run any ancillary scans that might be necessary before analysing your brain while you're experiencing a phantom headache. I'll look at your base data results as soon as I can. If I see anything unusual I'll tell you immediately. Okay?'

'You'll at least think about what I told you?'

'Of course. I'll investigate every avenue fully. You've come to me to cure your phantom headaches. I'll look at anything and everything relevant to that. But I can tell you now, there'll be a rational medical explanation for this. There always is.'

Amber frowned, clearly unconvinced. 'Is there?'

'Yes,' he said confidently. 'Always.'

15

The Think Tank

By eleven o'clock Fleming was beside Rob's bed in the Think Tank. The team had assembled. Standing next to the NeuroTranslator was Greg Brown, a pale, bespectacled Australian who had studied computer electronics in Sydney and California before coming to Cambridge to work as Fleming's technical assistant and computer specialist. Frankie Pinner was by the bed, checking Rob's life signs on the surrounding monitors.

Fleming bent down to his brother. Rob's eye-activated communication screen had been removed for the trial and he was reduced to one blink for no and two for yes. 'Rob, you do understand what's going to happen today?'

He blinked his left eye twice.

Fleming and Brown had spent months calibrating Brian not only to amplify and interpret brain waves but also to correlate their patterns to words. For the last month Rob had been poring silently over selected text passages while Brian read his mind, correlating his thought patterns to the words he was reading and finding simple connections. By linking the machine to a voice synthesizer Fleming hoped to translate Rob's thought words into speech. And today was the day.

He decided to be direct. 'There are risks, Rob. You must understand that although this trial poses no direct threat to you, you're in a weakened state – particularly your heart – and any exertion may place a potentially fatal strain on it. We can still put off the trial. There's no pressure to carry on. I want and need to make that clear. Do you still want to go on?'

Rob's eye blinked twice.

'Rob, you know the drill by now,' Fleming said. 'Some words are going to scroll down on the stimuli screen, representing all the words the computer recognizes from your exercises over the last month. When that's finished, take your time and think each word you want to say. Concentrate on just the word you want. Keep it simple and don't worry about grammar. You understand?'

Two blinks.

'Excellent.' Fleming glanced at the others in the room. Frankie was checking the life-signs monitors – Fleming noted that the ECG was steady, showing an even heartbeat, additional oxygen was on hand and a back-up nurse waited by the door. Greg stood by the NeuroTranslator, monitoring the split sections on the plasma screen.

The upper half, displaying Rob's brain-wave activity, showed a grid covered with fine horizontal lines, oscillating and peaking independently. On the lower half, words scrolled down like the credits of a movie. They reflected the text Rob had input into

Brian's neural net over the last four weeks. They were simple, *help*, *love*, *go*, *need*, *play*, *ball*, the vocabulary of a child a little younger than Jake. But they were words, vital building blocks to bridge the communication void between Rob and the world.

As each word flashed up Fleming saw the lines in the upper screen change – the pattern of wavelengths forming a unique thought signature for that word. Fleming watched the flashing words until the list was exhausted.

'Programming complete' appeared on the lower screen.

Fleming glanced at Greg and Frankie. 'Ready, everybody?'

They all nodded.

Then he turned to Rob. 'Ready?' His gaze fixed on his brother's left eye, and he waited for the double blink.

It didn't come.

Instead, as he stared at Rob's immobile left eye he heard a hiss of static come from the two speakers above the bed and then, in his peripheral vision, noticed movement on the upper half of the plasma screen. He turned to see 'Yes' flash on the lower screen. But what made the hairs stand up on the back of his neck was hearing an unmistakable voice issue from the speakers, saying the same word. Yes.

Not daring to look at the others, Fleming kept his eyes on Rob. He would try another closed question. 'Would you agree that I'm the better-looking brother, Rob?'

Again there was a pause, a longer one this time,

and for a moment Fleming thought that the 'yes' had been a fluke. Then Brian's screen flashed. The lines on the top half pulsed and a word flashed on the lower half. Followed by three more.

'No,' said the voice from the speakers. 'No. No. Ugly.'

A ripple of relieved laughter swept through the room.

It was time for an open question. 'Can you tell me how you feel, Rob?'

Another pause, then three words flashed up on the lower half of the screen. Almost immediately the disembodied voice spoke again from the speakers: 'Good. To. Talk.' Tears dripped down Rob's face and Frankie stepped forward to wipe them away. 'Like. I. Am. Climbing. Freedom.'

Fleming had programmed in a 'natural' speaking voice, so Brian's over-deliberate word-by-word utterances were less robotic than earlier voice synthesizers.

'It's working,' Greg hissed beside Fleming. 'It's goddamned working.'

Again the static followed by the lag. 'Yes. Good. Speak. Thank. You. Thank. You. Milo.'

'It's wonderful to hear you, Rob,' said Fleming. 'Mum and Jake are waiting down the corridor. Is there anything you'd like to say to them when they come to see you?'

Hiss. 'Love Jake. Love Mum. Love Dad. Love You Milo.'

'We love you too, Rob.'

'Talk. So Much Say. But Can't Say.'

'Don't worry, Rob. Take your time. It's just you

and me for now, and you can say whatever you want to me. You know that. Anything at all. Okay?'

'Feel Bad About Susan. And Jake. Feel Like Killed Susan. Feel Like Hurt Jake.'

Miles met his brother's eye. 'Rob, what happened was awful but it wasn't your fault. You suffered a stroke to your brainstem. There was nothing you could do.'

'No. No. No.'

'Rob, there was nothing you could have—'

But as the steady beeps of the ECG lost their rhythm and merged into a continuous alarm, Miles realized that Rob wasn't disagreeing with him. His brother was shouting in distress. 'No what, Rob?' he demanded, his own heart somersaulting in his chest. 'Talk to me, Rob!'

Static issued from the speakers and Rob's paralysed body began to shake.

'What's wrong, Rob?' said Fleming. 'Tell us what's wrong!'

Silence, except for the incessant alarms of the medical equipment.

Frankie leant over Rob, trying to hold down his convulsing body. Her calm voice was urgent. 'BP seventy over ninety. Breathing laboured. He's gone tachycardic and he needs oxygen.' She reached for the mask and placed it over his mouth.

The ECG flatlined.

'Charge up the paddles,' Frankie ordered. The other nurse rushed to the defibrillator. The life-support systems were flashing and beeping madly.

Frankie took the paddles. 'Stand back.'

107

Fleming stared at the ECG as the volts surged through his brother's paralysed body.

Nothing happened.

Frankie tried again.

The line stayed flat.

And again.

The line peaked erratically before flattening again.

She tried a fourth time.

Then Fleming heard static on the speakers followed by four distinct words that almost stopped his heart. 'Cut. The Rope. Milo.'

In that instant he was on the Eiger with his brother, looking down at Billy French. *You're never more alive than when you're close to death. But you're never more dead than when you're stuck with a life you don't want. If this ever happens to me, Milo, let me go. That's what I'd want. A little pain, don't mind that, a little fear and then nothing.*

Fleming stared at the ECG line, which remained stubbornly flat after four attempts to restart his brother's heart. 'Rob, talk to me.'

'Cut The Rope. Milo,' his brother repeated.

'We need the epinephrine!' Frankie barked at the younger nurse, who was fumbling with the vacuum-sealed foil packaging. She grabbed the pack and ripped off the foil, exposing the pre-prepped syringe of stimulant. Holding it like a dagger she prepared to plunge it straight through Rob's ribcage into his heart.

Before she could bring it down, Fleming reached out and held her wrist.

'*What are you doing?*'

'Let him go,' he said gently. Tears stung his eyes. 'Let him go.'

'But, Miles,' Frankie objected, 'he's—'

'Let him go,' he repeated, as he watched the ECG and heard the flat tone of the alarm.

He lost track of how long they stood there before he released Frankie's hand and she said, softly, 'He's gone.'

The nurses and Greg stared at Fleming and he felt something sag inside him. Only a few moments ago he had witnessed an incredible breakthrough, and now it had all gone wrong. This wasn't supposed to happen. He was supposed to help Rob speak and then, in time, get his body to work again. He was supposed to protect and save his brother, as his brother had so often saved him in the mountains. He wasn't supposed to stand by and help him die.

He stared at Rob on the bed. He seemed to be sleeping, but when Fleming looked closer his brother had become a stranger to him. The corpse looked exactly like Rob, but at the same time different, as if the essence of Rob had slipped away.

He checked his watch and swallowed hard. 'Time of death, eleven fifty-eight a.m.' Silently, the team spent the next few minutes clearing up while Fleming braced himself to break the news to his mother and Jake, news he hadn't accepted yet. All the time he kept telling himself, At least Rob's free from pain now. He's gone where no suffering can reach him.

Then, turning to leave the Think Tank, he froze.

Fresh static crackled from the NeuroTranslator speakers. The noise was louder than before and the voice sounded different, slurred, as if the signal was breaking up.

'Milo. Help Me Bro. I Can't Hold On Much Longer. I'm Falling. Pull Me Up.'

Fleming's mouth was dry but he willed himself to stay calm. How could this be happening? What had he done? 'Rob, what's going on?' He looked to Frankie for reassurance, but she was checking the monitors.

The static came back even louder.

'I'm Falling. Can't Hold On. Promise Me You'll Take Care Of Jake,' the voice said.

'I promise,' Fleming gasped. 'But hang on, we haven't lost you yet.'

The voice was breaking up but perversely it sounded more fluent. Glancing at the top half of the NeuroTranslator screen, Fleming saw that all brain-wave traces had gone. Taking the controls from Greg, he scrolled frantically down the display but all the brain-waves were flat, the signals inert. Then he scrolled up and saw activity on a brain-wave signal at the highest end of the frequency spectrum.

'God, Bro. Help Me. This Isn't Good. There's Something Bad Here. I Need To Tell—'

'Tell me what, Rob?' Fleming said desperately. 'How can I help you?'

Sounding more and more agitated, the words crackling from the speakers began to break up.

'No . . . Help . . . You Must . . . Important . . . Dangerous . . . Take Care Of Jake . . .'

The chilling words faded to hissing static and then, finally, silence.

'Come on, Rob,' Fleming rasped, his mouth drier than sandpaper. 'Talk to me.'

He turned to Frankie and caught her studying her wristwatch before she looked up. Her usually rosy cheeks were deathly pale and her eyes were as wide as plates. 'He's long gone, Miles,' she whispered. 'We lost him in the first seizure and he never revived.'

'That's impossible! Where did his last cries for help come from?'

'God only knows,' said Frankie. 'But he's been clinically dead for almost six minutes.'

111

16

Marin County, California. The next day

Amber's flight arrived late at night and she returned to her airy, echoing home in Pacific Heights. The next morning she awoke to a blue-sky California day. The bright sunlight and warm breeze blowing in from the bay helped thaw the lingering chill from the dream of dying that still made her shudder. She climbed into her Mercedes and drove across the Golden Gate Bridge to Marin County, and the Church of the Soul Truth Hospice.

The nun in scarlet robes at the reception desk in the sun-washed lobby was brisk and efficient. 'Your mother's being bathed at the moment, Dr Grant,' she said. 'If you wait in the visitors' reception room, I'll collect you when she's ready.'

Amber was pleased to see that the linoleum on the hospice floor was new and the paint fresh: she owed Gillian Grant more than if she'd been her natural mother, and whenever she felt guilty about paying another Church to care for her Amber reminded herself that this hospice, which the Church of the Soul Truth had taken over from the Catholic Church, was the best in the bay area.

Like so many other Catholic organizations around the world it had fallen into decline as the Red Pope's breakaway Church of the Soul Truth had surged in popularity. Nuns in black habits had once walked these corridors, but now they wore scarlet. The hospice offered the best care available, in beautiful surroundings. Each occupant had their own private apartment, with access to the communal pool, restaurant and the exquisite gardens, with which her mother had fallen in love.

Amber had wanted Gillian to stay with her when her father died five years ago but her mother had hated the idea of being a burden to Amber and giving up her independence. When she had fallen ill she had asked to come here where she had the best of both worlds: round-the-clock professional care and her own private space.

A picture of the Red Pope looked out from the wall above Amber. Even in a photograph the man was charismatic. He had a fine aquiline nose, chiselled cheekbones, and a smooth olive skin that belied his sixty-eight years. On his head he wore a scarlet skullcap that matched his splendid robes and the crucifix that hung on his chest from a gold chain. There was also a photograph of a magnificent red ship with a gleaming white superstructure designed to resemble a Gothic cathedral, the famous Red Ark, the so-called Floating Vatican, which toured the world continuously, eschewing any national flag of origin on its endless global pilgrimage. It was from the Red Ark that the Red Pope now preached to the world via the first ever electronic Church. In a corner of the room a television set, with the volume turned down, showed the Red Pope in action, conducting one of his online services aboard the Red Ark. A flashing message scrolled across the bottom of the screen: *Attend the service online: www.RedArk/Church_Soul_Truth.com*.

Behind the chair to her left was a ledge with three KREE8 WebCruisers lying idle. Each was a standard wireless headset with a surround-vision display visor, earphone, microphone and nasal scent pad. A sign on the ledge invited Amber to 'Board the Red Ark and attend a service live with the Red Pope'. She put on the headset, inserted the foam earpieces and angled the nasal pad.

The first thing she saw was a home page and an MTV-style video montage introducing the Red Pope.

'Viewing his near-death experience as a signal to focus all his drive and passion on the spiritual,' the voiceover said, 'Cardinal Xavier Accosta became a Catholic priest and soon ascended the hierarchy until he was summoned to Rome, to the Holy See. By the age of fifty-four His Holiness was already one of the most powerful men in the Catholic Church, one of the so-called Three Popes of Rome. Alongside the Pontiff, the White Pope and the Superior General of the Jesuits, the Black Pope, Cardinal Accosta was the Vatican's Grand Inquisitor, the Red Pope. But even then the Roman Catholic Church was in turmoil, struggling to survive the corruption, misogyny and scandal that permeated the Curia and many bishoprics around the world.

'His Holiness made a stand for reform on many fronts, including allowing women more say in the Church, permitting priests to marry and changing the objectives of the Institute of Miracles from validating miraculous claims to using technology positively to seek out evidence of the hand of God. But the reactionary right and their puppet Pope continually blocked his endeavours.

'He waited for the sick Pope to die before he made his stand. As one of the few members under seventy of the College of Cardinals, Cardinal Accosta was *papabile* and he attracted support. If he became pope he could fashion the Church into the powerful spiritual body he knew God desired.

'But it was not to be. Other cardinals feared his ambition and appetite for dramatic reform. They voted in one of their own to maintain the status quo. His Holiness could stay silent no longer and was forced to attack his own Church, advocating aggressive reform to ensure survival. He was heartened by the support he gained from within and without the Church, including the powerful lay organization Opus Dei. Eventually he was summoned by the new Pope and excommunicated.'

Amber listened to how, within six months, an impressive array of powerful, wealthy backers had lined up to support him, helping him found the world's first electronic Church – the Church of the Soul Truth – and how Accosta retained many of the trappings of his old office, with the sobriquet the Red Pope.

The video montage concluded with triumphant scenes of the Red Ark on its global pilgrimage as the voiceover explained how, over the last ten years, Accosta's electronic ministry had blossomed into what it was today: a vital and integral part of the modern world, founded on technology and receptive to new ideas.

At the bottom of the virtual homepage there was an instruction: 'Click button on headset to attend service.'

She did so and was immediately transported to an alternative reality. No longer was she in the visitors' reception room of the hospice, or watching a video, but in the front row of a surreal amphitheatre. If she turned her head she could see fellow members of the congregation as if she were sitting among them. She could almost feel the fabric of her neighbour's coat. Ahead of her she could hear the Red Pope's rich voice as clearly as if he was only a few feet away.

'Technology need not undermine religious faith,' he was saying, in reply to a question. 'It was Einstein who said that religion without science is blind, and science without religion is lame. Science should support faith and turn it into something more potent. Not just knowledge but something far more ambitious. Truth.'

The Red Pope sat on a raised dais on a simple chair. The informality of the setting reminded Amber more of a television talk-show than a structured church service, but that was partly why the Red Pope's ministry had proved so popular with old and young alike. Its potent alliance of charismatic leadership, transparent religious values and state-of-the-art technology was

116

irresistible. Movie stars, rock idols and leading political figures from around the world often made guest appearances at the services. All were keen to bask in his reflected glory.

Amber was aware of the sniffles and shuffles of the people around her, and her nostrils detected incense. She took in the sweeping pillars and arches that soared up to a perfect sky. It was as though she wasn't in an earthly space at all, but in some celestial temple. The congregation appeared limitless, representing all those, like her, who were attending virtually, online.

To her left, suspended in air, a number scrolled upwards continually, like a meter in a taxi. This represented the total number of people attending the service online via the Optinet and those watching via the television stations that paid for the broadcast rights. If the figure was correct, the Red Pope was currently talking to over five hundred million people world-wide: almost half of the total number of Catholics in the world at Rome's prime. The Church of the Soul Truth already had a global following in excess of one and a half billion.

A red light flashed in her peripheral vision, alerting her to a signal from the real world, and Amber felt a hand on her shoulder. She took off the headset and turned to the nun standing over her. 'Dr Grant, your mother is ready to see you now.'

17

When Amber entered Suite 21 on the second floor her mother was sitting in her wheelchair, her fine grey hair freshly washed and brushed. The french windows leading on to the walled sun terrace were open and a gentle breeze rustled the transparent curtains. After her bath, in the diffuse sunlight, she didn't look ill. Although she was painfully thin her cheeks were pink and her pale eyes bright. There was little sign of the cancer that riddled her body.

On the bedside table stood three framed photographs. The first showed Amber's parents smiling on a beach. The second showed Amber and Ariel when they were children, wearing matching blue dresses. The third showed the whole family in front of St Peter's in Rome with Amber's godfather, Papa Pete Riga, standing slightly apart in black robes, hands behind his back.

Her mother's face lit up when Amber entered the room and embraced her. 'Amber, how are you feeling? I heard about the headaches on TV. Why didn't you tell me before?'

Amber felt a stab of guilt that her sick mother should be so concerned about her health. 'I didn't want to worry you, Mom, and anyway I'm okay. It's nothing.' She sat down beside her mother. 'I'm seeing Papa Pete for dinner tonight. He said he came to see you the other day.'

Gillian Grant nodded. 'We talked about old times and he lifted an enormous weight off me by giving me his blessing for choosing to live here.' She paused. 'But something's up, I know. What is it?'

Amber sighed. Then she told Gillian everything – the headaches, Miles Fleming, the Neuro-Translator, her dream. 'The weirdest thing is I feel Ariel's trying to tell me something. It's like she's never been out of my head since she died.'

Her mother smiled. 'That's not so strange, Amber. Ariel's rarely been far from my thoughts either. Your sister and your father will always live on in me. And when I go I'll live on in you. We are our relationships. Increasingly, as I get nearer to the end of my life, I think that's *all* we are.'

Amber wanted to explain that it was more than that, but she let it go because she recognized a deeper truth in what her mother had said. The quantum world was all about relationships and entanglements between elemental particles: why should humans be different?

'You need to go back to England to cure your headaches?' her mother said.

'For about a month, yes.' Amber frowned. 'But I'm worried about—'

Her mother waved her hand dismissively. 'Worried about what? You must go. Don't worry

119

about me. I'll be here when you get back. The doctors say I've got a year, so it's better you go as soon as possible.' She reached for Amber's hand and squeezed it. 'I'm so proud of you, Amber, and all you've achieved, but perhaps these headaches are a blessing in disguise. A chance to stop blaming yourself for what happened to Ariel and start getting on with the rest of your life. Ariel would want you to be happy. She always looked after you and she'd hate to think she was causing you distress. Let things take their course.'

Amber sat back in her chair and allowed herself to bask in her mother's love and wisdom. She would miss her when she died. Though it was hard to think of death when she was here because Gillian was so full of vitality.

Later Amber accompanied her outside, pushed her wheelchair around the garden and reminisced, made plans.

At lunchtime she wheeled Gillian back to her room and helped her into bed. Before she left, she kissed her forehead, just as her mother had kissed her and Ariel when they were children. As she turned to leave, she stopped and tried to freeze in her mind the peaceful scene of her mother asleep in bed, sunlight filtering through the thin curtains, the greenery on the terrace beyond.

As she committed the calm scene to memory she couldn't have foreseen the storm to come. Or known that she would never again see her mother in this tranquil sun-filled room.

'The thing is, Papa Pete, I don't think what I experienced really was a dream.'

'Why not? If your discussion with Dr Fleming was making you focus on Ariel, it musta been a dream.' Years with the Society of Jesus had softened Father Peter Riga's New York accent, but it was still there. Now Amber and her godfather sat in her spacious kitchen. Dressed in black, with tightly curling grey hair and piercing blue eyes, he looked tired but ageless. Amber had sent the maid home and herself conjured up his favourite spare ribs and pasta. Now she and Papa Pete sat over empty plates drinking the Barolo he had brought from Italy. She was telling him about her dream.

'Papa Pete, I *never* dream. Remember? Ariel used to dream but I never did – that was one of the differences between us. What happened the other night reminded me more of the weird near-death experience I had during the operation. It wasn't like a dream.'

'So what was it?'

'That's what I want to find out. You remember telling me your first thoughts when you saw Ariel and me in the hospital in São Paulo after our natural parents had abandoned us?'

He sipped his wine and nodded. 'Sure. Though the doctors called you a single biological organism, I saw two separate souls.' His eyes narrowed. 'Where you going with this, Amber?'

She tried to frame her impossible question. 'Miles Fleming said I possessed part of the living

121

brain of a dead person. Could I still possess that person's soul too?'

Riga frowned and swirled the wine in his glass.

She continued, 'What if Ariel's soul has not been allowed to die because part of her mind still lives in me? What if, after all these years, she's using headaches and dreams somehow to contact me – to get me to release her?'

The frown deepened.

'Papa Pete? Say something. I know it sounds crazy but I've got to know what you think.'

'My child, I don't know what to say. This isn't something to which I can give a quick answer. I've seen too many things in my years as a priest to know that – particularly in view of how uniquely close your relationship was with Ariel. Ancient philosophers right up to Descartes believed that human consciousness, or the soul, resided in the brain.' Riga tapped his head. 'Even gave the exact location. Said it was in the pineal gland. But what you just said is so . . . unusual that I've got no instant spiritual, philosophical or rational response. I need to give it more thought.' He sat back in his chair. 'But you really think Ariel's still alive somehow? What's this Dr Fleming guy say?'

Amber shrugged. 'He's smart and I like him, but he's a scientist and not really interested in theoretical stuff. He wants practical solutions, doesn't like things he can't explain, and he sure as hell doesn't believe in an afterlife. He's promised to examine everything when I return, but I know he's convinced that I just had a dream.'

'Being practical ain't always so bad,' said Riga.

122

'Look, Amber, I return to Rome tomorrow, and I'll give it some more thought. Anyway, see what Fleming says and call me with any news. I'm sure there'll be a rational medical explanation.'

'I hope so,' said Amber, pushing the wine bottle towards him.

Riga placed a hand over his glass. 'Not for me, thanks. I suddenly got a headache.'

18

Optrix Industries.
The next day

In the morning Amber felt more optimistic as she drove across the Bay Bridge to Optrix's Berkeley headquarters. Talking to her mother and Papa Pete had encouraged her to believe that Fleming and his NeuroTranslator would indeed find a rational cause for her problem.

Yet as she sat in the insulated cocoon of the Mercedes, it didn't seem so impossible that some vestige of Ariel, the *wave* state of her metaphysical consciousness, might still exist in the *particle* state of the shared section of their physical brain. At a level she couldn't articulate, Amber still felt that her headaches might be a symptom of a greater malaise, and that to cure her Fleming would have to do more than use his NeuroTranslator to exorcize her phantom pain. He had somehow to understand her connection with Ariel.

As she put her foot on the gas and the Bay Bridge receded in the rear-view mirror, she could see the dark glass tower of Optrix Industries loom into view, gleaming like a pillar of polished ebony. As she approached the imposing gates she turned to the black granite slab beside the gatehouse. The words etched into it in silver read:

Optrix Industries
Optoelectronics Research Headquarters.
Let There Be Light.

The guard waved her through on to the campus and she parked by one of two ultraviolet-proof colonnades that allowed visitors to enter the building without being exposed to direct sunlight. She scanned the parking lot, and recognized the customized black Lexus with heavily tinted windows.

Inside the reception atrium, heels clicking on the polished marble, Amber greeted the security woman behind the desk.

'Welcome back, Dr Grant. I hope you're feeling better.'

'Much better, thanks, Irene.'

She entered the first elevator and pressed the button for the top floor. When the doors opened, she walked down the curving corridor to her office where her secretary, a tall brisk woman with short fair hair, was waiting. 'Dr Grant, how you feeling?'

'Fine, thanks, Diane. Any urgent messages?'

'Professor Mortenson in the main lab rang to say they're having problems with the Lucifer optical memory pixels.' Diane checked the electronic notepad in her hand. 'He says the electron-hole pairs are proving unstable. They aren't staying apart for as long as they should at room temperature.'

Amber frowned. Mortenson was one of her senior physicists but, like many of her team, he lacked initiative. She accepted that, as a workaholic who wanted to be involved in all aspects of development, this was partly her fault. It was time, however, to make people think for themselves. 'Tell him to review the ratios of the gallium arsenide and aluminium arsenide layers in the semiconductor – and to check the photon energy levels at the same time. If that doesn't do the trick then ask him to suggest how he intends to solve it.' She handed her brochure-thin briefcase to Diane. 'Would you put this on my desk? I gotta go see Bradley.'

Because of his condition Bradley Soames spent much of his time away from the bright sunlight of California, overseeing his VenTec foundation in Alaska, a private venture technology company that developed cutting-edge initiatives for a variety of specialist clients. He left Amber to look after most of the day-to-day running of Optrix.

VenTec's location, north of the Arctic Circle, was a closely guarded secret. When Amber had worked there ten years ago, managing the task force that developed the optical computer, she had never known its precise co-ordinates. Although she visited the place often, she would be hard pushed even now to pinpoint its exact whereabouts. Since few top scientists were prepared to work in Alaska for extended periods, even for Soames, Optrix had established its main research site here in the San Francisco bay area. VenTec was a bonus.

From her office Amber walked the circuit of the dark tower's top floor, passing the offices of the finance director, the human resources director and the commercial director, who were the three other members of the five-strong operating board that oversaw Optrix's worldwide business interests. Her office and theirs enjoyed spectacular views of the bay area but Bradley Soames's office occupied the centre of the circle and had no windows. Two doors protected it from the outside world.

Amber knew the drill and closed the first door before knocking on the inner one. It opened and Bradley's receptionist ushered her into the ante-room with a smile. 'Good morning, Dr Grant,' she said. 'He's expecting you. Please go right in.'

Amber opened a door of dark frosted glass and entered an enclosed corridor that twisted in ever-decreasing circles towards Soames's office. As she walked, the light dimmed gradually, enabling her eyes to accustom themselves to the gloom of his inner sanctum. The office was circular. There were no pictures on the soft-textured walls and no windows. A vague smell of medication hung in the filtered air. At the back of the room there was a couch and a glass-fronted refrigerated cabinet stocked with Coca-Cola.

Soames reclined on his chair, trainers resting on the curved desk that dominated the centre of the room, surrounded by the computer screens that allowed him to keep an eye on his global empire. He wore a pale grey cotton one-piece with inte-grated cowl and gloves. Inside, safe from sunlight, the cowl hung around his shoulders and the gloves were rolled back, exposing scarred, freckled hands.

Behind him, in the gloom, she could see two large shapes lying on the ground, staring at her with yellow eyes. Soames had brought with him his two timber wolves from Alaska. He had adopted them as pups to keep him company, feeling some affinity with their nocturnal habits. Everyone at Optrix called them 'the shadows' because they were silent, grey and stayed close to Soames when they were with him. He spoke to them in a strange guttural tongue that Amber didn't understand. He treated them as pets and encouraged her to treat them the same way, but she had once read that you should never hug a wolf or forget it was a wild creature. She had only to look into their bright, unblinking eyes to know that this was good advice.

The larger one glanced at her then turned away. Amber shifted her attention to Soames.

Apparently unaware of her, he was talking into a headset, monitoring the screens and reading the *Wall Street Journal*. He blinked constantly.

'Marty, I don't care, Matrix have gotta play ball with us if they want to survive. Look what happened to Intel chips and Microsoft Windows when the Lucifer came out. Now it's the world wide web. The entire Internet's gone optical – shit, it's *already* called the Optinet. And most of it relies on Optrix technology, Marty. This is the light age. Data transfer at the speed of light is what it's all about. Matrix have gotta work with us on our terms or stay in the dark ages and die.'

For a moment she stood and watched, studying his pale face, disconcerting blue eyes and golden hair. Many felt uncomfortable in Soames's presence. She didn't. She had never warmed towards him and did not regard him as a friend – he was too emotionally insulated to understand the concept of friendship – but her own childhood had conferred on her an affinity with him. It was also a privilege and an inspiration to feed off his intellect. Working with him made her life valuable, her contribution to the world significant.

'No, Marty, there's nothing to discuss,' Soames said abruptly into the mouthpiece. 'Think about it. 'Bye.' He pressed a button on one of the screens in front of him, killing the link, and turned to Amber with a grin. 'How'd it go?' Before she could answer he said, 'You heard? The Nobel committee finally decided to give me the physics prize but I told 'em I don't want it. I don't need the money and I sure as hell don't need the approval of that bunch of mediocre old jerks.'

Before she had time to respond, he moved on. Reaching under the desk he took out what looked like a credit card. 'Check out this optical prototype VenTec came up with. Fax, EVmail, video phone, wireless Optinet connectivity and the power of a full-size computer all in the palm of your hand. Awesome, ain't it?'

Keeping one eye on the wolves, she took the device from him and sat down. 'It's great . . . I didn't know you were working on this.'

Soames wasn't looking at her any more. He was scanning the newspaper again. 'We gotta discuss the China initiative. I know VenTec can create an entry-level optical computer so cheap that Optrix can get one into every household there by . . .'

Amber Grant gave a weary sigh. It was like dealing with a child – a brilliant, powerful, mercurial child, but a child nevertheless. She raised her voice and said, 'Bradley, land on earth for one minute and focus.' She waited for him to look up. 'I've just got back from the clinic.'

'I know,' he said. He gave a small smile then, his scarred lips curling up to expose incongruously perfect white teeth. 'Discovered anything?'

'Course not. I only just completed the first scan. You were right about Miles Fleming, though. He's real smart. How'd the rest of the Lucifer softscreen presentation go in London?'

'Great – after everyone stopped worrying about you, that is. Had to fly back to VenTec that night but they seemed mighty impressed with the launch. Anyway, I want to know exactly what Fleming's first thoughts are.'

'Don't know yet. Gotta go back for a longer spell. A month.'

Soames shrugged. 'Whatever. I need to find out what's behind these headaches of yours.'

She laughed. '*You* need to? I figure I need to find out a hell of a lot more than you do, Bradley.'

'Oh, yeah, sure,' he said awkwardly. 'Just keep me posted on what Fleming says.'

Half of Amber wanted to tell Soames about her dream, but there was something about his almost clinical interest in her condition that stopped her. 'I suggest we keep my treatment discreet,' she said. 'We don't want the investors getting unduly concerned about my health. I think we should link my collapse at the presentation with stress and concern for my mother, and tell the Optrix board I'm taking compassionate leave. I know at least two people competent enough to run the main projects. Any other issues can handle themselves while I'm away.'

Soames nodded. 'You seem to have everything under control. I suggest you tie up any loose ends and get back to your doctor.'

She smiled. 'Thanks for being so supportive, Bradley.'

'No sweat,' he said, his scarred face creasing unnaturally as he returned her smile. 'I understand how important it is to look after your health.'

As she turned to leave, she heard him clear his throat, the signal that he was on the verge of uttering what he liked to pretend was a casual afterthought. 'Just an idea,' he said, 'but don't let Fleming be too linear in his diagnosis. If I were you I'd encourage him to think outside the box. You know, explore every eventuality, however bizarre.' He shrugged. 'Just a thought.'

Amber frowned. It was a good thought and echoed her own concerns about Ariel so closely that she felt uncomfortable. 'Thanks, Bradley,' she said. 'I'll bear that in . . .'

But he'd already zoned out, immersed in his computer screens. That was the thing about Bradley: just when you thought he was being human and caring, you got a sharp reminder that he didn't think like other people.

19

The Red Ark. 33° 26´ S, 16° 12´ E.
The next day

Aboard the Red Ark, the Red Pope drummed his
fingers impatiently on the desk as he waited for the
KREE8 high-resolution holographic plasma screen
to fizz into life. When the Doctor appeared, a blood-
red cruciform brooch pinned to his white coat, the
screen gave his face an eerily effective three-
dimensional appearance. Cardinal Xavier Accosta
studied it for a second, careful to hide his disgust.
He needed this brilliant man and was grudgingly
grateful for his dedicated and selfless support. Not
only had the Doctor secretly helped fund the start-
up of Accosta's electronic Church but his technical
expertise had enabled it to spread at a speed that
had baffled the world. His genius had also been
instrumental in fulfilling Accosta's dream of making
the Soul Project a reality. But he still couldn't bring
himself to like the young man.

The Doctor aggressively protected the secrecy
of his allegiance to Accosta's Church, and
although he always deferred to Accosta there was
insolence in his eye and tone, which Accosta
disliked. He was the only person who could

address Accosta as 'Your Holiness' and sound condescending.

Accosta stared at him and smiled. 'You have something to show me, Doctor?'

Bradley Soames bowed his head deferentially. 'Yes, Your Holiness. I've conferred with Frank Carvelli and the third member of the Truth Council on all one hundred and eight trials.' A pause. 'The last experiment's the most representative of our progress.'

The plasma screen next to Soames buzzed into life. A woman was lying on a laboratory couch, her smooth shaven head encased in a glass sphere with a visor like that on an astronaut's helmet. Embedded in it was a small concave square of smoky glass resembling a tiny television screen.

The visor was up, revealing the woman's pegged-open eyelids. Lightly tinted lenses had been inserted in her eyes covering the eyeballs.

At first Accosta didn't know who the bald woman was, but as the camera zoomed in on her he recognized Mother Giovanna Bellini. Outraged, it took all his control not to cry out. He glared at Soames, trying to read his face, but the scientist's blank expression revealed nothing. 'How dare you do this?' he demanded. 'On whose authority?'

Soames shrugged apologetically. 'But, Your Holiness, I had no choice after Monsignor Diageo informed me you'd told him she was endangering the project . . .'

Accosta's jaw clenched. He hadn't expected Soames to go this far. Monsignor Diageo was always discreet whenever necessary measures needed to be taken, but Soames seemed to enjoy testing him. 'She was loyal. I didn't expect you to – do *this*.'

'What did you expect me to do with your troublesome priest, Your Holiness?'

Silence.

Soames smiled. 'Mother Giovanna didn't die in vain, Your Holiness. By watching her death you'll see how much we've already achieved.'

Accosta hated Soames then. He hated his youthful arrogance and his relish for the ruthless decisions that so taxed his own soul. But most of all he hated Soames for not allowing him to pretend that betraying Mother Giovanna Bellini, one of his most loyal subjects, wouldn't result in her death. He had learnt to accept casualties of war in the navy and had resigned himself long ago to making sacrifices to protect God's work, but he still felt guilty.

'Dr Soames,' he said curtly, 'in future on all matters regarding the Soul Project you will act only on my authority. Now show me the experiment.'

Soames nodded. 'As you wish, Your Holiness.' He cleared his throat. 'Before we start, some background: through quantum physics we've learnt that human consciousness can exist both as a particle, our physical brain, and as a wave, the thoughts in our mind. Physics also teaches us that energy can't just disappear, it has to go somewhere. Life energy's no different. And through recent quantum experiments we now know that at the moment of death our life force – our consciousness – leaves our body as a coherent

134

collection of subatomic photons. To detect these photons leaving the body we use a modified photon-detector screen. Interestingly each individual leaves a unique wave interference pattern. To avoid static the subject's head is shaved and to make the life force visible to the human eye we use polymer filter contact lenses, Flavion gas and green-light spectra to modify artificially the electromagnetic radiation frequency.'

Accosta stared grimly at the screen, eyes locked on the woman's, forcing himself to watch.

On screen a green gas invaded the glass sphere, giving her face a sickly actinic aura. On the right of the screen he could just see the electrode attached to her left temple. Off screen he heard a countdown.

Four . . . three . . . two . . . one.

The electrode sparked, followed instantly by a flash of light so fast and intense that even on screen it made Accosta blink. Suddenly, like a blown bulb, Mother Giovanna's eyes were blank beneath the lenses.

Accosta was sweating as he watched those unblinking eyes, his heart pounding in his chest. Despite his guilt the thrill was almost sexual. What had she seen when she died? What was she seeing now?

'Let me talk you through what happened, Your Holiness. This was typical of all the latest trials.'

The screen changed to reveal the same experiment from a wider angle. Accosta could now see Giovanna Bellini's whole body lying on the laboratory couch. At the foot of the couch were two monitors.

'I'll play it back again but this time slowed down over two hundred thousand times. Light travels one hundred and eighty-six thousand miles a second. Only by slowing the film can we track how successfully we channelled the life energy. I'll start from when the electric shock's administered, which sadly is the only way we can pinpoint the exact moment of death.'

This time when the lightburst occurred Accosta saw it as a spark emanating from the woman's eyes. Somehow a single spark passed through both tinted lenses simultaneously before colliding with the screen in the visor, leaving a zebra pattern of white stripy lines on the previously dark monitor.

'Note the quantum wave-particle duality exhibited here. For reasons we don't yet fully understand, life energy leaves through the eyes, allowing us to re-create the classic double-slit experiment. As the life energy leaves Mother Bellini's body it passes through both eyes before hitting the photon-detector screen in the visor. See how the screen records a classic wave interference pattern as the collection of light particles, or photons, leave the body and interfere with themselves. This stripy pattern is unique to Mother Giovanna Bellini, a barcode that's effectively her soul signature.'

Accosta nodded, absorbing the technical commentary as he followed the spark's progress past the screen and into the outer layer of the sphere. Here, although the film had been slowed to a snail's pace, the spark raced along every millimetre of the densely coiled translucent fibre

136

in the outer layer in the blink of an eye, momentarily lighting it up like a halo. Then the light was gone.

'This is the problem,' said Soames. 'We can now identify and channel the passage of the Bose-Einstein condensate but—'

'You mean the soul,' Accosta said.

'Yes, Your Holiness. The Bose-Einstein condensate's merely the correct quantum term for the boson system that forms the soul.'

Accosta frowned. 'So in plain English you're saying that you can channel the departing soul but you still can't hold it long enough in the head sphere to get a trace?'

'I'm saying it'll take time, Your Holiness. In the same way electricity always seeks earth, this energy always seeks the heavens. Stopping it for even a millisecond so that we can get a trace is difficult. You must appreciate that proving the quantum duality between brain and mind, or body and soul, is a significant achievement. Just proving the existence of the quantum soul as a boson system of photons is a breakthrough.

'But *tracking* the soul goes beyond the realm of quantum physics and into the realm of quantum metaphysics. The window of death is so small it's virtually impossible to take the learning from one experiment to the next. Each individual's death is different, so we're reduced to trial and error, hoping eventually to stumble on the right tracking frequency. If people died more than once we'd be able to focus on one person, running self-correcting iterative experiments each time they died. We'd find the locking frequency of the Bose-Einstein condensate – the soul – in no time.'

'But people don't die more than once. So how close are you to locking on to the soul?'

'Real close. The principle of what we're trying to achieve already exists in optoelectronics. In the same way that an optical computer captures a coherent collection of light photons encoded with data, we should be able to capture an intact soul as a coherent boson system of life photons for long enough to lock on to its frequency. We just need time.'

'We haven't got time. What other contingencies are in place?'

'The Truth Council's explored all related technologies, however diverse, to see which may prove useful. The most promising are being monitored and offered significant donations so we'll gain the inside track on any that show potential, but this technology is still our best bet.'

Accosta frowned. 'Frank Carvelli said you were confident of a breakthrough.'

'There's an unexpected recent development that I'm watching closely but I want to confirm a few aspects before I discuss it with you.' He paused. 'However, perhaps you want to call a halt for a while, take stock . . .'

'No. No. Not at all,' Accosta said hastily. 'If anything, you must speed up the experiments. What we're embarked on is too important to delay and if your confidence in the technology is justified we're tantalizingly close. We're almost there. There's too much at stake.'

'But after your reaction to Mother Giovanna's death, surely we should . . . ?' Soames trailed off.

Accosta glared at him, hating his need for this man, wondering, not for the first time, at the scientist's real motives for helping him. Keeping his voice icily controlled, he said, 'Now that you have killed Mother Giovanna, Dr Soames, it's even more imperative that we succeed with the Soul Project. I'll not allow her death to have been in vain.'

20

Surrey, England.
The next day

Sitting in the front pew in the old church, Miles Fleming kept his eyes straight ahead and told himself again that when he returned to Barley Hall he would discover a rational explanation for why his brother had spoken six minutes after death. It troubled him more than he could articulate.

The small ancient church, close to his parents' home in Surrey, smelt of incense, beeswax polish and the dust of the past. Its dark wooden pews were worn and its stone wall-plaques commemorated local parishioners who had died in wars that were now centuries past.

Someone once said that funerals were for the living and not the dead, and it felt that way to Fleming today. Despite his atheism, he had unquestioningly arranged a church service for the sake of his parents and Jake. His mother and father needed to believe their son was going to a better place, and the ritual made it easier for Jake to understand and accept what had happened.

The church was full and people were standing at the back. As well as family, many of Rob's friends were there: an eclectic mix of ramrod straight military types in full uniform, people in suits and even a few climbing bums with badger-eye tans and crumpled fleeces had converged on this small village south of London to pay their respects and mark Rob's passing.

When Fleming carried the coffin into church with five of Rob's army colleagues he had felt an overwhelming need to shout that he'd let his brother die and had heard him speak after death. But instead he'd helped the others to lay the coffin before the altar, then taken his seat at the end of the front pew next to Jake and his parents. Sitting there now, he could feel Jake's warm thigh next to his and hear his breathing as the child stared at the coffin. Fleming was aware of the Anglican priest's measured tones but he didn't hear his words. All he could focus on were his nephew's ragged breaths, as he listened for any sign that the little boy was breaking down.

In the four days since Rob had died, Fleming had kept himself from dwelling on his brother's death, immersing himself in practicalities. After notifying Virginia Knight and completing the death certificate, he had taken leave from Barley Hall to join his parents and Jake and arrange the funeral. His professional persona had taken over but inside he felt numb, his shock and loss bubbling away beneath a fragile lid of control.

He almost lost it in Cambridge when he had broken the news to his mother and Jake. She had crumpled briefly, then rallied and hugged an uncomprehending Jake to her chest. But it was

141

when she had hugged Fleming and tried to comfort him too, saying, 'Miles, you did all you could. No one could have done more for him. He's safe with God now,' that he'd had to bite his lip and blink back tears. Because he hadn't done all he could to save his brother. Although he knew the stimulant probably wouldn't have saved Rob, he lived with the guilt of holding the nurse back and allowing his brother to die. He still hadn't told his parents what he'd done, and probably never would, because they wouldn't understand – to them life mattered more than suffering.

'O almighty, all-knowing, compassionate Lord . . .' The priest's words cut through Fleming's thoughts and dark rage rose within him. As far as he was concerned, here in front of him was the essential conundrum of faith. Either God knew about suffering and could stop it but didn't care, in which case he wasn't compassionate, or he knew about suffering and cared about it but couldn't do a damn thing about it, in which case he wasn't all-powerful, or he could do something about suffering and cared about it, but didn't know about it, in which case he wasn't all-knowing. It was *impossible* for God to be almighty, all-knowing and merciful.

He looked across at his parents. His mother looked small and frail and his father, a retired architect, looked old for the first time. Both were gazing at the priest, needing their faith to sustain them and make sense of suffering, which Fleming had long accepted as cruel and arbitrary. He wished *he* had the comfort of blind faith now. But things weren't so simple.

Although his brother had been virtually dead when he had asked Fleming to 'cut the rope', and Fleming believed he'd done the right thing in releasing him from suffering, he was haunted by the knowledge that not only had Rob spoken again six minutes *after* he had died, but he hadn't sounded as though he was free of suffering.

Wrestling with the responsibility of what he'd done, Fleming tried to still the conflicting thoughts in his head, refusing to believe that Rob was anywhere but in oblivion. There must have been a lag in the NeuroTranslator, which gave the impression that he had spoken after death, some electronic glitch, and what Miles had heard weren't the words of a soul in torment but the last frightened gasp of a dying mind before oblivion claimed it.

Fleming had to believe this, because his credo wouldn't allow him any alternative. He could not bear to think that his beloved brother's consciousness lived on and continued to suffer. Particularly when he hadn't tried to save him.

An officer from Rob's regiment was speaking of his friend now. The man's soft Irish accent and understated recollections seemed to bring him back to life. Hearing Rob described as 'the best of fathers, the best of sons and the best of brothers, but above all the best of men', brought tears to Fleming's eyes.

But it was only when he heard Jake sobbing beside him and imagined his loss that he felt the dam burst within himself. The tears were painless when they came, a release of pent-up pressure. He

143

pulled Jake into his arms and they wept together
with unrestrained grief.

Three hours later

When the last of the mourners had left the wake at
his parents' rambling house, Fleming wandered
out into the garden. It had been good to see Rob's
friends but he felt raw and bruised. As dusk
gathered around him he sat on the bench beneath
the sycamore he and his brother used to climb
when their parents had moved here from the Peak
District.

He found this place and its memories comforting, but part of him was itching to get back to
Barley Hall. He had wanted to run a check on the
NeuroTranslator to put his mind at rest before
leaving the clinic, but then his priority had been to
join his family. Now, the longer he allowed the lag
to fester in his mind the more prominently it
featured in his thoughts. It wasn't enough to
believe it hadn't been significant; he had to *prove*
it.

A small figure ambled out into the gloom from
the kitchen. 'Milo?'

Even though the prosthetic legs were still new
to him, Jake walked so naturally that Fleming
found it hard to imagine anyone detecting any
awkwardness in his gait. 'Hi, Jake. Come over
here.'

The child sat on the bench beside him and
leaned against him.

144

'Milo, why did they have to go?'

Fleming wrapped his arm around Jake. For the last four days Jake had been asking his grandmother what had happened to his mum and dad and she had talked of heaven and God. Fleming had been more preoccupied with Jake's future: after lengthy discussions it had been decided that his grandparents would take care of him in the short term, but that Fleming would adopt him. 'Well, sometimes we don't know why things happen in life, Jake,' he said. 'They just do. But I know your mum and dad loved you a lot, and that I love you, and your grandma and grandpa love you too. We've all still got each other, Jake.'

'Where are Mum and Dad now, though? Have they got e-mail?'

Miles smiled at that. 'If they do, they haven't told me the address.'

'But where do you *think* Dad is? He must be somewhere, Milo.'

'Well, I suppose he's alive in our memories and our hearts.'

'But what's he thinking now? Can he see me?'

'I don't know,' answered Fleming. 'I think your dad's just gone to sleep. He was sick and now he's resting.'

'What's he dream about, then?'

Amber's dream and her notion that her sister's mind lived on in her flashed into Fleming's thoughts. 'If he dreams of anything I'm sure it's happy things – like you and all the people he loves.'

'What happens when he wakes up?'

145

'Perhaps he doesn't wake up. Perhaps he has a long, peaceful sleep that goes on for ever.'

'Grandma says Mum and Dad are in heaven.'

'Perhaps they are.'

'She says heaven's really high up and it's full of nice things.'

'Well, if it's a nice place and it's high up then your dad will have found it. He's a good climber.'

Jake looked up at the stars and sighed. 'Milo,' he said, frowning in concentration, 'if God makes heaven, which is good, why does he make this happen, which is bad? Why did he take Mum *and* Dad? He doesn't need them both.'

Fleming wondered what his mother would say to that. Jake hadn't even mentioned that the apparently almighty, all-knowing and compassionate God had also taken his legs. 'I don't know, Jake. If there is a God, perhaps he's greedy and thought your mum and dad were so special he wanted them for himself.'

'Heaven's a *good* place, isn't it?' Jake's earnest face was worried.

'Sure,' said Fleming, and ruffled his nephew's hair.

'So Mum and Dad are happy – because in heaven everyone's happy, aren't they?'

Fleming met Jake's intense gaze. 'Yeah, Jake, I'm sure they are,' he said.

But, of course, he couldn't be sure.

How could anyone?

21

The Think Tank.
Nine hours later

At twenty to three in the morning Amber was sleeping soundly in the Think Tank at Barley Hall. Earlier that afternoon she had returned from San Francisco and heard from Virginia Knight of Rob Fleming's death. The nurses had helped her settle into her cubicle where Amber had been delighted to find a card from Father Peter Riga with a box of her favourite Belgian chocolates. 'I'm sure that all the tests will reveal is that you have an excellent mind. Call me when you want to talk. Papa Pete.'

Then she had been wheeled into the Think Tank to continue her exercises and analysis. Eighteen minutes ago, she had fallen asleep and was now moving into REM, the dream state.

As her unconscious mind was pulled from her body, she twitched, then thrashed about on the bed. Moments later she was still and her eyeballs began their rapid movements. Her eyelids opened, and she stared blindly at the ceiling. Amber was being pulled away from her body even faster than before – so fast she could barely breathe – rushing at terrifying speed towards the bright light. Everything was compressed, the darkness blacker, the light brighter. She was sure that this time the light would reveal some terrifying truth and engulf her for ever.

As she raced towards it she could do nothing but scream soundlessly into the void . . .

Miles Fleming drove through the gateway of Barley Hall and up the gravel drive. He parked outside the front door. The entrance portico, flanked with Doric pillars, was imposing in the glare of the security lights but Fleming didn't look up as he entered the house and headed straight for his office.

After his talk with Jake he had turned in early and fallen into a fitful sleep some time after ten. Two hours later, a dark but forgotten dream had woken him in a cold sweat, galvanizing him to leave his parents' home and race here. He had to know why the NeuroTranslator had enabled Rob to speak after death. He had to explain rationally what had happened and he had to explain it *now*.

Striding down the dimly lit corridor of Barley Hall's east wing he ignored the night nurse dozing at her desk but slowed when he heard a child's plaintive cry coming from the Think Tank. There were no children staying at Barley Hall currently. When he heard what the child was saying, the hairs stood up on the back of his neck.

He inched open the door of the Think Tank until he could see Amber Grant lying rock still in bed, wearing the blue skullcap. Her skin was shiny with perspiration and her eyes were open. The sight of her was unsettling but it was the childish voice coming from her lips that made Fleming catch his breath.

She was calling, 'Amber, Amber, where are you?' sounding frightened and frustrated.

He padded across to the NeuroTranslator, pulsing in a spectrum of rainbow colours as its optical parallel processors performed countless simultaneous calculations. He made two adjustments to the circular dials on the lower panel beneath the sphere and flicked a switch. As the speakers hissed into life he had no idea what he was listening for. He waited for a few moments and was about to switch them off when a sound broke through the static.

The wailing scream was like nothing he had ever heard before. All he could think about as he scrambled to switch it off was a biblical quotation at which his brother and he had laughed nervously during Divinity classes at school. 'But the children of the kingdom shall be cast out into outer darkness: there shall be wailing and gnashing of teeth.'

For all his adult scepticism, that desperate keening unmanned Fleming. It hadn't been from this world: it was the sound of a soul in torment.

He collected himself and turned to the bed. Amber was now calm and breathing regularly, her eyes were closed and she was quiet. He left the Think Tank and carried on to his office. He was no longer anxious that he couldn't explain how Rob had spoken after death. He was now terrified that he could.

22

The Red Ark. 33° 15´ S, 16° 06´ E.
That night

Xavier Accosta hated the night. There was still so
much to do and while he slept he achieved
nothing. There had been a time when he had
hardly needed sleep but it had passed. The night
also brought introspection: when he was alone
with his thoughts the doubts came. His faith was
tested.

'Tell me honestly, Monsignor,' he asked, as his
assistant helped him prepare for bed in his private
stateroom aboard the Red Ark, 'do you believe that
the Doctor and the scientists will succeed?' Paulo
Diageo was the only person on earth to whom he
could voice his doubts. The huge man had worked
for him ever since Accosta ascended to the Curia in
Rome over twenty years ago. He had been the first
to swear his allegiance when Accosta left the
Vatican. A graduate of the slums of Naples, Diageo
once told him that he had experienced two
religious conversions: one had been earthly, when
he joined the Dominicans to escape his upbringing, the other spiritual, when he first heard
Accosta preach and determined to follow him. He

was a hard man, with a sharp, feral intelligence, who still had contacts with the secular underworld – some even said the Mafia – and Accosta knew he would do anything for him.

Diageo took Accosta's scarlet robes from him, folded them and placed them in the laundry basket. Then, with surprising gentleness, he reached for the fresh set by the door and peeled off the plastic wrapper, then hung them in the tall mahogany wardrobe for the next day. Finally he reached for the white towelling bathrobe on the bed and held it for Accosta to put on. 'It isn't the scientists who'll ensure your destiny is fulfilled, Your Holiness,' Diageo said, in his slow deep voice, as Accosta put his arms into the sleeves. 'It's God who'll make this happen. He won't allow time to run out. You're too important to His plans.'

Accosta took comfort from the man's quiet certainty.

Diageo walked into the adjoining bathroom. 'The bath is ready, Your Holiness,' he said when he returned. 'Your pain-killers and medication are beside your bed. You require anything else?'

'No. God bless you, Monsignor.'

'And you, Your Holiness. If you—'

'Thank you, Monsignor. I'll ring if I need you.'

After Diageo had gone, Accosta limped across the rug towards the bathroom. His private quarters were plain. The most valuable single item was a ceremonial sword, hanging in its scabbard above the bed. He kept this one memento of his years as a captain in the Argentine navy, seeing it as a symbol of the eternal war he fought for the salvation of humanity.

In the bathroom he let the towelling robe fall from his shoulders and removed his undergarments, then stood naked before the mirror. He still looked remarkably fit, considering his age and the battering his body had taken over the years. The most noticeable damage was the scar tissue on his wasted left leg and deformed pelvis, evidence of the injury that had changed his life all those years ago.

He had been a different man then, a young, red-blooded warrior who took God's support for granted. Conquest was all that mattered in battle, in his career and in the pursuit of women. Then the British Harrier jet had sunk his cruiser off the Falklands. He couldn't remember the explosion or being airlifted from the sinking battleship. But although it had happened over thirty years ago he could still recall every detail of the eleven-hour operation in Buenos Aires as surgeons fought to save his life. He had been unconscious throughout but he had seen the surgeons pin together his fractured pelvis from a position above the operating-table. He had wondered whether he would live or die.

When he woke from the operation, he had known his life must take another course. God had singled him out, sparing his soul but damaging his body to shift his focus from the physical to the spiritual and fulfil His grander purpose. He had given Accosta the blessing of suffering so that, in continuous pain, Accosta was perpetually reminded that he was God's envoy on earth.

He limped to the bath and tested the water before climbing in. As he lowered himself and felt the heat seep into his aching bones he comforted himself by thinking of all he had achieved since leaving Rome. In only ten years he had fashioned the Church of the Soul Truth into the single most important ministry on earth.

Still, when he got out of the bath and dried himself he realized that even this phenomenal success was meaningless. He pulled on his nightclothes and reached for the glass of water and tablets on his bedside table, taking each pill in the order Diageo had laid them out, saying a brief prayer as he did so. He hoped that Diageo was right and that God would allow Bradley Soames enough time to succeed with the Soul Project.

As he laid his head on the pillow he switched off the light. In the darkness he saw Mother Giovanna's pegged-open eyes stare at him accusingly and turned his face into the pillow. The Soul Project *had* to succeed to justify her death – and those of the others. His destiny had to be greater than being God's minister on earth. For his life – and Mother Giovanna's death – to have any purpose, he had to become God's minister on earth *and* in heaven.

23

Barley Hall

After leaving the Think Tank, Fleming ran down the dark, deserted corridors of Barley Hall to his office where he powered up his computer and accessed the Data Security Provider, using his password to open Brian's restricted files. He scanned the NeuroTranslator database until he saw the folder icon marked 'Rob Fleming'. He drew a deep breath, touched the folder on screen and opened it, revealing a series of more folders.

Within seconds he had arranged the screen display into two halves, the left showing the pulsing brain-wave patterns of Rob's brain, the right the Quicktime video footage from the cameras in the Think Tank that showed his death. Along the bottom of the screen a clock allowed him to synchronize each action on the video footage with Rob's brain activity.

Distancing himself from what he was witnessing, he replayed the experiment from the beginning, watching the brain-wave signals oscillate as Rob 'talked' for the first time. Each word had a unique signature pattern involving a number of brain waves, and as Fleming scrolled up the left side of the screen he saw nothing unusual.

Until Rob had his seizure.

The right side of the screen showed Frankie applying the defibrillator paddles to Rob's chest. The left side showed Rob's brain waves oscillating wildly, as if in great distress. Then, one by one, they faded away into flat lines, signifying brain death.

Over the next six minutes the brain waves didn't revive. Except one. A wavelength so high up the frequency spectrum that it was almost off the scale. It fluctuated randomly as Rob uttered his final words. It appeared solely responsible for his ability to speak after death. It was different from anything Fleming had seen before. He finger-tapped the screen and a dialogue box appeared. He looked at the title line but there was no name, just one word: 'Unknown'.

Fleming tapped the reverse double arrow on the timeline at the base of the screen, rewinding the Quicktime video to the beginning of the experiment. This time when he scrolled up the left half-screen he noted that the unknown brain signal was at rest until the moment Rob died.

Fleming tried to comprehend what had happened. He replayed the experiment twice more with the sound up so he could hear Rob's computer-assisted speech. All the time he studied the wavelengths, particularly the unknown one at the top of the screen.

Eventually he made two observations. The first was that the new wavelength appeared to enable

Rob to speak more fluently after death than he had before, almost as if it was faster at learning to use the NeuroTranslator than all Rob's other brain waves combined. The second observation was that although the wavelength was activated when Rob died it didn't *appear* on the screen then. Dormant and unnoticed at the top end of the register, it had been in Brian's neural net at the beginning of the experiment.

Fleming couldn't explain the first observation but the reason for the second was obvious: the NeuroTranslator hadn't discovered this mysterious new wavelength in Rob's death. Its neural net had learnt it from an earlier patient and a recent one at that.

Leaning forward, Fleming tapped the screen and went into the NeuroTranslator's list of files. He watched Amber Grant's details appear before him.

On the right side of the screen was the Quicktime recording of her first night in the Think Tank. She was tossing and turning in her sleep when her body suddenly calmed, her eyes opened and she cried out in the voice of a young girl. She was calling her own name repeatedly as if she had lost herself.

Fleming glanced at the left side of the screen and his throat constricted. First, the wavelengths scrambled and oscillated frantically, just as Rob's signals had when he died. Then the screen distorted, the wavelengths flat-lined momentarily as if she was brain-dead, and a unique pulsing signal appeared on the screen at the high end of the frequency spectrum.

Fleming knew without checking that it was the same new wavelength as the one that had allowed Rob to speak after his death. He stared at the screen. Then, with slow, dazed movements, he reached for the on-screen icons, opened tonight's files on Amber and played back the sequence he had just witnessed in the Think Tank.

He watched her sleeping, noting her physiological behaviour as she entered REM. She was struggling as if she was being pulled somewhere she didn't want to go. When she entered the dream state her body slackened. When most people enter REM they go into a state of paralysis, because the pons and medulla at the base of the brain send signals down the spinal cord to inhibit muscle activity and stop them acting out their dreams. Her signals were weak and she opened her eyelids as if searching for something. She talked – in the voice he had heard moments before, that of a young girl.

As he watched the brain waves flicker and die on one side of the screen and saw Amber sleep-talking on the other, he saw himself come into the Think Tank and approach the NeuroTranslator, turning on the speakers. When he heard the unearthly scream played back he studied the single unknown brain wave on the left side of the screen. It flickered in tune with the scream, as if reflecting every agony expressed within it. And all the time he could hear Amber calling her own name.

Fleming understood the human brain better than most men and he wanted more than anything to dismiss this as an anomaly of a troubled psyche, or delayed-memory syndrome. But he couldn't.

He remembered what Amber had told him about her dream of dying and a question nagged at him. What if she had been right? Because she possessed part of the living brain of a dead person, perhaps there *was* some connection between her living consciousness and that of her dead twin. Perhaps her dream of dying had been a memory of her near-death experience on the operating-table, and the scream he had heard was the death-cry of her mind, articulated through the unknown wavelength. And perhaps the child's voice hadn't come from Amber's consciousness but Ariel's.

Hadn't Amber said something about her and her twin trying to contact each other but being unable to, like two magnets of the same polarity? Fleming leant back in his chair and rubbed his temples. His head felt hot, as if he was running a temperature, and his hands were trembling. He wanted to go to bed and forget about this but the sound remained with him. However he twisted the data in front of him he kept coming back to one possible – impossible – explanation.

Somehow, when Ariel died a trace of her consciousness remained in the living section of Amber's brain that Ariel had shared. Unlike other parts of the human body, brain cells aren't renewed, and a vestigial mental link remained between the twins. A part of Ariel's consciousness seemed to be trying to contact her living sibling, while a part of Amber's had embarked at least twice on the traumatic journey of dying. At some unconscious level, they were seeking a reunion in the no man's land between life and death.

If the hardware connection between the twins was their shared brain tissue, then the software link was the unique and unexplained brain wave. But this wavelength didn't just link Amber and Ariel, it had allowed Rob to communicate. This neural signal, this soul wavelength, might be the universal link between the abstract mind and the physical brain – between life and death.

As he replayed the video of Amber sleep-talking and the scream issuing from the NeuroTranslator speakers, Fleming remembered his dream and Jake's question about heaven. A chill ran down his spine.

There had to be a rational explanation for this.

He was so engrossed in his thoughts that he jumped when he noticed the figure standing a few feet away from him, staring at his computer screen. The director of Barley Hall was holding two cups of espresso.

'Virginia, what are you doing here?'

'Insomnia's my excuse, Miles. What's yours?'

'How long have you been standing there?'

Knight looked at the computer screen again. Her face was white. 'Long enough. What the hell's going on?'

Fleming was glad to unburden himself. 'Take a seat, Virginia. I'm not entirely sure what I have here but there are a few things you need to know.'

Xavier Accosta was fast asleep when there was a sharp rap on the door of his stateroom. He opened his eyes and tried to orient himself. 'What is it?' he barked.

The door opened a crack, spilling a triangle of light on to the jewel-like colours of the worn Chinese rug. Monsignor Diageo pushed his head round the door. 'Your Holiness, forgive me for disturbing you but there's an urgent call.'

'Can't it wait?'

Diageo opened the door further, widening the triangle of light, and stepped into the room. 'No, Your Holiness, it can't.' He was holding a cordless digital phone.

'What time is it?'

'Three thirty, Cape Town time.'

Accosta groaned and took the phone. He didn't recognize the caller's voice at first, but when he did his irritation evaporated and he became instantly alert.

As Accosta listened euphoria rushed through him. He controlled the urge to bombard the caller with questions, although there was so much he wanted to know. He listened patiently, until the caller stopped talking, then asked three questions. After listening intently to the replies, he issued four instructions. Finally he thanked the caller and hung up, returning the phone to the waiting Diageo.

He threw back the bedclothes, sprang up and

rushed to the bathroom with virtually no trace of his limp.

'Monsignor Diageo,' he called over his shoulder, 'we have to prepare for the new day. There's much to do. Our Lord's finally provided, and we mustn't disappoint Him.'

24

Barley Hall. The next morning

Amber woke exhausted. The memory of last night's dream was sinister and seemed more significant than the first. She had the frustrating notion that there was something she should remember, something to do with Ariel. It was as if she could see her sister calling to her through thick distorted glass but couldn't hear what she was saying. As she prepared for the day ahead she looked forward to seeing Miles Fleming again and hoped that the initial analysis from the NeuroTranslator would shed some light on her predicament. She would call Papa Pete in the afternoon.

She was feeling more optimistic when there was a knock on the door and Professor Virginia Knight entered the Think Tank. Her hair was flat and her suit looked as if she had worn it all night. 'Excuse me for disturbing you, Dr Grant, but I have bad news. Your mother's condition has deteriorated. The hospice advises you to return as soon as possible.'

It was the last thing she had been expecting. The shock hit her like a physical blow. Amber had known that her mother was dying but until now she hadn't accepted it. Her phantom headaches and dreams seemed unimportant. She had to go home.

'There's a flight in a little over two hours. If you leave in the next fifteen minutes you can make it. A limousine's waiting to take you to Heathrow,' Knight said, with a sympathetic smile. 'I'm so sorry. If there's anything I can do let me know.'

Amber checked her watch. 'Is there any chance of speaking to Dr Fleming before I go?'

'Not if you want to make your flight. If he comes in at all today, it won't be for some time.'

Amber was disappointed. Now she would have to wait for the NeuroTranslator results. 'Could you please pass on my condolences about his brother, and thank him and his team for me? And I need to arrange to come back and finish my treatment.'

'Don't worry about that now. The clinic will contact you to continue where you left off. That's no problem.'

By nine fifteen she was in a limousine pulling out of Barley Hall. In the rear-view mirror she watched the majestic house recede into the distance. As the car passed the turning to Cambridge, she didn't see the Jaguar heading in the opposite direction.

Fifteen minutes later the uniformed driver offered her a small bottle of Evian. She was thirsty, and as she watched signs for the M11 and London come into view she sipped it.

A sudden lethargy struck her on the M11. When the car reached the M25 she was unconscious. At the turning for the M4 it drove past the signs for

Heathrow and carried on to Maidenhead. Here the driver turned into the drive of a large red-brick Victorian property with a white sign by the gates: The Church of the Soul Truth Hospice. The Church's symbol, a stylized representation of the Red Ark with a cruciform mast, featured beneath the text.

The car drove straight into a garage behind the property. Amber's prostrate body was moved from the limousine, carried into the hospice mortuary and placed in a ready-prepared insulated burial casket with oxygen tanks and an intravenous drip.

The necessary customs papers and death certificate were prepared in the name of Jane Smith and stamped with the hospice name. Two doctors' signatures had been scrawled on the blank forms. The personnel who processed Amber and the relevant administration did so with a calm, unquestioning precision that indicated they had done this before. Finally the white coffin was closed and the locked casket was placed in a hearse then driven to the freight area of Terminal 4.

Two hours later Amber Grant's unconscious body was in the air, safely stowed in the climate-controlled hold of a Boeing 747, flying in more comfort than the most pampered first-class passenger ever did.

The Red Ark. 18° 06´ S, 16° 03´ W

The Red Pope was filled with energy, and he was oblivious to the pain that racked his body. Dressed in full-length starched scarlet robes he paced around his office in the prow of the Red Ark. The anticipation that he might be close to the end of his quest was so strong he could almost taste it.

'Everything in place at your end, Doctor?' he demanded of the shadowy face on the television screen above his desk.

'The laboratory's being prepared now, Your Holiness,' Soames said. He was smiling. 'It'll be ready soon enough.'

'Are the Truth Council on standby?'

'As soon as you get here they'll all be available – in person or online.'

'Excellent.' Accosta turned to Diageo standing silently by the door. 'Monsignor, you have made the other arrangements? Tied up all the loose ends?'

'Our contacts in London and—'

Accosta smiled at Diageo. 'No details, Monsignor Diageo.' Diageo's shadier contacts in the secular world had their uses but Accosta's burden was heavy enough without knowing about them. 'Do what you must do, Monsignor. Simply tell me that everything is in place.'

Diageo nodded impassively. 'It is.'

'Excellent.' Accosta turned and looked out of the vast picture window at the limitless ocean stretching before him. He retrieved a handkerchief from his robe pocket and coughed violently into it. Diageo stepped closer to him but Accosta waved him away. 'Tell the bridge to head north, full speed ahead. And prepare both helicopters. I want to be at the Foundation within twenty-four hours. Make my apologies to those on board with whom I was to speak, and run looped repeats of my sermons for today's services.'

He looked down. The white handkerchief was flecked with spots of red. He felt no fear: he was confident that when the time came he would be ready.

25

Barley Hall. 9.30 a.m.

Despite his exhaustion, Miles Fleming's mind burned with possibilities as he parked his Jaguar and hurried in to see Amber. After the excitement of last night or, more accurately, this morning, Knight had sent him home to snatch a few hours' sleep. When he did doze off he had slept through his usual six o'clock alarm call.

He couldn't stop thinking of what this new wavelength might mean. There had to be a rational explanation for it; he was sure of that. He just needed time to research it. The scientist in him was driven to know more, recognizing that this finding eclipsed the discovery of microwaves a few decades ago. However, another part of him wished he could undiscover the new wavelength because its existence threatened everything he believed in. What if there was more to our existence than this life? What if there was a hereafter? What did that mean for his exclusive focus on the here and now? And what did it mean for Rob's soul? And, as Jake had demanded, was heaven a *good* place? Did he really want to know the answers?

'Miles, we need to talk,' Knight called, as Fleming passed her office. She sounded grim as she ushered him in and sat him down. After Rob's death she had been sympathetic but detached, keen to know exactly what had happened. Last night when he had told her about Amber Grant, she had been cautious. 'Miles, I've been talking to the other trustees and there are a few concerns I need to make you aware of,' she said now.

Fleming frowned. 'What concerns?'

'I wanted to wait but you're here now so we may as well cover them. Since Rob died during an experiment here we have to ensure that Barley Hall's reputation for safety is whiter than white.'

'Virginia, he was my brother. I feel awful about this but the trial didn't cause Rob's death.'

'Miles, this is about perception. I know it wasn't your fault and the independent inquiry won't—'

'Inquiry? What the hell are you talking about?'

'Just a formality. These are delicate times. There are sponsors to think of and significant donations at stake. There's a rumour that you didn't do all you could to save your patient and we want to nip it in the bud before the press blow it out of all proportion. It's simply a case of sending you away on leave for a few weeks and then, once the inquiry has vindicated you – as we know it will – you can come back. Full pay, of course, and—'

Fleming was astonished. 'You're suspending me? Come on, Virginia, you must be joking. I already told you that after *four* ineffective attempts to revive my brother I stopped the nurse using epinephrine. I feel terrible about what happened

168

but I'd do it again. To all intents and purposes he was dead and I didn't want to prolong his suffering. I did nothing wrong. There's no cover-up. It's all on video, for Christ's sake. Let me talk to the trustees. I can sort this out.'

Knight shook her head. 'I'm sorry, Miles, but I agree with the trustees on this one. We have to protect Barley Hall's reputation in the short term and yours in the long term. This way we can clear the air and avoid even the suspicion of a cover-up. The press—'

'What have the press got to do with this? They don't need to be involved. Why should they suspect a cover-up? Rob was my brother, for Christ's sake.'

'I'm sorry, Miles, this isn't up for discussion.'

Fleming was barely able to contain himself. 'This is ludicrous, Virginia. What about Amber Grant and the new wavelength? We're tantalizingly close to something amazing and you want to examine whether or not I'm to blame for my own brother's death.'

'That's something else I need to discuss with you, Miles. There's to be no mention of what happened in the experiment. It's bad enough that Rob died and we don't want to fan the flames of interest with stories about communicating from beyond the grave. I've spoken to the others involved in the trial and have explained that what happened was nothing more than a lag effect. As far as they and anybody else are concerned the official explanation is Rob's neural signals were active *before* he died but were only transmitted

169

after his death because of a delay in the Neuro-Translator – a technicality.'

Fleming slammed his fist on the desk. 'What about Amber Grant?'

'As of now that's not your concern. She's had to return to California. Her mother's close to death.'

'She went this morning? You told her about the—'

'She's got enough to worry about now, Miles. I guess we should leave her alone for the time being. When the situation with her mother is resolved and you get back from leave—'

'Suspension.'

'Look, Miles, I'm truly sorry about Rob and know as well as you do what a potentially huge discovery this wavelength is. But we need to be real careful how we handle it. At the moment we don't want or need any half-assed leaps in the dark. Go away for a few weeks – it is *not* suspension – and think things through. When this episode blows over you can come back fully vindicated and continue your work, including this new wavelength. Your patients will all be looked after, including Jake if he needs any follow-up treatment before you get back. All trials will be carried out according to your wishes. Go home and relax. Take some holiday, spend some time with Jake, get your head together.'

Fleming paced around the room. 'How can I relax, Virginia? This isn't right. This is bloody stupid. What if I refuse?'

'Miles, you've got to trust me. Don't make this any more difficult than it already is. I don't want to call Security and escort you off the premises but I will if I have to.'

'What? You want me to leave *now*?'

'It's best. Clear your desk and go home. Don't worry about telling anybody or explaining anything, I'll do that.'

Fleming took a deep breath and held his arms tight down by his side, not trusting himself to control his anger. 'I don't know what's going on here, Virginia, but this is bullshit. I'm going to fight it. It isn't going to end here.'

Knight stood up. 'Miles, be reasonable. You need time out. Rob's death has been a greater shock than you realize. If you go against the trustees' wishes I can't protect you against punitive action.'

'*Protect me?*' Fleming walked round the desk and stood inches from his boss, looking her in the eye until she turned away. 'I always knew you were a bureaucrat, Virginia, but I never thought you could be so petty. I'm going to do what I need to do. No more. No less. If you don't like it then do what *you* need to do. Trust me, there are plenty of other institutions who would welcome my work with open arms.'

Ten minutes later Fleming was speeding through the narrow country lanes towards home. The Jaguar's soft top was down, and as the trees raced by their golden leaves waved in the breeze. Listening to it he was reminded of the scream that had issued from the NeuroTranslator speakers, and his dead brother was on his mind.

At that moment, turning his car towards

171

Cambridge, Fleming's molten anger cooled into something harder. He knew he couldn't wait patiently for the inquiry to run its course. He felt an obligation to Amber, Rob and Jake – and to himself – to explore this further and find some answers.

Answers to questions about life and death, which no other mortal man had yet been in a position to supply.

26

The VenTec Foundation. Alaska.
Eighteen hours later

The Chinook flew low over the Brooks mountain range in the Arctic sector of northern Alaska. Accosta wiped the glass window beside him and looked down, straining to see the Foundation. He knew the converted oil-rig must be close now but there was no sign of it in the rocky white wasteland below or in the towering mountains on either side of him. Then he glanced up, above the helicopter's churning rotor blades, and saw a glint of weak sunlight on the highest peak.

Peering through the grimy window he could just make out a structure on the flat summit. Supported on eight angled struts, the black glass dome resembled an enormous spider squatting on the mountaintop. A satellite dish and a pylon stood beside it and a funnel pushed upwards from its glass skin. Beneath the dome he could just see a vast central pillar rooting the structure deep into the mountain, and housing the old drilling machinery and borehole. Jutting out from one side of the dome, an apron of steel formed a semi-circular platform. Accosta's stomach lurched as the helicopter dropped towards it.

It was an early afternoon in October and the light was already fading. The days were now only a few hours long and in a few weeks there would be no sunlight at all for almost five months. Accosta had no fondness for this bleak place, but he understood why Soames insisted on being based here and he himself valued seclusion. Above all, he needed the expertise and resources housed within its walls, which were funded and administered by Soames.

When the helicopter landed on the platform, his entourage ushered him out into the biting cold before escorting him through thick tinted-glass sliding doors into the warmth of the main reception area. The doors had a large V engraved into the glass and a logo: 'VenTec – *Past the Present to the Future.*'

Inside, Accosta's coat was taken from him as the security door leading to the unrestricted white sector hissed open. In the subdued light of the windowless corridor Dr Bradley Soames was waiting in a white bodysuit. Accosta was relieved to see that his wolves weren't with him: there was something otherworldly about them that he hated – and feared. The scientist greeted him as a host would an honoured guest: he genuflected and kissed the crucifix that hung from the Red Pope's neck.

'Welcome, Your Holiness.'

'Thank you, Doctor.'

'The other members of the Truth Council are—'

Accosta raised his hand and smiled. 'Can we

discuss that later? I'm impatient to see her. Is she here?'

'Follow me, Your Holiness. She's secured in the black sector.'

Accosta followed Soames down the corridor through the white sector. VenTec was laid out like a pie: four colour-coded slices surrounded the central pillar of the dome. The front white sector was unrestricted and contained the communal areas and general laboratories. The blue, green and black sectors were all restricted, open only to those with the necessary clearance. Accessed by an elevator in the central pillar, there was a fifth sector beneath the dome, deep in the mountain itself. This was the red sector, also restricted.

As they passed through the white sector, their heels clicked on the varnished beechwood floor. The conditioned air was devoid of odour but held a hint of static. To his left Accosta could see a series of open-plan laboratories. Some were empty except for unrecognizable apparatus; others were peopled with technicians and scientists in white bodysuits like the Doctor's. One was filled with row upon row of computers, whose screens flickered with intense white light.

In the residential quarters, Accosta barely glanced at the white chevrons on the sheer walls, which gave directions to the various facilities: the accommodation suites, restaurants, the cinema, medical suite, swimming-pool, gymnasium and a prayer room. The few external windows were tinted blue and gave the external Arctic landscape an even more frigid outlook.

Reaching the central pillar, the elevator leading to the red sector was marked with red chevrons and warnings: *Authorized Personnel Only. Eye Shields Obligatory.* Turning left, they passed another sealed security door, which led to the green sector.

Finally the corridor curved round to the northernmost slice of VenTec, the black sector, home of the Soul Project.

Opening the glass security door by placing his palm on a sensor beside the locking mechanism, Soames led Accosta through the complex, passing the conference room and communication room to the main laboratory. Outside he introduced Accosta to a striking blonde woman and a tall black man in glasses. Both wore the enamelled cruciform of the Church of the Soul Truth on their white bodysuits. The woman wore a musky perfume that Accosta found overpowering.

'Dr Felicia Bukowski and Dr Walter Tripp have been helping me on the Soul Project. Most of the work we've done so far is largely down to them.'

Accosta shook their hands. 'You are embarked on a sacred and glorious venture and I thank you for all your work and ingenuity.'

'It's an honour to be involved,' Tripp said.

'A privilege, Your Holiness,' added the blonde woman.

Accosta studied them for a second. Both were respectful but there was something about their manner and the way they returned his smile that didn't ring true. He prided himself on being able to see into a person's heart, and although he couldn't pinpoint exactly what was wrong, he felt as if the scientists were humouring him – two precocious children indulging a dull relative. He brushed these thoughts aside, and allowed Soames to usher him into the black sector's private accommodation suites.

Soames stopped at the first door and gestured for Accosta to look through a round porthole in the wall. 'She's asleep in there. The drugs will wear off soon.'

Accosta stepped close to the glass and stared at the woman in the single bed. She was attached to an intravenous drip and a life-signs monitor, which beeped with reassuring regularity. 'How is she?'

'Fine. She'll be kind of woozy when she wakes, but she'll be strong enough when we're ready for her.'

'Excellent,' said Accosta. Her dark hair was splayed out on the pillow, her olive skin glowing against the white linen, her long lashes flickering on her cheeks. As Accosta watched the sleeping Amber Grant, her ethereal beauty pleased him.

She was more than simply beautiful, though: she was a gift from God.

The drugs blurred Amber's already muddled sense of what was and wasn't a dream. Opening her eyes, she discovered that she was lying in an unfamiliar room, with her wrists strapped to a strange bed. Her heart raced when she saw the intravenous drip and monitor. Was this real or another nightmare?

A sudden movement in her peripheral vision

made her turn her head towards the small circular window to the left of the bed. Through it a pair of dark eyes stared at her. The hunger in that intense stare unravelled her courage far more than the wrist straps and the drip. The man's face was disconcertingly familiar, but in her post-drugged state she didn't recognize the aquiline nose and chiselled cheekbones. Then the face moved back an inch from the glass so that his whole head was framed in the window, including his scarlet skullcap. With a stab of fear so intense that it made her gasp, she realized who he must be.

This has to be a dream, she told herself. *A nightmare*.

For he was the Devil, come to take her soul.

27

The black sector conference room.
VenTec

The lighting was muted and Accosta sat at the head of the long, rectangular table. Flanking him were Monsignor Diageo and Bradley Soames. Soames's wolves sat behind him, still and silent as grey statues. Bukowski and Tripp were further down the table, hands resting in front of them.

On one of three holographic plasma screens facing Accosta, Frank Carvelli could be seen, absently fingering his unnaturally black ponytail. The head of KREE8 Industries, and member of the Truth Council responsible for media presentation and public relations, was dressed in his trademark black, including a cashmere jacket and roll-neck sweater.

However, for all Carvelli's media contacts, today's breakthrough hadn't come through him. It had come through the third member of the Truth Council who, to Accosta's annoyance, still hadn't come on-line. 'You said they'd all be here?' he said, turning to Soames.

The Doctor shrugged. 'They should be, Your Holiness.'

Accosta frowned and looked over Soames's shoulder. Behind him, through the two-way mirror that acted as one of the walls of the conference suite, Accosta could see into the gleaming white splendour of the main laboratory. The glass head-sphere lay with its visor open in a protective transparent cabinet beside the laboratory couch, at the foot of which was a battery of ancillary monitors and apparatus.

'Let's start,' Accosta said abruptly. 'Tell me again why Amber Grant is so important.'

Carvelli craned forward on screen and Soames smiled, revealing his perfect white teeth. 'I've known Amber Grant for many years as a business partner and have always admired her abilities,' he said, 'but I'd no inkling of her real talents till we started the first soul-capture experiments nine months ago. Of course, she was unaware of these experiments but it was about then that she began to experience unusual migraines. As time progressed it became apparent that her headaches coincided exactly with the experiments.' He explained Amber's unusual medical past. 'Ever heard of entanglement, Your Holiness?'

'No.'

'It's a ghostly, almost telepathic link between quantum particles that have interacted at some time in the past. The connection is instantaneous and works even if the particles are on opposite sides of the universe. Because of her unique medical history I think Amber is entangled with her dead twin. I've already explained how particles in the double-slit experiment change

180

their state when observed, as if conscious of the set-up of the experiment. Well, I'm convinced that when we conduct a soul-capture experiment we collapse the particle wave duality of the soul, causing a disturbance felt instantaneously throughout the universal boson system connecting all souls.'

On screen Carvelli nodded. 'And because of her entanglement with Ariel, Amber feels the disturbance as a phantom migraine.'

'You got it,' said Soames, and went on to tell Accosta about Fleming and the NeuroTranslator. 'What Miles Fleming unwittingly discovered was that Amber's the perfect lab rat for the Soul Project.'

'Why?' demanded Accosta, still unsure of the relevance of the complex quantum concepts.

'As I said once before, Your Holiness, what we really need is an impossibility, someone who can die more than once. Amber Grant possesses part of the living brain of a dead person, and if her neural signals are suitably stimulated when she enters REM her subconscious tries to contact her dead twin, and mentally she leaves her mortal body. By inducing the dream state we can track her mind's – soul's – journey each time she leaves and returns to her body. And because we can repeat her dying again and again we can run iterative loops to lock on to the holding frequency.'

'How can you be so sure of this?' Carvelli said, from the screen.

At that moment the second plasma screen fizzed into life and the third member of the

Truth Council appeared. She wore a navy suit with the obligatory scarlet cruciform brooch on her lapel. A qualified medical doctor, she treated only one patient nowadays: Accosta. In addition to managing a major clinic in Britain she also held a number of other posts, and had overall strategic responsibility for the Church of the Soul Truth Hospices around the world. She was the source of the secret flow of untraceable terminal patients to Soames's soul-capture experiments. 'Apologies for being late, Your Holiness, but I had to attend to matters affecting this meeting.'

Before Accosta could say anything, Soames gestured to her. 'We were just wondering how we can be so sure that Amber Grant has a unique talent, Virginia. Perhaps you could explain.'

Virginia Knight looked at Accosta. 'I heard her soul cry out, Your Holiness. And I've seen all Fleming's data. The evidence is compelling.'

Accosta tried to keep his excitement in check – the project had already yielded a bounty of disappointments. 'Thank you, Dr Knight.' He turned back to Soames. 'But how do we keep Dr Grant here without alerting the authorities?'

Soames smiled again. 'No problem. She's formally signed out of Barley Hall and Optrix aren't expecting her back for a month. Our only real area of exposure is her mother.'

'And I've seen to that,' said Virginia Knight crisply. 'Since Gillian Grant is in one of our hospices it was relatively easy to arrange.'

'In that case,' said Soames, 'I guess we've got

about a month before Amber's disappearance starts raising difficulties.'

Knight coughed. 'What about Miles Fleming?'

'What about him?' said Accosta. 'I thought he'd been isolated, suspended from Barley Hall.'

'He has, Your Holiness, but Dr Fleming's determined. He doesn't like things he can't explain, feels compelled to understand them – particularly as it was his brother's death that alerted us to Dr Grant's abilities. That's why he's so good, and that's why we've got to watch him.'

'Sure we'll watch him,' Soames chipped in. 'We need him. Take a look at the stages of the project so far.' He began to tick off points on his fingers. 'We've *detected* the existence of the human soul, *made it visible* to the human eye and *identified* each soul's individual signature through the photon-detector screen. Now we've got Amber Grant we ought to be able to *capture* its tracking frequency. But for the Soul Project to succeed in its entirety . . .' Soames looked meaningfully at Accosta '. . . and for *your* destiny to be fulfilled, we must complete the final stage.' Soames turned to Carvelli. 'Frank, though your particular expertise is undoubtedly key in making this final stage happen, Miles Fleming's contribution will be of critical importance, particularly as our earlier attempts to replicate his technology haven't been entirely successful and it'll take too much time to perfect it ourselves.'

'So we just watch him and wait?' Knight asked.

Soames grinned as though this was a game he

was enjoying immensely. 'We use his determination to find answers to make him help us.'

'That'll be dangerous,' Carvelli said.

Soames's grin became broader and Accosta had to suppress his distaste for the man. 'Of course it'll be dangerous. Especially for him.'

PART 2

THE SOUL TRUTH

28

Rome. Four days later

The Eternal City was unseasonably warm and humid for October and Fleming's shirt clung to his back as he wove his way through the tourists in St Peter's Square. In the hazy sunlight he squinted at his watch, noting he had twenty minutes before his two o'clock appointment.

In the last few days he had tried in vain to contact Amber Grant. He didn't have her private cellphone number, and her home phone at Pacific Heights in San Francisco was on answer-machine. When Optrix had informed him she was on leave of absence for a month, he explained that he was her doctor but was told that they could not provide him with a contact number: according to the Barley Hall authorities, he was under investigation for malpractice.

When he called the hospice in Marin County to inquire about Gillian Grant and leave a message for her daughter, the receptionist was similarly tight-lipped, which made him realize that Virginia Knight was subtly undermining his reputation. Unsubstantiated reports of him as 'brilliant but ruthlessly ambitious' and 'sacrificing his own brother in the pursuit of glory' were already appearing in the press. And when he'd called his office yesterday even Frankie Pinner had sounded nervous, cutting him off apologetically: she wasn't allowed to talk to him, she said, until 'everything had been sorted out'.

Finally, after every avenue had closed, he had come to Rome.

Despite the heat, fumes and noise that filled the stifling air, St Peter's magnificent dome shimmered against the sky. The outstretched arms of Bernini's flanking colonnades seemed to draw him into the bosom of the Mother Church. As Catholicism had declined this fortress of faith had become little more than a stunning theme park, a museum to a once great empire. Few of the crowds who thronged here were pilgrims; most were tourists attending the cultural equivalent of Disneyland. The final humiliation was that many wore the red crucifix of the Church of the Soul Truth.

As he entered the quiet cool of the great cathedral and looked up at Michelangelo's vast dome, Fleming felt no instinct to gloat. St Peter's ageless beauty was humbling, the fabric of the place so saturated with its past that he had only to press his ears to the pillars to hear its secrets. Rome had existed as a city for over twenty-five centuries, and for fifteen of those this had been the centre of the Christian faith.

He lit a candle for his brother and watched the flame send curls of wispy smoke high into the air. Whatever he thought about religion, scholars here had been studying matters of the soul for centuries. Fleming was an atheist embarked on uncharted seas with only some scientific certainties to guide him.

But that wasn't why he had contacted Father Peter Riga. He had called him because Amber had cited him as next-of-kin on her Barley Hall admission form. He was Fleming's only remaining link with her. Although Riga had been guarded on the telephone he had agreed to see him.

He left St Peter's and went into the sweltering streets to the nearest taxi rank. The cab took only a few minutes to cross the Tiber and deposit him outside the world headquarters of the Society of Jesus: the begrimed baroque splendour of Borromini's Collegio di Propaganda Fide.

He entered the building – and stepped into a different world, away from the bustle, glare and noise of the Roman streets. Inside, all was marbled stillness. He identified himself at the reception desk and was led up the grand staircase by a young man in black robes.

Father Peter Riga's office was on the top floor at the end of a long, dark corridor, and Fleming could tell by the deference with which the younger Jesuit knocked at the door that Riga was of high status within the Society.

'Come in,' boomed an American voice.

The room was simple yet comfortable: a desk with a brass reading lamp and a laptop computer, crammed bookshelves, two high windows, a worn rug on the marble floor, and two simple chairs flanking a small table. Each item was beautiful in itself – the bookshelves were carved with arabesques, the books bound and tooled in leather – but the antique walnut desk was exquisite.

Sitting behind it, framed in the golden light from one of the high windows, was a broad-shouldered man with close-cropped curly grey hair, a strong, weathered face and piercing blue eyes. When Fleming entered he stood up: he was short, no more than five foot six, with a barrel chest like a wrestler. He had to be about seventy but he looked in good shape. Beside him on the desk was a simple silver frame containing two photographs. One showed a younger Riga standing beside a smiling couple with two small girls apparently embracing. The other, more recent, picture was of Riga with Amber Grant and her mother. In both, as now, he was attired from head to toe in black.

'Welcome, Dr Fleming,' he rasped. Riga wasn't the classic soft-spoken priest – but then Jesuits, the intellectual Special Forces of the Catholic Church, rarely were. His accent reminded Fleming of a friend at Harvard, a scholarship boy from the streets of New York. Fleming shook his hand firmly.

Riga's intelligent eyes fixed on his, appraising him. 'So, how's my goddaughter?' he demanded, a protective note in his voice.

'I rather hoped you could tell me.'

Riga nodded slowly but his expression didn't change. 'Saw her a few days ago in San Francisco. Said you were testing her for phantom headaches and that she'd had a dream of dying – a dream she didn't believe was a dream. She believed Ariel's soul was somehow tied up with hers. Last thing she said was she was going to see what you and your technology made of it. You discovered something?'

Fleming studied Riga's face but couldn't fathom how much he did or didn't know. The Jesuit would probably have discovered by now that he had been suspended from Barley Hall so he'd better start at the beginning. He explained about the Neuro-Translator and the experiment with his brother. He told Riga about the night he had heard Amber's disembodied scream in the Think Tank, and that he had been suspended, pending an investigation into his brother's death.

Riga's poker face gave away little, but when Fleming explained about the soul wavelength he thought he caught a flicker of something cross the Jesuit's impassive features ... something that looked like fear.

'And she left before you could explain all this to her?'

'To go to her mother, yes.'

Riga nodded. 'Yeah, Gillian's real sick. So you ain't spoken to Amber since you left your clinic?'

'No.'

Riga narrowed his eyes. 'Okay, so how come this soul wavelength of Amber's has got you so fired up?'

'Isn't it obvious?'

'But what's it to *you*, Dr Fleming? Amber didn't figure you for a religious type.'

'I'm not. I'm a man of science. I don't believe in God or an afterlife and don't want to believe

191

in one. But I'm also someone who likes to under-stand things and this has given me an itch I can't scratch. It's put me in a position where I need to reassure myself that I'm right. For my own peace of mind I've got to prove that this wavelength is some kind of aberration – a mental last gasp or trace signal of the dying physical brain. And I can't do that without Amber.'

'What if you're wrong? What if you find there *is* an afterlife? What if your scientific questioning finds *proof* of it? What then, Mr Atheist?'

'I'll deal with that when I come to it. The point is, with Amber's assistance I might be able to help answer mankind's biggest question – and that's something I can't walk away from. I thought you'd understand that. You Jesuits are famous for your intellectual rigour and curiosity, your desire to know.'

'It's more a desire to *understand*,' Riga said. 'We don't want knowledge for knowledge's sake.' He flashed a wry smile. 'That's why mankind got thrown out of Eden in the first place. The Society's motto is *ad majorem Dei gloriam* – to the greater glory of God. Everything we do is aimed at reveal-ing *His* glory, not ours.'

'What are you saying? That there are some things God doesn't want us to know?'

'What I'm saying, Dr Fleming, is that some knowledge is dangerous and easily abused. Particularly nowadays.' For the first time the Jesuit's rock-like calm deserted him and his words were laced with controlled anger. 'My Church is at risk of extinction. And the threat doesn't come from atheists, Jews or followers of Islam, but from fellow Christians, inside and outside the Mother Church. Our current pope is weak and the right-wing factions within the Holy See cling to their power and wealth by ignoring necessary reforms and becoming even more controlling and dogmatic as the Church erodes around them. All the time the Red Pope's Church gets stronger. I knew Xavier Accosta when he was a cardinal in the Vatican, and there was a lot to admire. He was a bright, passionate guy. He'd have made a good Jesuit. There were many parallels between him and our founder St Ignatius Loyola – both Hispanic, highly charismatic, warriors whose wounding in battle converted them to devote their lives to God. But where Loyola strengthened the Mother Church from within, Accosta had no qualms about leaving it and exploiting its weakened state.

'He set up his rival ministry when infighting was rife within the Church. Pope John Paul II was ill, and had become a puppet of the powerful reactionary right. In Europe and the United States Catholic youth were falling away in vast numbers. In Latin America there were huge losses of Catholics to evangelical Protestant teachings. It was a terrible time. Accosta should have stayed and reformed the Church from within, but instead he put himself first. His obsession with technology and what he calls truth is no less dogmatic than the blind arrogance of those fools in the Curia.'

Riga paused for breath and his voice became softer, but no less passionate. 'We in the Society have one clear goal. Survival. We gotta save our Church from itself and those like the Red Pope who'd destroy us. Dr Fleming, you've stumbled into a war zone and you gotta be careful what you do with the technology you've found and the knowledge you seek. There are those in the Vatican and those near the Red Pope who'd do anything to possess it and *control* it.'

'But that's the whole point,' said Fleming. 'Once we know what awaits us after death no religion can control us.'

Riga released a dry, humourless laugh. 'You figure that's gonna fill the Vatican or the Red Pope with joy? Just think about the spiritual as well as the scientific implications of what you're seeking. You're putting yourself in the way of powerful forces – and you and Amber in a ton of danger.'

'Shouldn't Amber decide for herself whether she wants to get involved? She came to me for help and this wavelength might be vital in curing her headaches.'

'Maybe. We ain't talked since I visited with her in San Francisco a week ago.'

Fleming frowned. 'She hasn't called you since?'

'I figure she's got a lot to think about, with her mother. But I'm hoping she'll call soon.'

'When she does call, will you ask her to contact me?'

'Sure.'

Fleming stood to leave, disappointed that he had achieved nothing by coming here. 'Thanks for your time,' he said, extending his hand.

Riga took it. 'Likewise, Dr Fleming. You still gonna go looking for her?'

'I've got no choice. There's nothing else I can do.'

'God speed, then, and watch yourself.'

Shortly after Fleming's departure, Father Peter Riga closed the door, returned to his desk and dialled Amber's number for the eighth time since Fleming had contacted him. The voicemail kicked in, but he left no message. Instead he dialled a three-number extension within his own building.

On the third ring a voice responded.

'It's Father Peter. Get me the Superior General.'

He didn't have to wait long before the rich voice of the head of the Society of Jesus was on the line. 'Superior General,' Riga said, 'we gotta talk. Urgent.'

29

Leonardo da Vinci Airport. Rome.
Three hours later

Fleming struggled through the milling crowd towards the British Airways check-in. As he approached the desk, he realized that the self-confidence he had always taken for granted had deserted him. His career, which had sustained him throughout his working life, was slipping away from him, his personal life was non-existent and he had nowhere to turn. He used to call his brother when something personal was troubling him, and talk through professional matters with the director of Barley Hall. But they were the source of his troubles.

There was only one person who could help him make sense of all this and she was inaccessible. All he could do now was go home and wait for Amber Grant's call.

Fleming looked around him, feeling the chill of paranoia as he remembered Riga's warning. A bland, mousy-haired man in a lightweight jacket suddenly averted his gaze, and for a second Fleming thought he might be following him. He retrieved the return ticket to Heathrow from his jacket pocket, looked up at the departures screen and suddenly had an irresistible urge to talk to someone who cared that he existed. He delved into his briefcase, reached for his cellphone and dialled his parents' number. His mother picked up.

After reassuring each other that they were okay, he asked to speak to Jake.

When he came on the line the six-year-old sounded breathless and excited. 'Hi, Milo. I played soccer today.'

Fleming's mood lifted. 'That's fantastic, Jake. Well done.'

'When you come back I'll race you.'

'Oh, I don't know about that. You've got bionic legs now.'

'Don't worry,' said Jake. 'I'll give you a head start if you like.'

'We'll have to see about that. You still looking after the legs like we talked about?'

'Yes.'

'How's everything else back there?'

'Okay.' Jake's voice changed, becoming more pensive. 'Milo?'

'Yes.'

'Where are you?'

'In Rome.' At that moment he heard his flight to London being called and he glanced up at the departures screen. But it was another entry that caught his eye. Noting the gate and departure time, Fleming checked his watch. The idea was so obvious that he was exasperated with himself. He had spent the last few days agonizing over how to contact Amber when what he should have done was take the most direct course of action. Even if it proved futile he had nothing better to do.

'You coming back soon, Milo?'

'Not just yet, Jake,' he replied, filled with fresh purpose. He headed for the Alitalia desk. 'Soon. But there's something I've got to do first. Give my love to Grandma and look after each other, okay?'

'Okay, Milo.'

''Bye, Jake. Miss you.'

''Bye, Milo. Miss you too.'

Seven minutes later, when Miles Fleming left the Alitalia desk and hurried to the departures gate, he didn't notice the bland, mousy-haired man punching a short text message into his WAP phone.

Fleming no longer on flight BA 671 to Heathrow.
Now on Alitalia AL 102. ETA. 09.15 a.m. local time.
Destination: San Francisco.

30

VenTec. Alaska

The first thing Amber became aware of was being awake, conscious, followed by an itching sensation all over her scalp.

She opened her eyes. Nothing happened. However hard she willed her eyelids to move they remained stubbornly closed. She tried to reach up to scratch her scalp but her arms remained inert at her sides. Frantically she tried to move some part of her body, any part, but she couldn't.

What was happening? Was she paralysed?

Nothing made any sense. Even time lost its meaning as she struggled to think amid the torpor that fogged her brain. In the last few days – or was it hours? – she had been vaguely aware of people around her but little else. Did this have something to do with what had happened at Barley Hall? Something Fleming had discovered about her through his NeuroTranslator? If so, what?

Think, damn you, think, she urged herself.

Something must have happened in the limousine driving her from Barley Hall. There was only one logical explanation, although it made no sense. She had been drugged and abducted. But why?

Suddenly she heard voices, a man's and a woman's. She dimly recognized the woman's and a distinctive musky scent hung in the air. She remembered it from the past.

The bed was moving now and, even from behind her eyelids, she could tell the light was brightening, as if she was leaving a room and entering a corridor.

A door hissed on her left, then the bed was wheeled into an even brighter area. Hands were on her now, lifting her from the bed and placing her on another. A hum filled the air around her.

Suddenly her eyelids were pulled open, making her want to blink at the lights overhead. A face appeared above her, wearing bulbous eye-protectors. Then stinging liquid was dripped into her exposed eyeballs, and pegs attached to the lids, pinning them open. The pain was excruciating but Amber couldn't squirm or turn away. Lightly tinted lenses were then inserted into her eyes.

Her head was raised and she saw a glass sphere resembling an astronaut's helmet being lifted over her head. In the curved glass she saw her image distorted like the reflection in the bottom of a spoon. What shocked her most was that her hair had been shaved off.

Amber was close to panic.

To her right, refracted through the helmet in her peripheral vision, she could see a phantom figure in white bodysuit and eye-protectors, holding up a hypodermic syringe. The woman's voice spoke: 'She's lucky, she's only going to die in her dreams.'

As the indistinct figure steered the needle closer

to the exposed flesh of her right arm she smelt the frustratingly familiar scent again. Before she could try to make any connections she heard a hiss and an odourless luminous gas seeped into the helmet, bathing the world in a green actinic glow.

Then her consciousness dimmed and darkness claimed her.

No sooner had she surrendered to the comforting embrace of oblivion than she was racing towards the cone of light, to where she might find peace. She tried to control her terror as she sped towards it but she could sense the forces holding her back, threatening to rip her apart. The elastic tension grew and grew until she was absorbed in the light and close to the source. But even as she felt Ariel's luminous presence reaching for her, almost touching, the force ripped her back again. Back into the darkness. Back to herself.

This time, however, there was no respite from dying, no return to the living. Instead of waking or returning to normal sleep, she was instantly catapulted back through the void towards the cone of light. Experiencing afresh the terror of dying she merged again with the light, this time going deeper than before, almost reaching its core, the source. Ariel was closer, she could sense it, but still out of reach . . .

Then Amber was yanked away from the light. Only to be hurled back towards it again. And again.

Each time she entered the light, she came closer to the source, to death and reunion with her sister. But every time she was thwarted. The closer she came to her sister, the greater the force that pulled her back.

She was a pendulum swinging from life to death and back again, inhabiting neither, damned for ever to remain in limbo between them, in a hell of sorts.

31

Black sector conference room.
VenTec

'Bradley, is she all right?' Accosta was tense, watching Amber Grant's pale, sweating face in the glass sphere.

Sitting in the conference room with Carvelli, Diageo, Knight and Soames, he looked into the laboratory through the two-way mirror wall. Now that the Soul Project was entering the critical stage, the entire Truth Council had taken leave of their other responsibilities to convene at VenTec. Each wanted to see this experiment in the flesh.

Bradley Soames calmly studied the readings on a screen above them. 'Her life signs are fine, Your Holiness. Her heart's a little excited, but well within the safe range.' If he felt a qualm about turning his erstwhile business partner into a laboratory rat he gave no indication of it.

Accosta told himself again that he should feel grateful for Soames's dedication to his cause. 'And the injection? Won't it interfere with her dreams?'

Without looking away from the screen Soames said, 'On the contrary, Your Holiness. Revelax is a neurological wonder drug that our own Virginia Knight recommended.'

Knight nodded: her pale face was drawn and perspiration beaded her high forehead. Her gaze fixed on Amber as she said, 'It'll help Dr Grant sleep and will also stimulate her brain to enter a natural state of REM quicker and for longer. It will help us harvest her dreams, increasing their frequency and longevity tenfold.'

'In essence,' added Soames, 'her episodes of dying will last longer and occur more often, so every time her Bose-Einstein condensate leaves her body during her dreams of dying we can monitor the passage of her soul. Using modified technology similar to that found in an optical computer, we should then be able to get a lock on the tracking frequency.'

At the foot of Amber's bed stood a bank of apparatus: an optical computer, several monitors and a black box the size of a large television with four vertical strips of lights laid out in columns. Each column contained four different-coloured lights flashing independently up and down it, and mirrored the smaller columns of light embedded in the top of the glass head-sphere. The lights on all four columns would align – forming four rows of colour – when they had established a trace.

Now that the moment of truth was drawing close Accosta felt drained. All the incandescent energy that had sustained him over the last few days had depleted what small reserves he had left. The rumour that he was dying, fuelled by his increasingly frail appearance and his recent absence from the Red Ark, had been fanned by the Vatican's press office. Without a successor, it was whispered, his Church would fold, leaving its members rudderless in a turbulent sea. Rome had indicated that it would forgive its fickle followers and welcome them back.

But the worst aspect of these rumours was that they were true. The prostate cancer diagnosed almost six years ago had spread to his bones and liver, and his lungs were riddled with metastases. The disease was reaching its final stages. With only a few months, if not weeks, of life remaining, he was a candidate for one of his own Church's hospices.

Amber Grant was his only salvation.

'She's entering the REM state again,' he heard Carvelli say. He sounded breathless.

Only Soames seemed calm, studying the monitors with an almost detached air. 'Excellent,' he said. 'That was the longest we've managed to hold on to the condensate as an integrated boson system.'

'Why is that excellent?' asked Accosta, looking at the randomly flashing columns of lights. 'You still didn't lock on to the soul frequency.'

'Not yet, Your Holiness, but by tracking these first episodes of Amber dying, these first excursions of her consciousness from her body, we've come closer than with all the previous real deaths combined.'

'So how many days before we get a result?' Accosta said.

Soames laughed, and the scar tissue around his mouth distorted. 'Days, Your Holiness? Not days, hours – if not minutes. With the drug, Amber is entering and leaving the dream state indefinitely. She'll simply die again and again until we zero in on the exact frequency – like tracing a telephone caller by making them keep phoning. In fact, she'll die so often she'll wish she was dead.' Soames laughed again. 'Don't worry, Your Holiness, locking on to the human soul is no longer an issue. What we've got to focus on now is communicating with it.'

Soames turned to Carvelli. 'Frank, help His Holiness make preparations for the final act. And we've got to start thinking about Miles Fleming.'

'He won't help us,' Knight said.

'He won't help *you*, Virginia, but he has no reason to distrust me,' Soames retorted. 'And I'm not going to ask Fleming to help us. I'm going to offer to help *him*.'

Just then there was a beep and the four columns of light stopped their random flashing, settling into four static rows of colour.

For the first time Soames lost his customary cool. 'Get the readings,' he shouted at his assistants in the laboratory. Then he turned to Accosta, with an excited grin of satisfaction. 'It's done.'

But Accosta was no longer looking at Soames or the lights. He was looking at Amber Grant, and wondering why she seemed to be smiling.

32

The Church of the Soul Truth Hospice, Marin County. The next day

The Sister's scarlet robes rustled as she checked the computer screen on the reception desk. She glanced up at the tall man, smiled and said, 'Mr Kent, I understand from your call that your father is ill and may need hospice accommodation.'

'That's correct. But I'd like to look around first.'

'Of course. I'll arrange for someone to give you a tour and get you an application pack, containing all the relevant information and forms you'll need to complete on your father's behalf. I'm sure you appreciate that accommodation here is limited, so we need to prioritize our care.'

'I understand. But you do have vacancies?'

The sister glanced at the computer screen and gave a serene smile. 'This is a hospice, Mr Kent. Vacancies always arise. It comes with the territory. If you don't mind waiting, I'll get your application pack and arrange for one of the sisters to show you around.'

'Thank you.'

'You're welcome.'

As soon as the sister turned and left the desk, the man reached over and rotated the computer screen towards him. It took only a moment to find the name and suite number. There was an asterisk by the name but he didn't have time to check what that signified. Instead he turned and walked to the waiting room. On the wall there was a photograph of Xavier Accosta, the Red Pope, and a picture of the Red Ark.

The man took a seat, and after a few moments another sister in scarlet introduced herself as Sister Angela and led him out of the waiting room on a tour of the hospice. The man listened attentively as she explained about the care and facilities available to the patients, but said little until they ascended the wide staircase to the second floor, where suite 21 was situated. Gillian Grant's private suite.

'May I use the restroom, please?' the man asked politely at the top of the stairs, and was relieved to be directed to the far end of the corridor.

'I'll wait here,' the sister said.

As he walked past the closed doors he paused when he reached suite 21. He checked that Sister Angela was out of sight and the corridor was deserted then moved closer to the door.

Hearing voices he stepped back as the door to suite 21 opened. A man and a woman in white overalls stepped into the corridor wheeling a sturdy white coffin bearing the Church of the Soul Truth motif. They stepped past him and carried on towards the far end of the corridor, leaving the door to suite 21 ajar. The man saw that the bed was stripped and the room empty.

He returned to Sister Angela. 'Thank you for your time. I think I've seen enough.'

Fleming strode out into the sunshine and went to his hire Taurus, got in, and drove back to the Golden Gate Bridge. He still wasn't sure exactly what he'd expected to achieve by coming here, but whatever it was he wasn't even close.

After his impulsive dash across the Atlantic to San Francisco he had driven to Amber's luxurious home in Pacific Heights, only to find it deserted. He had then called Father Peter Riga to check if he had had any news. He was unable to speak to him directly but received a cryptic message from the Jesuit's secretary: 'Father Peter Riga wants you to know he shares your concerns and has taken steps to assist you.'

'What steps? What are you talking about?'

But the secretary either couldn't or wouldn't clarify the message, leaving Fleming more confused than reassured. One of the remaining avenues of investigation was the hospice.

Since there was no longer any doubt that Virginia Knight was poisoning his reputation, he had resorted to the subterfuge of the lowliest tabloid reporter to reach Amber, but even concealing his identity in an attempt to contact her through her hospice-bound mother hadn't worked. Gillian Grant was dead.

Driving across the Golden Gate Bridge, he didn't

notice the brown sedan following two cars behind. His eyes were focused on downtown San Francisco and the Bay Bridge beyond. He was concentrating on his last chance of contacting Amber Grant.

33

Optrix Industries

The receptionist's practised smile was welcoming but her words were not. 'I'm afraid Dr Soames has just returned from Alaska and is seeing no one at the moment.'

As he glanced around Optrix's large marble lobby, and noticed the CCTV cameras and discreetly placed uniformed guards, Fleming kept his frustration in check. 'All I'm asking is that you tell him I'm here and that I need to speak to him about his partner, Dr Amber Grant. I'm her medical doctor and have some information of which she needs to be made aware.'

The petite blonde's smile didn't waver. 'I'm sorry, but if you haven't got an appointment I can't—'

'Won't you use your headset to contact his office? At least let his secretary know I'm here.' There was a whirring sound as one of the cameras focused on him, then one of the guards ambled over in his direction. He was holding a finger to his earpiece as if listening to instructions. He smiled at Fleming: a corporate smile identical to the receptionist's.

'Would you please come with me, sir?' he asked pleasantly. He was big, Fleming's height but heavier.

Instinctively Fleming moved his weight on to the balls of his feet. 'Look, I don't want any trouble, I just want to speak to Bradley Soames.'

'I understand, sir,' said the guard, cocking his head as he listened to something in his earpiece. He pointed to the bank of elevators, indicating the black tinted glass cabin on the end. 'Please take the executive elevator to the top floor. Turn right when you step out and Dr Soames's office is the first door on the left.'

Fleming couldn't conceal his surprise. He looked up at the camera then turned back to the receptionist, whose expression remained unchanged. He moved towards the elevator and heard her utter a breezy, 'Have a nice day, Dr Fleming,' as the doors closed behind him.

He pushed the top button. Seconds later the elevator stopped on the fortieth floor and he stepped out on to a plush carpet. The circular corridor was deserted and silent, the occupants of the top floor ensconced in their hermetically sealed offices. All the offices were on the outer side of the circle, facing out of the tower.

Except one.

On its light oak door were two words. No title, position or qualifications, just a name. Bradley Soames.

He opened the door and was confronted by a tall, smiling woman with big hair. She gestured to a door of tinted glass to the right of her desk. 'Dr

212

Fleming, Dr Soames is waiting for you. Please go through that door.'

'You beat me to it,' Soames said, as he rose from behind the curved desk in his windowless office. 'If you hadn't found me, I'd have found you. Can I call you Miles? Please call me Bradley.'

Trying to hide his surprise, Fleming took Soames's extended hand. The man's grip was weak and Fleming responded in kind – he had seen the scars and didn't want to hurt him. 'I was half expecting you to throw me out,' he said.

Soames laughed. 'Oh, I never throw anybody out.' He gestured casually behind him. 'They do.' In the subdued lighting at the far end of the circular office Fleming could make out two dark shapes lying on the floor. Between them was what looked like a large bone. Only now did he detect a damp, feral smell in the mildly medicated cool air. 'But don't worry about them. Like I said, I'm glad you came. Take a seat. Have a drink.'

Sitting on the office couch with a can of Coke, Fleming looked at his host, whose manner was disconcerting, and whose physical appearance was worse than it appeared in any photograph he had seen of him. His body was rake thin, and the exposed flesh had been ravaged by invasive surgery. The bright gold hair and pale blue eyes only exacerbated the strangeness of his scarred face. Even so, Fleming could sense a fierce intelligence in him.

'Unfortunate business about your brother,' Soames said suddenly. 'I'm real sorry about that. Virginia Knight always was a political coward.'

'How do you mean?'

'Let's face it, she's a great administrator and a great maintainer, I understand she was once an outstanding medical doctor too – but, unlike you and me, she's no pioneer. She's not a risk-taker. She's a politician, and you've fallen victim to her fear of anything reflecting negatively on her.' Soames reached under his desk and pulled out a copy of *The Times* from London. It was open on page four and an article was ringed in red: 'Leading Neurologist Suspended, Pending Investigation into Research Patient's Death'. Fleming's photograph featured below the headline. 'I take it you've heard of the VenTec Foundation?' Soames asked.

Everyone with even a vague interest in science had heard of VenTec. More myths than facts circulated about the highly secretive place, including one that the ground-breaking optical computers the Foundation had helped develop for the world were as nothing compared to a secret supercomputer of fabulous power Soames kept in his mountain retreat. Specializing in radical innovation at the cutting edge of computer technology, VenTec was famous as a seedbed for blue-sky technologies, which were then developed and commercialized in the mainstream laboratories of Optrix or other major client businesses. 'I've heard of it,' said Fleming, still unnerved by his casual reception. He had come here prepared to grill Soames about Amber Grant – but instead found himself on the back foot.

'I'll cut to the chase, Miles. As you know I'm an avid fan of your work on the NeuroTranslator. It's probably the best application of the Lucifer chip optical technology I've ever seen. That's why I convinced my partner, Amber Grant, to come to you for treatment. And that's why I earmarked a significant donation towards developing it. But since you're no longer at Barley Hall, I've withdrawn my offer. Much to Virginia Knight's annoyance, I gather.' Soames grinned. 'The point is, I'm hoping that Barley Hall's loss may be VenTec's gain. I want you to use the donation and the not inconsiderable facilities at VenTec to develop your NeuroTranslator.'

Fleming wondered what response to make. He was flattered that someone of Soames's brilliance thought highly of him after Knight's character assassination. Plus the facilities at VenTec were reputed to be second to none. It would be an ideal way to continue his research into the soul wavelength. Except, of course, for one key ingredient.

'It's an interesting thought, Bradley, and in my current predicament I would normally leap at it but—'

'But what?'

'I didn't come to you looking for a job. I came here to make contact with Amber Grant—'

'Why? She's no longer your responsibility.'

'It's more complicated than that.'

'How much more complicated?'

'I need to speak to her and I wondered if you'd tell me where she is. There's something she needs to know, something related to her headaches.'

'What?'

Fleming repeated the story to date. When he'd finished Soames gave a low whistle, stood up and

215

began to pace around his office. His protective hood was rolled back on his ultraviolet-proof sweater, accentuating the stoop of his thin shoulders. 'This is incredible. You've *got* to let me help you continue your research. If I've understood you correctly, you want to confirm that this wavelength is just a temporary aberration, the vapour trail of a dying mind before it disappears into oblivion. Because that means your brother can't be suffering and you were right not to fight to keep him alive. Is that broadly correct?'

Fleming was impressed with Soames's grasp of what he'd told him. 'Broadly.'

The other man's eyes sparkled with excitement. 'Fascinating. This wavelength has made you doubt what you've always believed in and now you want to explain it?'

'I suppose so, yes.' For a private man, Fleming found himself strangely willing to answer this stranger's searching questions about his deepest fears.

'But in purely scientific terms, by trying to prove that the soul wavelength *doesn't* confirm the existence of an afterlife, aren't you in danger of making a serious error?' Soames asked. 'Don't forget, it's virtually impossible to prove something *doesn't* exist. It's much easier to prove that something *does*.'

'What are you saying?' Fleming asked. 'That I'm going about this the wrong way?'

'Absolutely. You've got no choice, Miles, not if you want peace of mind. Instead of using the soul wavelength to disprove the existence of an afterlife, use it to look for proof that it *does* exist. And if you can't find it, then at least you'll be able to tell yourself it probably doesn't exist because you've looked real hard. That's what I'd do.' Soames paused. 'There's one risk with this strategy, though.'

'Yes, I know,' said Fleming, understanding now why his overheated mind had overlooked this approach. 'I might find what I fear.'

Soames smiled. 'But it's too massive to turn away from. Surely you've got no choice but to continue with your NeuroTranslator research – as a scientist but also as a brother.'

'Yes, but I need access to Amber Grant. And I think she needs to be told about this. At the moment, she has no idea. That's why I've been trying to contact her.'

'Yes, of course. But her mother's just passed on and Amber's gone off to have some time to herself. I don't know exactly where she is and, frankly, it ain't my business, especially as she arranged a month's leave to cover her treatment with you. However, she does call me from time to time.' Soames stopped prowling and stooped down to the wolves. Absentmindedly he spoke to them in an unintelligible guttural tongue, then picked a scab off one of the scars on his hand and fed it to the larger wolf before ruffling its fur.

Fleming grimaced. Although the wolves paid him no heed, he still found their presence unnerving.

'Tell you what,' said Soames. 'Take me up on my offer anyway. You can have whatever you want to build an improved version of the NeuroTranslator. Without wishing to sound arrogant, I've got the best computer people at VenTec. They could help you develop a significantly more sensitive and powerful NeuroTranslator than the one at Barley Hall.' He stood up. 'To come clean with you, Miles, a client of ours, KREE8 Industries, is particularly interested in your technology, especially the educational and entertainment applications of thought-controlled computer-generated images and prosthetics. They've already asked VenTec to build what we regard as an improved version of your NeuroTranslator prototype. But without your understanding of the neural wavelengths it could take us years to make it operational. With your co-operation it would take days. In return you could follow up your soul wavelength research with the full resources of VenTec at your disposal. Just think what you could achieve with some real computer power behind you.'

'I'd need access to my files at Barley Hall.'

Soames waved his right hand in the dismissive way of the truly rich and powerful. 'Virginia's easy. I understand how she works and what she wants. So long as she gets money and a share of the credit for whatever you come up with – but none of the blame if it all goes to shit – she doesn't give a damn what you do. Trust me on this, Miles. I can get whatever you need from Barley Hall.'

'And Amber?'

'Start work now, and the next time Amber contacts me I'll put you two together and you can speak with her. I see no reason why she shouldn't co-operate. She needs to resolve her headaches and her issues with Ariel. She may even find it therapeutic regarding her mother.' Soames was plainly excited. 'What do you say, Miles? This discovery of yours is incredible. You *must* take it forward and you *must* let me help you. This is exactly the kind of radical research that VenTec was founded to promote.' He reached for the phone on his desk. 'Laura, get the plane ready for Fairbanks with a connecting helicopter for the Foundation. Don't worry about notifying VenTec, I'll call ahead myself. I need certain things put in place. Yes, I'll ask him.' Soames looked up, his grin so boyish and his eyes so bright that in the half-light he looked almost handsome. 'Miles, how much time do you need to pack?'

Swept along by Soames's enthusiasm, Fleming didn't hesitate. This was more than he had dared to hope for. 'All my luggage is in the hire car parked in a lot across the street.'

Soames slapped him on the back. 'C'mon, then. What are we waiting for?'

34

Black sector secure accommodation.
VenTec

When Amber Grant first rose to consciousness she felt such peace that she was sure she must have died.

A hand was squeezing hers. And there was a presence beside her, familiar, calming. Even the terrifying memory of dying again and again didn't trouble her any more. Something had changed deep within her. Whatever her abductors had done to her had somehow unlocked a blockage in her psyche. As if by capturing her body they had freed her mind. She no longer felt alone. Her sister was with her, not trapped or struggling to make contact like before but there, choosing to stay with her. Even her concern for her mother seemed easier to bear, as if she was sharing it.

No longer drugged or shackled, Amber reached across herself to touch Ariel with her right hand but there was only crisp, smooth bed linen. Although she could feel Ariel's hand in hers, clasping it as tightly as she had when they were children, and she could sense her sister beside her, comforting her, giving her strength, she was alone in the bed.

She opened her eyes, and found herself alone in a plain suite devoid of decoration and windows. At the end of the bed was a living area with a couch, television, chair and desk. Beyond that was a door, through which she could see a bathroom. The Spartan surroundings, white walls and simple furnishings were oddly familiar.

She sat up and discovered she was dressed in a white bodysuit. She felt physically exhausted, as if convalescing from an illness, but she was relieved to find herself once more in charge of her body.

It was so strange. She should feel desperate, terrified and alone. But she didn't.

'Where are you?' a voice asked. A voice that was both part of her and apart from her.

'I don't know,' she heard herself reply.

She stood up and felt somehow that she should recognize her quarters. They reminded her of a place she had visited in the past. She went to the main door and tried to open it but it was locked.

Then she saw the white bathrobe hanging on the back of the bathroom door and saw the V logo on the breast pocket with the tag line beneath: *Past the Present to the Future*.

Suddenly her brain fired with connections. The familiar musk scent and voice she had recognized when paralysed: Felicia Bukowski, one of Bradley's pet scientists, whom Amber had met when visiting his Foundation in the past.

She was at VenTec. Which could only mean one thing.

Bradley Soames was involved.

Her own partner was behind this.

35

Alaska

Miles Fleming had never been this far north before. Three years ago he and Rob had gone to Alaska to climb Denali, the highest mountain in North America. Soames's jet had already flown over the Alaska range on its 2,500-mile flight from San Francisco to Fairbanks. From there they had taken the helicopter into the Arctic region towards the Brooks mountain range and the oil fields of Prudhoe Bay and Point McIntyre.

'You'll see the Foundation soon,' Soames said, beside him, pointing out of the tinted helicopter windows to the white-capped mountains piercing the clouds below. 'A few miles to the east lies the Arctic National Wildlife Refuge, but my grandfather bought most of the mountains you can see to your left. Aeons ago they were under the sea. Formed from marine rock, they contain huge deposits of petroleum. My grandfather created Alascon Oil but it was my father who built up the company after the big oil strikes in the sixties and seventies. He perfected the process of drilling through the mountain core. It made his fortune, which, of course, formed the basis of mine.

'When he died I sold Alascon to BP to fund Optrix but kept about a thousand acres. I like it here; the climate agrees with me. From November to early February the sun doesn't rise at all, which is ideal. And in the summer, well, I don't go out much and privacy is never a problem here.'

Fleming looked down at the sea of white-crested peaks and felt a flutter of excitement. He saw the mountains as a good omen, reinforcing his impulsive decision to accompany Soames. What better place to ensure that Rob's soul was safe than in his beloved mountains?

Through a patch in the clouds he saw an isolated collection of cabins studding one of the valleys. 'Is that it?' he asked.

Soames laughed so loudly that in the window's reflection Fleming saw the two wolves raise their heads. 'No,' Soames said eventually. 'That's the rangers' station for the wildlife refuge.' He indicated the wolves behind him. 'That's where I got them as abandoned cubs. My Foundation's just ahead.'

A particularly high peak appeared in front of them and the helicopter rose. As they neared it Fleming caught himself analysing its slopes for the best ascent, evaluating the angles and how best to tackle each section. It represented a decent challenge with a variety of inclines.

A voice broke into his thoughts. 'That's VenTec.' Soames pointed to a black dome supported on eight angled struts on top of the flat mountain peak. Large plates of tinted black glass covered the massive construction and as the helicopter rose above it Fleming saw a large neon H in a circle on a steel platform projecting from the northern side.

'It was originally an oil-rig, intended to link up with that refinery in the next mountain.' Fleming saw a huddle of incomplete buildings, abandoned processing plant and skeletal metal frames on the lower peak. 'The plan was to have a system of pipes running through the mountains, connecting the rig to the refinery and eventually via a main pipeline to the coast. I sold Alascon before the plan was completed and converted the rig into a blue-sky science institute. According to the geologists it's still sitting on barrels of oil but the black stuff is old news. Oil is a product of the past, a million years in the making. I prefer products of the future.'

Fleming's stomach lurched as the helicopter dropped towards the helipad.

As the wheels touched down, the rotors' down-wash churned up the snow on the steel deck. When Fleming stepped on to the landing pad, his body felt as if it was being filleted by a thousand cold knives: the icy wind didn't seem strong but it cut through him.

'Come inside. The wind chill's at least ten below out here,' Soames said, unleashing the wolves, who raced away to the snowy slopes, grateful to escape the confines of the helicopter.

Although he could no longer see them, Fleming could hear them howl. 'Where are they going?' he asked, as two orderlies took his and Soames's bags and ushered them into the main doors of the Foundation.

'Wherever wolves go to, I suppose. They come and go as they please. They're at home.'

Inside the main lobby Fleming noticed a fire-proof glass door to his right, which bore medical and clothing symbols. Inside he could see state-of-the-art Arctic coats, boots, climbing gear and lockers – the survival room, containing all the clothing, medical supplies and rations that would be needed in the event of evacuation. On the wall beside the door was a colour-coded plan of the VenTec Foundation, with its five distinct areas: a central red core with four sections radiating out.

'C'mon, Miles,' Soames said. 'I'll show you to your room, then give you the tour.'

36

VenTec. Forty minutes later

Fleming kept rubbing his ears, wondering if the hum was emanating from within the Foundation, or from his own weary brain after all the flying.

'Your room okay?' Soames asked, as he led Fleming through the white sector, following the chevrons pointing to the blue sector.

'Fine.' Fleming's suite in the white sector was functional rather than luxurious but it had all the necessities. 'I notice the phone won't give an outside line.'

'That's mainly security. We handle confidential research here and there's an understanding that outside contact's kept to a minimum. It also cuts down on distractions. You're not completely cut off, though. Each sector's got its own communication room with sat phone for emergencies. And, naturally, we've got full modem access for data downloads. You got a problem with that?'

'Not really, no.'

'Okay. This is the white sector and most of its facilities are self-evident. It's the communal area and, like all the white corridors, it's open to everyone in the Foundation. There are some laboratories here but all the truly confidential work is done in the coloured sectors, and each coloured area is kept discrete from the others. We've got Chinese walls in here and inter-sector security is taken seriously.'

They reached a smoked-glass security door leading to the blue sector, and Soames pointed to a small finger-pad next to the disk slot. 'Only I have access to all sectors. That pad's a DNA scanner, takes a micro-thin layer of skin and if it matches my DNA – and only my DNA – the lock opens.' He raised his hands and extended his fingers like a fan. 'My skeleton keys. Ownership has its privileges.'

He pointed beyond the glass door. 'In the blue sector we specialize mainly in VR work. Many of our clients come here to work with our scientists and our computers to see how they can take their business to the next level. You know all about KREE8?'

Fleming nodded. 'Sure.' KREE8 were famous for their hologram communication technology and creating the first virtual movie actors, including famous dead stars. Only last year a computer-generated Marilyn Monroe had played opposite George Clooney in what had become the biggest box-office draw of the decade.

'Well,' said Soames, 'I don't think I'm giving away too many trade secrets when I say KREE8 effectively use VenTec as their R and D department. I'd guess that eighty per cent of their new product programme has come from behind that glass door in the blue sector.'

Soames stopped and indicated a slight figure walking purposefully down the corridor towards them. Aside from a small red crucifix on his chest, the man with the perma-tan and jet-black ponytail was dressed in black: polo-neck, trousers and patent leather shoes. Fleming recognized him from pictures in the media.

'Ah, speak of the devil,' Soames said. 'Miles, I'd like you to meet Frank Carvelli, the head of KREE8.'

Carvelli smiled, but the smooth olive skin around his brown eyes barely creased. Fleming guessed he had undergone plastic surgery, although it was too subtle for him to be sure. 'Dr Fleming, I'm a great fan of your NeuroTranslator,' he said.

'Thanks.'

'Miles has agreed to help us out on some of the refinements of the KREE8 version,' Soames told him.

A glance passed between Carvelli and Soames, and Carvelli raised an eyebrow in what Fleming took to be impressed surprise. 'Really? That's excellent.' He checked his watch. 'Sorry, but I've gotta get to a meeting.'

'Don't worry, Frank. I'll brief Miles on everything.'

'Real glad you're helping us out. Look forward to talking soon,' Carvelli said pleasantly.

After he had disappeared into the blue sector, Soames turned to Fleming and gave him a lopsided smile. 'You're something of a coup for me. I told Frank we'd need your expertise, but he bet you'd never agree to help us out.'

'Will I work in the blue sector?'

'No, because there are other projects in there that Frank's paranoid about. More important, though, I want you to have your own space so you can work on your soul wavelength without interference. Come, I'll complete the tour then show you your work area.'

Soames doubled back, retracing his steps around the central section, leading Fleming through the white sector to the green. 'In there we do mainly government work,' he said. 'Not just for our government either.'

They went on around the perimeter of the central circle, Fleming following Soames to the top of the red sector and the bottom of the black sector. Twice they passed scientists in white bodysuits, which appeared to be the regulation uniform. Both smiled briefly and passed on without speaking. The atmosphere was of quiet industry and didn't encourage idle chatter. In spite of the high-tech setting, Fleming was reminded of his visit to the Jesuit headquarters in Rome with its similar hush of intense activity.

Soames stopped in a square hallway. To his left, black chevrons gave directions to the black sector. To his right a large red chevron pointed to the central elevator protected by a glass security door with *Authorized Personnel Only. Eye Shields Obligatory* etched into the glass. The dull hum Fleming had detected on first entering VenTec was louder here.

'The red sector,' said Soames. He reached into his jacket pocket and retrieved a transparent plastic envelope. It contained a silver disk with a red chevron in the centre. He handed it to Fleming. 'This is your smart disk. It gives access to all white areas including your residential suite and the red sector, where you will work. The disk is specific to you and will record everything you do here – every door you open, every meal you order, every piece of apparatus you use, every consumable you take from the supply inventory. Try not to lose it.' He stood back from the door and indicated that Fleming should insert his disk into the lock mechanism.

'What's in the black sector?' he asked casually, surprised that Soames, who had been so open about the rest of his kingdom, had failed to mention it.

A strange look crossed Soames's face, as though he had a secret he was dying to share but couldn't. 'Later, perhaps,' he said. 'Come. I'll show you where you're working. The red sector's dedicated to pure computer power and houses my pride and joy.'

Fleming glanced once more at the signs to the black sector but said nothing. He inserted his disk in the red sector door lock and when the elevator opened he stepped inside.

The floor was of heavily tinted glass, illuminated from below by a bright, almost blinding light. The hum was definitely louder now and seemed to be coming from the light. They began to descend.

Soames rolled down the sleeves of his sweater, and Fleming saw how the ends formed gloves, which Soames placed over his hands, checking that no skin was exposed. He covered his head and face, then put on a pair of tinted spectacles. 'I haven't yet found a way to neutralize the ultra-violet in there,' he said, reaching for a pair of mirrored eye-protectors on the rack beside the elevator doors and passing them to Fleming. 'The light won't harm your skin but you'd better put these on.'

The elevator doors slid open and Fleming squinted through the eye-protectors as a tidal wave of light met him. Blinking, he followed Soames out. At first, he couldn't see anything, so dazzled was he by the brilliance, and he was reminded of Amber Grant's description of dying, of becoming part of the light, merging with the photons that formed it. But soon his other senses came to the fore. The hum was no longer a background distraction but a definable noise, and he could smell heat and static in the heavy air, as if a thunderstorm was imminent.

His pupils, shrunk to pinpricks, began to adapt to the light overload and to take in his surroundings. As his brain interpreted what he was seeing he heard a loud gasp. He didn't register straight away that it had come from his own lips.

37

The red sector

Fleming found himself standing on a broad circular gantry that ran round the rim of a cylindrical chamber. The sheer scale was dazzling. But it was the sight below him that had made him gasp.

He walked tentatively to the gantry rail, leaned over and looked down into the centre of the cylindrical abyss. Suspended in space, some ten feet below, was an orb of light as bright as a small sun. At least twenty feet in diameter, it pulsed and hummed. The wall surrounding the orb was comprised of tinted-glass windows, behind which were laboratories and control rooms.

'What is this place?' Fleming asked.

'We are now inside the mountain, in what was the main bore-hole when my father originally drilled for oil here. Far below us, perhaps miles below us, there is an untapped supply of oil, which has been sealed up. I increased the diameter in this upper area to house the laboratories below us. For my purposes it's perfect: cool temperature, privacy and protection – I couldn't ask for more.' Leaning over the gantry, Soames pointed at the orb. 'This is my baby, the mother of all optical computers. This is the Last Computer – the ultimate. It can assimilate and process vast amounts of information in the blink of an eye. Scouring the world wide web for anything new, the computer stores it within its almost limit-less memory of light. If the world collapsed tomorrow, Miles, virtually everything it has ever known would be secure within its vast quantum system of photons encoded with data and in-formation. And this brain below us can access any and all of that information at the speed of light. This is Mother Lucifer, the true bearer of light – or should I say enlightenment?'

Fleming was silent, staring in awe at the brilliant, pulsing orb. Soames laughed self-consciously. 'Some of my colleagues tease me about my creation. They say it reminds them of the old story – you know the one, where a mad genius is driven to build a supercomputer powerful enough to know everything in the universe and answer the one question that obsesses him. Eventually, using all his ingenuity, money and time, the scientist completes his supercomputer and on the very first day of its creation he asks his question: "Is there a God?"'

Soames looked down at his fiery creation.

Unable to pull his eyes away from it, Fleming asked, 'What did the computer say?'

'Nothing at first, so the scientist repeats his question. "Is there a God?" he asks again. Finally the supercomputer replies: "There is now."'

Fleming smiled politely.

'Imagine harnessing this power to your new NeuroTranslator,' Soames whispered. 'Imagine being able to use it to discover something not only in this world but *beyond* it, to communicate with the minds of those who've gone before. Not just for a few fleeting minutes, like you did with your brother, but indefinitely and at will. You could ask any question of those who've died. You could ask what it's like beyond the veil of death. Whether there's a heaven or a hell. Whether your loved ones are free of suffering. Perhaps you could even know the mind of God.'

The back of Fleming's neck prickled. He had come here to explain away the soul wavelength, to rationalize it as nothing more than the last gasp of a dying brain and reinforce his conviction that there was no afterlife – without it Rob was beyond pain – but here it was hard to hold on to his certainties. The heady vision of limitless opportunity laid out before him was dizzying. At that moment he felt nothing was impossible, on this earth or beyond it.

Then Fleming became aware of two other people standing with Soames. One was a tall black man with thinning hair and steel-rimmed glasses behind his eye-protectors. His forehead was lined but the skin around his eyes was smooth, as if all his life he'd only frowned and never smiled. The other was a woman. The white bodysuit flattered her trim figure and her long blonde hair was tied back in a bun. She was beautiful, with high cheekbones and striking pale blue eyes. He found himself comparing her icy loveliness with the exotic warmth of Amber Grant.

'Meet your two assistants,' Soames said, and introduced them as Dr Walter Tripp and Dr Felicia Bukowski, specialists in hardware and software respectively. 'I assure you,' he went on, 'both these fine scientists eclipse most so-called experts in either field.'

As he shook their hands, Fleming noted that Bukowski's unblinking gaze never left his face.

Soames half smiled. 'As I mentioned before, we and our client KREE8 have been looking at improving your invention for some time. Our most up-to-date prototype has been moved from the blue sector to a laboratory below this gantry. Most of the hardware is complete. The analogue-digital converter should be superior to the one you're used to, as should the neural signal amplifier.'

'Absolutely,' confirmed Tripp. 'In essence we've tried to rebuild your NeuroTranslator with certain enhancements while avoiding patent infringements.'

'I'm flattered,' said Fleming.

'But, of course, we'll need your expertise and the files of human neural signals you've collected over the years,' Bukowski said quickly. Her voice was surprisingly smooth and soft. It reminded Fleming of the Boston accents he had heard during his Harvard years. 'Your input is vital to calibrate our device properly so that it correctly interprets each neural instruction, whether for individual brain waves, or for a combination of waves.'

'Well, if I can access all my Barley Hall files from

here, as Bradley says, that should be relatively straightforward.'

'Oh, all your files are accessible,' she said, and led them all into the elevator. She pressed a button and the cabin descended. 'You can check them whenever you want.' The doors opened and she took him into an impressive laboratory, the orb pulsing on his left behind the glass.

He recognized the two NeuroTranslators, although they looked different from his Barley Hall prototype. This design was more finessed, featuring a sphere in a translucent blue cube with rounded corners supporting an integrated plasma screen with touch controls. The device was at least 20 per cent larger than Fleming's prototype with in-built speakers. It was also significantly more powerful.

'Why two units?' asked Fleming.

'VenTec policy,' Soames said. 'We always develop prototypes in pairs – so we have a back-up.'

'It's beautiful,' Fleming said, looking over it. At the back were two wireless infrared connectors he had never seen before. The left bore the legend 'receive' and the right 'transmit'. 'I don't recognize these ports, though. A new type of communication sensor?'

Tripp gave a dismissive shrug. 'Sort of. We've only included them to ensure that the Neuro-Translator's compatible with our latest optical networking technology.'

'Look, Miles,' said Soames. 'We've even built our own body surrogate.'

Fleming turned and saw the life-size mannequin standing by the door. It was eerily similar to Brian. 'I'm impressed, Bradley, but also a little spooked. How long have you guys been copying my work?'

'About a year,' said Soames, without any hint of shame. 'If you recall, we did try to recruit you in the past, but when you wouldn't join us we had to develop our own thought-control system.' He smiled. 'And after all, your invention was based on the Lucifer, *our* invention. Just be glad we're this far along the development track. It'll make your research easier.'

The small voice of protectiveness rumbled at the back of Fleming's mind but he silenced it.

Soames looked at him. 'So?'

Fleming decided he might as well go forward as back. 'So, when can we start?'

'I thought we already had,' Soames said.

38

The blue sector.
One hour later

A few hundred yards away, Xavier Accosta stood in the virtual reality media suite of the blue sector wearing a skin-tight bodysuit studded with electrodes that accentuated and defined every contour and muscle group on his head and body. To his right, on a large screen, an animated figure comprised of dots reflecting each position of the electrodes mirrored his every move. The room contained matt black sound, audio and digital video-capture equipment as well as a bank of white optical computer consoles.

Carvelli sat before a computer terminal, dividing his attention between the large screen by the wall and his monitor. 'Could you walk on the treadmill, please, Your Holiness?'

'Is it necessary to exert him so much?' Virginia Knight demanded. She stood beside Monsignor Diageo checking the oxygen station she had prepared. 'His respiratory system is weak. He mustn't be pushed.'

Carvelli looked up and smiled apologetically. 'I understand, but I need to get all the movements into the computer if it's to be realistic.'

Accosta grimaced through the pain that, since his arrival in Alaska, had worsened. He reached for the oxygen mask and took a deep breath, sucking the sweet pure air into his diseased lungs. 'Relax, Virginia. Frank's only doing what's necessary.'

Knight sighed. 'Just take it easy. Please.'

'We've almost finished anyway,' Carvelli said, making some further adjustments using the spherical mouse beside him. 'We've captured all the facial expressions we need. Could you do the arm again one last time?'

Accosta did as he was told and went through the full range of movements, bending his elbows and stretching out his arms, exercising every single muscle, then working his fingers.

'Excellent, Your Holiness. Do you want to see how it'll look?'

Accosta was still unsure of how realistic the end result would appear, although he had heard of the wonders this technology had already performed in Hollywood. Carvelli had explained that three of last summer's biggest box-office hits had starred 'virtual actors' and the audiences hadn't been able to distinguish between them and the real ones. With the increasingly prohibitive fees paid to movie stars and the seamless digital effects made possible by optical computer technology, virtual actors were now a viable alternative.

Carvelli clicked three buttons on his monitor and, within seconds, the animated figure on the large screen filled in from the feet up to become a man wearing only a pair of boxer shorts. Accosta recognized the body as his own but it was only when he saw the head definition filling in that his eyes widened. The person on screen was him – as lifelike as if he were looking in a mirror.

'What you're seeing, Your Holiness, is a composite figure taken from your physical genetic profile, adjusted by age – the movement scans I've just completed, and all those digital photographs we took of you earlier. The digital photography is what allows us to get such an exact likeness. That face up there is a computer-generated amalgam of your genetic makeup and a high-resolution multi-billion pixel digital image of you. The movement exercises we've been conducting ensure that the image obeys all your facial muscles and moves naturally. Now watch.'

His eyes fixed on the screen, Accosta saw his screen persona being dressed. Socks appeared on his feet, then shoes, followed by each layer of clothing, culminating in his scarlet robes, skullcap and chains of office. Even the official rings appeared on his fingers.

'That's incredible,' he said.

Carvelli beamed. 'With all due respect, Your Holiness, I believe you'll find this far more impressive.' He flipped a switch, illuminating a small red diode on a horizontal, four-foot-diameter, black enamelled disk at the back of the room, which began to hum. 'It takes a little time to warm up,' he said.

Red changed to green.

Then a figure appeared on the pad, building

upwards in fully rendered laser stripes as if painted by an invisible hand. This time when it was complete and Accosta recognized it as himself it was fully attired in all his scarlet splendour, matching the image on the screen. But this was no two-dimensional screen image: this was a real person. It was as if Accosta had been frozen and placed on the black disk. He doubted whether even he would be able to tell the difference if he saw himself standing beside it, dressed in the same attire.

Then Carvelli touched the monitor beside him.

And Accosta watched his image come to life.

First he noticed the subtleties: the breathing, the chest subtly rising and falling, the lips parting slightly. Then the heavy-lidded eyes blinked and the mouth smiled.

To Accosta's astonishment he found himself mimicking his double, as if he were the mirror image. It was like looking at his reflection but having no control over its movements. When it stepped towards him Accosta moved back involuntarily.

'The image can't move beyond the boundaries of the holo-pad,' Carvelli reassured him. 'It will do whatever the computer operator tells it to but the hologram can only exist on the pad. What do you think, Your Holiness? You happy with your image? After all, eternity is a long time.'

Accosta stepped forward and reached out, almost touching the phantom, mesmerized by the likeness. It was – to all intents and purposes – him. But this embodiment, this vibrant rebirth of his own fading body, would never succumb to disease or death. 'Yes,' he said with a sigh, 'I'm happy with it.'

Suddenly the hologram moved and Accosta watched the image smile as it knelt before him.

'You want to give him your blessing, Your Holiness?' Carvelli said.

'Yes,' said Accosta blankly, extending his hand and resting it on his phantom head, shocked to find no substance there. 'But it has to be able to speak. What about its voice?'

'You mean *your* voice?' Knight said behind him.

Accosta nodded.

Carvelli pointed towards the bank of audio equipment and two microphones beyond the holopad. 'Well, that's what we plan to do next.'

39

The white sector canteen.
Three days later. 11.18 p.m.

'Thought I might find you here, Miles. Had much sleep over the last few days?'

Miles looked up from his Caesar salad and gave Soames a weary grin. 'No, not much. But after I've eaten this I'm going to collapse in my room for at least eight hours.' It was late in the evening: Tripp and Bukowski had retired hours ago. He was almost too tired to eat.

Soames sat down next to him. On his tray he had a bowl of fruit, a can of Coke and a bread roll. He appeared eager to discuss Fleming's progress. 'So, how's it going?'

'Good.'

'Walter and Felicia been attentive?'

'Sure.' At times Bukowski had been almost too attentive.

'Walter told me you've finished the mods.'

'I've set up a small demo for you and Frank tomorrow.'

Soames's eyes lit up. 'Great. Good work.'

Fleming allowed himself a smile. He was satisfied with the progress they'd made in just three days.

It had taken over sixty hours, stopping only to eat and grab a couple of hours' sleep, for Fleming to arrive at this point. As he had suspected, the hardware in the spotless white and chrome laboratory was excellent, and the NeuroTranslator was superior to the prototype he had developed at Barley Hall. True to his word, Soames had arranged for Fleming to download his files from the database at Barley Hall. He'd spent hours wearing the Thinking Cap in front of the body surrogate, calibrating the NeuroTranslator so that it would correctly decode the complex patterns of neural signals that instructed even the simplest tasks. It had taken six hours alone just to fine-tune the device's interpretation of eye movements.

Once these early adjustments had been achieved to his satisfaction, the other body movements followed more quickly as the device's neural net learnt for itself. And, with the relevant calibrations made, this NeuroTranslator was so fast that there was no lag between thought and action. Immediately he thought about raising an eyebrow, the body surrogate did the same. In the pure world of the abstract it was perfect.

Movement control, however, had been a relatively easy precursor to the more difficult task of interpreting thought speech. Again he had started at the beginning, going through the basic vocabulary, feeding back glitches to Tripp and Bukowski, who had diligently obeyed his every order. Gradually he had enriched the vocabulary until the computer's neural net had taken over.

Earlier that evening, after Tripp and Bukowski had

retired to their quarters, Fleming put on the Thinking Cap and powered up the NeuroTranslator for a final check. Scrolling up and down the screen he'd registered the standard brain waves spiking across the monitor: alpha waves, mu waves, theta and beta waves, as well as the others. Everything appeared to be in order. Every recorded wavelength was in evidence.

Except one.

Now that the new NeuroTranslator was up and running, he downloaded Amber Grant's neural scan with its unique wavelength from his Barley Hall files. By the time he'd done this and turned back to the NeuroTranslator a new line had appeared at the top of the screen, soaring above the highest megahertz band of the other wavelengths. And within a few hours of studying the soul wavelength he had reached an inescapable conclusion.

'How do you feel?' Soames asked.

'Dog tired.'

'I mean about the NeuroTranslator.'

'Pretty good. You'll see tomorrow.'

For a few minutes they sat in silence, Fleming eating his salad, Soames drinking his Coke and picking at his fruit.

'How about your soul wavelength?' Soames asked. 'I mentioned it to the others and they're fascinated. You had a chance to look into it yet?'

Fleming frowned. He had only talked about the soul wavelength with Soames, and was unsure how he felt about involving the others.

Soames read his expression. 'They want to help,

Miles. You're among friends here. Carvelli's a smart guy, and Walter and Felicia aren't stupid. Use all of us to bounce ideas off. That's what we're here for.'

Fleming felt a sense of release: it would be good to share his concerns and feed off their collective intellect and experience. 'Thanks.'

'So, you had a chance to look into it?'

'Briefly. It's early days, but I can already see two big issues I need to resolve.'

'Want to talk about them?'

Fleming was too tired. 'I'd welcome your opinion. I really would. But not now.' He rose from the table. 'I'm sorry but I'm dead on my feet. My brain's frazzled and I've got to crash. I'd love to discuss it tomorrow, though, after the demo.'

'Sure.' Soames stood up and rested a hand on Fleming's shoulder. 'Get some sleep, Miles. Tomorrow promises to be a big day.'

Later that night

Sleep came as soon as Fleming had stripped naked, climbed into bed and placed his head on the pillow.

Hours later, however, Amber Grant intruded on his dreams about Rob and Jake. She was whispering in his ear, her hand brushing his thigh, her touch so light and sensuous it brought goosebumps to his skin and made the hairs rise on his legs. Her cool fingers travelled up to his groin, gently massaging him until he became erect.

246

Night air cooled his skin as the covers were pulled back and someone slid in beside him. A soft form moulded itself to his, hot, sweet breath warmed his cheek, and the insistent fingers quickened their motion.

He moaned in his sleep as he felt hot breath move down his neck, to his chest and then his stomach. For a delicious moment a tongue licked his belly, while the fingers circling his straining erection slowed to a teasing feather-light caress. Surrendering to the sensation, he yearned for release and as the tongue moved lower he unconsciously clenched his buttocks, thrusting his pelvis upwards.

'Amber,' he groaned aloud, as the searing mouth enveloped him, waking him with a start. Then he realized instantly that it hadn't been a dream.

And that it wasn't Amber.

'What the hell?'

Felicia Bukowski's blonde hair looked luminous in the glow from the illuminated alarm clock as her head gently bobbed up and down on him. And when she looked up her pale irises shone in the light like metallic discs. Every physical instinct told him to let her continue. But something compelled him to reach down and push her away. 'No, no. Stop. I'm sorry, but this is wrong.'

He wasn't sure why he stopped her, except that he knew he had to. Perhaps it was because of what he had seen in her glinting eyes: the flash of naked triumph that made him fear that if he yielded to her he would somehow surrender far more than he realized.

He suspected, however, that his compulsion had more to do with betrayal. It was irrational, particularly for a man who had hitherto placed so little value on commitment, but Fleming suddenly knew that he felt a strange allegiance to Amber Grant. So strong that, until he reached some kind of resolution with her, any other intimate relationship would be tantamount to treachery.

Felicia's eyes hardened but he saw no hurt in them. Only disappointment and anger. Saying nothing, she held him for a moment longer, squeezing him tight as if testing his resolve, and then she rose, put on her robe and left.

After she had gone, Fleming lay in the dark, listening to his pounding heart, knowing that, despite his exhaustion, sleep would elude him.

Unknown to Fleming, a few hundred yards away in the black sector, Amber Grant was also unable to sleep.

Over the last few days she had been recovering her strength and observing the guards, registering the time when they checked on her, the time when they brought her food and the time when they collected the meal trays. Looking for patterns in their behaviour, she watched and waited.

Plotting her escape.

40

The red sector.
The next day

Both Walter Tripp and Felicia Bukowski were at the demonstration in the red sector laboratory the next afternoon. Fleming had considered mentioning Bukowski's intrusion to Soames – how had she been able to gain access to his room? – but since it would serve no purpose he had said nothing. And now, in the light of day, he could almost convince himself that it had never happened. If he didn't mention it again he was sure she wouldn't. He hoped it wouldn't sour their working relationship. So far, aside from a discernible coolness, he was relieved to see that she was acting as if nothing had happened.

'That's fantastic,' Soames said, as the mannequin extended its right arm.

Making a point of staying still and silent, Fleming worked his way mentally down the body surrogate, starting at the mannequin's eyes and travelling down its body, flexing the shoulders, extending the arms, bending the torso and knees and finally wiggling its toes.

Frank Carvelli grinned from his seat beside

Soames. 'You can do all that through thought?'

'Thanks to some help,' Fleming said, indicating Tripp and Bukowski standing by the Neuro-Translator. Tripp smiled. Bukowski lowered her eyes.

'Can it control on-screen images as well as the mannequin?' Carvelli asked.

'Absolutely. It can control whatever medium you like. The body surrogate is the hardest. On-screen or computer-generated images are much easier.'

'How about making it talk?' Soames asked.

'I'll show you.' To impress someone like Soames, who was as enthusiastic as he was brilliant, was a challenge. 'Making it talk isn't very convincing because its lip movements are so crude, but I can put words into its mouth. It won't look great but you'll hear the words clearly from the speaker in its head. What do you want it to say?'

Soames handed Fleming a sheet of typed paper he must have prepared for such an eventuality, a text from the Bible. 'Seemed appropriate,' Soames said. 'Creation. That kinda thing.'

Fleming tapped the screen above the NeuroTranslator, ensuring that communication mode was activated. Then he picked up Soames's text and read the first line in his head. Immediately he saw the words appear on the screen as the computer translated his thoughts into on-screen text. Then the body surrogate seemed to speak. Or, rather, words issued from the speaker embedded inside its smooth latex head.

'And God said, Let there be light: and there was

250

light. And God saw the light, that it was good; and God divided the light from the darkness. God called the light Day, and the darkness he called Night. And the evening and the morning were the first day.'

'Amazing,' said Carvelli. He sounded genuinely impressed.

After two more equally successful exercises, Soames nodded in satisfaction. 'What about your soul wavelength?' he asked. 'Want to talk about it now?'

Fleming looked at their expectant faces. 'Sure. I need to study it some more but looking at the data from my brother's death and from Amber Grant's stay at Barley Hall there are a few obvious issues.'

'Such as?' asked Carvelli.

'Well, as we discussed when Bradley and I first met in San Francisco, in order to show that the soul wavelength *doesn't* represent evidence of an afterlife or a link to the other side, I'm trying to prove the opposite. And to prove that the soul wavelength isn't just a dying signal picked up momentarily by the NeuroTranslator at the point of death I need to *maintain* contact with the soul after death by finding a way to lock on to it, and so keep the soul wavelength open indefinitely. That's the first problem – proving the existence of the soul by tracing it after death. Incidentally, trying to find this locking frequency without Amber would require experimenting on countless people at the exact point of death until a lock-on was found, which, of course, would be ludicrous and unethical.'

'And the second issue?' said Soames, without a pause.

'Assuming I could lock on to the soul of a *dying* person and prove the existence of an afterlife I still wouldn't be able to contact the soul of a person who has *already* died – such as my brother. To do that I'd need some kind of identifier – a unique address – that would allow me to page a particular soul, for want of a better way of putting it.'

'Okay,' said Soames, stroking his chin. 'So you figure that if you could lock on and page individual souls, and use your NeuroTranslator and the soul wavelength to communicate with them, you'd prove their existence?'

Fleming was impressed with how quickly Soames grasped concepts that he was only just getting his head round. 'Or not, depending on what I discover. And that's why I need Amber. By studying her freak dreams of dying – when, in neurological terms, she does actually die – I might be able either to find a locking-on frequency to contact the other side or, as I hope, a more rational explanation . . .'

Carvelli frowned. 'How about your problem of identifying and paging souls who are already dead?'

Fleming smiled. 'I'll cross that bridge when I come to it. Since, ultimately, I'm hoping I'll find no evidence of a genuine afterlife, the problem of paging souls should be of purely academic interest.'

'And you're saying that you can't go any further without Amber?' said Soames.

'Yep,' Fleming said. 'I can tinker around the edges but without Amber I can't prove anything, one way or another.'

'Okay,' said Soames, with a thoughtful frown. 'That makes sense. In which case I suggest you get some rest while I see about contacting Amber.'

41

The black sector conference room.
One hour later

'The test will happen tonight,' Soames said with a triumphant smile.

Knight turned towards him from her seat at the conference table. 'Fleming's delivered?' she asked. 'Already?'

'I saw it,' confirmed Carvelli beside her.

Soames nodded. 'The NeuroTranslator is there, fully calibrated, complete with all the communication modifications necessary to link up with the soul-capture hardware. We're ready to go.'

'Tonight?' Accosta said, still not believing it. Progress on the project seemed to be accelerating as the end of his life drew nearer – as if God was speeding him on. From his seat beside Monsignor Diageo he looked through the two-way mirror into the laboratory. Two orderlies were preparing the bed and the glass head-sphere.

'Tonight,' Soames confirmed. He turned to Knight. 'We have a test candidate from the hospices?'

Knight hesitated. 'Since Amber we've cut back on collecting terminal subjects,' she said. 'As you know, one terminal patient is stored in a life-support casket in the green sector, but she was brought here for a different reason.'

'There's no real reason why she can't be a candidate, though, is there?' demanded Soames. 'I mean, she fits most, if not all, of the usual criteria, doesn't she?'

Knight nodded reluctantly. 'Yes, I suppose so, but are—'

'There's no time for buts, Virginia. We'll use her.'

'How soon can we do this, then?' Accosta asked.

Soames checked his watch. 'Tripp and Bukowski should be ready in six hours.'

Six hours. Reaching for the mobile oxygen station Accosta felt a rush of anxiety. His destiny rested on this experiment. If it was a success, the future was virtually assured. Everything he had been working towards, every sacrifice and every ruthless decision he had made would be vindicated. He was so close to the culmination of all his dreams that it was almost unbearable. All the disappointments of the past were as nothing compared to his anxiety now. Despair required little more than stoic acceptance. Hope, with all its tantalizing promise, was far crueller.

He calmed himself and turned to Soames. Once again, the scientist had been true to his word, recruiting Fleming to the cause without the Englishman even being aware of it. For all his reservations he had to admit that Soames had delivered everything he had promised. 'You have done well, Bradley. Thank you.'

'Don't thank me yet, Your Holiness. Not till after the experiment. But I'm confident.'

Accosta turned to Carvelli. 'And if it works?'

Pulling up his sleeves, Carvelli leant forward on the table. 'Well, Your Holiness, all the multimedia equipment has been set up on the Red Ark. You've seen the plans and the layout for the cathedral, which should give maximum impact on camera. The seating also allows those physically attending the event to be close enough to verify the authenticity of what they witness.'

'What about the other equipment?' Accosta asked, retrieving a white handkerchief from his pocket.

'That's not a problem. We've already delivered duplicates of most of the soul-capture hardware to the Red Ark. Assuming that this experiment is a success, when it's over specially commissioned freight aircraft will transport the additional apparatus.'

Accosta wheezed and coughed into his handkerchief, then folded it into his hand without looking at the bloody contents. Wordlessly Monsignor Diageo leant across, took it from him and handed him a fresh one. Accosta smiled his thanks and turned back to Carvelli. 'Assuming this experiment is a success, how long before we can hold the event?'

'Thirty-six hours.'

'Is that all? What about publicity? It's vital that the Day of the Soul Truth is seen by as many people as possible.'

Carvelli smiled and ran a manicured hand over his unnaturally black hair. 'Trust me, Your

Holiness, publicity isn't a problem. With all the uncertainty about your health there's already huge interest in you – and not just from your followers. Even as we speak my contacts in the media are waiting for a press release. As soon as we know this experiment has been a success I'll announce the event.'

He paused. 'Rest assured, Your Holiness, this is going to be everything you need it to be. Bigger than any media event in history. When people learn what the Day of the Soul Truth is, I doubt that anyone – whoever they are or whatever they believe – will choose to miss it.'

42

The white sector

Sleep wouldn't come. Lying on his bed, Fleming's eyes stung with fatigue and his head ached, but he couldn't calm his thoughts. After a bath and an early supper he had dozed, only to wake even more restless. It was now ten o'clock in the evening and he couldn't sleep, even though he hadn't enjoyed a proper night's rest since he left San Francisco.

Without Amber he couldn't go further, but his mind continued to mull over the data he had seen in the NeuroTranslator files. Perhaps he'd missed something. Overlooked some small aspect of the soul wavelength that would help explain it as nothing more than the temporary anomaly he believed, and wanted, it to be.

The more he thought about it, the more he knew the truth of what he intended to prove. The dying of the mind was a fleeting moment of nature – dewdrops in the morning sunlight evaporating into a steamy mist before finally disappearing into the warm air. Rob's frightened words after death were little more than that same mist, signifying nothing but the stressful transition from life to oblivion. If only he could be sure of this, though, he could put his fear for Rob out of his mind and return home to Jake with a clear conscience.

Again, he told himself to relax. He could do no more until Soames contacted Amber. But however many times he rolled over in bed and told himself to go to sleep, he couldn't. His mind nagged at him. And not just about Rob.

He thought about Bukowski, listened for noises outside his door, then returned to Amber – as a patient who needed to be cured, as the key to laying Rob to rest, and as an attractive woman – and Rob, the NeuroTranslator and the soul wavelength.

Taking deep breaths he tried to clear his mind of everything: after a good night's sleep everything would fall into place.

'Goddamnit.' He sat up. There was no point in lying there, tossing and turning. He had learnt from bitter experience that the only cure for insomnia was to work, until he either solved his problem or convinced himself that he couldn't.

He threw on a pair of jeans and a VenTec T-shirt, slipped into his shoes and left the room. The corridors were deserted and the lights were even lower than usual. Careful to tread quietly, he left the residential quarters, passed the restaurant and cinema, turned left towards the green sector, and reached the square hall outside the red sector elevator. He had no idea what he expected to find by re-analysing the NeuroTranslator data but it had to be better than doing nothing. As he put his hand into his pocket for the access disk he heard a noise and voices. Then the door to the elevator slid open. Instinctively he stepped back against the wall.

'Careful,' he heard Tripp hiss at two orderlies. Fleming recognized the apparatus on the trolley they were pushing. Why was the NeuroTranslator being moved at this time of night?

He almost stepped out to challenge Tripp, but stopped himself when he saw the party turn down the curving corridor that led towards the black sector. Despite his natural curiosity he had been so consumed with getting the new NeuroTranslator operational that he hadn't given any more thought to the mysterious black sector. But now, hungry for answers, he was intrigued.

He waited for them to disappear round the corner, then stepped out of the shadows and followed.

As he stole down the dimly lit corridor Fleming was acutely aware that not only was he alone in this isolated mountain complex but no one even knew he was there. Not his family, not Barley Hall, no one. His heart beat faster in his chest.

'Come on,' Tripp muttered, ahead of him. 'Dr Soames is waiting.'

Keeping close to the wall, Fleming peered round the curving walls and saw Tripp insert a disk into the access slot of the black sector door. It hissed open and all three men passed through it with the trolley. When they had disappeared, the door stayed open and Fleming ran towards it. As he got there it hissed shut. In desperation he inserted his own disk in the slot but the light by the handle remained red.

'Shit,' he said and retreated back into the shadows, wondering what to do next.

Moments earlier, in her secure suite in the black sector, Amber had also been restless. The male guard assigned to her appeared to have a set pattern. Each evening at six he delivered her supper. Then, at some time before eleven, he would knock softly on the door. If Amber responded he would enter and take away the meal tray, but if she remained silent he would wait until morning.

She had spent the whole day trying to find a weapon but everything in the featureless room was screwed down or harmless. Eventually she had gone to the towel rail in the bathroom and gradually prised apart the fittings, releasing the hollow chrome bar.

After her meal had arrived she had quelled her nervousness, eaten what she could and placed the tray by the bed, which she made up to look as though she was lying in it.Then she retreated to the bathroom, holding the chrome bar like a base-ball bat.

She waited in the gloom, her shaven reflection staring out at her from the mirror. Every time she checked her watch, only a few minutes had passed. Then, just when she'd thought he wasn't going to come, she heard the knock on the door.

'I've done here,' she said.

She heard the lock click and the door opened.

First the subdued light from the corridor leaked into the room, then the guard followed. For a moment she lost her nerve, convinced she couldn't hit him in cold blood. Then she thought of her abduction, everything she had undergone subsequently, and gripped the bar tighter.

'You enjoy the fish?' the man said, walking towards the bed, his back to the bathroom. Amber stepped behind him and, with all her strength, brought the bar down on his head. It buckled with the first blow so she hit him again.

'Not much,' she said, as she watched him grunt and fall to the floor.

Within two minutes she had him on the bed, gagged with one of the pillowcases, his hands tied behind his back with the other. Then she pulled the covers over him, checked that she had his black access disk and left the room, hoping she had a few hours before he was discovered.

She had no real plan for getting out of the Foundation. Short of commandeering a helicopter there was no way off the mountain – she was all too aware of its isolation. Her appearance was so altered by her shaven head that she doubted anyone would recognize her, but even if she managed to alert people in the white sector about her abduction she wasn't sure that they would help her escape. This was Soames's kingdom. People here depended on him for everything. Her only hope was to reach a satellite phone in one of the communication rooms and call someone on the outside. Someone she trusted, like Papa Pete Riga.

In the corridor she followed the signs for the

black sector exit until she heard voices. She waited, and watched three men approach with a piece of apparatus on a trolley. To her relief they turned right in the direction of the main laboratory. Hugging the walls and staying alert for any other noise she eventually reached the exit door. She inserted the guard's disk, and it slid open. She stepped out into the corridor and tried to decide whether to follow the white chevrons to the left or the right.

Then a man moved out of the shadows and whispered her name.

Fleming didn't recognize the shaven-haired figure at first. Not until he saw the eyes. He'd have known those eyes anywhere. She looked as startled as he felt. They stared at each other, not sure what to do.

'What the fuck are you doing here?' she hissed.

'Trying to get in there so I can find out what Bradley Soames is up to with my NeuroTranslator. What are you doing here?'

'Trying to get out.'

Before he could ask her why, he heard footsteps to his left. He reached for her, pulled her towards him and backed into a dark recess. He could hear her breathing, feel her heart beating. He watched three figures approach from the direction of the green sector. This time he recognized Bukowski, and he could tell from the way Amber tensed beside him that she recognized her too. Bukowski was escorting two men pushing a gurney. On it was a white coffin.

One of the men slipped and banged the coffin against the far wall.

'Whoa,' whispered Bukowski, almost laughing, 'the old bird's not dead yet. Can't have her croaking before we're ready.'

Bukowski opened the door to the black sector and Fleming's mouth dried.

He recognized the motif stamped on the coffin, the stylized red ark with the cruciform mast. Even in the dim light he could just make out the wording beneath it: *Church of Soul Truth Hospice*.

In that instant, as she watched the coffin, with its distinctive logo, being wheeled into the black sector, all thoughts of escape left Amber. All she cared about was stifling the hideous fear uncoiling in her belly.

It couldn't be. It simply couldn't.

Clutching the smart disk she stepped out into the corridor and headed back to the black sector. Silently, Miles Fleming followed her.

43

The black sector conference room

The wolves behaved as though they were invisibly attached to Bradley Soames. Flanking his chair at the head of the conference table, tongues lolling from slack jaws, they stared down the table, unnerving, unfathomable, untouchable. Occasionally Soames would dangle his hand beneath the table and one of the wolves would take something from it.

The others in the room, including Accosta, sat further down the table. Most feared the wolves, but Accosta hated them. There was something pagan about them – ungodly almost. He rose from his chair and walked to the two-way mirror, supporting himself on Diageo's strong arm. The white coffin was laid out on the gurney beside the laboratory couch. Watching the lid being removed to reveal the body, with its saline drip, oxygen mask and other life-support systems, saddened him. But this would be the last necessary killing. The last sacrifice – before he sacrificed himself.

'You see the NeuroTranslator, Your Holiness?' Soames asked, pointing at the translucent blue cube containing a pulsing sphere of light and topped with a computer monitor. 'With its modified infrared communication ports it can connect with the head-sphere's photon-detector screen, which records the subject's unique soul barcode.' He pointed to the foot of the laboratory bed, at the black box displaying four columns of flashing lights. 'And by setting the locking signal we gained from Amber we should be able to keep the communication line open indefinitely. With this experiment we intend to let the soul escape. Then, seconds later, using both the subject's unique soul barcode and the locking signal, we'll page it, as it were. Immediately we've done that, we'll communicate with it through the soul wavelength and the NeuroTranslator.'

Accosta watched as the frail patient was laid on the bed and her eyes were pegged open. He envied her imminent release, half wishing he could take her place. But his time would come. 'After tonight we can put an end to all this suffering,' he said, as the glass sphere was placed over the subject's head. 'And after the Day of the Soul Truth there will be no need to do anything like this ever again, because when the truth is revealed for all to see, evil will have no more place in this world.'

'Yes, Your Holiness,' agreed Soames. 'Yes, indeed.'

'Look,' Amber hissed at Fleming.

Crouching in the corridor, he peered through the circular windows of the main black sector laboratory. Through the heavily tinted glass he could see the white coffin being opened and a body lifted out. Bukowski and Tripp obscured his view but he could tell that it was wearing an oxygen mask and had an intravenous drip in its left arm.

'Whoever was in that coffin isn't dead,' Amber whispered

'I can see that,' he replied. He was about to say something else to her, when the translucent cube resting on the table beside the laboratory couch caught his eye. 'That's the improved Neuro-Translator I helped Bradley's people build.'

Amber frowned. 'Why build one for Bradley?'

'I'm beginning to ask myself the same question.'

He looked around the laboratory. A bank of apparatus stood at the foot of the bed, and he could hear a hum. There was a blank monitor on one of the units and four columns of randomly flashing lights on another. One of the scientists moved. Through the dark glass Fleming could just make out that the person on the couch was a woman and that her head was being shaved. Then something was put into her eyes.

'That's what they did to me,' Amber said, as they placed a glass sphere over the woman's head.

'How do you mean?'

'When they experimented on me.'

'What?' He turned to her in disbelief. 'Who experimented on you? Soames?'

'Who else?' she said. 'It seems he's been using you *and* me. But I don't know why. All I do know is that it's got something to do with Ariel and my dreams.'

He didn't understand, and continued to stare through the tinted window. Above the bed two large screens showed close-ups of the subject's face but because of the reflections in the glass Fleming couldn't see it clearly. One of the scientists, Tripp, turned towards the mirror that lined the left-hand wall and raised a thumb as if giving a signal to himself – or to someone beyond the mirror.

Still unable to explain what he was witnessing, Fleming turned back to Amber. She was staring intently at the scene unfolding before them, trembling with barely controlled rage. 'How could he do this? How *could* he?' she whispered.

The humming grew louder and the scientists stood back from the laboratory bed and put on eye-protectors. Then, through the tinted glass, Fleming saw a dazzling spark of light illuminate the sphere around the woman's head. It seemed to come from her eyes before pulsing around the outer layer of the sphere like a halo.

In that instant there was a high-pitched beep and the four columns of lights, which had been flashing randomly, were suddenly in perfect alignment. On the previously blank monitor beside the lights he now saw a zebra-striped pattern of white photon dots, which he recognized as the classic wave interference pattern from a double-slit experiment.

Then the light faded from the head-sphere.

Seconds later, before he could process what he had seen, the halo returned, as if summoned back. For one chilling moment the light was such that the reflections shifted on the monitors suspended above the bed and the close-up images of the subject's face were clearly visible.

Amber jumped as if she had been scalded, tore herself out of Fleming's grip, burst through the doors and ran screaming into the laboratory.

Fleming had no choice but to follow her.

Bukowski turned first and tried to block her, but such was Amber's momentum that she was pushed aside as though she was made of paper. Amber let out a desperate cry. 'Bastards,' she shouted. 'You fucking bastards!'

Above him Fleming could see the close-up monitors, and the frail face staring out from the screen. The pegged-open eyes staring out through bizarre contact lenses were lifeless now.

'Mom,' Amber yelled, reaching for the couch. A male scientist lunged at her but Fleming pushed him away before hitting him hard on the chin with the heel of his hand. Tears streaming down her face, Amber pulled the glass sphere off her mother's head and plucked the lenses from her eyes, but she was dead.

'Bastards!' Amber cried again, gently laying her mother's head on the bed. Lifting the glass sphere, she turned to face the mirrored wall.

The hair rose on the back of Fleming's neck when he saw the soul wavelength on the NeuroTranslator monitor pulse into life and heard a cry as strident as Amber's issue from its speakers: '*Amber.*'

In that instant Fleming understood how Soames

had used him, and he knew with a certainty that went beyond scientific proof that the mind could exist beyond death. All his scientific reasoning and scepticism withered under the onslaught of pent-up rage voiced by the wronged soul whose body lay dead on the couch.

'*Murderers!*' screamed the NeuroTranslator speakers, and Amber flung the head-sphere at the wall mirror. For a moment it remained intact, then cracks darted across its surface, reaching every edge and corner.

Then, with a resounding crash, it collapsed in a symphony of shattered glass.

And there stood Xavier Accosta, Bradley Soames and Virginia Knight.

The ensuing silence transcended the noise of the shards ricocheting off the floor.

44

After two armed VenTec security guards escorted Fleming and Amber through the broken glass and into the conference room, it was Accosta who attempted to restore some dignity to the situation. 'Please sit down,' he said courteously. 'You deserve an explanation.'

It was only now that Amber saw the wolves, standing behind their master, hackles raised.

'Yes,' Soames nodded, 'I'm sorry we weren't able to reveal more to you sooner.' He proceeded to introduce Monsignor Diageo and Frank Carvelli, as if they were all at a cocktail party.

'What the hell's going on?' Fleming demanded.

Amber lunged for Soames but was forced into a chair. 'What have you done, Bradley? What the *fuck* have you done?' she screamed at him. 'How could you? We were partners, for Christ's sake.'

Soames looked genuinely shocked. He seemed not to understand her outrage. 'We only had her here because of you, Amber, and she was dying. Because of her death no one need be harmed any more. Not you, Miles or anyone.'

Amber stared blankly at him, her rage so intense it choked her. It was as if her earlier shock at seeing her mother's death and her subsequent outburst had leached all the energy from her. Fleming laid a hand on her shoulder.

The need to comfort Amber was strong but it was beyond Fleming. He couldn't even reassure himself.

Seeing Virginia Knight with Soames and Accosta, wearing the red cruciform brooch of the Church of the Soul Truth on her chest, helped him snap out of his shock. And the sight of Accosta's haggard face, suffused with its smile of triumph, brought back Father Peter Riga's words of warning.

He and Amber had been set up. He had been so driven to seek out the truth about his brother that he had been blind to Soames's lies. At least Amber had been used against her will, but he had *helped* the bastards. Fleming was filled with such a profound sense of humiliation that he wanted to lash out. But he wouldn't yield to emotion. Not yet.

Soames looked at him. 'You remember our first meeting? You wanted to explain away the soul wavelength as proof of an afterlife and I told you that you should try to prove it instead. Remember? Well, how does it feel to know that such things are possible?'

Fleming kept his face impassive. 'How do I know they are?'

'You heard Gillian Grant's soul.'

'I heard her call you murderers. A delayed reaction of some kind.'

272

Soames shook his head impatiently. 'No, you heard her soul. Not at the point of death like you heard your brother's but after we had paged it. We let her go and then we called her back. You see, you were right when you said that to prove the real existence of an afterlife you'd need to find a way to lock on to the soul and contact it after it had gone. That way you could establish that contact wasn't just some last gasp, as you called it. Well, we've done that. We used Amber to gain our lock-on – like you wanted to. She just gave us the co-ordinates first. Incidentally, we tried with a number of terminal patients too – as you mentioned so disapprovingly.' Soames seemed pleased to impart his knowledge. 'You want to know how we page the soul, how we identify the individual consciousness?'

'I suspect you're going to tell me, whatever I say.'

'You aware of the double-slit experiment, Miles?'

Fleming nodded.

'Well, I modified it from detecting photons of standard light energy moving through a double slit to detecting *life energy* photons leaving a dying human body. We've done it over a hundred times and each individual soul leaves a different striped wave interference pattern, not unlike a barcode. It seems that each of us not only has our own unique genetic blueprint for our physical body but also a photon blueprint for our metaphysical soul.' Soames smiled. 'Quantum duality is everywhere.'

Fleming and Amber both stared at Soames in disbelief. 'A hundred?' they said in unison.

'You've killed a hundred people for this?' Fleming gasped. He turned to Virginia. 'And you helped him. Christ, you set us both up. You needed the lock-on from Amber and the NeuroTranslator soul wavelength from me.'

Knight had the grace to look uncomfortable. 'It's for the best, Miles,' she said. 'You'll see. Believe me.'

'*Believe you?* How the hell can I believe a word you tell me? You were my boss, for Christ's sake, I was supposed to be able to trust you, and all the time you've been involved in this crock of evil shit.'

'This is not evil, Dr Fleming,' Accosta interjected calmly. 'On the contrary. Dr Grant should be proof of that. When we most needed help she was delivered to us. Amber is unique, a gift from God. You don't believe me now, but in time you'll see that I'm right.'

'But you didn't just abuse Amber, you killed her mother. And what about the other poor bastards you murdered? How the hell can you justify that?'

'They were dying, as I am. We merely eased their passing. And this final experiment was a success. Amber's mother served her purpose, as we all serve our purpose in the eyes of God.'

Fleming knew it was impossible to continue the argument. He had once heard it said that faith was something people died for, whereas dogma was something people killed for. Riga had been right: Accosta was as arrogant and dogmatic as the fools in the Vatican – and even more dangerous. 'But what can you possibly hope to achieve by meddling with souls?' he asked.

'Salvation,' Accosta said simply. 'The salvation of billions of souls. And you ought to be proud of what you've done to help the cause. You've both performed a great service to humankind. We live in a technological age inundated by choice. People need direction today more than they've ever needed it. No longer are they prepared to trust in blind faith or useless reams of information. They want – they *demand* – the truth.

'With this technology I'll remove all doubt about the greatest question still troubling mankind. What happens to us after we die? And unlike other religious leaders I won't demand faith, I will *show* them the truth about the human soul. I will *embody* the truth so that no one – atheist, Jew, Roman Catholic, Moslem, Buddhist or humanist – will have any cause to doubt my vision. All will join the Church of the Soul Truth because they'll have no *rational* reason not to.'

'Assuming, of course, your vision is correct,' Fleming said.

Accosta gave him a pitying smile. The smile of someone who is so certain of a belief that the more you argue rationally and coherently against it, the more they become convinced of your blindness and their insight into the truth. 'I understand from Dr Soames that you're concerned about your brother, that he has a soul and he might still be suffering. I believe it's a valid concern, Dr Fleming. But whatever I tell you about his fate, or the fate that awaits you, is irrelevant because I belong to a Church in which you have no faith. But after the Day of the Soul Truth I'll convert you, just as I'll convert everyone else, regardless of their current beliefs. I'll *prove* to you that I alone know the truth about what happens to the soul after death.'

'How on earth will you do that?'

'Because I will no longer be on this earth when I prove it,' Accosta said calmly.

Before Fleming could absorb this, Soames stepped forward and patted him on the back. 'I can't see what you're so upset about, Miles,' he said. 'You got what you asked for. You came here to find out about your brother and in due course you will. In fact, I'd planned it as a surprise. There's no need for this ugliness.'

Fleming looked at him: the man had had a component removed. Somewhere along the line, during his mixed-up life, he had had what amounted to an empathy bypass. Fleming spoke slowly, enunciating every syllable. 'Bradley, you abducted and experimented on Amber, murdered her mother and a hundred other people for some half-baked crazy scheme, and you deceived me along the way. And yet you wonder why we're angry.'

'Yes, I do.'

Fleming shrugged, as if in defeat, and gave Soames a broad, apologetic grin. 'You're right, I overreacted.' Still smiling, he clenched his right hand into a fist, tensed his shoulder and punched Soames as hard as he could in the face. The guards were slow to react but the wolves were on him in seconds, their damp feral smell stifling him as they covered his body. The larger one clawed at his arm as he tried to protect his throat.

'Call them off!' the Red Pope shouted. 'There's no need for any more violence.'

Grudgingly Soames issued an unintelligible command and the wolves backed away. Amber reached for Fleming's arm – the claws had left only a scratch.

As the guards moved to escort him and Amber from the room, Fleming took some satisfaction from the anger in Soames's eyes as he gingerly touched his chin. As they passed him, Amber turned and spat in his red, contorted face.

'I can't see what *you*'re so upset about, Bradley,' Fleming said, 'You got what you asked for.'

'What are you going to do with them?' Accosta asked Soames, once Amber and Fleming had left.

Soames was nursing his jaw. 'Keep them out of the way until the big day, Your Holiness. We cannot allow them to jeopardize the preparations.'

Accosta tried in vain to read his expression. He wanted to believe that the reason Soames had poured so much of his money, time and intellectual resources into this grand scheme was solely because of his faith in God and his conviction that Accosta was His chosen minister. But even now the Red Pope was unsure of Soames's true motives. 'I don't want them harmed, Bradley,' he said carefully, 'not before the Day of the Soul Truth and not after it. Is that clear?'

Soames frowned, like an awkward adolescent who can't comprehend why he is being lectured on something that has nothing to do with him.

'We've almost reached our sacred goal and I've you to thank for that,' Accosta continued. 'Regrettable actions were necessary to reach this moment. But after the Day of the Soul Truth there should be no cause for violence or disagreement. Is that understood?'

'Of course, Your Holiness.'

Accosta turned to the others. He understood them better. Carvelli was vain and shallow, but he had served the church unquestioningly. Knight was a true believer, who didn't trumpet her faith but shared Accosta's turmoil when it came to making difficult moral decisions to fulfil God's will. And Monsignor Diageo had always been his right hand, his rock. Soon their loyal service would be rewarded. Soon they would be able to bathe in the warm certainty that they had contributed to something righteous and wonderful. 'Dr Soames has expressed his desire to remain here for the Day of the Soul Truth, out of the spotlight,' he said.

'And the sunlight,' Soames said.

Accosta smiled understandingly. 'The rest of us shall return now to the Red Ark and make our preparations.'

They looked sad but Accosta said, 'Don't be so downcast. This is not an end but a beginning. Rejoice with me. We're on the brink of a golden age of enlightenment.'

A sweet smile illuminated Virginia Knight's troubled features. 'Yes, Your Holiness, it'll be a glorious day,' she said.

'Glorious,' echoed Diageo.

Carvelli was more expansive. 'The Day of the Soul Truth will be a revelation.'

Soames nodded as if in agreement. 'It will indeed be the day of Revelation, Your Holiness – or, as the Greeks would say, the day of the Apocalypse.'

45

The blue sector.
Two days later

'It doesn't look much now,' Soames said as he led Fleming and Amber into the virtual reality suite housed within the blue sector, 'but you wait. You haven't been in here before, Amber, have you? It's something VenTec have been developing with KREE8 Industries.' Amber refused to meet Soames's gaze. She still found it difficult to accept the extent of his betrayal, to reconcile the man who had abducted her and authorized her mother's murder with the man she had respected and admired for years. 'And obviously this is a first for you as well, Miles,' Soames said. His face was still swollen and the contusion drew attention to a fresh scab on his already scarred chin, but his anger had gone. The events of thirty-six hours ago might never have happened.

But Fleming's anger, like hers, was still alive. Ignoring the two security guards hovering inches behind him, he didn't acknowledge Soames. Fleming and she each wore a deep blue, skin-tight bodysuit, gloves and slippers with sensor pads. The blue smart fabric was made up of thousands of microscopic beads, like pixels on a computer monitor. Soames and the two guards were similarly attired.

The room itself was a large but unprepossessing space. The floor, walls and ceiling were the same deep blue as the bodysuits. The floor felt solid, and she guessed that, along with the walls and ceiling, it was a high-resolution screen. In the centre of the room were three rows of two seats. 'Since this is going to be essentially a spectator experience I thought we should be comfortable,' Soames said, ushering them to the two front seats. The guards sat behind them and Soames at the back. Soames had a palm-top computer in his left hand and tapped the touch screen with his right. 'How shall we dress?' Soames said. 'Formal, I think.'

Immediately the blue suits were transformed. Fleming was in a dinner suit, complete with bow-tie, and she wore a strapless black dress. Amazingly the area of bare flesh on her arms looked real and her hands were apparently no longer in blue gloves. Moreover, her hands didn't feel as if they were wearing gloves. If she looked very hard and moved her hand quickly against the blue backdrop she could just about see the joins, but when Soames transformed the room she was transported to another place and the illusion was seamless.

Now she and Fleming sat in the front row of a vast congregation, in an auditorium that resembled a cross between a theatre and a cathedral. Columns flanked both sides, like a nave, and ahead there was a stage. Overhead there wasn't so much a vaulted ceiling as the illusion of a sunlit sky dotted with puffy white cumulus clouds. At any moment Amber expected cherubim and seraphim to appear. There was a balmy freshness in the air and, bewitched by the surroundings, she surrendered herself to the guilty frisson of excitement. She recognized the cathedral on the Red Ark from her VR excursion at the hospice.

Over the last two days, grieving for her mother and trying to come to terms with her death, she had sought distraction by watching television in her secure quarters. Constant news coverage from CNN and the BBC had explained the Day of the Soul Truth and she now understood the breathtaking arrogance of what they had planned. But, try as she might, she could not understand their strange alliance. She had known Soames for years and had never seen any evidence of a religious streak in him. The idea of him serving or following Accosta was ludicrous. Soames only associated with people who could serve *him*, never the other way round.

A murmur rippled through the audience, like wind through a field of barley, then a tall figure in red entered from the left and stood in the centre of the stage. Watching Accosta's self-satisfied smile, she was determined that he and Soames would pay for what they had done. She didn't know how or when, but they would pay.

Turning her head she caught Fleming's eye, and her courage swelled when she saw her own determination reflected there.

46

The Red Ark. 18° 55´ N, 16° 99´ W

Xavier Accosta had never felt more alive than he did now, minutes from death. Standing on the dais in his cathedral aboard the Red Ark he gazed out at the physical audience of little more than a hundred. Invitations to attend his service aboard the ark were randomly despatched to a few among the millions of e-mail addresses of his registered followers, depending on their location at the time. This practice hadn't changed for the Day of the Soul Truth, although a limited number of special invitations were sent out to the major religions. Interestingly, not one declined. All had sent a senior delegate, no doubt to witness and subsequently deconstruct whatever took place.

Accosta had heard that many of those lucky enough to be attending today had been offered thousands, even millions, by media representatives and wealthy individuals to attend in person. He was gratified that few, if any, had sold their ringside seats to this turning-point in human history. But the physical audience was only a fraction of the true audience. According to

Carvelli, the numbers watching on virtual head-sets, Internet screens and television exceeded four billion – 90 per cent of the wired world. Carvelli had been right. This was the biggest media event in history.

Before the main event, Accosta presided over a short service in which he paid tribute to all his dedicated followers and extended his blessing to all of those watching, regardless of their faith. Then, barely pausing for breath, the Red Pope raised his arms, summoned all the remaining power in his diseased body and spoke to the world: 'Today I am going on a journey. Many have gone before me on this journey from life to death, and in due course every one of you will follow me. It is unfortunate that dying is the last thing we ever do, because it could teach us so much about living. But this final journey still remains a mystery to us all.

'The uncertainty about what happens to our souls after death lies at the heart of religion, with every creed demanding that its followers believe exclusively in its view of the afterlife. Each – including the Church of the Soul Truth – demands this, based on nothing more than an act of faith.

'Two thousand years ago a man was crucified for our sins. The man we Christians believe was the Son of God came to live among us and tried to help us go beyond faith to see the truth. But even then many were blind to his lessons. His parables and teachings were interpreted in ambiguous ways, and only a few saw him or his miracles with their own eyes. Even his death and resurrection were inconclusive to all but true believers.

'Today I won't preach to you. I don't want you to believe in me or have faith in God. I will show you the truth – all of you. You will all *see* my resurrection with your own eyes and *hear* my truth with your own ears.

'I have been chosen as God's second messiah to die and be reborn, so that I can stand astride both worlds, one foot beside God and the other beside you, my fellow man. Today I, Cardinal Xavier Accosta, will blunt Satan's horns by removing for ever from your hearts the spiritual doubt that the Devil exploits to create conflict and evil. After today there will no longer be any excuse for yielding to Satan's temptation, because you will know that God, your true God, exists.

'At the end of my journey today, I will return to share the secrets of life and death with you. I will reveal to you the Soul Truth and, with this act of sacrifice, I will gain salvation for your soul and the souls of all humanity.'

When he finished there was no applause, just a hushed, awed silence.

Diageo and Virginia Knight appeared beside him and escorted him to the left of the stage, to where Bukowski and Tripp were waiting by the couch and the apparatus.

Diageo had tears in his eyes when he helped Accosta lie down on the laboratory couch that would be his deathbed. 'Don't be sad, my friend,' Accosta whispered. 'I'm not leaving you. By doing this I will stay with you for eternity.'

Diageo tried to smile as Knight placed the electrode on Accosta's temple with trembling hands.

Bukowski came then and gently pegged open his eyes, before inserting the dye and the lenses. His eyes stung but he told himself that soon his pain would be gone. Soon he would be filled with peace and joy as he bathed in the love of God.

Tripp helped raise Accosta's upper body and placed the glass sphere over his head.

Then Carvelli appeared from the left of the stage, beside the bank of sound equipment and the KREE8 holopad. He double-checked with Tripp that the wireless interface between the NeuroTranslator and the other equipment was operational. Then he scrutinized the cameras and media equipment. The audience watched their methodical movements with awestruck reverence.

Bukowski moved to the NeuroTranslator, ensuring that the soul wavelength was on screen.

Knight waited for each of the team to nod their readiness before crossing herself and turning to Accosta. 'All is in place, Your Holiness.'

Accosta sighed, with a blissful sense of release. He was so close now. Moments from his apotheosis.

'We're starting, Your Holiness,' Carvelli said. 'If for any reason—'

Accosta cut him off. 'I'm ready.' He had never felt more prepared for anything in his life.

Carvelli's face was tense. 'May God go with you.'

'God awaits me,' Accosta said quietly, as the switches were pulled and the humming grew in intensity. Gas entered the sphere and bathed the already distorted world outside it in a green glow.

286

To his left he could see Virginia Knight praying. He smiled. She had no need to pray.

Above the hum he could hear another sound. A deep wordless cry, a collective intake of breath, rose from the audience. He wished then that Carvelli had arranged music and, for a second, he wondered what music he would have chosen to accompany this moment.

Then the countdown started.

10 . . . 9 . . . 8 . . . 7 . . .

To his right he saw Virginia Knight's trembling hand holding the palm pad that controlled the electrode attached to his forehead – the electrode that would release the lethal electric shock, killing him instantly. He realized then that this would be the last thing he would ever see as a mortal man.

6 . . . 5 . . . 4 . . .

Like a spiritual cosmonaut Accosta took one last deep breath and waited for launch.

3 . . . 2 . . . 1 . . .

At first there is a black void. Then he is aware of a light in the distance and rushing towards it. The speed is breathtaking, exhilarating. He feels no fear. The faster the speed, the quicker he will reach his journey's end.

Within the blink of an eye he is inside the cone of light, moving so fast that it seems to stand still around him like a shimmering blizzard of silver particles. He is merging with the light, becoming indivisible from the photons that surround him. He is aware of being both a discrete entity – *himself* – and a part of a greater whole, a greater self.

A feeling of bliss flows through him as he nears the source of the radiance. Filled with rapture he surrenders himself to the luminous host, bracing himself for the moment of revelation – for the moment when he will be at one with God and he will know all there is to know.

The instant he reaches the source, a blinding, blue-white supernova blots out everything. He is consumed in a swirling maelstrom of colour and light, a burst of energy so powerful it explodes his whole being and reconstitutes it, again and again and again.

Suddenly the blinding light-storm is gone and his vision returns – but not as it was. He can see new colours, shapes and dimensions. A host of previously unimagined sights are revealed to him. It is as if he can see *everything*.

Then he understands what he is seeing.

And it is at this moment that the departed soul of Xavier Accosta wishes he could speak.

But he has no voice and can only cry out in silent despair.

47

Virtual reality suite.
The blue sector

Fleming watched the glass sphere on Accosta's head as the spark of life leapt from the Red Pope's dying eyes, hit the photon-detector screen and formed the distinctive halo of light in the sphere's outer layer of optical fibre. He now understood the procedure: the beeping noise and the four columns of light coming into alignment on the unit at the base of the bed signified lock-on, enabling them to trace Accosta's soul. The barcode interference pattern displayed on the monitor next to the lights signified Accosta's unique soul signature. With these two pieces of data – the lock-on signal and the signature – they could now make contact. And with Fleming's NeuroTranslator and Amber's soul wavelength Tripp and Bukowski should be able to communicate with the Red Pope's soul.

At that moment Fleming's anger was suspended. He wasn't thinking about the morality of how this had come about: Soames's deception, the murders, and the Red Pope's ruthless, vaunting ambition were all forgotten. His only thoughts, as he watched the line between life and death being redrawn, were of his brother and Jake.

When he had first sat down in the VR suite with Amber, he had been determined not to give Soames the satisfaction of reacting to his technical wizardry or the Red Pope's circus act. But it was impossible not to be consumed by the spectacle, not to be awed by the import of the event unfolding before his eyes. His helpless fascination went beyond mere scientific curiosity or even his concern for Rob's soul. It was more primal. All his life he had assumed that there was no afterlife and certainly no interventionist God. Even the recent events had been tantalizingly inconclusive, yielding more questions than answers. Soon, however, he would no longer be able to choose what to believe in: he would *know* the truth and the thought terrified him. But still he couldn't turn away.

The light had dissipated from the glass headsphere when Knight and an independent doctor checked the Red Pope's life signs and declared him officially dead. Carvelli seemed preoccupied with the black equipment to the right of the scanner, focusing on the black circular disc on the floor, checking its infrared connection to the NeuroTranslator.

'Watch the KREE8 holopad,' Amber whispered in his ear, and Fleming understood what was intended to happen next.

Not only were Soames's people going to use the NeuroTranslator to allow Accosta's soul to speak to the world, they were also going to control a hologram of him in the same way that Fleming controlled Brian. What was about to take place was nothing less than the virtual resurrection of the Red Pope. He shifted his gaze to the black pad and a shiver ran down his spine.

Seconds later the KREE8 holopad hummed into life. The halo reappeared in the glass head-sphere on the Red Pope's corpse and Fleming imagined the soul wavelength on the NeuroTranslator split-screen monitor starting to spike.

Then it began.

Horizontal line by horizontal line, an apparition appeared before his eyes. Accosta seemed to solidify out of thin air. To all intents and purposes, the Red Pope was standing not ten feet from his own corpse. Every detail was perfect, down to the expression on his face.

Then his head turned, as if to survey the crowd, in a slow, deliberate movement, like a newborn child flexing a hand. His face looked grave and the mesmerizing dark eyes seemed to address each member of the audience individually. Fleming didn't need to imagine the effect on the billions watching around the globe. His own palms were sweating and his heart was pounding in his chest.

There was a moment's silence and then Accosta's lips moved, saying the words that would for ever divide human history into two. The time before this moment. And the time after.

'I am a servant of the Lord. I have seen His power and I know His will. He has ordered me to return to you and reveal the Soul Truth.'

Another pause, and Fleming strained forward in his chair.

Accosta's deep voice was uncannily the same as the voice he had had in life. 'I have always believed in God,' he said solemnly, '*my* God, who created mankind in His own image to worship Him. An all-powerful, all-knowing, compassionate God.

'When I was younger I was troubled by what the philosophers call the Problem of Evil. Given all the evil in the world, how can an all-powerful, all-knowing, merciful God exist? Either God knows about evil, cares about it, but *can't do* anything about it – in which case He is not all-powerful, or He cares about it, can do something about it, but *doesn't know* about it – in which case he is not all-knowing, or he knows about it, can do something about it, but *doesn't care* about it – in which case he is neither merciful nor compassionate.'

Fleming felt gooscbumps on his forearms. It was if the Red Pope was speaking directly to him, directly addressing his own argument against God and religion.

'I have always squared this inconsistency,' continued the Red Pope, 'by believing that my powerful, omniscient, benign God *allowed* evil in the world to give us, his greatest creation, the gift of free will. To trust us with the ability and opportunity to choose between good and evil, even in the face of our harshest trials and tribulations. I now know the truth about good and evil. And now I know this truth it seems so obvious to me. After all, what God would create man simply to worship Him? What Supreme Being could be so vain, so *petty*?' He spat out the last word, as if it were a bitter taste in his mouth.

'There is no Problem of Evil because our Lord did not create us to worship Him. I always assumed God created a perfect ordered world – an Eden – then introduced the serpent of evil to test us. But this isn't true. Our Lord created an evil world then introduced good. The natural state in this world and the next is chaos – entropy. Evil is the normal way of the world, and good was only introduced as a capricious whim. The Lord only created us to enhance his amusement. That is the sole reason for our existence.

'As a child builds a stack of bricks only to knock it down again, our Lord allows us to climb higher and higher, believing in virtue and goodness and honour, only to dash us down with random acts of evil.

'There is no heaven, only arbitrary suffering. Life beyond death is as cruel and random as life on earth – except that it is eternal. There is no escape. There is no karma. No justice. No Elysian fields where the good may find peace after a hard life. There is no divine order, just chaos. The Soul Truth, which I can reveal to you now, is that God – the God to whom I dedicated my life on earth – doesn't exist.'

Accosta's face seemed to sag, the hologram capturing with sickening accuracy the horror and despair etched in his features. 'I am a soul in torment. The Lord I have willingly served all my life, and the Lord I am now condemned to serve for all eternity, is not God. There is only one Lord and he is the Lord of chaos and darkness. He is the Devil. Satan himself.'

A gasp rose from the audience. In any other context, Accosta's words would have sounded deranged, but now they sounded anything but. Fleming could feel Amber searching for his hand and gripping it.

The Red Pope raised his arms. 'Our Lord Satan will prove there is no God by using an agent on earth to reveal four signs,' he rasped, in the tones of an Old Testament prophet. 'These four horsemen of the Apocalypse will be unleashed upon this blighted world to spread terror before them and despair in their wake. The first will ride this night. The second will follow two days hence. On the next day, the final two horsemen will appear together, riding side by side.'

Accosta paused, and his face looked more lifeless than his corpse. His very soul seemed saturated in despair. 'Forgive me. I took my journey full of hope but I have returned with none. There is no hope. There is no God. I cannot even pray for you.'

A moment of shocked silence followed.

Then Accosta's image disappeared and the world was plunged into darkness.

Stunned and frightened, Fleming blinked, searching for light in the sudden blackness.

Seconds later, a sound broke the unearthly hush but it brought Fleming no comfort.

It was the sound of wolves howling outside, in the dark.

PART 3

LUCIFER

48

Like the shadow of an eclipse moving across the globe, electricity fled from city to city as night fell, only returning with the dawn. Starting from the west coast of America, the darkness followed the setting sun west across the Pacific, hitting Honolulu in Hawaii at sundown, 6.53 p.m. local time. For the next twenty-four hours, as the earth completed its revolution around the sun, virtually every major city throughout the world experienced a power cut from sundown to sunup.

The darkness inspired an extreme range of emotions, from panic to denial to anger. A small minority joyously celebrated what was understood to be the first sign, the first horseman of the Red Pope's apocalypse. It was as if humanity had regressed to a pagan time when it worshipped the power of the sun, believing that it alone pushed back darkness and brought forth all that was good in the world.

Many cowered in their homes until the dark angel passed. Others rushed out into public places to gather together, seeking comfort in numbers.

By midnight in Australia most of Sydney was teeming with hysterical people waving candles, trying to fend off the darkness. This was echoed across Asia and Europe as the setting sun moved across the world. The international media tracked the passage of darkness, reporting on how their regional bureaux were going off the air, literally powerless, as darkness fell.

Some tried to counter the panic, arguing that this was an insignificant fluke; that the Red Pope's revelation had been staged and the darkness was coincidental. But as the extent of the phenomenon became evident, fear turned to terror and then anger. A growing majority felt the need to make someone accountable for their despair and disillusionment.

During the night of darkness, widespread looting was rife. Large areas of London's East End, Paris and New York City's Lower East Side were vandalized by roaming mobs. But the greatest violence occurred in the main centres of worship. The principal targets of the mob's anger were the robed priests, who had lied to them about heaven and God. The Churches had been their spiritual advisers, demanding that they invest in them all their faith, holding themselves up as God's sole agents. But the Red Pope's revelation had wiped out the value of faith.

And someone had to pay.

The bigger the church the greater the anger: from Hagia Sophia in Istanbul to Canterbury Cathedral in England to St Peter's in Rome to the Jewish Synagogue in Jerusalem. The denomination didn't matter. Priests sought sanctuary in their now redundant churches as torch-bearing crowds surrounded these ancient places of worship whose spires pointed confidently to a heaven that the Red Pope had exposed as a lie.

A state of emergency was called in many countries as the authorities tried to explain the darkness. The following day, when the power returned with the sun, the American president appealed for calm and logic to prevail, making a robust televised address to his nation and the world.

'There is no proof yet that this is related to the Red Pope's address, or indeed that the Red Pope's address was genuine,' he stated. 'The FBI and the coastguard have taken the rare step of boarding the Red Ark, while it is still in international waters, and a full investigation is under way. More important, whatever Cardinal Accosta did or did not say is irrelevant to the laws of this land. I cannot control what does or doesn't happen in heaven or hell, but here in this world I can. Whatever anyone else chooses to believe, I believe that the law stands and it must be obeyed. I don't know who will or won't be punished in the next life but I can promise you one thing: if you break the law you will be punished in *this* life. If you've lost faith in everything else, have faith in that.'

Sitting alone in the conference room in the black sector, Soames stroked his wolves and watched the news bulletins. Even as the CNN and BBC anchormen both claimed that an uneasy calm had been restored, he smiled. He knew that the world was bracing itself for the real storm to come.

49

VenTec. The next day

A storm was brewing outside VenTec. Dark snow-clouds blanketed the mountain peaks and gusting winds buffeted the helicopter flying the Truth Council back to the Foundation.

'C'mon, it ain't necessarily a disaster,' Soames said soothingly, as he stood in the lobby to greet the shell-shocked Carvelli and Knight. Carvelli appeared dazed: his handsome olive-skinned face was pale, and his usually immaculate hair dishevelled. Virginia Knight looked worse: the horror of what she had witnessed aboard the Red Ark was written across her face. She seemed on the verge of collapse.

'After we left the Ark was crawling with FBI agents,' Carvelli said. 'Must have been monitoring it ever since we announced the Day of the Soul Truth, and when the first sign threw the world into panic they boarded us. If we'd waited any longer we'd be answering difficult questions now.'

'You're safe here,' Soames said, laying a reassuring hand on Knight's forearm. 'We've just got to reconvene and think through what this means.'

He looked across at Tripp and Bukowski, who were following the two members of the Truth Council into the Foundation. Their faces were expressionless as they brushed snow off the shoulders of their Arctic jackets and turned towards Soames. Catching his eye, they both nodded understandingly and hurried purposefully to the lift that connected with the red sector.

'Where's Monsignor Diageo?' Soames asked. 'I thought he might come back here with you for the . . .' he searched for the appropriate phrase '. . . post-mortem.'

Virginia Knight shook her head, unable to speak. Her fair hair seemed more streaked with grey than when she had last been there, a few days ago.

'He's dead,' Carvelli said slowly. 'Threw himself off the Red Ark's highest deck.'

'Even though he knew he would find no escape in death,' Knight said.

'He panicked,' Soames stated, 'and we must avoid doing the same.'

He led them to the black sector. The corridors of the Foundation were deserted. VenTec was self-sufficient with its own generator and utilities, and a sterile environment that required minimum maintenance. Except for a skeleton crew, he had evacuated almost everyone on the day before the Red Pope's revelation.

The broken glass had been cleared from the conference room in the black sector but the mirrored wall hadn't yet been replaced. The echoing blue-white space of the adjoining laboratory changed the acoustics of the enlarged room and made it feel colder. The wolves sat motionless as Knight and Carvelli took their seats at the table.

Soames poured them some coffee from the flask beside him and took a sip from his can of Coke.

Knight put her head in her hands. 'Everything we did was in vain – all the killings, all the time we spent. There was no justification for any of our crimes.'

Soames smiled. 'It hardly matters now, does it?'

Knight turned to him, appalled. 'We were used by Satan to do what we thought was God's work. We did evil, believing it was good. Of course it matters.'

Soames's smile grew broader. 'Why? Okay, God turned out to be Satan – but so what? In fact it's good news. If there's no God, you won't be punished for your sins.'

'How can you say that, Bradley? You were a believer too. How can you be so unaffected by this?'

'Let's just say I'm not unduly surprised.' He pointed to his scarred face. 'You aren't born like this and immediately think that God's a good guy. I've always suspected the bastard was a sadist, so to have Him unmasked as the Devil comes as something of a relief. It sure explains a few things and cuts through all the contorted bullshit the Churches have been churning out, trying to make sense of how their all-knowing, all-powerful God could allow so much misery into the world.'

He smiled at Knight, who was sitting open-mouthed. 'If you think about it, what the Red

Pope's soul revealed was a refreshing, liberating truth. That's why it doesn't matter. After all, nothing's changed.'

'Of course it has,' Knight said angrily. '*Everything*'s changed.'

Soames laughed. 'No, it hasn't. The only thing to change is what *you believed in*. Stop being so melodramatic, Virginia. It's not like God's suddenly packed His bags and gone. He was never there – you just didn't know it. Now, at least, you know life's basically a crap game with the dice loaded against you, so you can stop whining and get on with it.'

Virginia sat very still, staring at Soames, eyes narrow with hatred and disgust. 'You never believed in God, did you?'

Soames said nothing. For a moment, however, he almost told her everything. The need to make her understand the secret knowledge he had kept locked in his heart was so strong. But he had to be patient. His long wait was almost over.

'Hey, hey,' Carvelli interjected. His broad smile was forced, but his smooth confidence was returning. 'C'mon, guys, let's not turn on each other. This has been a setback, a major disappointment, but we've got to be practical. Virginia, Bradley's right. Perhaps we should accept the new way of things and try to adjust accordingly.'

Knight let out a long sigh.

Soames leant towards her. 'Virginia, we've got to make the best of this. And, as you so clearly pointed out, we have transgressed – not necessarily in the eyes of our new Lord and Master, but we have broken the law.'

Carvelli looked alarmed. 'Will the FBI find anything on the Red Ark to implicate us in the killings and . . . ?'

'Don't worry about the Red Ark. The authorities have got their hands full trying to explain the first sign and preparing for the next ones. However, perhaps we should be concerned about the witnesses to our over-enthusiastic and, on reflection, misguided acts of murder and abduction.'

The horror on Knight's face deepened. 'What are you saying?'

'Amber Grant and Miles Fleming are serious liabilities.'

'But the Red Pope said we shouldn't harm them,' Knight said automatically. 'He said the violence—'

Soames guffawed. 'But he was *wrong*, wasn't he? You still haven't grasped it yet, have you, Virginia? The Red Pope was a self-deluding arrogant fool who knew nothing.' He looked directly at Carvelli, then Knight. 'Look, it's simple. Fleming and Grant have to be silenced permanently so that we can put this sorry episode to rest and get on with the rest of our lives. And, Virginia, stop looking so horrified. Your conscience is redundant now that there's no longer a God to give you credit for doing good.'

'Damn God,' Virginia shouted. 'What about our *humanity*? What about our *human* belief in what's right or wrong?'

Soames spoke in a contemptuous whisper. 'What about it, Virginia? What about this precious

304

humanity you've suddenly discovered? Is it the same humanity that allowed you to collaborate in the deaths of a hundred terminally ill patients just because you thought you were serving God?'

50

Black sector secure accommodation.
Two hours later

In the secure suite two doors down from Fleming's, Amber was sleeping. After her mother's death she had been too traumatized to rest, but after the Red Pope's Day of the Soul Truth and the subsequent chaos a strange calm had descended upon her. She had fallen into a deep sleep unlike any she had experienced before. It seeped through her bones, relaxing her muscles and dissipating the stress and anxiety.

She entered the dream state with calm serenity; she didn't struggle or exhibit signs of disquiet. Instead she lay still and although her eyeballs exhibited the classic signs of movement when she entered REM the lids remained closed and her breathing regular.

Then, as it had so often before, her mind took the journey to death.

The darkness envelops her in a velvet cocoon and a numbing calm possesses her. No harm can come to her here. Even when she sees the now familiar pinprick of light and experiences the rush through the black vortex towards it she remains un-troubled. This time she is not alone on her journey. A presence is with her, leading her. It's as if she and Ariel have never been apart as they approach the cone of light. They fuse and become as one, and Amber knows all that Ariel knows.

Racing through the darkness she understands that Ariel has been waiting for her in the no man's land between life and death. Her sister's patience only ran out on the day that Bradley Soames first detected the human soul in his early experiments on terminal patients. That day, the wave particle duality of soul and body collapsed, which so warped the universal membrane connecting life and death that its disturbance affected Ariel and caused Amber, her entangled twin, to feel phantom pain.

Amber's dreams of dying were caused by Ariel's bid to warn her to stop Soames's tampering. The nature of their bond meant that every time Ariel tried to use Amber's descent into the dream state to inhabit her living consciousness she pushed her sister away. The more aggressively Ariel pushed through the rotating door towards life, the faster Amber spun away towards death. Ironically, Soames's experiments on Amber released Ariel to make contact with her before continuing her long-delayed passage towards death. And now as her sister guides her into the light Amber knows that Ariel is saying goodbye. She also knows that Ariel intends to show her something.

Entering the cone, they are moving so fast that the light seems to stand still around them like a frozen blizzard of silver particles. No longer is she travelling through the luminescence, but merging with it, becoming indivisible from the photons that surround her. But she feels no fear now that Ariel is with her. For the next few timeless moments they are joined again, the dancing twins, moving together in concert, in perfect accord. And as they near the peak of the cone a feeling of bliss flows through Amber as they reach the apex and merge with the source of the radiance. Then Amber is aware of being both a discrete entity – *herself* – but also a part of her sister and a part of a greater host, a greater self.

Then a blinding blue-white supernova blots out everything and a swirling maelstrom of light consumes her, pulling her apart and reconstituting her, again and again.

Suddenly the light-storm is gone and she is alone, waiting to be plucked back from the light, back into life. But she feels no sadness or loss. Instead, for the first time, she feels complete. Lingering at the apex of the cone, her vision is restored and the bright light which once dazzled now illuminates. Like a climber standing on a peak and looking out over a sunlit plain she can see clearly where her sister has gone. And her adoptive mother. And all those she has loved.

In one stunning revelatory instant, before she is yanked back into the vortex, she catches a glimpse of what lies beyond the source of the light and inhabits the next world.

'Amber, wake up! Wake up!'

Confused and disoriented, Amber couldn't

distinguish whether the familiar voice was real or in her dreams. Then she opened her eyes and saw Soames standing in the half-light of the open doorway, flanked by the two wolves. 'I just wanted to check everything was okay with you,' he whispered. After all that Amber had experienced over the past week, his concern was ill-timed and inappropriate.

Amber slipped out of bed and padded over the carpet to him. 'I could never understand why you and Accosta were in league together ... but you never believed in him, did you? Somehow you knew what he'd discover. You knew it would be terrible.'

'Amber, I simply wanted to find out what happens when we die. No different from what Miles was trying to do – or any scientist worth their salt would do if they had the technology. I had the technology, which you helped me to develop. All I did was seek the truth. Is that so bad?'

'What about the way you did it, murdering and abducting people?'

'It was necessary, Amber.'

'Why?'

'To find the *truth*.'

'But this is the weird thing, Bradley. I'm not even sure it *is* the truth. Not the whole truth anyway. There's something more to—'

'You think?' Soames interrupted. In the half-light his face wore a quizzical frown, as if trying to figure her out. 'No,' he said abruptly. 'There's nothing more. There's only one truth. And when the signs come you'll understand it too.'

She stepped closer. 'But what if Accosta was only speaking a half-truth, Bradley? Don't you even care if he was wrong? Hell, I want him to be wrong. It's only natural. Even you must want that, Bradley, surely?'

He turned to leave and as he did so the shaft of light from the corridor crossed his face, illuminating his eyes. Ever since she had met him she had known he was strange, but had always put it down to his powerful intellect and a strange upbringing due to his illness. But in that instant when she looked into his eyes she realized it was more than that. He wasn't just eccentric or lacking in empathy, he was emotionally absent. She didn't see evil in his eyes; she saw something far more frightening.

She saw a vacuum.

51

Black sector secure accommodation

Twenty-seven hours after the Red Pope's announcement, the media leaked the secret joint findings of the FBI technical agents aboard the Red Ark, an invited group of top scientists and a delegation from the Vatican's Institute of Miracles. Testimonials had been taken from all those of the audience who had physically witnessed the events, including the invited senior members of the major religions.

All parties were keen to expose the Red Pope's revelation as a hoax, but after analysing his corpse and poring over the complex technical equipment, they had been forced to acknowledge that the only input into the hologram had come from the NeuroTranslator, and the only source for the NeuroTranslator signals was the soul-capture sphere around the head of Accosta's corpse. This technical admission and the testimony of those who had been on board the Red Ark during the announcement had left the committee with no choice but to conclude that there was no 'earthly way to explain what had happened'. Another unofficial source was quoted as saying that if this was a technical trick then 'the hoax was no less miraculous than Accosta's soul actually speaking after death . . .'

Associate Director Morgan Jones, the tall black FBI chief in charge of the investigation, gave two press conferences in which he appeared confident in the official diagnosis while strenuously and eloquently saying nothing. But his reticence and the Vatican's initial 'no comment' when asked to refute the Red Pope's revelations were seen as confirming the leaked findings and supporting Accosta's final words.

Locked in his suite, watching the events unfold on television, Fleming could only pace out his frustration. He was incapable of sitting still, and his mind was similarly agitated, battling to process all the information he had received so he could clarify what he now believed. He had been unable to sleep since the Red Pope's words, and he had become increasingly certain that they contained some truth. What Accosta had revealed dovetailed too closely with the one theory that made any sense of his atheistic sensibilities: religion as a malevolent force in the world.

A noise outside the door halted him. It opened to reveal Bradley Soames. The wolves stood panting quietly at his heel. He was smiling, jubilant. 'How you feeling, Miles?'

Fleming didn't answer.

'Tell me,' Soames asked, leading the wolves into the room and closing the door, 'how does it feel to have your gravest fears realized?' He sounded coolly interested. 'How does it feel to know your brother's probably suffering now and you didn't try to save him? How does a guy like you, who has spent his life trying to ease suffering in this world, and has depended on the sweet release of oblivion in the next, handle the fact that death brings only more arbitrary suffering *for ever*?'

Fleming said nothing, and did not look at him.

'How would your parents feel, knowing that their beloved elder son is dead and in pain because their younger son refused to save him? How would your nephew feel? It's Jake, isn't it? How would he handle this knowledge? I think it would destroy him. Don't you?'

Still Fleming was silent.

'Don't feel too bad, Miles,' Soames continued. 'In many ways you were right. There is no divine God. There is no ultimate judge who ensures everyone gets their just deserts in the hereafter. There's just a malevolent Lord of Chaos. The only difference from what you believed then and now *know* is that when you die, the chaos and suffering continue for eternity.'

Fleming crumpled to his knees, with tears streaming down his cheeks.

Soames stepped closer. 'I pity you. It must be difficult living with yourself, knowing the fate to which you've consigned your brother.'

Suddenly Fleming reached for Soames's right hand and gripped it hard in both of his. The wolves tensed but Soames signalled them to stay back. 'There's no point begging, Miles. I can't help you. Not now.' A small laugh. 'Or perhaps you're praying? No, that would be stupid.' He pulled away his hand. 'Why pray when there's no one to hear you?' He led the silent wolves from the room.

Hands clasped together, Fleming remained on the floor until he heard the door close. Then he sat up slowly and opened his hands.

52

The white sector communication room

Grey-faced and expressionless, Virginia Knight felt numb, enveloped by the vacuum of her now absent faith. She replaced the satellite phone on its cradle. There was only one option left to her.

Leaving the room, she walked like a zombie through the deserted white sector, towards the exit where, through the glass doors, she could see the gathering snowstorm lit up by the external security lights. Using her disk, she opened the door to the survival room next to the reception hallway. Not knowing what to select, she rifled through the supplies and chose prepacked items, stowing them in a rucksack.

Then, with a deep sigh, she left the survival room and walked back into the heart of the Foundation, towards the black sector.

Black sector

Amber paced around her room, her frantic steps mirroring the turmoil in her mind as conflicting thoughts warred inside her head. What she had seen in Soames's eyes had increased her anxiety about Accosta's revelation. She had already seen the first sign he had predicted, which indicated that there was some truth in his words. Yet her dream had suggested there was a contradictory truth.

She sat on the bed with her head in her hands. She was still unsure of exactly what Ariel had tried to show her, but she knew that her sister had gone to a very different place from that described by the Red Pope.

To calm herself she cast her mind back to the last time she had seen her mother alive, sleeping in the hospice, afternoon sunlight filtering through the translucent curtains, the green of the terrace plants beyond. The serenity of that moment soothed her as surely as if her mother had laid a cool hand on her forehead.

'Perhaps Ariel was trying to tell me something,' she said aloud. 'Something I need to tell the world . . .'

Amber gazed around at her secure cell in remote, inaccessible mountains north of the Arctic Circle. Even if she knew what she wanted to tell the world, how could she contact anyone? This place didn't even seem part of the world.

Click.

Amber swivelled and stared at the door.

She had never been frightened of Soames before but now apprehension built within her as she braced herself for another confrontation. Standing ramrod straight, she faced the door.

It opened hesitantly.

The silhouette wasn't Bradley Soames's. It was too tall.

'Amber,' the figure whispered urgently, stepping into the room. 'Let's get out of here.'

Amber's jaw dropped and her heart lifted. 'Miles, how the hell did you get in here? More to the point, how the hell did you get *out*?'

'Let's just say I borrowed a key off Bradley. I'll explain later. First we've got to get out of here.'

53

Black sector

The dark, deserted corridors were as quiet as treachery. 'You've got a plan?' asked Amber.

'One step at a time,' Fleming said. 'First we get out of the black sector. Then we head for the white sector communication room and use the sat phone to make a call.'

'Who to?'

'The FBI – anyone who'll listen.' He didn't care who they called as long as they got word out about their predicament and revealed Soames's role in recent events. His main worry was what to do after that. It would take time for help to arrive and until then they were at Soames's mercy. If he had been on his own he might have tried to climb down the mountain and head for the rangers' station he'd seen when flying in. But there was Amber to consider.

They were yards from the secure door leading from the black sector and he was about to approach it when he saw a security guard through the glass. He pushed Amber into the shadows and hissed, 'When he walks out of sight I'll try opening the door.'

Seconds later, the guard walked on. 'Let's go,' he whispered, leading Amber to the door.

'How you gonna open it?' Amber whispered.

'With this.' He opened his right hand. 'I took it from Bradley.'

Amber peered at the small black fragment on his palm, one side glistening darkly in the half-light. Then she grimaced. 'Gross.'

'It got us out so far so don't knock it.' He balanced the scab on the tip of his right index finger, and pressed it against the fingerplate next to the door lock.

He felt a hot sensation as the DNA scanner peeled off a microscopic section of tissue, then watched the red light, praying the guard wouldn't come back. The light stayed red, and he imagined an alarm alerting Soames.

'Come on, you bastard,' he muttered, jiggling the scab. He could feel the anxiety radiating from Amber as she huddled closer to him.

Suddenly the light changed to green, and they sighed with relief.

When the door opened they stole out of the black sector and turned left away from the direction the guard had gone. Entering the white sector Fleming had the strange sensation that they were being followed, and twice he turned round to check, but it soon became evident that the place was deserted. On his left he could see a heavily tinted glass window, showing a blue vision of the Arctic landscape outside. Heavy snow furled and billowed against the night sky.

Amber pointed to a door down the corridor on the left. 'There it is,' she said.

The communication room door stood open and three matt grey satellite phones sat in a regimented row on the central workstation. Feeling his anxiety abate, Fleming reached for the first and held it to his ear. 'Who do we call?' Amber asked beside him.

Fleming tried to recall the name he'd heard in the news reports. 'The FBI agent heading up the investigation.'

There was a sound behind them, but before Fleming could turn his head he heard a voice say: 'You're not going to call anyone. All the phones are down. Communication with the outside world has been cut.'

A cold lump in his stomach, Fleming wheeled round. Virginia Knight was standing in the doorway, her eyes bloodshot, her face deathly pale.

She reached into her pocket.

'This is for you, Miles,' she said. 'I'm so sorry it had to come to this . . .'

54

Fleming moved so fast that Amber forgot to draw breath. One moment he was standing beside her, holding the satellite phone, and the next he was leaping through the air, knocking Virginia Knight to the floor.

Knight didn't try to struggle as Fleming reached into her pocket, retrieved the access disk and stood over her. 'Why are the sat phones down?' he demanded. His voice was taut with anger.

Knight stared dully at him. 'Bradley's cut off all contact with the outside world,' she said. 'Even I can't get a line out. Only he's got access.'

'Why?'

'I don't know. The guy's lost it. All I know is he intends to kill you. You gotta get out and get help.'

'How the hell are we going to do that?' blurted Amber. 'We'd have to climb down the mountain.'

'That's the only way,' said Fleming grimly.

Knight looked up at him. 'Let me help you. I've got area maps and plans of the site.'

'Where?'

'In a rucksack in the survival room.'

Fleming studied her for moment, then pulled her up. 'Let's go.'

They passed through the remainder of the deserted white sector and within minutes were in the reception area. Ahead Fleming could see the blue-tinted glass exit doors with the V etched into them, and the thick swirling snow beyond. To his left was the survival room, stocked with climbing gear, rations and clothing for the harsh conditions outside. Using Knight's smart disk he opened the door and ushered the women inside.

One wall was lined with survival suits, all bright red, branded North Face. Unlike normal clothing, they didn't hang from hooks; instead they were self-supporting, like armour. Each suit had a wire extending from the ankle cuff of the left leg which was plugged into an electric wall-socket, and beneath stood rows of kinetic energy boots. A shelf contained insulated helmets, with integrated snow visors and lamps. Along the opposite wall a row of open shelving displayed rations and climbing paraphernalia: axes, ropes, snow saws, ice picks. Fleming was impressed, particularly with the survival suits: they were state-of-the-art smart clothing, similar to the gear he had used on a trip to Chamonix eighteen months earlier.

In the left-hand corner of the room two sets of clothing were neatly laid out on a bench, one large, the other smaller. A bulging rucksack lay on the floor beside the bench. 'There's one set each and I've filled the rucksack with climbing gear and rations. You're probably more familiar with this stuff than I am, Miles, so I suggest you check what else you need and help Amber kit herself out.' Reaching into the rucksack, Knight retrieved a palm-top computer and handed it to Fleming. 'This contains a full map of the area and plans of the old Alascon Oil site. There's a rangers' station to the east of here.'

Fleming nodded. 'I noticed it from the chopper when I flew in.'

'Your smart suits are equipped with microphones and transceivers to contact each other and send distress signals a few hundred yards, but to make long-distance contact up here you've got to get to the rangers' station. Apparently no one mans it at this time of year, but it's got a fully equipped communications suite. You can get a message out from there. Now hurry – there isn't much time.'

Fleming began to check the contents of the rucksack as Amber got into her smart suit. 'Why are you doing this, Virginia?' he asked.

'I wish I could do more, but the helicopter's off limits.'

'Why's he so keen to kill us?' Amber said. 'I know we're a liability but we're stuck here and it's—'

'It makes no sense. I tried to call the authorities before I came to get you. I wanted to turn myself in and call for help but, as you saw, that's not an option. Anyway, even if I had got through there's such chaos out there it'll take ages before any sort of normality is restored.' Her shoulders sagged. She looked lost, broken. 'If it ever is restored.'

'Why are you helping us, Virginia?' Fleming asked again. 'Why now?'

'I did wrong and I'm trying to put it right. I'm sorry for what I allowed to happen – what I made happen.'

'But why?' Fleming probed, as he checked that the power leads in the lower legs of Amber's survival suit were plugged into her kinetic boots. 'If there's no God, there's no reason to stick your neck out for us. Aren't you concerned about what Bradley will do to you?'

'Yes, but it hardly matters now. I did everything – good and bad – because I thought I was serving God through the Red Pope's grand mission. Now, after all that, there's nothing anyone can do to me. Got nothing left to lose, nothing left to believe in – except myself. And to be true to myself I've got to help you. If I can't hang on to the belief that my life's been worthwhile, everything's been for nothing.'

Fleming saw her despair and confusion, caught a glimpse of the woman he had known at Barley Hall. 'Come with us,' he said.

'No, I can't. I gotta keep an eye on Soames. He's not who I thought he was. It's like he knew what the Red Pope would reveal. There's something more to this.'

'You think the Red Pope's revelation wasn't necessarily the whole truth?' Amber said.

Fleming turned questioningly to Amber, but before he could say anything Knight said, 'You saw the first sign – the darkness and what happened afterwards. That was the first horseman of the Apocalypse. In the Bible, the Book of Revelation says that the first horseman will spread unrest around the world. The other horsemen will follow and I'm afraid they'll prove beyond doubt that the Red Pope's revelation was the whole truth.'

'It's not as simple as that,' Amber said. 'It can't be. There's more, I can feel it.'

Then Fleming heard a sound which triggered something primal in his brain. His heart beat faster and his muscles tensed in preparation for flight. He reached for Amber, checked that the zips were done up on her survival suit, that the collar microphone and helmet speakers were operational, and that the kinetic boots were delivering power to the rest of the suit when she moved her feet. 'Can you feel warm air between you and the suit?' he demanded.

She nodded.

'Good. Keep your zips sealed and follow me.' He turned to Knight, who was staring out of the glass door into the reception lobby and to the exit door beyond. 'You sure you're not going to come with us?' Fleming asked.

She didn't answer, just opened the door to the survival room and made for the exit door.

Slinging the rucksack over his shoulder, Fleming ran to the exit. Then he heard the sound again.

Wolves howling.

From the corner of his eye he saw a movement, and turned. Soames was standing fifteen yards behind him in the lobby, just beyond the survival room. His wolves stood at either side of him, yellow eyes staring, hackles raised.

Fleming stopped beside Knight in the doorway and wondered how much protection the survival suits would give against the wolves' attack. An aluminium frame ran through them but it was designed to support climbing ropes. And the layers that made up the space-age fabric were lightweight and designed to withstand cold, not teeth and claws.

'Leaving so soon?' Soames said quietly. His scarred face was flushed, his eyes wide and staring. He looked as if he could barely contain himself.

'Let them go, Bradley.' Virginia Knight's voice quavered with fear. 'It's over. The Soul Project doesn't matter any more. You never believed in it anyway. You were never one of us.'

'Oh, but I was. I was always a believer, Virginia. I still am. It's just that neither you nor Accosta ever thought to ask me *who* I believed in.'

A visible tremor ran through Virginia Knight. 'In that case, you got what you wanted. You won. Surely that's enough. You don't need to hurt or kill any more people.'

'Is that what you wanted, Bradley?' Amber asked suddenly. 'To show the world that the Devil was in charge?'

Soames smiled slowly. 'It hardly matters now, Amber, does it?'

'But it does, Bradley,' said Amber, 'because the Red Pope's Soul Truth might not be the only truth.'

Soames's eyes narrowed and Fleming saw a look of understanding pass between him and Amber. 'I think *you* understand why I can't let you or Miles live,' Soames said.

Carvelli appeared from the white sector behind Soames. 'Bradley? Virginia? What's going on?'

At that moment Knight did two things. First, she pushed Fleming hard in the chest. Off-balance, he stepped backwards, across the threshold into the freezing night. As he did so he pulled her and Amber with him. Then she reached in and pulled her disk from the locking mechanism, closing the sliding doors and locking them outside.

She stared at Soames through the glass. Wearing only her thin navy suit, she shivered but her face was devoid of fear. Even as Soames reached for the locking mechanism, she shouted at him, 'Bradley, I know why the Red Pope's revelation was no surprise to you.'

Fleming and Amber pulled at her, but she wouldn't move. She glanced at Fleming, and said, 'Go.'

'Not without you,' he said.

'*Go*,' she spat, then turned back to Soames, who was muttering at his wolves as they howled and scrabbled at the door, desperate to get out. As he placed his finger on the DNA pad and the door unlocked the animals became frantic.

Fleming grabbed Amber's arm. 'We better go.' Then he turned back to Knight but he knew from the look in her eyes that she wouldn't come.

'Go, Miles,' she shouted. 'I can buy you time.' Then she turned back to Soames. Even as the first wolf scrabbled through the door and leapt at her, he heard her say calmly, 'You don't just worship Satan. You—'

It might have been the gusting winds or the first

327

wolf ripping at her throat that stole her words. As the second wolf tore at her hamstrings, Fleming willed himself to focus on saving Amber. He didn't see the snow turn red around Virginia's writhing body, or Carvelli staring out from behind the glass door, pale with uncomprehending horror. Or Bukowski and Tripp rushing towards the exit from inside the Foundation.

All his energy was concentrated on pulling Amber through the cutting wind and into the snow-laden night.

328

55

Amber welcomed the freezing cold and Fleming's staccato orders: they kept her mind from what she'd seen and what was behind her in the dark.

'Keep close to me and do exactly as I tell you,' she heard Fleming shout through the speakers in her helmet. Running across the steel platform towards the helipad, he pulled a rope from his rucksack. He clipped one end to an alloy hoop on the waist of her suit and the other end to a similar hoop on his. 'We'll rappel wherever we can get an anchor, otherwise we'll down-climb. Okay?'

'Okay,' she replied, although she didn't understand what he was talking about. Running in the boots was difficult because the crampons on the soles dug into the ice. 'Where are we going?'

Fleming pointed into the snow-flecked darkness. Beyond the scope of VenTec's high-beam security lights, she could see nothing. 'Turn on your helmet lamp.'

Tapping the button on the strap, as he'd shown her in the survival room, she heard a click then saw the light beam out into the night. She was glad of it, but it seemed pathetically inadequate in this dark and inhospitable place.

Fleming stopped a few yards ahead, bent over, then disappeared. Running forward into the wind she turned her head madly from side to side trying to find him in the dark and the swirling snow.

Then she heard his voice. 'Stop and look down.'

Four feet in front of her she saw the railing that marked the end of the steel gantry and the helipad. Beyond that there was nothing. Craning over, she saw Fleming securing himself to one of the spider's legs that underpinned the structure. She was amazed at how quickly he had shimmied over the railing and made his way down to the under-belly of the rig. He looked completely confident dangling above the abyss, every movement fluid and assured. Then he raised his right hand and signalled for her to follow him.

She hesitated.

'Come on,' his calm voice urged, through the speakers in her helmet. 'Just climb over the railing and make your way towards me. I'm secured to the stanchion and you're tied to me, so if you fall I've got you.'

She hated heights, always had.

'Come on,' he soothed. 'It's a lot safer to climb down here than it is to stay up there.'

Still she hesitated, screwing up her courage.

Then she heard the wolves, sensed them running towards her, and one fear overcame the other. She climbed on to the railing and inched her way over the side. Her heart racing, she looked down and manoeuvred her head so that the beam of her helmet lamp rested on Fleming. His right arm was reaching for her. But there was a seven-foot gap between them.

'How the hell did you get over there?' she asked.

'I fell.'

'What?'

'On purpose. I dropped down to the next beam then climbed across here.'

She heard scampering above her and growling.

Jump now! Fleming ordered.

Taking a deep breath she stretched out her feet, and slipped off the platform. To her surprise, her boots and crampons crunched on the girder, which was broader than it had appeared from above, and she made her way to Fleming, feeling a huge wave of relief when his arm encircled her waist.

'Well done,' he said. 'Now we need to climb to that ice ledge. From there we can rappel down—'

'Rappel?'

'A fancy term for going down using a rope, so I can support you. Don't worry, it's a walk in the park.'

'Honestly?'

She could see him grimace through his snow visor. 'Not really,' he said. 'In these conditions it's going to be fucking difficult.'

'Right,' she said slowly, wishing she hadn't asked, and tried to copy his every move as she followed him down the rig on to the ice ledge of the mountain. He seemed to know the best route down instinctively.

On the ledge, it was misty and less exposed. She

wanted to rest but Fleming was already rummaging in the rucksack, taking out ice screws, rope and chocks. He pointed to another ledge below. 'We've got to rappel down to there, then hopefully zigzag our way down this face until we reach the shoulders of the mountain. Then we turn east. The descent to the rangers' hut's going to be tough, but if you do as I say we'll make it.' He paused for a second. 'Shit. How the hell did it get down here so fast?'

Fear ran down Amber's spine as she saw a pair of yellow eyes coming at them from out of the mist.

Fleming swore and indicated to their right. The second wolf was coming from the opposite direction.

Before she had time to think, Fleming had two ice picks in each hand. He handed a pair to her, and shimmied over the ledge. Kicking his boots into the ice wall below he made footholds while he used the picks to pin himself to the almost sheer face. He made it look easy. 'There's no time to rappel,' he said. 'Put your feet in my footholds and dig the picks into the ice to support your upper body. Don't worry, I'll keep the footholds close together.'

This time she didn't hesitate, just clambered over the edge, found Fleming's footholds and began the descent.

The next ledge was probably thirty feet below but to reach it they had to traverse diagonally and it seemed further. Within a few yards her calves were cramping, but her arms were worse, and soon her back muscles were burning. But whenever she faltered, the howling of the wolves spurred her on.

Embed right pick. Embed left pick.

Hold.

Shuffle right leg along to next foothold. Shuffle left leg along to next foothold.

Hold.

It was torture, the rhythm accentuating the pain.

Pick, pick, hold. Shuffle, shuffle, hold.

There was no respite and the simple act of staying on the vertical mountainside was agony, let alone moving down it. All she could see in front of her was icy rock, inches from her eyes, illuminated in greens and blues by the helmet lamp. Her lungs were so starved of air that she felt as if she was under water, suffocating beneath a beautiful but deadly frozen sea.

Just when she thought she would pass out, two strong arms eased her on to the lower ledge. Her legs collapsed beneath her and she fell to the snow.

She could hear the wolves howling overhead as Fleming massaged her calf muscles. 'Well done,' he said. 'That was hard. There shouldn't be many as sheer as that and we can rappel from here. Once we get to the shoulder of the mountain we can rest for a while on the flat.'

She was almost weeping with frustration and pain. 'I don't think I can do it.'

'You can,' he insisted. He didn't even sound out of breath.

'Go on without me. One of us has to stop Bradley. Something's not right about what the Red Pope said – and I think Bradley's behind it. One of us has to survive to stop him.'

'Ssh. Save your strength for getting down the mountain.'

'But I'll hold you up. You must go on alone.'

'No. We're in this together.' Fleming yanked her to her feet. 'How the hell did they get down here so fast?'

Over her shoulder, she saw two grey shapes further along the shelf. The wolves were racing towards them. Fleming pulled her up and along the ledge with him, towards the heart of the mountain. She imagined the wolves closing in: this was their terrain.

Suddenly Fleming stopped. She followed his gaze and saw that the ledge ended some twenty yards in front of them, hitting a sheer wall of the mountain, cutting off their escape. About ten feet above where it met the ice face an eight-foot-diameter circular pipe jutted out.

Fleming unclipped the rope that connected him to her, and pushed her forward along the ledge. 'Go to the end and wait for me.'

Amber looked nervously over her shoulder at the wolves. They were close now. 'What are you going to do?'

'Hope I get lucky,' he said, as he held both ice picks high above his head and began to jump up and down on the ledge. 'Run, damn it, run!' he shouted, as she stood watching him. Galvanized, she made for the mountain face.

When she got there she turned and saw Fleming still jumping up and down, while the wolves raced closer and closer. Just when she thought the nearest wolf was going to leap at him, he fell through the ledge, and vanished in a flurry of snow and ice.

The wolves careened to a stop. A ten-foot gap in the ledge now divided them from her. But where was Fleming?

'Miles, you okay?' she said into her microphone, trying to control her rising hysteria. 'Miles, talk to me. *Miles*.'

56

The security suite. VenTec

'Jesus, Bradley, what have you done?'

Frank Carvelli's face was a sickly green as he followed Soames down the white sector corridor away from the reception lobby where the patch of red snow on which Virginia Knight's mutilated corpse had lain was visible through the glass doors. Vomit stained his immaculate black cashmere polo-neck, and all trace of his smooth confidence had disappeared. 'Why didn't you call off the wolves? We hadn't even agreed to get rid of Fleming and Amber so why kill Virginia for letting them go? This is getting way out of hand, Bradley. This is too—'

Soames raised his hand impatiently and studied the snow-flecked security monitors. The cameras on the outside of the rig were picking up nothing on the helipad or the steel platform outside the reception area – except two security guards, looking aimlessly out into the snowy night. 'Where have they gone?' he asked, puzzled rather than angry.

Tripp and Bukowski appeared in the doorway.

Both were kitted out in survival suits and carried guns. Their gloved hands were smeared with blood and their suits were streaked with dark stains. Carvelli leant against the wall to steady himself.

'You've cleared away the mess?' Soames asked.

Bukowski nodded.

'Well done. Now go outside and find the wolves. Bring back whatever they've left of Fleming and Amber.'

Bukowski and Tripp turned away.

'One word of advice,' Soames said, before they left. 'Don't disturb them if they're still eating. Let them finish before collecting what's left.'

'Bradley, what's got into you?' Carvelli moaned. 'Why are you doing this? It's madness. Why's it so important to you that Amber Grant and Miles Fleming die?'

Soames's disconcerting eyes appeared to look deep into Carvelli's soul, evaluating, deciding. 'Do you *really* want to know?' he asked eventually. The way he said it made it sound like a challenge. *Can you handle the truth?*

Carvelli's mouth felt dry. 'Yes,' he croaked.

For a second Soames didn't respond. Then he gave a small smile and led Carvelli out of the security suite. He passed through the white sector and pressed the elevator button.

Fleming's luck had changed: the weak part of the ledge had broken away, creating a barrier between Amber and the wolves – but plunging him, for one heart-stopping second, into the void. It had taken all his strength to implant his picks into the icy rock-face beneath the ledge on Amber's side. His first attempt didn't hold, but the second – which almost wrenched his right arm out of its socket – did.

Then he clawed his way up and on to the ledge.

Amber rushed to help him up. 'Why didn't you answer me?'

'I was kind of preoccupied.'

'You scared me,' she said, holding him close.

'I scared myself.' The wolves were pacing around the ledge on the opposite side of the gap, mustering the resolve to make the leap. 'Come on,' he said. 'We can't stay here.'

'There's no way I can climb down there,' she said, pointing to the sheer rock-face, which disappeared into the darkness without any hint of a ledge or natural break.

Fleming reattached Amber's rope to his own suit, then reached into his rucksack for the palm-top computer Virginia had given him, laid it in his hand and checked the screen. 'We're not going down. We're going up.' He waved at the open pipe ten feet above them. 'If I've read this plan correctly, that's an overflow pipe from the original Alascon oil-rig. The pipeline probably cuts through the mountain towards the refinery on the eastern mountain, which isn't far from the rangers' station. It should be relatively easy to move along – it's protected from the elements and those bastards shouldn't be able to follow us.'

Even as he indicated the wolves, the larger animal was backing away from the ledge preparing for a leap.

Fleming moved to the ice wall at the end of the ledge. 'Stand back from the edge and keep your hand on the carabiners – sorry, that's the snap rings on the rope linking you to me. If I fall, unsnap them or I'll drag you down with me.'

She gave him a horrified look. 'And let the wolves get me? I'm not touching any damn snap rings. Just make sure you don't fall. You're supposed to be good at this.'

Fleming planted his left ice pick in the sheer face, used his right boot to kick out the first foothold and pulled himself up. Then he planted his right pick higher up and kicked in his left boot. Climbing fluidly, he reached the pipe with little difficulty. Inside it resembled a manmade cave, damp and dark but infinitely more inviting than the bleakness and the wolves outside. He could feel a current of warmer air blowing from inside the mountain.

He looked down, and saw the first wolf leap across the gap. He braced his legs and tugged on the rope, hoping Amber wouldn't slip, but the wolf gave her impetus and he pulled her into the pipe before it caught her.

They paused for a moment to watch the wolves baying helplessly below, then turned and walked into the mountain.

There was an uphill gradient to the pipeline but a flat track running along the base acted like steps. They walked in silence for almost fifteen minutes, when Fleming became aware of a change in the air. The subtle current was now a warm breeze and he could smell something too. 'That's odd.

Bradley told me his father never produced oil here.'

'He didn't,' said Amber. 'He made a strike but died before the rig began to produce. Bradley closed everything down and sealed up the borehole when he sold Alascon Oil and converted the rig to VenTec.' She stopped in her tracks. 'Look!'

Ahead, through the gloom, Fleming could see the most bizarre sight: a stroboscopic light show accompanied by a whirring hum. The breeze was now so strong he felt the warm air pushing against him. As he approached he had to turn his eyes away from the source of light above him because it was so bright, but by keeping his eyes down and squinting he could take in his surroundings. They had arrived at a crossroads where the pipe they were walking along bisected the central borehole. Below was a vast circular hole, at least thirty feet wide and blocked with an iron plug some twenty feet down. In the centre of the plug was a projecting pipe, which Fleming guessed was the top of the drill bit. The smell was strong here and he guessed that somewhere down in the murky abyss beneath the iron cap was oil. A dilapidated gantry ran across the borehole offering access to the other side.

A glance upwards told Fleming that a vast fan, sucking in cooler air, pushing out hot air, was producing the light show. Above it he could hear a now familiar hum. This and the bright light told him what was overhead.

Stepping forward, he checked the gantry: although it was corroded, it seemed sound. 'Come on,' he said, 'let's get a move on.'

The wind from the fan threatened to blow him off the gantry, and the blinding light meant he had to look down into the unnerving pit.

'God, it looks like it goes down to hell itself,' he heard Amber say behind him. She rested a hand on his shoulder, and when they reached the other side they breathed audible sighs of relief.

From here the pipeline sloped downwards and Fleming was encouraged. The lower the pipe exited on the other side of the mountain, the less climbing Amber would have to do. They walked in silence for half an hour until they came to a fork.

'Which way?' Amber said.

'I have no idea, but my hunch is to take the easterly one – the left. That should take us closest to where we want to be. I can also feel some air coming from there.'

'Okay,' she said, and stepped forward into the left tunnel, taking the lead.

As he watched her small form walk ahead, his mind wandered to the strange look of understanding that had passed between Amber and Soames when she had challenged the Red Pope's announcement, and Soames's cryptic remark: *I think now you understand why I can't let you or Miles live.*

What the hell had he meant by that?

'Amber?'

'Yes?'

'What did Bradley—'

Amber stumbled and disappeared. She screamed, 'I'm falling, Miles!'

Fleming braced his legs, gripping the rope that

341

still joined them together. She was falling too fast, though, and it snapped taut. He fell on to his stomach and was dragged along the pipe. Ahead the incline fell away sharply, like a chute, and beyond he could see only snow and the dark, cold night. This was another overflow pipe. It had spewed Amber out of the mountain into thin air and was trying to do the same to him. He tried to dig in his crampons and boots but couldn't get any purchase on the sheer iron.

'Cut the rope!' Amber shouted. 'Please cut the fucking rope!'

In desperation he thrust his ice picks into the metal pipe, trying to get a grip, the friction sparking like a subway train with its emergency brakes on.

Just feet from the mouth of the pipe he heard a crack and experienced the white-heat of pain in his right arm as he flipped round to dangle feet first out of the pipe. But at least he had stopped falling. Somehow the tip of the pick in his right hand had anchored itself to a protrusion in one of the weld seams. Quickly he thrust in his left pick to ease the pressure on his strained right arm. The rope round his waist was pulling at his arms but he was grateful for the survival suit's internal wire framework, which helped spread Amber's weight through his body. But he had no foothold. He couldn't pull her up. Gritting his teeth, he wondered how long he would be able to hold on.

In her dreams of dying, Amber was falling through blackness towards death. But this time there was no light ahead of her, only more darkness. And this was no dream.

The first thing she was aware of was that the ground had fallen away from her feet and then, almost immediately, she was out of the pipe and in free fall.

When she felt the first yank as the rope went taut she sighed with relief, but then she began to fall again and realized she was pulling Fleming with her.

Seconds later her fall was broken for a second time. Suspended by the ring on the front of her suit she lay on her back in the dark, the light from her helmet torch illuminating the flecks of snow swirling around her in the void.

'Miles, what's happening?'

'It's not good.'

'Cut the rope, then.'

I'm not cutting any more goddamn ropes.'

She was surprised by the aggression in his voice. 'But . . .' She paused. 'I'm sorry.'

There was a moment of silence.

'What were you going to ask me before I fell?' she asked.

'It was about Bradley and what the Red Pope said. But it hardly matters now. I guess I'll find out the answers myself soon enough.'

'I guess we both will,' she said.

Hanging in the gusting air, looking down into the gloom, she thought, This is it. I'm going to die. I'm actually going to die. At last.

She felt no fear: instead there was anger and a burning sense of injustice. She also experienced

343

a sudden and surprising stab of sadness for Fleming and herself, which filled her with a wistful sense of what might have been.

Miles knew he was near the end, but inches to his left he could see a tantalizingly close series of handholds in the form of a line of proud rivets running down a vertical seam in the pipe. Just above his feet the bottom of the pipe was curled into a broad lip, which formed the perfect foothold if he could just raise his feet high enough to perch on it. But with Amber's body weight pulling him down, these havens, inches away, might as well have been miles out of reach. He would only find safety if he released Amber's rope, but after Rob he wasn't about to cut any ropes and help anyone else go to their death.

'I guess we've all got to die some time,' he heard Amber say. There was no fear in her voice but he detected sadness. And a frustration that matched his indignation.

'Yep. We're going to die some day,' he muttered, through clenched teeth, 'but it's not going to be today.'

57

The red sector

Frank Carvelli was not a brave man: he had poise, a certain presence when required, but this wasn't one of those situations. Following Bradley Soames down into the red sector made his bowels feel loose. He had never been to this part of the VenTec Foundation before and was unsure of the dubious privilege of being invited down here now.

Carvelli had always prided himself on his ability to turn events to his advantage by understanding the ebb and flow of human needs and desires. His media and film production empire was founded on it: he knew what the public wanted and could charm his business partners. His affiliation with the Red Pope had done wonders for the KREE8 profile: his company's presentation technology had helped the world's first electronic Church come into existence and his grasp of public relations and producing movies had allowed him to guide Accosta's use of the technology to make an already media-friendly personality into a phenomenon.

But if Accosta's Church had provided the opportunity to showcase KREE8's products on the world stage, Bradley Soames had provided the technological expertise and resources to maximize them. Without Soames and VenTec's research input, KREE8 would have remained unexceptional in the communications technology arena.

Carvelli thought he had played Soames well, convincing the man to give him the fruits of his genius for a fraction of their market value, all in the name of helping the Red Pope's grand plan, the Soul Project. But now he realized that in fact Soames had managed him. It was becoming increasingly evident that Soames had manipulated everyone, including the Red Pope, to satisfy his own agenda. Whatever that agenda was.

'Put these on,' Soames ordered, handing him a pair of eye protectors. As the elevator stopped, Carvelli could see a blue-white light leaking in beneath the door. Soames was rearranging his clothing to cover his skin, and by the time the doors opened he resembled a cowled monk.

'Do you understand what this is?' Soames asked, as Carvelli stood on the steel gantry and looked down the borehole into the sphere of pulsating light energy.

Carvelli stared at the orb for some moments before replying. He marvelled at the sparks flickering inside the sphere like sunspots. As his eyes became accustomed to the light he noticed the laboratories that encircled the orb. Through the curved tinted viewing windows of one he could see a replica of Fleming's NeuroTranslator and

Soames's soul-capture head-sphere. But the main viewing area was decked out with consoles and monitors, and a host of peripheral equipment. 'It's a computer,' he whispered, in awe of the vast power the twenty-foot-diameter sphere must contain. 'It's a huge optical computer.'

'It's more than that, Frank. Far more.' Soames's voice changed. His usual aloof detachment was gone, replaced by pride. 'This is our Lord's power made manifest, the instrument for spreading his dark enlightenment across the globe. This furnace of white-hot heat and light will forge the four nails to be hammered into the coffin of faith. Through its power the four signs promised by Satan and revealed by the Red Pope's lost soul will be delivered.'

Carvelli's anxiety increased. It was all he could do to stop himself shaking. His voice didn't sound like his own when he said, 'That's why you weren't surprised by the Red Pope's revelation. You already knew who our master was, because you've always served him.' He was horrified by the depths of Soames's deceit.

There was a sound to his left and Carvelli turned to see the elevator door open. Bukowski and Tripp stepped out, followed by the wolves, their muzzles caked with blood.

'Amber and Miles?' Soames demanded, as the wolves moved to stand beside him.

Her face impassive, Bukowski shook her head. 'No sign. The wolves returned without finding them. They've probably fallen off the mountain. And, if not, it's unlikely they'll survive. The weather's getting worse, and although Amber Grant's many things, she isn't a climber.'

'But Miles is,' said Soames.

Carvelli ignored the exchange. He was still trying to come to terms with Soames's agenda. 'You've *always* served Satan,' he said again, as if hoping that by repeating it the revelation would become less shocking.

'No,' barked Bukowski and Tripp in unison, turning on Carvelli as if he had uttered a blasphemy.

'Don't you understand?' demanded Bukowski, with a chilling half-smile as she and Tripp looked towards Soames. '*We* serve him.'

Turning to the cowled figure of Soames, who was silhouetted with his wolves against the bright light radiating from the sphere, Carvelli's bowels loosened. He couldn't help it: he had never known fear like this before. 'Who are you?'

'Who do you think I am?' Soames answered.

Whimpering, Carvelli could only stare. Suddenly he understood, with sickening, terrifying clarity.

Soames stepped towards him. 'Now, let me explain why Amber and Miles can't be allowed to threaten what's in place.'

Trembling, smelling the reek of his own fear, Carvelli listened.

'Now that you understand everything, only one question remains,' Soames said, when he had finished. 'Are you with me or, like Virginia, against me?'

Carvelli looked at Soames and then at the wolves, standing tense beside him. He tried to speak, but his mouth wouldn't function. All he could do was kneel and hang his head in submission.

'Would you do something for me?' Soames asked.

'Anything,' Carvelli rasped. 'Anything at all.'

Soames nodded with satisfaction. 'Take the helicopter to Fairbanks. You can use my plane from there. It's a little matter. An extra insurance policy.'

58

Climbers call the phenomenon the third-man syndrome: the sense, when climbing in pairs, of an invisible but benign guiding presence. Arctic explorers have reported the same sensation. Fleming had experienced it on a few occasions with his brother, usually when they were exhausted, hungry and at the end of their endurance. Afterwards, Rob always confirmed that he had felt it too.

This time it was different. As Fleming gripped the ice pick handles, his joints and muscles burning, there was no third presence. But even as his hands numbed and it became hard to breathe he did feel something: the strange sensation of strong hands closing around his wrists. Husbanding his remaining reserves he prepared for one last desperate lift, hoping he could gain enough height to plant his feet on the bottom of the pipe and take the weight off his arms.

He hadn't been able do it before when he was relatively fresh, but now he had nothing to lose. He gritted his teeth, tensed his biceps and tried to raise his body. He strained as hard as he could but barely lifted himself an inch. Then he felt the hands around his wrists grip him tighter, as though supporting him.

He pulled with every vestige of strength he had left and raised his right leg as high as he could. To his surprise his foot came to rest on the lip of the pipe. A burst of energy surged through him. He brought his other foot on to the lip, then reached across for the handholds provided by the rivets.

Pausing momentarily for breath, terrified that if he stopped for long his new-found energy might leak away, he clambered up the holds supplied by the rivets using his boots, crampons and ice picks for purchase, lifting his and Amber's weight higher up the pipe.

With each inch gained his strength seemed to grow, until he found himself back in the horizontal section of pipe and could hear Amber scrabbling over the lip, gaining her own purchase on the metal. When the rope went slack and they were safe, his strength evaporated and he rolled on to his back. Seconds later Amber was bending over him, her eyes wide with concern and something else: something he couldn't place.

'How did you do that?' she asked.

He was too breathless to speak.

'That was impossible.'

'Strange things happen in the mountains,' he rasped.

She laughed at that and despite Fleming's exhaustion, a core of hope glowed within him.

He pulled himself to his feet and took Amber's

arm. 'We can't hang about here. We need to get to the refinery and find our way down to the rangers' station.'

After the initial elation had subsided, Amber didn't care how Fleming had saved them. The fact that he had was enough.

Retracing their steps to the fork, they headed in what they hoped was the direction of the refinery. As they walked on in the darkness, it dawned on her that although he knew her medical past and most of the significant events in her life, she knew little about him, but before she could question him he said, 'It's pretty clear to me that what we heard and saw was no hoax. I've seen the technology – hell, I developed some of it – and one of the signs that Accosta's soul predicted has already manifested itself. But you aren't convinced, are you?'

'I had another dream,' she said, 'but I know what you think of my dreams . . .'

Fleming grinned. 'I deserved that. But that was then and this is now. I've become a lot more open-minded. Tell me about your dream – or whatever it was.'

'Like you, I believe the Red Pope's announcement wasn't a hoax, but I also think it wasn't the only truth or all the truth.'

'Why?'

'Because I think . . . I *know* I've seen what happens after death. I know where my sister's gone because she showed me. I can't go into specifics because what I saw was indescribable – but she's gone to a good place. Not only did I see it, I *felt* it. It's a place beyond suffering. A safe, sun-lit plane where the shadow of pain can't reach. The nearest I can get to describing it is as a state of bliss.'

Fleming was staring at her, his face luminous with fresh hope. She knew he was thinking of his brother and wanted to reassure him, as Ariel had reassured her. 'All I know,' she said softly, 'is that what I saw wasn't the hopeless, damned place the Red Pope described.'

'I want to believe you,' he said.

She smiled. 'Well, believe me. All you need is faith.'

Fleming gave a noncommittal shrug. 'What I can't figure out is why Bradley revels in the Red Pope's announcement. It's like he wanted it, hoped for it.'

Amber struggled to bring into focus a bunch of unformed thoughts that swirled in the back of her mind. 'I know,' she said. 'That worries me too. And that's why we've got to get word out because I've a scary feeling he's enjoying this.'

A gust of cold wind blew across them and Fleming's arm shot out to stop her walking any further forward. 'This must be the end of the pipe.' He pointed ahead and Amber could see moonlight and stars. 'The storm seems to have passed. Look, you can see what's left of the refinery out there.'

She was relieved to see that the pipe led out on to level ground, although it was thick with snow and the lower section of the exit was submerged in a drift. Beyond it, looming in the moonlight, she could make out the framework of various unfinished structures, including two vast cylindrical cages, designed to house oil-storage tanks. 'It's so cold out there,' she said. 'Why don't we stay in here and get some rest before heading off in the morning? We've still got time before the next signs appear.' She glanced hopefully at Fleming.

'Okay,' he said. 'We can eat some of our rations from the bag and get some sleep. There's some warmth in here but it's going to get pretty cold once we stop moving and the energy in our kinetic boots runs out. We'll be okay if we huddle up close, though.'

She kept her voice deadpan. 'I've experienced worse horrors recently.'

59

Atlantic Ocean

Further south, day had dawned, and Carvelli sat wide awake in the only occupied passenger seat of Soames's private jet as it sped to London. He felt as if he would never sleep again. He had only one aim: to fulfil his mission.

He dismissed any notion of defying Soames or running away. There was nowhere he could run to – in this life or the next. Just thinking about Soames and what he'd told him made Carvelli break out in a sweat. His once immaculate appearance was deteriorating: his skin was pale and blotchy, his hair dishevelled and his black clothing rumpled.

The phone rang in the armrest of his leather seat, making him jump. He picked it up. 'Yes?'

'I was told to ring this number,' said a mild Scottish accent. 'I understand you're to collect a package and it isn't to be harmed.'

Carvelli had never met the man before but he had seen a picture of him and recognized the voice. Soames and Knight had used him in the past – on the Soul Project. *God, that seems so long ago now*, he thought. 'That's right. And I'm supposed to bring the – the – *package* safely back to America today. As soon as possible.'

'No problem,' said the voice. 'We'll be waiting at Heathrow for you. We've done a recce and we know where it is. Judging from its size and condition, it'll be easy to handle.' A laugh. 'Should be child's play.'

Carvelli didn't feel like laughing as he hung up. He felt sick.

The sound of wolves howling woke Fleming before the light did. Ignoring the pain in his muscles, he shook Amber awake.

She sat upright immediately. 'What was that?' She blinked, 'Where are they?'

'Don't know, but we've got to get a move on.' He looked out of the pipe at the incongruous shapes of the refinery construction site. The sun was low and bathed the scene in a weak, flat light. In a few weeks it would disappear for the winter. A thick crust of fresh snow lay everywhere but the wind wasn't as strong as it had been last night and the sky was relatively clear.

Amber stood up then collapsed again, holding her right leg. 'Shit.'

He grabbed it, and could feel straight away the knotted thigh muscles through her suit. Silently he kneaded them, despite her cries of protest, and only let go when he was satisfied the muscle was adequately loosened.

She scowled as she tested her leg.

'Sorry, but at least you can walk now,' he said.

'And it'll hurt a lot more if the wolves get us.'

Despite the thick snow they made good progress, and although they heard wolves they didn't see any as they passed through the refinery. It was eerily still and silent, the structures towering above them like snow-covered tombstones.

After three hours, they stopped for a break, ate chocolate from the rucksack and melted some snow in the portable stove to make coffee. For a few glorious moments the sun came out and Fleming even dared to forget their circumstances.

Then they heard the wolves again. Closer.

Perhaps it was because they were nearing the bottom of the descent, or perhaps because he was enjoying being out there with Amber, but when he swung the rucksack back on to his shoulder he took his next step without probing the ground ahead. He plummeted through the snow, through a gap in the ledge, dragging Amber and the overhang of fresh snow with him. Then he was careening blindly down the mountain, cursing his stupidity, bracing himself for impact with rocks. The rucksack was pulled off him, and twice he felt Amber's boots in his back. Curling into a ball, he lost track of how long they fell but it seemed interminable. When he stopped he was submerged, unsure which way was up. He pulled the rope and was encouraged to feel Amber tug the other end.

He straightened from the foetal position and allowed a dribble of spit to fall from his mouth – Rob had taught him to use the flow of saliva to test the direction of gravity. Now he knew which way was up and began to dig. Soon he could see watery sunlight filtering through the translucent snow above.

Within seconds his head was exposed and he was looking at a copse of firs, then Amber popped up beside him, gasping for breath. He clambered out of the snow and pulled her after him. Then he brushed himself down, concerned about the missing rucksack and the palm-top. But just as he thought of going back to look for them, Amber pointed down the valley. 'Look.' Following the direction of her finger, he saw a collection of huts nestling in the snow. 'Is that it?' she asked.

He looked around him, at the vast, mountainous, uninhabited, snow-covered expanse, and had to smile at the question. 'Yep,' he said. 'I guess it is.'

60

Rangers' station. National Wildlife Refuge Reserve

As Virginia Knight had told them, the rangers' station was deserted. A large sign by the snow-covered main cabin explained that from mid-October to late March the site was manned on a temporary basis. It consisted of three cabins and a series of computer-controlled concrete bins that released animal feed, depending on temperature and elapsed time, throughout the winter. When the human population moved out the animals moved in. The place was crawling with well-fed wolves and the sky was dotted with high-flying birds of prey.

Amber marvelled at the mountain behind her. She could see the plateau at the top but no sign of the refinery or the peak of the higher mountain next to it. It disappeared into the clouds so there was no way of knowing if VenTec was ever visible from here.

Fleming went to the main cabin, which had a laser communication antenna and satellite dish on the roof, and was about to break open the door when Amber pointed at a wooden box to the right of the door. A small neat sign informed them that:

All travelers are welcome to take shelter in this cabin and use the facilities within. All we ask is that you leave it as you found it, replenish all supplies and keep animals out. Any donations can be left in the metal tin and visitors are requested to complete the guest book. Lock up when you leave and place the key in this box.

Thank you for your interest in the wildlife of our beautiful state.

John Mahoney. Head Ranger

National Wildlife Refuge Reserve. Arctic region. Alaska.

Amber fished out the keys and opened the door. Inside, the cabin was surprisingly sophisticated, well insulated and furnished, with all the technical equipment they could wish for. There was an optical computer in the corner, with its own monitor, and a video-conference plasma screen beside a matt black communication unit, complete with video-link camera, satellite phone, keyboard and fax. After her initial surprise, Amber realized that the equipment was a necessity in this isolated place. 'Good kit,' she said, powering up the Lucifer optical computer.

Fleming picked up the satellite phone. 'Works too. Place must have its own generator.'

Amber gave a nod of satisfaction when she saw the Optinet portal appear.

Fleming dialled a number on the phone keypad. 'Can you put me through to the FBI? I don't know.

Headquarters? Washington's fine.' There was a pause, then Amber heard him say, 'Hi, I need to speak to the guy heading up the inquiry into the Red Pope investigation. Sure. I understand you're busy with all that's going on. Just get a message to him. I assure you he'll want to talk to us. Tell him Amber Grant and Miles Fleming need to contact him. I was the guy who helped create some of the equipment used by the Red Pope for his announcement. Tell him we've got information. Yeah. Can you get him to call me . . . Hello? What? Sure, I'll hold.'

Within four minutes a video-link had been established with Associate Director Morgan Jones's temporary command centre aboard the Red Ark. The definition was excellent and on the plasma screen above the communication console Amber could see the cavernous ballroom. In the background technical agents in shirtsleeves were sitting at trestle tables poring over computer screens. Styrofoam coffee cups littered every available surface while large video screens showed news coverage from around the world. In the foreground a lean black man, Associate Director Morgan Jones, in a dark blue suit, white shirt and shoulder holster, paced around a conference table at which three other men were sitting.

'Could you both move closer to your vidcam. I need to verify your IDs,' Jones said.

Amber and Fleming took off their helmets, moved closer to the console and peered into the camera lens. Amber was suddenly self-conscious about her shaven hair: it was growing back and her head was covered in a downy fuzz, but she guessed that she didn't closely resemble any reference shot Jones had on his screen. Nevertheless, he seemed satisfied, and was either too gallant or preoccupied to comment.

'We've been looking everywhere for you guys. Dr Grant, you were reported missing some time ago and the fellow who reported it has been working with us on this Red Pope mess.' He turned and gestured behind him to a figure in black, threading its way through the rows of tech agents, towards the conference table. Amber smiled when she recognized her godfather. 'Father Riga was at the service as one of the senior members of the Catholic Church invited to witness the event. He and other religious leaders have been trying to help us make sense of what happened.'

'Amber, thank God,' Papa Pete said, as he reached the table. 'Dr Fleming. Where are you now? After you came to visit me, we had you followed – for your own protection,' he added hurriedly, 'but we lost contact with you in San Francisco.'

Fleming frowned. 'You suspected something when I saw you in Rome?'

Riga sat down and folded his arms across his chest. He looked unrepentant. 'Yeah, but I wasn't sure what. The Jesuits had monitored the Red Pope's services for some time and we figured he was planning something big. When you contacted me about Amber's soul wavelength, I made some connections.'

'And we've been trying discreetly to find Amber

362

Grant ever since,' added Jones. 'But after the Red Pope's Day of the Soul Truth we've had our hands full trying to control the panic. Tell us where you are and what you know about the event.'

Amber and Fleming exchanged a look. Between them they explained how they had escaped to the rangers' cabin, then filled in the details of the last week. Amber recounted her abduction and the experiments. Fleming talked about how he had been duped by Soames into developing a more advanced NeuroTranslator compatible with Soames's soul-capture technology. He explained how Soames had already proved the existence of the human soul, making it visible at the moment of death and capturing its signature on a photon-detector screen, but needed Amber to find the locking frequency to trace the departing soul and his NeuroTranslator to communicate with it.

'Basically, between us, Amber and I gave him the missing pieces of the jigsaw to make the Day of the Soul Truth possible.'

'So it was genuine, then?' asked one of the FBI technical agents. He had a portable optical computer in front of him. 'We couldn't find any sign of a hoax but I kind of hoped you were going to explain how they'd rigged it.'

'It might have been genuine,' Father Peter interjected. 'Our own scientists in Rome concede that. But it was still a trick of sorts.'

Fleming sighed. Amber could almost hear him thinking, Why are priests always so bloody sure of everything? 'I wish I could tell you it wasn't true,' he said. 'I really do. But the technology is genuine.

That was the Red Pope's soul we heard, I'm sure of it.'

'So there really is no God and we've got to prepare for the other signs?' the associate director asked baldly. His lean dark face looked grey.

'Not necessarily,' Amber said, making a sudden connection.

Fleming turned to her and smiled. Then he looked back at the vidcam. 'She had a dream.'

'No,' she said, reaching for the computer beside her. 'It's more than that.'

61

It was something to do with the way in which
Soames had reacted to the Red Pope's revelation
. . . not just accepting it, but welcoming it – almost
expecting it. What had he said to Virginia Knight
when they were escaping?

'Oh, but I was. I was always a believer, Virginia.
I still am. It's just that neither you nor Accosta ever
thought to ask me *who* I believed in.'

It was the combination of his eagerness to
embrace the Red Pope's revelation and the contrasting vision Ariel had shown her in the dream
that had made her reach for the computer.

Using the track pad on the top right of the keyboard, she activated the on-screen Optinet icon to
get access to the optical Internet. Within seconds
she had called up the Optrix portal and used her
own personal access code to enter Optrix's Data
Security Provider. With the advent of the optical
Internet, speed and weight of traffic were no
longer an issue but security was: data travelled at
such quicksilver speeds on the Optinet that information thieves could raid a company or an

individual's data files and escape with their booty before the victim could blink.

Since the international data security agreement of 2004, hardly any company or individual stored their own data. Virtually everyone was now linked up to the Optinet and subscribed to third-party Data Security Providers or DSPs. Using quantum codes, these data banks were regarded as hacker-proof and security was guaranteed. Each subscriber was given a randomly generated code, known by no one else, including the DSP.

Using her code, Amber accessed the Optrix DSP. Once she was in, she used the search engine to check the Optrix corporate client archive, paying particular attention to international utilities. It took her less than three minutes to confirm her suspicion.

'What's this dream you had, Amber?' the associate director asked.

Amber rubbed her eyes then briefly explained, concluding, 'All I'm saying is that it convinced me the Red Pope's truth wasn't the *only* truth.'

'Of course it wasn't the only truth,' Riga agreed. 'What Accosta saw was the truth of a damned man, a man excommunicated from the Mother Church. What your sister saw was the virtuous truth of the Catholic—'

Angrily Fleming shook his head. 'Have you learnt nothing? How do you know this has anything to do with being a Catholic – or even a Christian? If Accosta saw a vision of Hell it was because he arrogantly thought he knew all the answers and killed people to prove it. Whereas

Amber's sister lived a good life – it's as simple as that. It's got nothing to do with religion.'

'The point,' said Riga, unfazed, 'is that we're at war for the souls of humanity. God has allowed the Devil to test us, and we must rise to the challenge. Until now everyone believed the greatest trick Satan could play was convincing us he didn't exist. But that ain't true. His greatest trick's convincing us that *only* he exists. That's why it's imperative the signs are stopped.'

'That's not the only reason,' said Jones. 'It might be your job to save our eternal souls, Father, but I'm more concerned here about our living bodies. If I remember my Bible then the four horsemen of the Apocalypse don't exactly bring health, wealth and happiness to the world.'

'Could someone remind an embarrassed atheist what each of these horsemen does bring?' Fleming asked.

Riga leant forward in his chair, his lined face grave and unsmiling. 'According to the Book of Revelation the four horsemen ride on different coloured mounts. The first is a white rider, who spreads civil unrest; the next a red rider who brings war, then a black rider with famine. The final horseman is the pale rider.'

'What does he bring?'

'Death.'

There was a beat, then Fleming spoke again. 'Will they come in that order?'

Riga shrugged. 'All we know is that the first sign has already spread civil unrest and, according to the Red Pope, the third and fourth will arrive together.'

'Otherwise we know diddly,' the FBI man said. 'We've got no real way of knowing in what order they'll come or in what form.' He checked his watch. 'Mind you, we'll know soon enough. The second sign's due at any time.'

'The signs will be engineered by man,' Riga declared.

'How do you mean?'

'God is testing us. He won't bring a natural disaster. He's testing our free will. The civil unrest, the first sign, came about as a result of power cuts and Accosta's announcement. I think the others will occur in a similar way. He'll use people, tempting them to do evil. The signs will be man-made. Accosta himself predicted that an "agent on earth" would bring the signs.'

'That's what I was trying to tell you,' Amber said. 'I think I know who the agent on earth is.'

Fleming understood. 'Bradley.'

'Yup. I've looked in the Optrix database and confirmed that every single city around the world that suffered power cuts employs a highly sophisticated computerized system to manage their utilities. All these systems are optical based and use key components bought, either directly or indirectly, from Optrix.'

Associate Director Jones frowned. 'You're saying that Bradley Soames was behind the power cut?'

'Yup.'

'But why?'

'He's a pawn of Satan,' said Riga, matter-of-factly. 'He has taken on the task of fulfilling the signs to convince the world that the Red Pope's revelation was the one and only truth. He serves the Devil and intends to kill faith in God.'

The FBI chief looked sceptical. 'What do you think, Amber? He was your partner.'

Amber had always thought she knew Soames better than anyone, but his recent actions didn't tally with the man she had thought she knew – the man who had changed the world for the good and given away millions in philanthropy and for medical research. *Could* he have some strange affinity with a darker power? A shiver ran through her when she remembered the time he had woken her from her dream and she had looked into his eyes. 'Frankly, I don't know why he's doing it,' she said. 'What do you think, Miles?'

He rubbed his chin. 'I wouldn't use quite the same language as Father Riga, but for once I find myself agreeing with him. Whatever Bradley's motives, he's committed to proving Accosta right.'

'How?' demanded one of the tech agents. 'All those systems are protected by qubit codes.'

'Yeah, and even if he could break some,' said another, 'just orchestrating every city to power up and power down with the rising and setting of the sun would require an incredible feat of computer muscle . . .'

Amber caught Fleming's eye and could see he was thinking the same as her. 'Soames is a very bright guy,' she said, 'and he's got a computer with the necessary muscle.'

'I saw it in the red sector beneath VenTec,' Fleming agreed. 'It's a massive ball of light in the main borehole of the rig. Right down in the heart of the mountain.'

'I helped build the early prototype,' said Amber. 'It was pretty powerful then, certainly capable of cracking codes and manipulating other computers on-line, and Bradley's refined it since. His dream was always to go beyond the basics of optical computers and create one with genuine quantum capabilities – what he called the Last Computer. It's capable of ten to the power of fifty-one operations per second – that's one with fifty-one zeroes after it – but its photonic quantum bits or qubits can employ an unimaginable number of superpositional states, allowing it to process infinite calculations simultaneously. Breaking quantum codes isn't a problem for a machine of this power.' She looked down at her computer and began tapping keys. 'I'll see if I can use a double S to find it on the web, and then I'll try to access its database, but it won't be easy.'

The two FBI technical agents at the table, who were specialists in state-of-the-art computer and electronics technology, were bewildered. 'What's a "double S"?' one asked.

'A stealth seeker,' Amber replied. 'Something we've been developing at Optrix. Basically it's an intelligent virus, a package of quantum code that I can send down the optical Internet to search for things. It will find any site I tell it to and then, without being detected, work out how to gain access to its data before reporting back.'

It took her seven minutes to construct the stealth seeker and tap in the search parameters before sending it on its way. 'Done,' she said, with a satisfied smile. 'It's on its own now, searching the Optinet. It should report back in about—'

Her screen froze and began to fizz, a stream of data scrolling crazily up and down the monitor. A bizarre screeching sound like a fax emanated from the speakers.

'What the hell was that?' the tech agent said, from the unaffected video conference screen.

'I don't know,' Amber said. 'I didn't do it.'

Pandemonium was breaking out behind Associate Director Jones. The lines of agents in front of their computers were staring at their screens and she could see, from the few that were visible, that they were all fizzing like hers.

The phone rang beside Jones and he picked it up. 'I understand,' he said. 'Yeah, I'll check it out.' He put the phone down. 'That was Washington. The Hoover building and the Quantico Academy have the same problem. Their databases are going mad and apparently it's not just the Bureau. This has been happening for the last few minutes and it's pretty widespread. Turn one of the screens to BBC.'

Suddenly there were scenes of the New York Stock Exchange: people stood in shocked silence on the dealing floor as, above them, the giant screens giving prices for blue-chip stock went as crazy as Amber's. 'Wall Street is reeling,' a commentator was saying. 'Institutions across the globe are trying to come to grips with a phenomenon that makes past fears of the Y2K bug a fond memory. A world already in shock is asking itself one question: is this the Red Pope's second sign?'

As if on cue, the giant Wall Street screen featured in the live report went blank. Moments later, so did Amber's. Then, almost immediately, she was back on-line, and so were the others.

With one important difference.

There was no longer any data on any of the screens. Every single monitor showed only row upon row of zeroes.

62

The black sector conference room

The chaos and panic of the second sign far outweighed that caused by the first. Every stock and share price in every bourse in the world, from Wall Street to the Hang Seng, was reset to zero. Every bank account of every corporation, government and individual was wiped out at a single stroke. Credit cards didn't work in stores or online. Cash machines wouldn't operate because they couldn't identify customers' smart cards or locate money in any accounts.

But it went much further than the financial markets and the banks. Criminal records were expunged from every computerized database in the world – from the FBI in Washington to Interpol in Paris and Scotland Yard in London. Government records of citizenship, tax liability and voting rights vanished. Medical insurance policies, academic records, including exam results and school registers, were wiped clean. Scientific research files and medical records were erased. Military data and personnel records disappeared. Each of the high security Data Security Providers on the optical Internet was raided and all the data stored in them deleted. Every online computer database, website, archive, library and storage facility in existence was purged. If something wasn't printed, stored offline, written down or remembered, it was gone. It was as if the mind and memory of the entire technological world had been obliterated.

Bradley Soames sat in the black sector conference room, watching the hysterical news bulletins from around the world. All was chaos and panic, and it was good.

Rising from his chair, he walked towards the red sector elevator. The wolves followed him. In the elevator the humming was louder than usual and he looked down through the tinted-glass floor of the cabin. The orb of light beneath him was fiercely beautiful, pulsing as he'd never seen it before. Streaks of lightning seemed to shoot around the inside of the sphere, giving it the appearance of a sunstorm. The elevator stopped just above it. The light-sealed doors opened on to the control room and the laboratories that surrounded the borehole.

Tripp and Bukowski stood at the bank of terminals that controlled the computer. Bukowski turned to him, her eyes shining.

'How's it going?' he asked. 'Any retrieval or capacity problems?'

Bukowski laughed. 'It's incredible,' she said. 'We haven't even deployed a fraction of its capacity and transmission has been even better than we could ever have imagined. No data corruption whatsoever.'

Soames wasn't surprised, but he was relieved. He tried to control his growing impatience to finish this, reminding himself that everything was on schedule and it was his duty to adhere to the predicted timings to fulfil the signs. The last two would arrive together and on time as announced, and then his mission on this earth would be accomplished.

A phone rang. Tripp picked it up then handed it to him.

It was Carvelli. 'The insurance policy is in place and on its way,' he said.

'Excellent,' Soames replied. 'Come directly to my quarters when you arrive.'

He sat down and watched the fireball of harnessed light through the tinted viewing window. Sighing, he picked a piece of flaking skin off his forearm and fed it absently to a wolf. Tiredness swept through him, born of decades of waiting, planning and knowing.

It's almost over, he told himself again, quelling the almost intolerable need to bring the final signs forward and finish it now.

You're so close now, he cautioned himself. *It's only a matter of time before your purpose is finally fulfilled.*

63

The rangers' station

Fleming didn't share the panic that had descended on the world. He was thinking about Soames. Knowing that the man was behind this helped somehow: it offered him the chance of redemption because at last he had someone to fight, someone who could explain the Red Pope's announcement.

And explaining Soames's technology to the FBI had rekindled a memory; something Soames had said about each soul having a unique barcode. It had given him an idea, which offered the hope of finally contacting Rob's soul and proving that he was free of suffering. For now, though, he had to help resolve the chaos and disorder that surrounded him.

Apart from a few blips, communications were largely unaffected by the data crisis, and computers were soon operational again, with software programs largely intact. However, the computers and their programs were empty husks, as if they had just been purchased. All stored information was gone; all databases had been erased. And it was the shocked expressions on the tech agents' faces that helped Fleming make the connection to the Red Pope's prediction. 'This is the second sign,' he said, looking at the zeroes on the screens.

Associate Director Jones stopped pacing and put down the phone into which he had been barking instructions. 'It's a goddamned disaster,' he said. 'The whole world's got Alzheimer's. Society's on its knees. The most basic transactions are impossible. Institutions have no way of knowing who anyone is or even what they are. But it doesn't fit with the four horsemen.'

'No, it doesn't,' agreed Riga.

Fleming rubbed his aching shoulder. 'Tell me again what the black rider brings?'

'Famine,' said Riga.

Fleming sat back and waited for everyone to stop their frantic activity and look at him. 'Isn't that exactly what we've got?' he said. 'An information famine.'

Amber patted his knee. 'Wait,' she said, tapping keys. 'I think you're right, Miles, but there's even more to it. The stealth seeker I sent out has returned. It couldn't hack into Bradley's computer – it's too powerful – but it has brought back some interesting information. There's been *colossal* data traffic going down the Optinet into it.' She exhaled. 'Do you want the good news or the bad?'

No one dared say anything.

'Well, the good news is that the data hasn't been deleted. It's potentially retrievable.'

'Where is it?' asked Jones.

'That's the bad news,' she said. 'Bradley Soames has it stored in his super-computer.'

'What?'

'It's possible,' said Amber. 'As far back as the turn of the millennium, scientists used Max Planck's "black body" formula to estimate that a photonic computer of one litre in volume could store ten to the power twenty times more data than an old ten-gigabyte hard drive. And the volume of Bradley Soames's computer is bigger than one litre.'

'It's a hell of a lot bigger,' said Fleming. 'The sphere I saw was at least twenty feet in diameter.'

'We've got to get the data back,' said Jones.

'We've got to do more than that,' said Fleming. 'Not only have we got to rescue the data, we've also got to close down his computer. It's obvious that Bradley Soames is using it to carry out the Red Pope's signs. He did it with the first and now this. It's safe to assume he'll use it to trigger the last two, which, according to the Red Pope, are due to happen together in a little over twenty-four hours. It seems he's decided to save the two big ones till last – his grand finale.'

'War and death,' said Riga, with a grim nod.

'Exactly,' said Fleming. 'And if they happen it's game over.' He turned to Amber. 'If you were Bradley, how would you use his computer to fulfil the last two signs?'

Amber leant back in her chair and rubbed her temples. Despite her exhaustion, her feline green eyes burned even brighter than usual and her fuzzy halo of hair had a softness about it that made

378

Fleming want to touch it. 'What would I do?' she mused. 'Well, given that virtually every computer system in the world is linked up to the Optinet, I'd activate one of the military installations. Perhaps one of the biological warfare containment labs at USAMRIID, or in Iraq or Israel—'

Associate Director Jones stopped his pacing. 'I wouldn't do that,' he said, with chilling calm. 'I'd open some missile silos and launch a few armed nuclear warheads.'

Fleming nodded. 'That would do it. That would lead to war and death – a lot of death. Any of this would be enough to precipitate war on a global scale.'

'We've got to destroy that computer,' Jones said quietly.

Amber grimaced. 'It's not as easy as that. If we destroy it we'll lose all the data. It could take years, decades, to restore the world's "mind". Some of the data is irreplaceable and if the current chaos isn't controlled soon, the world economy and infrastructure might be so damaged we won't be able to restore any of it – ever. This is entropy on a grand scale and it must be reversed. We must rescue the data before we destroy the computer.

'Also, Bradley will have installed electronic alarms and mines, so the instant the computer comes under attack it will trigger its commands. Any outright assault on VenTec or the computer will be counter-productive – bringing forward the last signs.'

'Can you disable it remotely, online?' asked one of the tech agents.

'It's too powerful and well protected. We've got to get inside VenTec and somehow physically reprogram the computer at source before Bradley becomes aware of it. That's the only way to retrieve the data and deactivate the computer's ability to trigger the final sign.'

'How the hell are we going to get at it without him triggering the signs?' asked Jones.

Fleming turned to Amber, who groaned when she realized what he was going to say. 'No way, Miles,' she said.

'Do you know anyone else who can reprogram that thing?' he asked.

Her shoulders slumped.

'Well,' Fleming said, with a grim smile, 'it looks like it's down to us.' He turned to the FBI chief. 'I think I know a way to get Amber in. We'll need equipment.'

'And back-up. The HRT team's on standby,' said Jones.

'HRT?' asked Fleming. *Hormone replacement therapy?*

'The Bureau's hostage rescue team. They're trained at getting into and out of places like this. We've got a squad at the Anchorage field office a few hours from you.'

'Okay,' said Fleming. 'We should also inform the army about the final signs.'

Jones gave a humourless laugh. 'Jeez,' he said, picking up the phone again, 'with something this big, I'm going to inform a hell of a lot more folks than the military.'

64

Ninety-two minutes later

Four additional video-conference screens had been set up in the FBI operations room aboard the Red Ark, positioned so that they were visible to Amber and Fleming. Three showed men in uniform.

One was Special-Agent-in-Charge Wayne Thomas, who headed up the hostage rescue team, and was currently in Anchorage, the FBI's field office in Alaska. A whip-thin man with a long face, he wore a dark blue FBI waterproof over a black flak jacket and combats. On the screen next to him was a man in army fatigues. Lieutenant-Colonel Mark Kovac, a career soldier with the prescription buzz-cut, headed up a section of Delta Force, the élite Special Forces division of the US army. He was communicating from a classified base two hundred miles south of the Canadian border. Kovac had a gift for looking bored, even when it was obvious that he was fully alert. Amber guessed his heart-rate was lower than that of most athletes. But for all his apparent casualness, she could tell he was itching to wrest command from the FBI.

There had already been a subtle jockeying for power: the Delta commander had intimated that this was a job for professionals, and the FBI agent had countered by emphasizing the need for 'appropriately trained' personnel. 'Surely you agree, Lieutenant-Colonel, that this mission requires the surgical precision of a scalpel rather than the brute force of a hammer.'

The testosterone-fuelled atmosphere made Amber uncomfortable but Fleming was unaffected by it – even when Kovac challenged him about returning to VenTec. 'You're a civilian, Dr Fleming. Just tell us all you know about the layout and leave it to us.'

Amber had turned to him in panic. She was frightened about going back up the mountain but at least she felt safe with Fleming. He exuded a physical confidence that Kovac couldn't match.

Fleming smiled at Kovac. 'I'm coming with you.'

'After we haul out of the Black Hawks it could still be a pretty tough climb,' Kovac said. 'We can support Dr Grant, but two of you will hold us back.'

'Don't worry about me,' Fleming said quietly. 'I'll keep up.'

'You climbed before?'

'A little.'

'What level?'

'What level are you, Lieutenant-Colonel?'

Kovac shrugged. 'Eighteen. But I've been trained.'

'How many levels are there?' asked Amber.

Fleming turned to her. 'The top level's thirty.

Rob was a twenty-seven. There are probably only a handful of people in the world over twenty-six.' He turned back to Kovac. 'But eighteen's excellent. Anybody over fifteen is very good.'

'Like I said, I've been trained,' said Kovac modestly.

'What level are you, Miles?' Amber asked.

'Nineteen.'

After that Kovac paid Fleming more respect.

Now Amber's attention was on the third screen where yet another man in uniform was scowling and shaking his head at Associate Director Jones. He was older, with silver hair and five stars on his uniform. 'If you figure we're going to take our missiles off-line, you've figured wrong,' the General boomed. 'We've laid down contingencies since Y2K to ensure we *never* need go off-line and we're not going to start compromising national security now. The world's in a heap of shit, in case you hadn't noticed.'

'But that's the point, General,' Jones said. 'If you close down all missile bases then Soames can't activate them. You'll be *protecting* national security.'

'Who says this psycho's not going to try to activate the Russians' missiles or someone else's? We've got to defend ourselves.'

Associate Director Jones shook his head. 'Surely, General, if we set the example and discreetly explain the position to the world we can ensure Soames can't use *anyone*'s ordnance to start a war. If everyone stands down, at least this risk will be taken out of the equation.'

'It's not going to happen – we don't know everyone else *will* stand down,' barked the General. 'As the saying goes, there's no point being a good guy until the rest of the world becomes one too. And if war is inevitable, I'm damned if we're going to be caught with our pants down.'

'Even if it means *starting* the war?' asked Riga.

The General's jaw muscles clenched. 'So be it.'

Fleming stood up and leant forward. 'But surely the President—'

'Look, Dr Fleming, I appreciate your assistance in these matters, I really do. However, as chairman of the joint chiefs of staff I've just been with the President, who is somewhat occupied with a number of other matters at this time, and he agrees with me that a joint Delta force and FBI incursion into VenTec is the only viable option.

'Lieutenant-Colonel Kovac is an excellent soldier and his men are the best we have. Fortunately they're on manoeuvres near the Canadian border and can rendezvous with the FBI in Fairbanks within a couple of hours. When they reach your location, they'll run defence, enabling you to lead Dr Grant and the FBI into the end zone and disable Soames's computer. Kovac's men will give you whatever assistance you require – but we cannot, *will not*, stand down our missiles. If, as we believe, the Red Pope's last two signs are war and death, then it's my duty to ensure this country is protected.'

Amber watched Fleming try to interrupt but the General went on, 'Don't misunderstand me. I fully

384

appreciate the gravity of this situation and the importance of your mission. It is vital you succeed, not only to salvage the world's computer records and protect the countless human lives threatened by the final signs, but also to restore our faith in God and the power of good in this world.'

He paused for a second, the power of his steely gaze connecting with everyone in the room and all those on the other video-conference screens: the Delta commander, the FBI agents, the Jesuit priest and the two scientists, Fleming and Amber. 'What you are all embarked on,' he said, 'is nothing less than a crusade for the salvation of the mind, the body and the soul of humanity. And if there is still a God, I pray with all my heart that He goes with you.'

65

Black sector. Six hours later

The storm had returned stronger than before and Carvelli was glad that the helicopter returning him to VenTec had been able to land before the worst hit. He could hear the snow and wind batter the glass outside the thick tinted windows on his way to Soames's private quarters.

The large anteroom in the black sector was an eclectic Aladdin's cave: the stripped maple floor was strewn with Afghan, Turkish and Persian rugs; exquisitely lit African masks adorned one wall, tapestries from Rajasthan and framed silk textiles from China covered another. Aromatic sandal-wood carvings from Saharanpur were displayed in a basket beside a fireplace of gleaming black jet. Corals and exotic stones lay on a glass tabletop above an up-lighter, which illuminated the jewels and projected their rainbow beauty on to the white ceiling above. A back-lit severed lion's head, with full mane, stared out from an alcove, and built into the wall beside the main door was a large aquarium containing a Technicolor kaleidoscope of darting tropical fish.

It seemed to Carvelli that Soames, a man cursed never to venture into the sun and experience at first hand the more exotic climes of the world, had used his massive wealth to bring the sensory beauty of those lands into his private kingdom of semi-darkness.

Carvelli shuddered. He had never been inside Soames's quarters before and, despite its treasures, he didn't care to be there now.

He knocked on the double doors and waited for permission to enter. When he heard nothing he stole into the large living area. On one wall there was a section of carved stone, taken from an ancient pagan temple, depicting exquisitely detailed figurines engaged in every imaginable sexual act. It made Carvelli's palms sweat to look at it as he moved quietly across the parquet floor. There were no personal artefacts, no photographs of friends or family, no novels, compact discs, no bottle of spirits or cigars. Except for a glass-fronted cooler of Coke cans in one corner there was no indication that Bradley Soames indulged in any of life's trivial pleasures. Indeed, even with the sensual trophies on show, the place reminded Carvelli of a museum devoid of joy.

When Carvelli heard the voice at the other end of the room he didn't recognize it at first. Then he realized it was Soames – and that he was pleading.

'But I've done all you asked,' Carvelli heard him say. 'I brought darkness and unrest and now I've brought famine. Can't I just move the final signs forward a few hours? What difference can it make after waiting so long?'

Carvelli froze, heart in his mouth.

'Please let me do this,' Soames wheedled. 'It's too dangerous to wait – I can sense it. Grant and Fleming know about Mother Lucifer. The longer I wait the more I feel certain they'll find a way to sabotage everything.'

Terrified but compelled to hear more, Carvelli moved closer to the ebony door at the end. It stood ajar, and as he inched towards it he could see that the room beyond was in darkness.

Soames spoke again, angrier now. 'Why's it so important to stick to the schedule? It's so close now, and the effect will be the same. It's only right that you let me finish it *now*. I've done everything you wanted. I'm tired. I want this over. I *demand* it.'

There was a crack, like a whip, then a strangulated sob.

Carvelli moved closer, and in the shaft of light from the door he saw that the room was bare except for a simple bed. Soames was kneeling at its foot, back to the door. He was naked, his skin mottled and pitted with scars from the numerous operations he had endured. And he was alone.

'I demand it,' he said again. 'I *deserve* it. You must let me bring forward the last signs. It's only fair after I've performed this great service for you.'

He lifted a small whip high into the air with his right hand and began to strike at his shoulders, all the time crying and asking forgiveness for his defiance. 'Forgive me for my arrogance and my impatience. I wish only to serve you and fulfil my purpose.'

Eventually he laid the bloodied whip on the floor and bent forward over the bed. He seemed calmer. Then, to Carvelli's astonishment, he clasped his hands together, lowered his head and began to pray: 'Our Father who art in heaven, hallowed be thy name . . .'

Carvelli stood in the doorway, frozen with shock, disbelief. He was unable to reconcile what Soames had revealed to him earlier with what he was witnessing now: a recitation of the only prayer in the Bible attributed to Jesus Christ. But before he could make sense of it, Soames lowered his hands and raised his head. Without turning, he said, 'Frank, you've brought my insurance with you?'

'Y-y-yes,' Carvelli stammered. 'In the white sector.'

'Well done.'

'You want to see him?'

Soames nodded. 'I'll be along shortly,' he said. Then he turned towards Carvelli, moving his profile into the beam of light from the half-open door. Carvelli looked away, covering his eyes with his hand, filled with the irrational certainty that if he saw Soames's face he would die.

66

The Brooks mountain range. Alaska

The storm buffeted the Black Hawk helicopter so hard its whole frame shook and creaked. Through the snow-lashed glass, Fleming could see fork lightning crack open the darkness, revealing flashes of white mountain peaks rising above him, like the cresting waves of a storm-tossed sea. If, as the General had hoped, there was a God, then as far as Fleming could see He wasn't with them on this mission.

Over the last few hours, he and Amber had remained in the rangers' cabin, becoming increasingly apprehensive as the weather deteriorated. Twice he had tried to contact his parents in England but there had been no reply, so he and Amber had used the time to eat and get some sleep while they waited for the helicopters. When they arrived, the weather was a whiteout and the pilots hadn't dared land. Instead Amber and he had been winched aboard.

'Buckle up and hold tight,' the pilot said grimly, as the helicopter rose higher. 'We're flying blind and this is only going to get worse.'

Fleming glanced around the cabin. Most of his fellow passengers looked equally grim. In addition to the pilot, there were four Delta Force operators, or D-boys, including Kovac, and two FBI tech agents who were assigned to assist Amber. She sat beside Fleming, looking small and vulnerable among the men in full combat gear.

The D-boys wore Arctic combat suits, white with a ghosted camouflage pattern. Each was weighed down with a backpack, grenades and a black oily CAR-15 pump-action shotgun or M-60 machine gun. The G-men wore the black Ninja suits favoured by the FBI hostage rescue team and carried more modest – Fleming thought more appropriate – rifles.

Somewhere out in the swirling darkness a second helicopter was carrying another four FBI HRT agents, including Special-Agent-in-Charge Wayne Thomas, and a further four Delta Force operators. A third back-up helicopter with another team was on standby just north of Fairbanks.

The plan was simple: fly low to avoid detection – maintaining radio silence as long as possible – to the unfinished refinery on the lower peak behind VenTec. Here the helicopters would hover as close to the ground as possible, allowing them to abseil – or, as the D-boys called it, fast-rope – on to the mountain. After regrouping at the refinery, Fleming would lead them to the pipe and retrace the steps he and Amber had taken when escaping. They planned to reach the borehole under the red sector and infiltrate Soames's computer from beneath. The first part, returning to the refinery, was supposed to have been straightforward.

But the storm had changed that.

Because the global positioning system relied on data that had been lost with the Red Pope's second sign, the pilot was forced to navigate in the old-fashioned way using maps and eyesight. But eyesight didn't work in a whiteout like this. In these conditions it was like speeding blindfold at Mach 3 through Manhattan, and any other mission would have been aborted. But if they didn't stop Soames's computer before the final signs were triggered, it would be too late.

Kovac tried to make light of it. 'The conditions are fine,' he said. 'We've got excellent cover and the element of surprise.'

Suddenly the chopper swerved to the left, and in the lightning Fleming saw the second helicopter appear on their right. *Shit*, he thought. *They can't even see each other in this mess*. Amber was staring at him – she had seen the near-miss too.

'How will we see the landing area in this storm?' she asked Kovac.

He turned to her, still appearing vaguely bored. 'You probably won't even see it,' he drawled, as if the landing area was some kind of need-to-know secret to which she wasn't privy, 'but don't worry about it.'

Fleming and Amber exchanged looks.

'You ever fast-roped before, Dr Grant?' one of the Delta Force soldiers asked her.

She shook her head.

'It's okay. I'm taking her down on my rope,' said Fleming.

'You sure you're happy to do that?' Kovac asked. 'She's mission critical. We don't want her damaged. Perhaps one of us should do it.'

'Thanks for your concern,' said Amber hurriedly, 'but I'm sure I'll be fine with Miles.'

Kovac looked hard at Fleming, then shrugged.

'Getting close,' said the pilot, in the calm, reassuring tone that all pilots acquire, but Fleming heard the underlying strain when he told them to 'prepare the ropes and get ready'. The chopper was rocking in the air, taking all the pilot's physical strength to control it.

Three bolts of lightning lit the sky, turning the black night a blue-white more blinding than the darkness. Then a garbled message came to them over the radio.

'Hit . . . lightning . . electric's gone . . . going down . . . Black Hawk down. Black Hawk down . . .'

Silence.

Fleming peered out of the window to his right. In the crackling, electrified air he could see the second helicopter reeling as it tried to steady itself. There was a black charred gash above the cabin beneath the main rotors, which appeared to stutter in the turbulent air. Then the chopper lurched forward and spiralled downwards like a leaf in autumn.

Fleming's heart dropped with the helicopter. He watched it disappear into the whiteout. The brightness of the subsequent fireball briefly illuminated the dark abyss into which the Black Hawk had plummeted.

In the ensuing silence no one in the cabin met anyone else's eye. They needed to absorb what had happened in their own way, each trying to fend off the paralysing fear that it might happen to them.

'Hatches open. We're going in,' said the pilot, pointing down into the churning snow, where Fleming could make out the two empty steel frames designed to house the refinery's vast drum-shaped storage tanks. 'Throw the ropes.'

The helicopter doors slid open and freezing air blasted through the cabin. Kovac kicked out the ropes – four on each side.

'I'll try and hold it steady,' the pilot said, 'but I can't guarantee shit in this.'

Kovac was shouting for his men and the FBI agents to go down in the agreed order: 'Two by two. Go! Go! Go!'

In turn each man gripped a rope, backed out of the hatch and jumped, sliding down the swaying ropes, towards the swirling snow and what they hoped was the ground.

Fleming reached for Amber and waited his turn. He could feel her trembling when he wrapped his arms round her and placed his hands on the rope above hers.

'Don't worry, I've got you,' he whispered, harnessing his suit to hers, using his body to block her view of the swirling storm outside as he backed out of the hatch and into the void.

67

Amber couldn't remember feeling more physically frightened. Her stomach lurched and her heart beat so fast she thought she might faint. The heavy rope swayed like cotton in the gale-force winds and her gloved hands burned with friction. The rope and the helicopter were swinging so much that she might as well have been attached to a pendulum. But whenever she lost control she could feel Fleming's body close in, gripping her to him, checking her speed.

The descent seemed to take for ever: everything happened in slow motion. Looking down, she had no idea where the ground was in the swirling snow. Then to her left there was a clear gap and for an instant she saw what was below. If she had been scared before she was terrified now.

The helicopter had been pushed out of position by the storm and was hovering over the edge of the mountain. Below the opposite rope on the other side of the helicopter there was nothing. She screamed a warning at the Delta Force operator on the rope as he reached the end of his descent, but the wind was so fierce she could barely hear her own voice. Helpless, she watched him abseil to the base of the rope then release his grip. He seemed to hang for a second in the air as if kept buoyant by the force of the storm. Then he slipped silently into the darkness. To her right another man did the same. Neither let out a cry.

She began to swing even more violently and realized Fleming was purposely shifting his balance as they neared the end of their rope. He was swinging into the mountain.

He shouted in her ear, 'Bend your knees and roll.'

Seconds later she felt the impact as she hit the ground on her feet and crumpled into a ball. Fleming rolled with her in the snow. Before she could get her breath Fleming was pulling her to her feet. 'You okay?' she heard him ask in her helmet speaker.

She nodded once, then doubled over in pain.

'What's wrong?'

'Nothing,' she gasped.

Kovac was on them, shepherding them away from the edge of the mountain, towards the refinery. 'You hurt?'

She grimaced. 'Just winded.'

'Walk it off,' he said. 'There ain't much time.'

Nearing the refinery area, there was more protection from the storm. 'How many of us are left?' Fleming asked.

'Five who are fit to go on,' said Kovac. His voice was even. 'We lost two off the edge and one broke his leg.'

Ahead, Amber could see two figures standing in the swirling snow; one was bending over a prostrate man whose left leg was bent back on itself. She was relieved that one fit man was in the black FBI uniform of the tech agents. At least she and Fleming weren't the only technically qualified members of the team.

Fleming was trying to get his bearings. 'There'll be shelter in the pipe. We need to get your injured man out of the storm. What do you want to do about him?'

Kovac didn't hesitate. 'We'll get him comfortable and warm, then leave him with a radio. If we're not back for him in six hours he can break radio silence and call the back-up helicopter. By then we'll have either failed or succeeded. It may be immaterial anyway.' He moved towards his colleague.

The weather was worsening. Their team was depleted. However Amber looked at it, the omens weren't good. It was almost as if God – or whoever was really in charge – didn't want Soames stopped.

Fleming turned to her. 'Don't worry, Amber, our luck must change soon. It can't get any worse.'

But it could.

Minutes later he shouted, 'I can't find the pipe. The snow's covered it. I think it's over there but we've got to dig for it.'

'Okay,' said Kovac, inured to changing plans and shifting fortunes.

'Okay,' agreed Amber. But she didn't feel okay. All she could think about was how everything that could have gone wrong had gone wrong. She had escaped intending to call the cavalry, not realizing that she and Fleming *were* the cavalry.

She thought of her godfather waiting on the Red Ark. 'I'll pray for you until you return victorious,' he had promised, confident that they would succeed in their mission because it was 'God's will'.

Gritting her teeth, Amber followed Fleming's footsteps in the snow. 'Papa Pete, I hope to God you haven't been praying until now,' she muttered, under her breath, 'because if this is what happens *after* you've been praying, then we're in deep shit.'

68

The white sector

Carvelli rubbed his clammy palms together, trying to dispel the disturbing image of Soames flagellating himself.

Soames was now fully dressed, standing in one of the deserted recreation rooms in the white sector, his wolves sitting patiently at either side of him. Bending over, he peered through the etched-glass door into the next room. He had already put through an excited call to Tripp and Bukowski in the red sector to check on the status of his computer, and in the last few minutes he'd twice asked Carvelli the time. With each update, he said, 'Almost there, almost there,' repeating the two words like a mantra.

As he looked through the glass he grinned. 'Well done, Frank,' he said. 'Was it difficult, getting hold of my insurance policy?'

Carvelli was unsure what to say. He wanted Soames's approval but he was frightened of deceiving him in case he was punished. If he was honest, he hadn't done much, except wait for the men to pick up the 'package' from school then spend the flight reassuring the kid that he was on a surprise trip to see his uncle. 'He's pretty together, if that's what you mean.'

'Not even a little scared?'

'He misses his grandma and grandpa and I'm not sure he believes my surprise-trip story. But he's a tough one.'

Soames gestured Carvelli over. 'Look what he's doing.'

Carvelli moved closer to the window, keeping as far from the wolves as possible. He already knew what the boy was doing: he had been playing with him for the last half hour.

'Look at him piling up my old bricks,' Soames said, with a distant smile. 'He's so meticulous with each tower, making sure every brick is perfectly placed.' Soames pushed open the door. 'I must talk to him.'

The boy was standing in the middle of the large room on a parquet floor strewn with battered old-fashioned toys – Lego, GI Joe and countless wooden bricks, which were now in towers, each almost four feet high. When he heard the door opening the boy turned.

'Hello, Jake,' said Soames. 'Great towers.'

'Where's Uncle Milo?' the child demanded. He examined Soames's scarred skin with frank scrutiny. 'What's wrong with your face?'

Soames stepped closer to him, bent down and brought his face to within inches of Jake's. 'I don't like sunlight,' Soames said, 'and sunlight doesn't like me. What's wrong with your legs?'

Jake didn't flinch. 'They're okay.'

'But they're not your legs, are they?' Soames sneered.

Jake kept his gaze steady. 'Yes, they are. Uncle Milo gave them to me.'

Soames straightened up and moved towards one of the towers. 'I used to love building towers as high as I could then knocking them over. Why don't you knock this one over first?'

'No, thank you,' Jake said quietly. His posture had stiffened and Carvelli could tell he was scared, but he kept his head up and looked straight ahead.

'Go on, be as rough as you like, throw the bricks around the room. No one's going to tell you off,' urged Soames. The wolves moved closer and sat, panting, a few feet behind Jake. 'Try the other tower first, if you like.'

Jake shook his head.

'Or both together perhaps.'

Still Jake didn't move.

'I think you should do it,' Soames said, his voice colder. The wolves moved closer, until they were almost breathing down the back of Jake's neck. The child's knees were shaking and his lip trembled, but he didn't move. Carvelli knew what Soames and the wolves were capable of, and he wanted Jake to give in and knock down the towers, but part of him cheered on the boy's defiance. He wished he had the same courage.

Soames bent down and again pushed his face close to the boy's – even if Jake had wanted to step back, the growling wolves barred his way. Soames was angry now: his scarred lips peeled back from his incongruously perfect white teeth in a snarl. 'Knock down the fucking tower.'

The boy's whole body was trembling, his face ashen, but he stood his ground.

'You think your uncle's here,' Soames taunted. 'Don't you, Jake?'

The boy looked accusingly at Carvelli: his eyes were bright with tears but not one leaked on to his cheek. Carvelli felt himself shrivel inside. 'No, I don't,' the boy said. 'But when Milo comes to get me he'll—'

'He'll *what*?' roared Soames. 'If Miles comes, he'll die, like your father and your whore mother died, and they'll meet up in Hell, like everyone's going to meet up in fucking Hell, including you!'

Jake scrunched up his face and put his hands over his ears.

Soames's face was red now – Carvelli had never seen him so angry. The wolves were panting, waiting for the order to attack. The back of Jake's jacket and trouser legs were flecked with their spittle. 'Your uncle Milo's probably already dead!' Soames screamed. 'Soon your grandparents will be dead too and then – and then—' Soames let out a roar of rage and pushed over the towers. Then he stormed out of the door, followed by his wolves, leaving Carvelli standing alone with Jake.

Filled with awe, Carvelli moved to the boy and laid a hand on his shoulder. 'They've gone.'

With his fingers pushed into his ears, the child shook his shoulder, trying to dislodge Carvelli's hand.

A wave of shame swept over Carvelli. He removed his hand and left the room.

It was only then, when he knew he was alone, that Jake collapsed on the ground and began to cry.

69

Four hours later

'There it is,' said Fleming, squinting at the spiralling light show ahead. As the rotating shards of brightness pierced the darkness he could see the borehole.

'God, it's hot,' said the FBI tech agent, a tall black guy called Howie.

'And bright,' said Kovac. 'Better put on your masks.'

After donning his, Fleming looked up at the vast rotating fan, blowing hot air out of the red sector above. The light beyond it was so bright that even with his mask Fleming couldn't discern anything through the rotating blades except a blinding radiance. 'Wait,' he said. 'The fan's slowing.'

'It's on a thermostat,' said Amber. 'Its speed's constantly changing. There are other more sensitive temperature stabilizers in the red sector. The fan moves hot air away from the sphere. Depending on the ambient air temperature it accelerates or slows to a virtual stop.'

'So if we wait for it to stop we can get through?' said Fleming.

Amber nodded.

'How will we know when it's going to speed up again?' asked the second Delta Force operator, a thickset blond man with blue eyes.

'We won't – except when it starts going faster,' Amber replied.

'The important thing at this stage,' said Fleming, 'is to get Amber and Howie to the computer so they can do what they need to do while we run defence.'

'I'll go through first,' said Kovac. 'I'll check out any problems and recon the other side.' He gestured to the other D-boy. 'You take up the rear, Olsen.'

Fleming watched Kovac dash across the gantry and scale the steel inspection ladder welded to the side of the borehole. At the top he waited just beneath the slowing blades. Now that the fan was virtually stationary Fleming could see that it had only four blades and that a man should be able to slide through the gaps between them.

Kovac extended his right arm to test the force of one of the blades coming to rest. Suddenly there was a click and the blades speeded up. Not too fast, but fast enough to give Kovac and those watching a shock.

'I'm not sure the blades actually stop,' Fleming heard Kovac say in his helmet speaker. 'I'll try while they're still moving.'

Then, before Fleming could counsel him to wait, the Delta Force leader lunged for one of the blades and gripped it. As the blade rotated above the pit, Kovac shinned up on to its curved surface and mounted it then vanished into the brightness beyond. Fleming felt dizzy.

'I'm through,' said Kovac casually. 'Looking good. There's a maintenance ledge to one side and the ladder carries on up. Who's next?'

They all looked at each other then up at the fan, which was still rotating a few clicks faster than looked safe. Fleming stepped forward and ran across the gantry. He climbed the ladder and waited, as Kovac had, just below the fan. Up close, even at this speed, the blades still seemed to be moving too fast. He waited, gathering his courage, feeling like a pedestrian trying to cross a Formula One racetrack. The blades slowed, there was a click and the fan stopped.

Two hands appeared through one of the gaps above him. 'Come on, I'll pull you through.'

He reached up and felt Kovac's powerful hands take his arms and lift him through the fan.

Half-way up, when the blades were level with his groin, he heard another click and the blades moved. His heart almost stopped and his first instinct was to let go, but the fan barely moved, just pushed him closer to the ledge where Kovac was standing.

There, Fleming looked around him. Soames's sphere of light was suspended within two intersecting hoops no more than ten feet above him. The fireball seemed brighter and more volatile than the last time he had seen it and, even with his eye protection, he had to squint. To his right was a ladder that ran up the side of the borehole to a doorway twenty feet above, which led into the control room and the laboratories that encircled the globe of light. He could just make out the tinted viewing windows and wondered if the doorway accessed the laboratory where he, Bukowski and Tripp had developed the upgraded NeuroTranslator for Soames.

'Come on,' Kovac whispered into his microphone.

Amber was next and since the fan remained static her light frame was easy to pull through the gaps. Special Agent Howie followed.

Only one more to come: the second Delta Force operator.

The fan clicked and picked up speed.

'Shit,' whispered Kovac. He checked his watch and glanced at Amber. 'We'll wait a few minutes for it to slow again but if it doesn't we'll have to go on without him. We've lost so much time and I don't know how long you're going to need to do your stuff.'

'Neither do I,' said Amber.

Another click. The fan slowed.

'Come on, Olsen,' Kovac whispered.

Fleming braced himself and, with Kovac, reached down as the blades came to a stop. He took the Delta Force operator's right arm and Kovac took the left. The man was heavy with all his kit but they wrestled him through the gap. He was almost clear of the fan when it clicked again.

Nothing happened.

The man looked up at Fleming and grinned with relief.

Then he was no longer grinning.

It happened so fast that Fleming could only stare in horror as the fan kicked into high speed, wrenching the man from his and Kovac's grip. For some seconds the Delta Force operator rotated with the fan blades as if he was on a carousel. But as the speed picked up he was squeezed down through the blades like a carrot through a blender. All the time, as the fan macerated him from the feet up, his surprised face stared up at Fleming.

It was over in seconds and Fleming didn't even hear the thump as the man's remains fell into the pit below. In many ways that was the most startling and unsettling thing: aside from the blades chewing up his body, the man had made no sound.

The FBI agent leant forward and vomited.

Kovac turned to Amber, who was staring into the whirring fan. His jaw muscles twitched but otherwise he showed no emotion. 'This makes it even more important to finish what we came here to do.'

Amber was still staring at the fan.

Kovac took her head in one massive hand and forced her to look at him. 'Are you up for this, Dr Grant? Because if you're not then this whole fuck-up has been a waste of time.'

Amber blinked.

Fleming put a hand on her shoulder. 'Come on, Amber, let's get on with it.'

She nodded. Her face was still pale but the fire had returned to her eyes.

'Let's go,' said Kovac, turning to climb the ladder.

70

The door at the top of the ladder opened on to a deserted laboratory. Following Kovac's lead Amber crouched low and shuffled into the white room behind him and Fleming. To her left, she saw a body surrogate like the one Fleming had shown her at Barley Hall. *What had he called it?* Brian.

Next to the mannequin, atop a gleaming workbench, she recognized Fleming's updated NeuroTranslator and Soames's soul-capture head-sphere. 'I thought that stuff was on the Red Ark,' she said.

'The bastard was leaving nothing to chance – he made a back-up.' Frowning as he spoke, Fleming stared at the apparatus as if he was thinking something through. Then he looked through the tinted window to the pulsing orb of light beyond. 'Amber?' His eyes were bright with excitement.

'Yes.'

'Ssh,' hissed Kovac ahead of them. He pointed to his right.

Amber looked through the tinted viewing screen, past the glass sphere of light and into the laboratory area on the other side of the borehole. A guard stood outside the sliding doors and inside someone was at a console staring into a screen. His tall frame and bald head were familiar: Walter Tripp. Amber scanned the laboratory circuit surrounding the glass sphere, searching for Bukowski, but there was no sign of her.

'That must be where the master controls are,' she whispered. 'We must get him away from the console before he can warn anyone. How do we do that?'

Kovac turned to her. 'You need to interrogate him?'

'Not really. I can find out everything we need to know from the computer, and I wouldn't trust what he told us, anyway. I just need him away from the controls. Can you do that?'

The Delta Force leader smiled at her; it was a cold, hard smile. 'Sure. Wait here.'

Crouched beside Fleming and the FBI agent, she watched through the tinted glass as Kovac stole round the circle of interconnecting laboratories, passing the steps to the raised elevator platform. She lost sight of him for a moment, then saw the guard on the other side of the borehole collapse. Seconds later Kovac rose in his place, crouching outside the sliding doors to the area where Tripp was standing.

She watched them open and Tripp turn. He appeared puzzled rather than alarmed, no doubt secure in this impregnable fortress of technology. She saw him say something, but couldn't hear what. Then he left his station and wandered to the door. He seemed to be calling someone.

Suddenly he disappeared below the viewing window and Kovac beckoned to them through the glass.

Amber followed in his footsteps and found herself in the main control centre. Both the guard and Tripp lay motionless on the ground, eyes wide open, their necks bent at an odd angle. Tripp looked as worried in death as he always had in life, and Amber turned away hurriedly: she had seen enough of death in the last few days to last her a lifetime.

The control room hadn't changed since she had been here last a few years ago, and she was relieved to see that the main screen in front of her was live. Tripp had been monitoring the progress of the vast computer and was already in the system, which meant she wouldn't have to break in.

At last their luck was changing.

Reaching for the on-screen controls, she touched the Datafile Manager icon and pressed the quick-browse button. The screen scrolled down lists of files so fast it was impossible to read each line. At the bottom there was a number of at least seven digits.

'What's that?' Fleming asked, over her shoulder.

'That,' said Amber, in awe, 'is the list of every single file stored within the photons of light in that glass ball out there. In essence what you're seeing is the roll call of every piece of electronically recorded data the world has ever amassed. This is the black hole into which all the world's lost data has been sucked.'

411

There was a beat of silence as the enormity of what they were looking at sank in.

'What do the digits at the base of the screen represent?' the FBI tech agent asked.

Amber sighed. She was used to working with mind-blowing computer power but she was still impressed at the scale of what Soames had achieved. 'That number is an estimate of how many *years* it would take to view every file in the Datafile Manager currently scrolling down the screen at the speed you're seeing it now. Not the total *contents* of the files, just the *titles*.'

'That's *millions* of years?' said Kovac. 'Jeez.' For once even he was impressed.

'How about sending the data back to all the places it was stolen from?' asked Fleming.

'Don't worry, that'll be pretty quick. Every transaction can be done at the speed of light. However, we need to check the original program and ensure the integrity of the data and pathways. Soames may have built in booby traps either to destroy the stored information if tampered with or to return it to the wrong addresses. Incorrect, corrupt or mis-placed data could be more damaging than none at all. We'll have to go through some standard hygiene procedures to ensure the correct data returns to the correct databanks. But with the power of this computer it shouldn't take longer than a few minutes.'

'What about stopping the final two signs?'

'While the return of the data is being monitored to make sure it's okay, I can search the computer's underlying programs for any pre-set instructions relating to relevant areas such as nuclear installations, warheads, that kind of thing. Then, once I've defused whatever Soames is planning, I'll key in a PIP.'

'A what?' demanded Kovac.

'A paradox implosion protocol,' she said. 'A PIP's basically a program that sets up a paradox in the photonic core of the qubit stream, turning the computer's vast power on itself.' She smiled at Kovac's bemused frown. 'It's what you soldier boys call a bomb. A *big* bomb.' She checked her watch. 'We've got a few hours yet, haven't we?'

'Unless Soames brings things forward,' said Kovac.

Amber turned to the FBI tech agent. 'You know how to install a CAS programme?'

'A "clean and screen"?'

'Yes.'

Howie nodded.

'Good,' Amber said. 'I'll activate the second terminal over there and you can use it to run a CAS on the data, ensuring it returns in the exact state it was taken and to the exact locations it was stolen from. Okay?'

'Whatever you say.' The tech agent moved to the second terminal as Amber powered up his screen from the panel on hers.

'The elevator's the only way into this sector, isn't it?' said Kovac.

Fleming nodded. 'Apart from the way we got in, yes.'

'I'll go up to the gantry level and keep a lookout. Stop anyone from disturbing you guys. Good luck.'

413

'Looks like everything's under control,' Fleming said, after Kovac had gone. Clearly he had something on his mind because he kept glancing back to the laboratory where his NeuroTranslator was stored. 'You don't need me for the next few minutes, do you?'

She was punching keys. 'Why?'

Fleming didn't answer at first. Then he pointed at the fireball and asked, 'That computer can perform *really* complex calculations at incredible speed, can't it? I mean, if this thing can't calculate a possible causal correlation between two apparently unrelated systems, then there probably isn't a connection or correlation to find. Right?'

She turned to him and narrowed her eyes. 'Yes. What are you getting at?'

'There's one thing I need this computer to do before you destroy it. It involves my Neuro-Translator and Soames's soul-capture headset and should take only a few minutes.'

'What is it?'

She listened as he explained. When he finished she shook her head. His outrageous hypothesis was almost certainly doomed to failure, but she of all people couldn't stand in his way. 'It's bad timing,' she said.

'It's the *only* time I'll have access to this computer power. Now or never.'

Sighing, she punched a soft key at the bottom of her screen. 'I've activated the dumb terminal in the laboratory where your NeuroTranslator is. Go in and use the search icon. Type in your questions and it'll seek out the data to prove or disprove your hypothesis. If you don't get an answer within a minute or so there ain't one. Okay?'

Fleming moved closer and briefly she thought he was going to kiss her. And she wanted him to. But he just smiled, said, 'Thanks,' and rushed off.

'How's it going?' she called over to the tech agent on the other terminal.

'Almost there. Oughta be done in a few minutes. How about you? Found out what the third and fourth signs are yet?'

'Not yet, but I'm ready to start searching the base instructions now.'

However, before she could key in the search parameters the screen changed. A grid of longitude and latitude lines appeared before her, and beneath it was a map of India and Pakistan.

Two dots, one over Delhi and another over Lahore, were flashing red. And in the top left-hand corner of the screen a slow countdown was under way. The figure 100 flashed yellow. Then, after a set number of flashes, it changed to 99 . . . then 98.

'Oh, my God!'

'What?' said Howie.

'I'm not sure,' Amber said, trying to keep calm. 'Just remind me again. India and Pakistan are both nuclear powers but not exactly best buddies. Yeah?'

The G-man nodded cautiously. 'Yeah.'

'Christ. I think that by returning the data stolen with the second sign, we've somehow brought forward the last two.'

'War and death?'

415

The screen changed again. This time she saw a larger map, showing Asia and Europe. Red dots flashed over numerous sites in the Middle East, and large swathes of Ukraine, Russia, North Korea and China. A similar countdown was in evidence at the top corner of the screen.

'Shit,' said Amber, reaching for the control keys. This was happening automatically. She had to get into the programming and stop it.

Bang.

A gunshot.

Then three more.

'What the hell was that?' asked the FBI man. He stiffened.

The sound of gears told Amber that the elevator was descending. 'Probably Kovac,' she said, torn between the countdown on the screen and the elevator.

'I'll check,' said the FBI man, and ran towards it.

Amber returned to the screen, punching in a program code as the countdown continued: 92 . . . 91 . . . 90 . . .

She heard growling behind her, then a scream. She whipped round. One of Soames's wolves leapt from the elevator platform and embedded its fangs in the tech agent's throat, stifling his cries. The second wolf leapt at his groin.

Then Soames appeared. Walking down the stairs, he stepped over the agent's writhing body, while Bukowski followed with a gun. The blonde scientist glanced at Tripp's crumpled body then glared at Amber, blue eyes as cold as ice.

'Amber, step away from the terminal and come here,' Soames said, with chilling calm.

She glanced back at the screen. The numbers were counting down: 88 . . . 87 . . . There was nothing she could do about it.

'Touch nothing, or Felicia will take great pleasure in shooting you,' Soames cautioned.

Amber didn't move.

'Where's Miles?' Soames asked. 'You two seem to have become something of an item.'

'He's not here,' she said, willing herself not to look towards the fireball and the laboratory beyond.

Soames scanned the area and smiled. 'What a shame. There's someone to see him.'

71

Fleming had just finished interrogating the computer in the far laboratory when he heard the gunshots.

Instinctively he turned back to look across the borehole to where Amber was working. He stared in disbelief as the FBI man was brought down by the wolves. Ducking out of sight, he searched the laboratory for a weapon, but there was none – all he could see were the NeuroTranslator and the soul-capture head-sphere.

He watched helplessly as Soames appeared with Bukowski, who was pointing a pistol at Amber.

Where the hell's Kovac? Shit, shit, shit.

Amber moved away from the console towards Soames, who stepped forward to meet her. At that moment, Fleming saw Carvelli in front of the elevator . . . with Jake.

What was he doing here?

Fleming had to restrain himself from leaping up and charging, armed only with his bare hands.

Leaning into Amber, Soames reached for her

collar. Seconds later, Fleming could hear his voice issuing from the speakers in his helmet.

'Hello, Miles. I'm using Amber's microphone so I know you can hear me. First things first. Your mission has failed. The final signs have been activated so you have no more reason to be heroic. Also, I have your nephew with me. We're going up to the gantry level now and I will give you two minutes to come up in the elevator and join us or I'll expose Jake's tender young eyes to the light. Then, if you still don't show, I'll feed him to my pets. They're partial to young flesh. The choice is yours.'

Fleming balled his hands into fists. He watched Soames's lackeys shepherd Jake and Amber into the elevator and felt sick with impotent rage.

All was lost. He had no choice.

If he could no longer help to save the world, then he must at least save Jake and Amber.

Time ticked by. It seemed hopeless. Amber needed to be back at the master console finding a way to stop the countdown. But only Miles Fleming could do anything now. And he didn't know how to reprogram the computer.

Standing by the elevator on the exposed gantry level, squinting through her eye-protectors, she saw Kovac's body lying on the steel platform beside another guard. Both looked dead. Kovac's neck area was torn and bloody and there were bullet wounds in his upper body. Carvelli stood alone to her left. He looked pale and sickly, as if he would much rather be somewhere else. By contrast Bukowski was obviously itching to use her gun. She stood with Soames and Jake by the railings. Soames wore his protective clothing and Jake's silhouette looked pitifully small beside him and Bukowski.

'You okay, Jake?' Amber asked.

He darted a quick look at the wolves, standing expectantly by the elevator, and nodded. The movement almost dislodged his over-large eye-protectors.

'He's fine,' said Soames. 'For now.'

'Why are you doing this, Bradley?' Amber asked.

'I'm not *doing* anything,' he said. 'I'm simply ensuring that what has been preordained happens. I didn't decide this, I'm merely fulfilling the prophecy. That's why you never stood a chance of stopping me. Even by reversing the second sign and restoring the world's data you've only made the final signs more potent.'

'You're going to launch nuclear missiles and wipe out most of Asia?'

Soames laughed. 'Of course not. That's the whole point. Mankind will choose to do this. The loss of power in the first sign didn't cause civil unrest – humanity's reaction to it did. The second sign wasn't real famine – it didn't starve humanity of what it needs physically to survive, only what it has come to rely on. And the final signs will be no different. Mankind will bring war and death upon itself through its own prejudice and choice. Certain nations are going to see phantom missile launches on their computer screens. They're going to think they're under attack but they still have a choice. They can either check whether the attack is genuine, trusting their enemies when they reassure them that no missiles have been launched, or start a real and costly war.'

Soames smiled. 'What do you think will happen, Amber? I'm not a gambling man but I wouldn't bet against war and death. Especially as the authorities are going to receive this misleading information just after all the world's data has been restored by your magnificent act of heroism. Undoubtedly they'll praise their good fortune that their data came on-line again just in time to detect an attack and retaliate.'

'Why are you so desperate to fulfil the Red Pope's prophecy when you know it isn't the only truth?'

Soames smiled. 'Because it will be,' he said, gesturing to the elevator. 'Soon it will be the only truth.'

The elevator was descending to the next level. Someone had summoned it from below. Miles Fleming was coming up. It was over. Soames had won.

She tensed and stared at the elevator. So did Jake. And the wolves.

'Watch out, Milo,' Jake shouted. Bukowski slapped him hard across the face, sending him sprawling.

'Don't do it, Miles,' Amber yelled.

But it was no use. Even as she willed the elevator to remain stationary the cabin began its ascent. Through the glass she could see the outline of his figure rising with it. When the doors opened, he raised an arm and stepped out.

Soames uttered a guttural command, and the wolves leapt at Fleming, knocking him to the ground, tearing at his clothing. Jake screamed, and Amber threw herself at the wolves, trying to pull them off, but they ignored her and continued their frenzied attack – ripping at Fleming's neck, pulling at his helmet.

When it came off she gasped. The head was plastic. It was the body surrogate. She turned towards Soames and Bukowski as a figure appeared like a dark avenger over the railing behind them and pulled Bukowski backwards, screaming, into the borehole.

'Take Jake and get back to the master console,' the figure shouted at her, reaching for Soames and pulling the protective gear off his head.

Amber grabbed Jake's hand and pulled him towards the elevator – just as the wolves stopped attacking the dummy and Carvelli ran at her. One leapt at her – but then Carvelli pushed himself in its way, opening the path to the elevator. 'Go,' he shouted, as he wrestled with the wolf, which was clawing at his stomach and lunging at his face.

Amber didn't need any second bidding. She flung herself and Jake into the elevator and reached for the down button. But the second wolf was already upon them, clamping its fangs around Jake's left leg even as the door closed. Panicking, she kept pressing the button, but Jake's leg was blocking the door as the wolf's jaws dug deeper into it. All the time the animal stared up at Amber with its evil yellow eyes. To her left, through the tinted glass, she saw Carvelli's body go limp as the other wolf sank its bloody jaws into his throat.

Then Jake reached down to his left thigh and pressed something. His leg came off and the wolf, with one last wrench, fell back, pulling the leg with it, freeing the door.

The elevator closed with a hiss, but as it began its descent Amber could see the wolves move towards the railings, where Soames was struggling with Fleming.

She couldn't think of that now, though. She had too much to do.

72

Soames was surprisingly wiry and strong, and when Fleming ripped off his protective clothing, exposing his hypersensitive skin to the light, he fought even more fiercely.

Fleming was weighed down with the bulky soul-capture head-sphere with its integrated electrode Thinking Cap. He had used it to control the body surrogate via the NeuroTranslator while he climbed out of the laboratory maintenance door and scaled the borehole.

The wolves were coming for him now.

Standing on the gantry, he punched Soames hard in the face, then wrestled him over the railings until he was hanging in space, gripping Fleming's wrist.

'Call them off,' he shouted. Below him the orb was pulsing like a small sun and Soames's skin was already turning red.

The wolves howled and whined but kept back, as if sensing that to attack would endanger their master.

'Call them off,' Fleming said again.

Soames gave a guttural command and the wolves backed away. 'Miles, you must stop Amber. She mustn't interfere with the signs.'

Fleming shook his head in disbelief. 'You're one evil bastard.'

'I'm not,' Soames pleaded. His voice became earnest. 'This is important. You of all people must understand. There's a reason for what I'm doing and you mustn't stop it.'

'What the hell are you talking about?'

'The Red Pope's revelation has a purpose and I must fulfil it.'

'But his revelation was a lie.'

'No, it wasn't. It was a half-lie and a half-truth. It was *his* truth.'

'But you want to make it the *only* truth.'

'I've no choice. I have to convince the world there's no God, that there's only the Devil. That's my purpose.'

Fleming reached down to hold Soames's other arm. The man's skin was blistering now but he seemed oblivious to the pain. 'Why is it your purpose, Bradley? Who do you think you are? The Devil?'

'It's much more complicated than that.' Soames looked directly into his eyes. 'I'm God's second son.'

Fleming almost dropped him. 'What?'

'Listen, listen,' begged Soames. 'Two thousand years ago, God sent down his first son. He was a good man who preached compassion and forgiveness – he even died on the cross for humanity to teach you the true way of God. But it didn't work.

425

Religions fought with each other over their interpretation of Christ's teachings. They got in the way of faith. It no longer became an issue of free will but of power and guilt. Where's the free will in a priest saying "Do what I tell you to do or you'll go to Hell"? That isn't free will, that's obeying orders because you fear punishment.

'Priests are only men anyway. They don't care about understanding God – they care about building power in this world. But God doesn't want vast churches and adoration. He's not that kind of father. He wants you, His most ambitious creation, to come of age and no longer need Him. That's what his first son tried to explain. Living a good life is its own reward – at death each individual will experience his own soul truth. But no one listened.

'So He sent down a second son, a darker son. Me. Not to preach good and kindness this time, but to prove once and for all that God doesn't exist. That only the Devil holds sway. Only then could mankind outgrow the shackles of religion and develop its own sense of right and wrong – *true* free will. After all, one can only make a truly virtuous choice when there's no promise of reward. So this is God's gift to you, to erase Himself from your consciousness. That's why I built up Accosta. Arrogant and dogmatic, he was the perfect symbol of religion. By having him, the leader of the most powerful religion on earth, disavow God from beyond the grave the world had to listen. And after the signs they'll have no choice but to believe.'

Soames smiled up at Fleming. 'You, of all

people, ought to understand this, Miles. You hate the self-important dogma of religion. You were an atheist who did good for no reward in the next life. And look at Virginia Knight. When she followed the Red Pope she was weak and cowardly, easily led to betray friends and even sanction countless deaths, telling herself it didn't matter because they were terminally ill and she was doing God's will. But it was only when she lost all faith in God that she found faith in herself and the courage to help you and Amber escape. It was only when she stopped depending on the promise of the next life that she acquired independence in this. Miles, you must stop Amber or all is lost.'

'You're insane! Millions will die.'

'Lives will be lost but souls will be saved,' Soames pleaded. 'You must understand. I am who I say I am. I knew what the Red Pope would reveal. That's why I fought so hard for the Soul Project. I knew what the signs would be. That's why I prepared for them. Believe me, Miles, I am both Lucifer and God's son. I am God's instrument. I am the fire of hell that brings suffering and despair, but I am also the purging flame that prepares the ground for hardier future growth. Miles, the future of mankind is in your hands. You must allow the signs to run their course, to burn out the weed of religion and allow a stronger strain of self-belief and genuine free will to grow up in its place.'

Soames paused, as if waiting for him to respond but Fleming didn't know what to say. There was a twisted logic to Soames's words.

Soames gripped Fleming's wrist. His skin was

blistering and tearing, revealing weeping red sores. Fleming tried to pull him up so that he could cover himself, but the more pressure he applied to the skin, the more it ruptured. 'Please, Miles, please,' Soames begged, ignoring the pain. 'Kill me but let the signs run their course. You *must* hammer the final nails into the coffin of religion. There will only be this one opportunity, Miles, and it rests with you. You *must* do it now, Miles,' he screamed. 'You *must*.'

73

09 . . . 08 . . . Amber's first glance at the screen told her she was too late. The countdown had almost run its course. The phantom strikes were about to start.

Leaving Jake to watch the elevator in case more guards appeared, she entered the base programming of the computer. It soon became apparent that Soames had been right. All the stolen data had been returned but the act of restoration had triggered the final signs.

06 . . . 05 . . .

She looked at the map of India and Pakistan and the larger map of Asia. All the red dots were still flashing. If she keyed in a photonic implosion program she could destroy the computer but not before it sent out its misleading information and set in play the war and death apocalypse prophesied by the Red Pope.

She had to overwrite the code.

. . . 04 . . . 03 . . .

Starting with the larger Asia map, she opened a small viewing box at the base of the screen, used it to access the base programming and search for the germ instruction that would seed the phantom launch message down the optical Internet. She found it quickly and within seconds had disabled it. The dots on the map stopped flashing.

Excellent.

... 02 ...

She flicked on to the map of India and Pakistan, replicated what she had done with the first map. Opened a viewing window to access the base programming code. Began searching for the germ instructions ...

... 01 ... 00 ...

Shit. Too late.

The red dot over Delhi stopped flashing. Then a red line arced out of Delhi towards Pakistan.

She checked the base programming. The germ instruction had already been sent to the missile command centre in Lahore, informing it incorrectly that India had launched a nuclear strike. Taking a deep breath, Amber rubbed her perspiring palms together then deleted the message.

The arcing line disappeared from the screen.

Amber's shoulders slumped with relief. Calming herself, she prepared to insert the PIP that would destroy the computer. But before she could start, a flashing dot reappeared on the map. Then, with no countdown or warning, a line arced out from Lahore towards India.

Frantically checking the base code to see whether she had missed something, she realized that this wasn't a phantom strike – this was

Pakistan's armed response to the earlier 'strike' from India.

Not taking her eyes off the screen, Amber dived back into the base programming of the most powerful computer in existence, and searched for a miracle.

'You must stop her, Miles,' Soames screamed at him. Soames's earlier calm had deserted him. The skin on his forehead was almost hanging off his face and his eyes were suffused with blood. 'Help me, and I'll help you discover your brother's fate. The computer's the key. There's a relationship between the soul signature and a person's genetic code. The interference pattern correlates with the introns, the junk code that makes up most of our DNA. The computer can work out your brother's soul signature from his genome. With my help you could page him. You could contact him.'

Fleming knew this already. That had been his hunch when he'd left Amber to interrogate the computer. 'I know what it can do,' he said.

Soames's lips contorted into a manic smile. 'So, you realize that the computer's vital if you want to satisfy your need to know – your need to *prove* he's okay. If it's destroyed, you'll never be able to contact him. Never be able to put your mind at rest.'

Fleming had already come to a decision. 'Rob's okay,' he said.

'But how do you *know*?'

'I don't, Bradley. I guess I'll just have to have faith,' he said, and a weight lifted off him.

Soames looked close to panic. 'But Amber must be stopped. She's the only one who can prevent the signs and you *must* stop her!'

'No, I mustn't,' he said slowly. 'Like you said, I'm allowed to exercise free will. And that's what I'm doing.'

'No! No!' Soames shouted. 'You're making a fatal mistake! This isn't meant to happen! You must stop her!'

'Too late, Bradley!' Fleming heard Amber shout behind him. Turning, he saw Amber standing by the elevator with Jake, watching the wolves who were watching him. 'I had a runaway, but I deactivated it and diverted it into the sea. It's over.'

Soames glared up at Fleming. 'You fool,' he spat. 'God gave mankind a second chance. He sent His second son. Yet you blew it. Again. You aren't worth saving.' He released his grip. Fleming held him for as long as he could but Soames's skin peeled off in his hands and the man fell backwards into the borehole, landing in a heap on the pulsing glass sphere.

The wolves howled behind him and Fleming turned just in time to see them launch themselves. Instinctively he threw his arms over his face and braced himself for the impact. But none came. They leapt past him and into the borehole after their master. He looked to see where they had fallen but could see no sign of them. It was as if they had disappeared, returning like demons whence they came.

Their master was still visible.

Staring down at the man who claimed to be both

Lucifer and God's second son, a shiver ran down Fleming's spine. Soames lay on the glowing glass sphere, his eyes open. His arms were splayed out as if he was being crucified on a ball of fire.

Fleming felt Amber lay a hand on his shoulder. 'I've got Tripp's access disk. We need to get out of here pretty quick,' she said. 'I've installed a PIP in the computer and it's about to burst.'

Fleming turned to Jake, who was salvaging his chewed leg. He scooped the child up and followed Amber into the elevator.

His back broken on his own creation, Bradley Soames waited for death. His skin was peeling off in layers as the heat and light from the glass sphere beneath him burned him with a pain more acute than any he had experienced in a life already rich in suffering.

He was on a wheel of fire in Hell itself.

But it wasn't his physical agony that distressed him.

It was his sense of failure.

'Forgive me, Father,' he yelled, in his despair. 'I tried to help them.'

Then the ball of fire beneath him cracked into tiny fissures before it exploded in a supernova of blue-white light.

Minutes earlier

Running out of VenTec, holding Jake close to his chest, the first thing Fleming noticed was that the weather had cleared. There was even a streak of orange on the distant horizon. The second thing he saw was the back-up helicopter approaching from the east.

Within two minutes they were on board. The Delta Force operator who had broken his leg was already in there. He had told the Black Hawk to pick him up then come to VenTec to check for survivors.

'No one else make it?' he asked, as Fleming settled Jake into the seat between him and Amber.

Fleming shook his head.

'How about you guys?' the man asked.

Amber squeezed Fleming's hand. 'We're okay,' she said. 'We're gonna be just fine.'

'If I were you I'd get as far away from VenTec as possible. And fast,' Fleming called to the pilot.

'Hearing you loud and clear. Setting a course south for Fairbanks.'

Even as the pilot turned the chopper south Jake twisted in his seat. 'Look, Uncle Milo!'

Fleming turned in time to see what looked like a rod of white light burst up from the top of the mountain, blasting through the spider-like structure of VenTec, and piercing the darkening sky like a vertical searchlight.

Then there was a secondary explosion and the base of the brilliant white light turned to fire. Fleming guessed that the enormous energy unleashed by the exploding fireball must have released the oil trapped deep in the mountain, forming a pillar of flame that seemed for a moment to connect Heaven and Hell.

'So,' the Delta Force guy said, with a tired grin, 'we saved the world, right?'

Fleming nodded, but all he could see, as he squeezed Amber's hand and pulled Jake closer to him, was a vision of Soames stretched out on his ball of fire, staring contemptuously at him. 'Sure we saved the world,' he said quietly, ruffling a hand through Jake's hair. 'Sure we did.'

EPILOGUE

Villa Ronda Jesuit retreat. North of Rome. Eighteen months later

The reception was held in one of the Society's grander summer establishments. It was a festive occasion, a celebration – not just of the appointment of the new Superior General of the Jesuits but of the broader renaissance of the Mother Church.

Guests in linen suits and ecclesiastical robes sipped drinks in the cool, arched terraces of the Palladian villa and meandered through its sun-dappled gardens.

As she straightened up from helping Jake adjust his laces, Amber nursed her round belly, feeling the new life kicking inside her. Her only regret was that her mother hadn't lived to see her first grandchild.

She thought back to when she had only half lived her life, always aware of Ariel and her own guilt, never of herself as an individual. Then she thought of her life since she and Ariel had released each other. What had her mother once said? 'We are our relationships.' She had been right, Amber realized now, both in life and in death. Looking across the gardens, she saw Fleming being beckoned to join the group gathered around Papa Pete Riga.

She thought of the quantum world, which had so occupied her life. In many ways Fleming had always been solely 'particle': individual and detached, scared of commitment, relying on the weapons of hard science and practicality to hold at bay the suffering and chaos in the world. She, on the other hand, had been 'wave': consumed by her relationship with her sister to the exclusion of any other personal attachment, reliant on her quantum work with Soames for distraction and her quest for understanding. But now that quest was over, and there was no need for distraction. Fleming and she completed each other, allowing each to be both individual and together, particle and wave, I and we. Perfect duality.

She smiled and stroked her belly again. Her work, which had been a wondrous distraction, was now only part of her life. Optrix was successful enough not to need her involvement in everything, and she'd been surprised by how easy she had found it to delegate many of her old responsibilities.

Holding Jake's hand, she watched Fleming approach Papa Pete. Her godfather was resplendent in the black robes of his new office: as Superior General of the Society of Jesus he was the head of the Jesuits, the so-called Black Pope. Fleming hadn't wanted to come to the reception, and only agreed to accompany Amber because of the debt she owed to her godfather.

Seeing Papa Pete, so proud, occasionally pausing in his conversation to acknowledge the respects of his followers, she thought of Soames's last words to Fleming. They had often discussed her former partner's stated mission to destroy religion and faith in God so that man might find true free will, but she had never reached a conclusion about him. He had been such a powerful and ultimately positive influence on her life. To her, Soames had been and always would be an enigma. And, despite all that had happened, whenever she thought of him she found it hard to feel anger or hatred for him – only sympathy.

Miles Fleming didn't entirely share Amber's philosophical outlook, but seeing her standing with Jake, he couldn't help smiling at how happy and natural they looked together. Jake had become part of their unit and Fleming no longer even felt he was honouring his promise to his brother to care for his son. Jake was part of him now, as Amber was.

In some ways his life hadn't changed much. After Soames's computer had been destroyed and the world returned to a semblance of normality, the media had tried to identify the 'saviours of civilization'. But there was such chaos in the ensuing months, and so many rumours flying around, that with the help of the FBI he had kept his and Amber's names out of the reports and returned to Barley Hall to continue the work he had started there. He had more power now that he ran the place, and his funding levels were higher, but otherwise life went on.

In other ways, however, he had been transformed. He remembered when he had tried to fight suffering not only by helping to rebuild shattered patients but also by keeping himself detached, but now, as he looked across at Jake and the woman who was about to bear his child, he realized that they represented his world. They might eventually cause him suffering but they also made him whole, gave his life meaning.

He often thought of Rob, but no longer felt the same guilt or concern for his soul. He would find out soon enough whether Rob was safe on that sunlit plane Amber had seen in her dream. Until then he would concentrate on living.

Soames still haunted him, though – and coming here today had only exacerbated this.

After the Red Pope's predicted final signs had failed to materialize, the world had breathed a collective sigh of relief. The failure of Armageddon to take place led many to dismiss the whole episode as a grand hoax, the act of an insane genius. What no one could explain, however, was how the insane genius had known what the Red Pope was going to announce. Despite numerous investigations and inquests, this had never been satisfactorily resolved.

Nevertheless, in the ensuing months millions of relieved people flocked back to the religions as if to atone for allowing the Red Pope to dampen their faith. Atheists, who had never thought of religion, now made it a priority. A huge vacuum had been left by the dissolution of the Church of the Soul Truth and there had been a backlash against new progressive ministries. People had been fooled once and didn't want to be fooled again.

One Church was suited to meet this massive demand for a return to core, stable values, a Church that had been on the verge of collapse before the Red Pope's announcement. As it flung open its doors to its prodigal flock, it dogmatically reinforced its sole ownership of the truth, laying down strict rules of worship and proudly proclaiming itself the Mother Church. In its entire fifteen hundred years of existence the Roman Catholic Church had never been stronger.

Even now, as Fleming greeted Peter Riga in his black robes of office, watching the stream of well-wishers stoop to kiss his hand, he thought of Bradley Soames's final words.

'So He sent down a second son, a darker son. Me. Not to preach good and kindness this time, but to prove once and for all that God doesn't exist. That only the Devil holds sway. Only then could mankind outgrow the shackles of religion and develop its own sense of right and wrong – *true* free will. After all, one can only make a truly virtuous choice when there's no promise of reward. So this is God's gift to you, to erase Himself from your consciousness.'

It was the ranting of a madman, but as he remembered seeing Soames stretched out on his ball of fire, yelling, 'You don't deserve to be saved,' Fleming shivered, despite the warm sun on his back.

After congratulating Riga, Fleming asked him a

question. He purposely didn't use his title. 'Peter, did we learn anything from the Red Pope's Day of the Soul Truth?'

'Of course, Miles,' Riga said, without hesitation.

'What?'

Riga frowned as if the answer was obvious. 'We learnt that people need guidance. That they can't be trusted to find God by themselves. Like sheep, they need a strong, confident shepherd to help them see the true glory of God.'

An involuntary shudder ran through Fleming. 'And you're the shepherd?'

Riga smiled then, and his smile expressed the same beatific certainty that Fleming had seen in Accosta's face.

For one surreal moment in that bright, white sunlight, Fleming couldn't distinguish between the two: all that seemed to separate the Red Pope from the Black Pope was the colour of their robes.

THE END

ACKNOWLEDGEMENTS

As ever, my greatest debt of gratitude is to my wife, Jenny. She, more than anyone else, helped bring *Lucifer* to light. Her inventive research and creative ideas were invaluable in developing characters and plotting story lines.

In our research the following books proved particularly valuable: *The Quantum Self* by Danah Sohar (Flamingo 1991), *Q is for Quantum* by John Gribbin (Weidenfeld & Nicolson 1998), *Eiger Dreams* by Jon Krakener (Pan 1990) and *The Tibetan Book of the Dead*.

I am extremely grateful to everyone at Transworld Publishers for their warm encouragement and continued support, especially my excellent editor Bill Scott-Kerr.

Major thanks are due to my friend and agent Patrick Walsh, and film agent Sam North.

I also thank the following for their help in researching the book: Commander Jerry Plant of the Royal Navy, Giles Palmer for his ideas on quantum physics and Pete Tyler for his insights on theology and the Catholic Church. Any mistakes are mine alone.

Finally, I should like to thank both my parents for their tireless enthusiasm and support. Outside the peerless Transworld sales force, they are the best sales team an author could wish for.

AS GOOD AS MICHAEL CRICHTON OR YOUR MONEY BACK.

If you don't think Lucifer is as good as Michael Crichton, just return this book along with your till receipt. Please tell us when and where you bought it and the reasons why you weren't happy with it and we'll refund your money.

CRIME ZERO
by Michael Cordy

When the ultimate solution becomes the ultimate crime. . .

The year is 2008. Violent crime has become a global epidemic, nowhere more so than in the United States. Everything from the death penalty to liberal reforms has failed. Nothing has been effective . . . until now.

Project Conscience promises to be the solution. It is a bold attempt by a powerful group of scientists, politicians and senior law-enforcement personnel to use gene therapy to treat criminals and cure violent crime. But among their number are those with a more sinister agenda, who would go further and turn the dream of Project Conscience into the nightmare of Crime Zero.

It is up to Luke Decker, a criminal psychologist disillusioned with the growing dependence on genetic science, and Dr Kathy Kerr, his one-time lover and ideological adversary, to fight this deadly new scheme, a scheme so ruthless in intent and so vast in scope that it will irrevocably change the evolution of mankind itself. . .

'A storming, action packed thriller'
Daily Mirror

0 552 14604 8

THE MIRACLE STRAIN
by Michael Cordy

'Jurassic Park meets the quest for the Holy Grail meets
Raiders of the Lost Ark'
Mail on Sunday

A heart-pounding international thriller of retribution
and redemption. One man battles for the life of his
daughter in the face of seemingly unbeatable odds. But
to save her he must first reach for the ultimate
knowledge. . .

Doctor Tom Carter, surgeon, geneticist, husband, father,
needs a miracle. As the inventor of a revolutionary
machine, the Genescope, he has the power to read a
person's genes, predicting the onset of disease . . . their
lifespan . . . their future.

But at the moment of his greaest triumph, the Nobel
Prize for Medicine, Carter's world is shattered by the
assassination of his wife. He knows that the killer's bullets
can only have been meant for him. In the aftermath of
her death, a scan reveals that his daughter Holly has an
incurable brain disorder and less than a year to live.
Even the most advanced conventional science cannot
save her. Something more radical is required.

A secret brotherhood, two thousand years old, may
have the answer. They need his new technology to
complete their own sacred quest. In return they offer
Carter the chance to look beyond the genes of man . . .
and into the genes of God.

0 552 14578 5

A SELECTED LIST OF FINE NOVELS
AVAILABLE FROM CORGI BOOKS

14783 4	CRY OF THE PANTHER	*Adam Armstrong*	£5.99
14497 5	BLACKOUT	*Campbell Armstrong*	£5.99
14667 6	DEADLINE	*Campbell Armstrong*	£5.99
14646 3	PLAGUE OF ANGELS	*Alan Blackwood*	£5.99
14775 3	THE EXORCIST	*William Peter Blatty*	£5.99
14586 6	SHADOW DANCER	*Tom Bradby*	£5.99
14871 7	ANGELS & DEMONS	*Dan Brown*	£5.99
14578 5	THE MIRACLE STRAIN	*Michael Cordy*	£5.99
14604 8	CRIME ZERO	*Michael Cordy*	£5.99
14654 4	THE HORSE WHISPERER	*Nicholas Evans*	£5.99
14495 9	THE LOOP	*Nicholas Evans*	£5.99
13275 9	THE NEGOTIATOR	*Frederick Forsyth*	£6.99
13823 1	THE DECEIVER	*Frederick Forsyth*	£6.99
13990 4	THE FIST OF GOD	*Frederick Forsyth*	£6.99
14717 6	GO	*Simon Lewis*	£5.99
07583 3	NO MEAN CITY	*A. McArthur & H. Kingsley Long*	£5.99
14591 2	REMOTE CONTROL	*Andy McNab*	£6.99
14592 0	CRISIS FOUR	*Andy McNab*	£5.99
14797 4	FIREWALL	*Andy McNab*	£6.99
54535 X	KILLING GROUND	*Gerald Seymour*	£6.99
14682 X	A LINE IN THE SAND	*Gerald Seymour*	£5.99
14666 8	HOLDING THE ZERO	*Gerald Seymour*	£5.99
14794 X	CRY OF THE CURLEW	*Peter Watt*	£6.99
14795 8	SHADOW OF THE OSPREY	*Peter Watt*	£6.99